THE FA[IRY]

M. Lucie Chin liv...
theatre. *The Fairy of Ku-She*...
She is working on her second.

M. LUCIE CHIN

The Fairy of Ku-She

FONTANA/Collins

First published in Great Britain by
Fontana Paperbacks 1990

Printed and bound in Great Britain by
William Collins Sons & Co. Ltd, Glasgow

For David and Memi Chin

And for Ben,
for giving me the chance to
know his entire family

Author's Note

First month	30 days begins early-mid February
Second month	29 days begins mid March
Third month	30 days begins mid April
Fourth month	29 days begins mid May
Fifth month	29 days begins mid-early June
Sixth month	30 days begins mid-early July
Seventh month	29 days begins mid-early August
Eighth month	29 days begins early September
Ninth month	30 days begins early October
Tenth month	29 days begins early November
Eleventh month	29 days begins early-mid December
Twelfth month	30 days begins early-mid January

The beginning of the Lunar New Year can vary as much as a month in relation to our own calendar, so the above equivalents are only approximate. The Chinese year was noticeably shorter than ours and not completely in sync with their own view of the seasons, so once every five cycles (sixty years or five times the twelve-year zodiac cycle) an extra month was added, usually in the spring.

For the sake of sanity I have not attempted to adjust the calendar to locate the proper starting point for each of the years spanned by the story. Nor have I assigned any particular years, either by their animal sign or Imperial reign (there were three ways of calculating the date, making precise pinpointing of events by later historians a miserable job). I have set the story somewhere in the Ming Dynasty without inflicting it to any specific emperor, since none of the disasters I have depicted actually happened, and history has enough to answer for.

The Fairy of Ku-She

Book One

In the last months of the year, when the dragons have retreated beneath the seas, the handle of the "Drinking Gourd" points toward winter and the sky becomes heavy with clouds dark as rust. Then the fairy Chou Ch'ung-i, whom the Heavenly Jade Emperor placed in charge of Hibiscus Village, home of the fairies and lowly earth spirits, summons those of her subjects in charge of winter. They leave their caves and dwelling places and dutifully gather at the Great Hall of her mansion in the center of the village.

The White Tiger of the Winter Wind appears from his lair. The Fairy of One Hundred Flowers presents the spirits under her care—Wintersweet and Plum Blossom and all the others who will bloom before spring comes. The Fairy of One Hundred Trees brings the spirits of the evergreens. The Frost Fairy and the Lady of the Winter Moon present themselves, as do the fairies Tung Shuang-Ch'eng, keeper of the Crystal Snow-vase, and the Fairy of Ku-She, keeper of the Golden Chopsticks. These two appear riding upon the White Mule, which is the spirit of snow.

When the summons is received, all the fairies so called don their finest clothes and ornaments and prepare to leave their caves and homes bearing small gifts as tokens of respect, for Chou Ch'ung-i is the greatest fairy of all. She alone must answer to the Heavenly Jade Emperor for the conduct of her subjects, and it is she who decides where and when and how much of the efforts of the lesser fairies must be applied to the world of men.

7

In the Great Hall, Chou Ch'ung-i receives her subjects, who perform obeisances, swear allegiance to the Heavenly Jade Emperor and present their tokens. Madam Chou instructs them in their duties to the emperor and their responsibilities for the coming winter. The formality is observed with all due pomp and ceremony. She tells each how he or she must prepare for the coming season and gives her written order to those whose duties commence most immediately. Then all withdrew to a fine and sumptuous banquet where they sit feasting and drinking, talking and playing games, dancing and singing for the amusement of their hostess for a day and a night.

At the rise of the next dawn they withdraw to their proper places and begin to prepare for the winter now at hand.

The winter tiger walks the Earth, and cold winds rattle the bamboo and freeze the water in the buffalo wallows. The fairies of One Hundred Trees, One Hundred Grasses, One Hundred Plants and so on, call home the spirits of summer growing things, and the land becomes brown and withered. Leaves fall to the ground and nothing new is born in the earth. Then the Fairy of Frost walks the land by night, chasing after the Lady of the Winter Moon, and soon becomes bold once more and sports about over fields and lakes and through the town streets in the day as well.

It is then that Chou Ch'ung-i summons Tung Shuang-Ch'eng and the Fairy of Ku-She. They appear before her with the Crystal Snow-vase and the Golden Chopsticks and are instructed in the placement and amount of the year's first snowfall. For every flake Ku-She removes from the vase with her Golden Chopsticks, a foot of snow will fall upon the Earth. If Ku-She drops the flakes delicately from atop a cloud, the snowfall will be gentle, the snow fluffy, soft and beautiful. If several flakes are given to the White Tiger to carry to earth in his mouth, there will be a fierce blizzard with great winds and bitter cold. Tung Shuang-Ch'eng must guard the vase carefully lest it become broken or overturned, for then the world below would be buried in snow nearly to the height of Heaven itself, and mankind would be in danger of perishing.

In the spring Chou Ch'ung-i calls them all together once more and reads a message from the Heavenly Jade Emperor himself, remarking on their conduct in the performance of their tasks, praising or admonishing as necessary and granting them release from their duties. Once more a feast is held, and the Fairies of Winter go home to rest. Tung Shuang-Ch'eng and the Fairy of Ku-She return to their snug cave and the Crystal Snow-vase and the Golden Chopsticks are put safely away.

It came about one fine morning in early summer that a youth appeared at the gate before the cave of the two fairies of the snow. Barely more than a child, he wore garments of soft blue and yellow, and leaf green—the livery of Chou Ch'ung-i's summer servants—and his face was bright and fair. At his call he was met by a little serving maid clad all in white.

"What is it you want?" she said. "My mistresses are asleep within and should not be disturbed, as their season of service is but recently past and the next is not due for many months."

The young man bowed his head and said, "My humble apologies to your ladies, but my mistress has sent me to summon them to her at once."

"But it is summer!" the maid exclaimed. "May I tell them the reason, so their preparations may be appropriate and their steps properly quickened?"

"I was not told the reason," the youth said. "But my mistress bids them come informally for tea in the Garden of Whispering Bamboo." At that, the young man vanished and the maid ran into the cave to alert the other servants and prepare her mistresses.

Lady Tung and Lady Ku-She dressed quickly in summer gauze and lightest silks. Powdered and rouged, jeweled only with earrings of white jade and slim, golden hairpins hanging with tiny snowflakes, they set out for the great house of Madam Chou. Each carried a box filled with tiny summer tea cakes and, in case it should be required, the scrolls with the new snowflake designs for the coming year.

When they were ushered into Madam Chou's presence, they found she was not alone. Seated beneath an awning of palest green silk was a man with the bearing of a great nobleman. He was dressed in green-and-gold mail over a tunic and skirt of silver-and-blue brocade embroidered with fish and sea serpents, and all about the hem the ocean waves rolled and crested, row upon row. His coat was all the colors of the rainbow, richly embroidered with patterns of clouds and waves and, worked as a series of medallions, the crest of the Dragon King of the Northwest.

Lady Tung Shuang-Ch'eng and the Lady Ku-She recognized the emissary of the Lung Wang at once, and prostrated themselves, knocking their heads upon the ground seven times in a gesture of respect. Chou Ch'ung-i bade them rise and presented them to the emissary as tea was served.

Both Tung Shuang-Ch'eng and Ku-She knew why he had come, but it would not have been polite to say so.

Lady Tung bowed politely and began. "You honor us beyond measure by this audience, My Lord. To what do we, your humble servants, owe the priceless treasure of your visit?"

The emissary was pleased by their humility as well as by their beauty and would have liked nothing better than to sit and exchange pleasantries, but today he was not in a position to do so.

"My lord the Lung Wang desires your service, as you must no doubt realize. As occasionally happens, the thaw in the Northwestern Mountains was unusually thorough this year. Even the tops of the greatest peaks in the country are nearly bare of snow—a fact which distresses my master greatly. Because of this depleted condition, there is not enough moisture in the High Heavens for the proper manufacture of clouds. Rising vapors from lakes and oceans have not been as abundant as in most spring seasons, and have only contributed sufficient moisture for lower level clouds and light rains. The great storm clouds must draw their moisture from both the landbound bodies of water and the vast snowcaps of the highest peaks together. The Lung Wang is concerned that there is already too little moisture in the high ranges to prevent drought by late summer. He has, therefore, petitioned the Heavenly Jade Emperor for an increase of twelve feet of snow in the Northwestern Mountains within the month, and the emperor has so commanded."

So saying, the emissary took from his sleeve a scroll sealed with the huge jade-and-gold seal of the Emperor of Heaven himself, which he handed to Chou Ch'ung-i with a bow.

Madam Chou, who was used to dealing with seasonal anomalies at the request of one major deity or another, opened the scroll with no more formality than was due, read it briefly, called for her own writing implements and set down the order to be executed before the next full moon. Upon this document she affixed her own seal, and handed the scroll to the two snow fairies.

Content that his master's interests were satisfactorily in hand, the emissary of the Lung Wang took his leave, having much other business of a pressing nature to accomplish before the day was out.

The fairies returned home to prepare for the journey, but later in the day, as Tung Shuang-Ch'eng was overseeing the grooming of the White Mule, the Fairy of Ku-She came running to her side greatly distraught. Her hair was disheveled and her gown undone. She was in a high state of distress and on the verge of tears.

"Oh, Sister, Sister," she pleaded. "You must come with me at once. Something terrible has happened."

Ku-She ran through the cavern to her own chamber, where she at last collapsed upon her couch sobbing.

"Ku-She!" Tung Shuang-Ch'eng said sternly, partly upset by her friend's difficulty, and partly annoyed at such irrational behavior, "you must tell me what has happened or we cannot decide how to remedy it. Stop crying and talk to me."

"Oh, Sister, it is the worst thing that could possible happen and I am done for!"

Tung Shuang-Ch'eng was exasperated. "This is utter nonsense," she said. "There is only one thing which could be that bad and—" Tung Shuang-Ch'eng abruptly stopped speaking and sat upon the couch next to Ku-She. "The Golden Chopsticks?" she said. "What has happened, Little Sister?"

Ku-She huddled against the cushions, hugging herself and looking bleak. "They are missing," she said in a very tiny voice.

Tung Shuang-Ch'eng nodded. Indeed, to lose that which was in one's charge was the worst fate that could befall an elemental guardian, and Ku-She's tears were not unjustified.

"How, Little Sister?" she asked gently, stroking Ku-She's hair, hoping to calm, if not quite to comfort, her companion.

"If only I knew. The chest is here by my couch and, until a moment ago, was still locked. I undid the latch myself. Inside, the satin cushions and silken bag were all in place, undisturbed, exactly as I had arranged them on the last day of our service. The chest was *still locked*, but the chopsticks were gone!"

As she spoke, Ku-She sat clutching the key about her neck. All fairies whose duty included the care of an artifact wore such a key. It was suspended upon a chain of gold and silver links that had no catch and was too short to remove over the head.

As she listened to Ku-She's words, Tung Shuang-Ch'eng also stroked the little key about her own neck. Then suddenly a single thought entered both minds, and the two women ran from the chamber to look in the casket where Tung Shuang-Ch'eng kept the Crystal Snow-vase. With great relief they found it in place and unharmed.

"It is safe," Ku-She sighed, "but perhaps only for the moment. Whatever magic has stolen my Golden Chopsticks could surely also be used against the Snow-vase or any other object in a fairy's charge. What can we do?"

"We must go to Chou Ch'ung-i at once," Tung Shuang-Ch'eng said, locking the casket again. "We must tell her what has happened and beg her forgiveness for the poor quality of our guardianship. I will ask that the Crystal Snow-vase and all the other fairy objects be kept safely in a guarded room in her palace for the time being, and you must promise to find the Golden Chopsticks and their thief."

As Tung Shuang-Ch'eng lifted the casket and stood to go, Ku-She collapsed in a heap and looked as bleak as before. The strength of what, for a short while, had seemed to be a common problem, had deserted her entirely and she sat on the floor shaking. Tung Shuang-Ch'eng put down her burden and sat on the floor also.

"Have courage, Little Sister," she said. "All is not lost. You have a month to carry out the search before any but Madam Chou and those few who must place their tools in her care must know. And an entire summer before our season of duty comes. Much can be done in that time. We will all help as much as we can."

"The Great Dragons are not known for their patience," Ku-She said. "And Madam Chou will be furious with me. It would be only right if I were to be banished from the village forever."

"That will not return the Golden Chopsticks," Tung Shuang-Ch'eng said. "It is up to you to do that, and if you succeed, no one can find fault with you."

"But if I do *not* . . ."

"Then you are no worse off than you are now. But if you apply yourself diligently in your search, even though you fail, your punishment could not help but be tempered by the sincerity of your effort. You must go, Ku-She."

"Yes," Ku-She replied, drying her eyes and sitting more erect. "You are right. I have no choice and it is my duty, but . . . if only I knew where to start."

Tung Shuang-Ch'eng rose and lifted her casket once more. "In the Great Hall of Hibiscus Village. Once we have informed Chou Ch'ung-i of the dilemma, and you have shown a proper respect for your position and fault, we may seek her aid and counsel. She knows much of the ways of the gods and the world of men and it is to her advantage to help us, since the Heavenly Jade Emperor will not hold her blameless for the conduct of her inferiors.

"Take heart, Little Sister. There is much to be done before failure is inevitable."

The strength of her companion's character and the wisdom of her words gave Ku-She great hope and determination. She rose from the floor and went to her own chamber, where she prepared herself in a manner befitting a formal audience.

In the meantime, Tung Shuang-Ch'eng had sent a servant ahead to beg an interview and to stress the urgency of the matter. By the time the footman returned, both were ready and the two fairies set out for the mansion of Madam Chou Ch'ung-i once more, Tung Shuang-Ch'eng with her casket and Ku-She with her empty chest in her arms.

Madam Chou was not pleased, but neither was she as surprised as they had expected her to be.

"Taoist magic," she muttered into her fan. "I should have petitioned the Jade Emperor ages ago and had that fellow struck down by a dragon."

Astonished, Ku-She raised her head from the floor and stared. "You know the thief?" she exclaimed, then remembered herself and ducked her head again as Madam Chou's gaze shifted to her.

"I know of a likely suspect," she said, and her voice sounded stiff with annoyance. "A great many years ago, by the lives of mortal men, our village was accidentally discovered by a Taoist monk. Such events are rare, but they happen from time to time. Till now, however, none has ever found us a second time, for, with respect to the world of men, we do not exist in any specific place. This monk was a particular nuisance, and swore to me that he could find the village whenever he wished; that he could come and go as he pleased, unstopped and unseen, and that he could take whatever he desired by way of proof."

"Then *surely* it is he!" Ku-She cried to the tiles beneath her nose.

"Ku-She!" Tung Shuang-Ch'eng whispered. "Shhhh!"

"Nothing is certain," Chou Ch'ung-i said sternly. "Nor will your task be simple because you have the man's name. You must still find him and retrieve the chopsticks.

"Go now, Ku-She, and prepare for your journey. Take nothing with you save what is absolutely necessary. You may take one servant, but Tung Shuang-Ch'eng and the White Mule must stay here. Shortly I will send a servant to you with the name of the monk and what little I know of him. You must seek him as best you can, and quickly, but take care, there are many dangers in the world."

"Madam," Ku-She said, "Will I be mortal in the world of men or will I still have all my fairy powers?"

"You will be more than they are but less than you have been. How much so I do not know, but it is one of the consequences of walking among them in their own world. Were we gods it would not matter, but we are merely fairies, and in some ways the Taoist magic may prove stronger than our own."

At dawn the next day, Ku-She bade Tung Shuang-Ch'eng and all her other "Sisters of the Winter" farewell and set out from the cave to find most of the Principal Fairies of the Spring, Summer and Autumn waiting at her gate.

"Do not fear, Little Sister," said the Fairy of One Hundred

Trees, "our spirits are everywhere in the world below, especially now that it is full summer. We will watch over you and aid you as best we can should you be in peril."

Ku-She thanked them sincerely, though she knew she must do this task alone. Then she set off into the hills with one serving maid following behind and two small bundles, neatly packed and hung on a yoke.

First she traveled to the underworld and sought an audience with the Judges of the Court of Death. The monk, Wei Pan Ch'ao, had been, by all accounts, an audacious man and, though he had learned much of magic and especially longevity, he was uncommonly fond of a good prank, and no doubt owed less to the secrets of longevity than to the luck of not having been killed by an angry victim.

Ku-She had brought gifts and the First Judge was very helpful.

"He is well known to us, Little Fairy," he said. "This man has cheated death more times than I can recall. He is regularly on the roll of those to be summoned to court, and yet he always finds a way to avoid his fate. He is due to be summoned again in two months' time, and once again I expect he will have a reprieve. Have you, perhaps, some means by which we may keep him at last?"

Ku-She bowed her head sadly. "No, Your Honor," she said, "I have nothing, and I cannot wait two months."

"Then neither of us can be of service to the other as he cannot be summoned earlier without some cause. You must seek him among the living, Little Fairy."

"Yes, Your Honor," Ku-She said, bowing deeply before the assembled judges. "But as this monk is a nuisance and a bother to be constantly upon your rolls, and as this unworthy slave will be in the world of men, it is not unlikely that she may find something of use to you. I therefore humbly beg your indulgence and ask if you could but tell me where in the world I might seek him."

The judges thought for a moment and conferred among themselves. Ku-She stood still as stone and barely dared to breathe. At last the First Judge took up his brush and ink and with a quick flourish, set down a neat row of characters.

"This is the province in which he is currently traveling," he said, handing her the note. "More than that I cannot tell you.

In two months' time we will know his location exactly, but for now this is all we can do for you. You must find him yourself."

Ku-She thanked them profusely, performed a great many kowtows and took her leave, finally emerging into the mortal world with her maidservant following closely at her heels.

The day had been long and hot and not at all fruitful. The two peasant women walking along the side of the road carried a sheaf over each shoulder and a small bundle at the waist. The sun was setting, but they turned from the road and walked toward a large grove of catalpa trees some distance across a meadow instead of traveling the four li to the town ahead; a thing to be greatly wondered at had anyone been about to see. For women to travel alone on the open road was unusual enough. Taking the sheaves to market was a barely sufficient excuse, but to be found camping by the roadside was not only shocking, it was dangerous. That was unimportant, however, compared to the task they faced. Thus they had lived for a month, and an end was nowhere in sight.

Neither woman was old but one was clearly younger than the other. At once she set about making a comfortable repose within the grove, loosening the sheaves and arranging them to provide a place to sit and later serve to cushion their sleep.

As darkness settled into the grove they built a tiny fire, sheltered from sight of the road by the thick trunk of an old tree, and there they settled in to quietly await another day.

From the little bundle she had carried, the young maid produced a kettle which she placed upon a flat rock at the fire's edge. As she reached into the pack again and withdrew a pair of fine and delicate porcelain cups, the kettle began to boil at once, though she had fetched no water. She next removed a small lacquered box, which contained a number of various tea cakes. She placed the box before her companion and poured the tea, sitting patiently to one side waiting for the other to begin. They ate and drank their fill and the kettle remained warm and brimming and the contents of the little box never diminished.

When she had finished eating, the little maid reached into the bundle once more and withdrew a comb of ivory and gold and a tiny alabaster jar filled with scented oil. Settling down behind her companion, she undid the untidy knot of hair at the back of her mistress's neck and began to carefully comb out the bits of debris which had caught there from the sheaves. She oiled the ends of her long, night-black hair and did it up again in an elegant coil held in place with silver pins and clips. This she did every night, and in the mornings she would once more bind it back into the peasant style before they set out upon the road, but for now she would give her mistress as much of her proper service as she could manage.

While the maid worked, the mistress gazed up at the stars in the night sky, bright among the dark branches, winking in and out as the warm breeze ruffled the leaves overhead. The moon was already up. It looked like a fat pearl, softly glowing like the dragon fire. Ah, the dragons. The Lung Wang . . .

In spite of the warmth of the night, Ku-She shivered at the thought. The little maid mistook the gesture, thinking she had caused her mistress pain.

"Forgive me, My Lady," she said urgently. "I did not mean—"

"Hush, child," Ku-She said, patting Yin-Whun's knee. "It is not you. You have served me well, and I am pleased at my choice of you."

Ku-She looked up into the sky once more. "In four nights' time the moon will be full, and we have not yet accomplished our task. I fear the wrath of the dragons, but even more I fear the displeasure of the Emperor of Heaven, for he may find fault with Chou Ch'ung-i and all of Hibiscus Village on my account."

"Tomorrow, My Lady," the maid said boldly. "The old men in the market felt sure we would find him in the city, and we will be there in the morning."

"Yes, Little One," Ku-She said. "Perhaps. But to find him is one thing. To get from him that which he has stolen is another. I have no idea how I may go about it."

Yin Whun slid the last of the pins into her lady's hair and went to the tea kettle, which grew warm again as she held it in her hands. "Have faith, My Lady," she said. "When the time comes you will surely know what to do."

The night was full of the sounds of its creatures, but as the women sat, sharing a last cup of tea before sleep, Ku-She became increasingly aware of another sort of sound. She did not know what it was, but it seemed to be all about among the trees, and it did not seem quite natural to the night.

When she heard her maid gasp, she looked up to find a tall man standing before her just within the sphere of firelight and among the trees were the shadowy shapes of four others—a band of brigands, Brothers of the Green Wood.

"Well, now, Brothers, what have we here?" said the tall man. "A very odd pair it seems."

He stepped closer and the others came forward into the light. One of them began to walk slowly around the two seated women, looking closely at their dress and the silver ornaments in Ku-She's hair.

"Such fine things for a sister of the land," said the smaller man, bending close, touching Ku-She's hair. Then he quickly withdrew his hand, holding it to his mouth as though nursing a burn, his eyes wide as he dropped to one knee before the women. "Or could it be you are really a great lady of the city traveling in disguise!" he gasped, mockery clear in his voice.

The circle of men laughed and came closer, one of them giving his kneeling companion a shove with his foot.

"Show a little respect, Brother," he said.

The man on the ground at once began to grovel, knocking his head upon the earth in a mock gesture of respect. "Forgive me, Great Ladies, for my treacherous and evil mouth. Your worthless slave kowtows before you and begs you to spare his miserable life."

His companions roared with laughter, and the tall man stepped forward and dragged the prostrate man to his feet by the back of his shirt, shoving him aside. He then gently prodded the silver teapot with his toe and looked at Ku-She.

"A fine collection of goods, Little Sisters," he said, smiling again. "It is not often one has the opportunity to steal items of such obvious worth. They should fetch a nice price in the city."

He squatted and took the gold and ivory comb from Yin Whun's lap. "I suspect there is more in that pack, too."

The maid said nothing and Ku-She turned her full attention to the man, a look of such great scorn upon her face, that for a moment the bandit thought his brother might, indeed, have been right.

"And a pair of fine beauties as well," he said in a low voice.

"Take what you will of our goods," Ku-She said angrily, "and be off. It is of no concern to us what you do with such things, but my maid and I shall not be touched."

Again the men laughed and there was a note of definite menace to it. The ugly little bandit who had mocked them hurried up behind Ku-She and began pulling the silver pins and clips from her hair, babbling, "Oh no, My Great Lady! We would not think of touching ones as highborn as *you*!"

The others drew closer now, too, and snatched up the teapot, the lacquered box and the porcelains. An older man stepped up and grabbed Yin Whun by the hair, nearly lifting her off the ground. "And the father of two daughters such as these could surely find buyers to pay a handsome price."

The ugly little man began to squeal with glee. "I have it now! Not the mistress but the *maids*!—made off with the old lady's silver and a taste for fancies above their station. Ha! Ha! And used goods too, I'll wager . . . with the old master after you both no doubt."

"Not a bad idea either," said the old man, dropping the maid and beginning to tug at his sash with an eager leer.

That look was on the faces of all the men in the grove, but Ku-She pulled Yin Whun closer to her and sat quite still, a look of defiant anger on her pale, beautiful face.

"I have said we shall not be touched and we *shall* not be," Ku-She said with a calm, chilling voice.

The men howled, but Ku-She's voice cut through the din of their laughter like an icy wind. "Sisters, hear me. I am in need of your aid in a small matter. If you would see fit to assist me I would be most humbly grateful."

The brothers were hysterical with laughter now. "And *mad* as well!" one called out. But as Ku-She's voice died, the grove grew noticeably colder. In spite of the fire and the heat of the summer night, the air was frigid, and a wind sprang up as though from all directions at once. It had no source, and swirled about the grove, casting the fire into twisting, crackling frenzy. The leaves of the trees rattled, and the branches beat against one another till the grove itself seemed alive.

The men looked about in fear now, and the leader, angered, advanced a step or two toward Ku-She, who sat quietly upon the ground with her little maid by her side. But before he could reach her the bough of the tree directly above him bent down and struck him a heavy blow on the top of the head. He howled, this time from pain, and ducked away, but it did no good. Suddenly the trees in the grove all began waving their branches wildly, striking hard and fast at the nearest Brothers of the Green Wood, beating them and bruising them till the blood ran from their heads, shoulders and arms, which they held up to protect themselves. Terror stricken, they ran from the grove, but the roots of the trees reached up to trip them as they passed, and the tall grasses whipped at their legs and tangled about their ankles, causing them to fall. The air grew colder, till they thought it must be as cold as the deepest day of winter, and the wind whipped at their faces and stung the cuts on their bare arms.

Screaming, the bandits fled across the meadow, but when they reached the road, all was calm once more. The summer night had returned, hot and slightly sticky, and the men, who had held onto their loot even as they ran, found they no longer carried the objects of value they had stolen from the women in the grove, but worthless trash—a lump of iron where the silver teapot had been; two clots of clay, wet and oozing where the porcelain teacups once were; and the lacquer box now just a handful of twigs and splinters. They threw these things away hastily, and ran down the road for their very lives, for they knew the place was haunted and that spirits were about.

In the grove Ku-She and her little maid settled down to sleep under the stars. The sheaves had now become cushions and they lay upon sheets of silk.

At dawn Yin Whun was up and tending to her lady's toilet. She dressed Ku-She's hair in the high and elegant style of a married woman of wealth, adorned with clips of gold and pins of silver with drops of amethyst and crystal. From the pack she drew forth a traveling gown of summer gauze and cloud-light silk richly embroidered with flowers, and a loose, linen coat of deep green worked with flocks of birds and banks of chrysanthemums.

Yin Whun unrolled the tight bundles, and with a slight shake all the wrinkles fell away. Thus garbed with jade and pearls about her neck and gold upon her fingers, Ku-She bade her

maid be off and settled down to wait in the grove, which had
suddenly grown dense and impenetrable with tall, thick stalks
of bamboo.

In good time the maid returned along the road upon a litter
she had rented in the town. Where the grove had been there
was now a cottage of modest elegance, and at the gate a
beautiful young woman.

The litter bearers settled Ku-She among the cushions and
before long they had entered the gates of the town. She
instructed the men to take her to the best teahouse in the city,
where she took a small, private room at the front of the second
floor. From there she could watch the street from behind the
balcony screen, and she once more sent Yin Whun out into the
town in search of Wei Pan Ch'ao. While the maid searched,
Ku-She, with the aid of two gold rings from her own fingers,
procured the assistance of the teahouse owner to enquire of his
customers who might know of the man she sought. This man
was, she said, her late husband's uncle, her only living relative
and, once the proper mourning period was over, she had set out
in search of him to beg his counsel and guidance in the matter
of her future and fortunes, as she was still quite young and had
no sons or living family of her own, but did possess a great
deal of land.

As her arrival at his door had been in a splendid litter and her
clothes and jewels and manner were equally impressive (and
the gold rings quite heavy), the man was cheerfully inclined to
render whatever service he could, and questioned all his
customers closely, but to no avail.

Near evening, however, Yin Whun returned, a flush upon
her cheeks and a glow in her dark eyes. She immediately cast
herself upon the floor at Ku-She's feet and performed numerous kowtows, talking all the while.

"Lady," she said. "I have failed to find the one we seek.
Indeed, I believe he is no longer within the city walls, but I
have other news of him which may please you well enough to
forgive my clumsy and fruitless efforts."

"Rise," Ku-She said. "Your bobbing up and down dizzies
me. Speak quickly and plainly, child, for this waiting about all
day has sorely tried my nerves."

The maid sat on the mat at her mistress's feet and did not
trouble with an exact account of the day, but went straight
about her news.

"I do not know for a fact that he is not here, but those who knew of him believe him to have gone two days ago. None has seen him for that time. But there is more. And perhaps it is even better news.

"While he was here he lodged at the house of a young scholar. The youth is of independent, though modest, means, and is without family, save a sister newly married. He has a small house on Black Lotus Street, and it is there that Wei Pan Ch'ao was lodged for a week. The monk is said to be the young man's uncle, though some say Wei Pan Ch'ao is of great age and several generations separate that kinship.

"It is also said that the young man, whose name is Wei K'e-yung, has only recently passed the Imperial Examinations with the highest of honors and that, on behalf this achievement, Wei Pan Ch'ao bestowed upon his nephew a fine and glorious gift, fit even for the emperor himself."

Ku-She's eyes brightened and the maid looked up in excitement. "Surely it must be what we seek. I cannot imagine one such as he with possessions of any value, save what he stole from you."

"Perhaps he knows we seek him and has left them behind to confound us."

"As this generosity does not seem to be a deep secret," said Ku-She, "it is more likely that he has simply tired of carrying them."

"I do not know the nature of the gift," Yin Whun said. "That particular I could not discover, but—"

"It is enough," Ku-She said, settling back upon her cushions and sipping at her tea. "It was well done, and I agree, the gift could be little else but what we seek."

Yin Whun accepted a cup of tea from Ku-She's own hand and trembled slightly with joy and relief until she noticed the shadow of melancholy still clinging to her mistress's eyes.

"Now," Ku-She said quietly, "it remains for me to know how I will rescue them from him."

Very early the next morning an old woman made her way slowly down Black Lotus Street to the gate of a modest house. A servant answered her knock, and she enquired if this was the home of the scholar Wei K'e-yung. When the boy allowed that it was, she announced herself to be Madam Feng who, because of her wisdom and skill in such matters, had been employed as go-between on behalf of a lady of means and, therefore, had an arrangement of considerable merit to discuss with the master.

Astonished, the boy hurried off into the house, but returned almost at once, bowing and very careful of his manners, and showed the old lady into the main hall where he offered her tea and cakes till his master, who had still been sleeping, could make himself presentable and come to her himself.

She acknowledged this with a curt nod but accepted only tea and looked about the room with a sharp and critical eye.

Presently a tall, slender young man entered the room, quiet and unhurried, but punctual. He wore the blue robe of a scholar of the First Rank but informally, without hat and bound only with a simple sash. His hair was dressed neatly in a modest style and his demeanor was entirely that of a serious student without airs or pretensions above his station. As soon as Madam Feng saw him, all the sharpness went out of her look and she shed her stiff and critical posture, for the grace and charm of his person were considerable, and his beauty was astonishing. They exchanged formal salutations and the match-maker began the business at hand.

"Young Sir," she said, "as you have no living parents or older brothers, I have come directly to you on a matter of great delicacy. One I think you will find of great advantage to you. I have taken on this employment on behalf of a Madam Ku who is herself a widow with no living relatives of either her husband's or her own. She has no children and is still quite young and, due to the circumstances of her husband's death, possessed of considerable wealth. It is not unusual for a woman in such a position, particularly one of such rare beauty as Madam Ku's, to find her virtue assailed from all sides by schemers and fortune hunters. Therefore, though she remains chaste and devoted to her husband even in the Land of the Dead, she feels it would be most wise to ensure the safety of her fortune and the perfection of her reputation against even the *possibility* of foul lies, by seeking an honorable marriage with a man of unquestionable principle and talent. Since her husband was nearly forty years her senior, she feels it would be unwise to seek someone who might once again leave her estate unprotected while she is still too young to be unreproachable. Her wealth and position make a marriage as Second Wife unsuitable. Therefore she has set me the task of finding a young bachelor of proper station and skills.

"You, Sir, are a most favorable candidate. For though your means are hardly worth considering, your reputation is exceptional and your success in the recent Imperial Examinations promises much for your career in the Emperor's service. Futhermore, the lady herself has expressed a desire that I investigate your suitability, as she feels you would make a good match if my enquiry proves fruitful and you yourself are willing."

Wei K'e-yung was somewhat taken aback by her forthright speech. It was a boldness he was not accustomed to in women, and which would have been unacceptable from any but a professional go-between. But he listened to what she had said and realized that fortune had, indeed, smiled upon him. Yet he was not at ease.

"Mistress Feng," he said. "I am humbled by the generosity of this offer but feel myself to be most unworthy of such a match. . . ."

"Do not reject this match too hastily, young scholar. Further enquiry on both sides can only be of benefit right now."

Wei K'e-yung agreed, and a series of formal questions was posed by both parties. Madam Feng examined him closely about the source and extent of his income, his lineage, as well as the tutors who had instructed him in the classics. Finally the old woman said, "Since you qualified so highly in the Imperial Examinations, why have you not been given an official post?"

"A position of Third Secretary to the District Magistrate of Lanchow was offered to me. A very important district and a fine post for a first appointment, but I felt my time would be better spent applying myself to further study so that I might place well in the Second Degree Examinations as soon as possible, and hence make use of the opportunity for higher honors while I am still young with a long career ahead. To this end I expect to commit all my energies and small resources rather than seek profit and a higher life-style *now*."

The old lady smiled slyly. "With a rich wife, young sir, you could do both and, when your Second Degree arrives, perhaps purchase a higher post than you could manage merely by appointment of an Imperial Minister."

"Mistress Feng," said Wei K'e-yung, "if I were to accept this proposition on those grounds, I would be no better than any fortune hunter. I do not see how this can be resolved."

"It is because of this very uprightness of character which causes you to hesitate that my employer would find you such a morally acceptable candidate. In addition to which there is the lady's own preference to consider. Since her position is not a usual one and her fortune is so great, she has insisted that I urge you to an unusual course of action and, therefore, requests to meet with you personally."

Reluctantly, Wei K'e-yung agreed, and a time was set to meet at a teahouse in New Moon Street the next afternoon. The young servant boy showed Madam Feng out and bade her good day, but no sooner had he barred the gate than a little maid ran up with the old lady's fan, which had been left behind in the reception hall. Hastily the boy threw the bolt and ran into the street, but to his surprise, the old woman was nowhere to be seen.

The fairy maid poured hot tea from a cold pot and produced sweets and delicate pastries from a simple, seemingly empty straw basket, which she placed before her mistress. But Ku-She neither ate nor drank. The little maid combed her lady's hair out of the matron's knot and oiled and dressed it with silver pins and a gleaming net, but Ku-She seemed unaware. Yin Whun laid out the sleeping mats but Ku-She would not lie down to sleep. "You must rest yourself, most excellent Lady," the maid begged. "There is much to be accomplished tomorrow. There may yet be a way to prove his possession of the chopsticks and learn where they are kept. You must not despair. You will win them from him yet."

But Ku-She merely closed her eyes and bowed her head lower, and a single tear jeweled her cheek.

The old woman who met Wei K'e-yung at the teahouse door and led him to the private room on the second floor did not look precisely as he remembered Madam Feng. She seemed smaller and more frail, but a woman often deceives the eye in public, and he could not deny he had known her at once. In a clear voice she thanked him for the return of her fan and begged him to accompany her upstairs to meet a young lady of her acquaintance to whom he might prove of some assistance with a small matter. Thus, well chaperoned and mindful of public propriety, Wei K'e-yung followed the go-between to have a look at the lady who had offered him her fortune and her person.

It required no further persuasion or negotiation on the matchmaker's part to convince Wei K'e-yung of the wisdom of the match. The lady could have been penniless and burdened with family debt, and he would gladly have taken her as his wife and given over all his means, sold his house and servants and even his books to unburden her if such had been required. For the instant his eyes fell upon her, with that one glance, he utterly lost his heart and much of his reason.

By the time he returned home, half the night had gone and the servants had begun to fear for his life, for he was not generally given to late carousing. When he entered the gate at last, their fears were only slightly diminished, for he did not seem himself. Though he had drunk many pots of wine, he did not seem precisely to be intoxicated. He could not recall if supper had been served, but he had no desire for food or tea. The old man and his wife who kept house for the scholar could barely get him to speak, and he wandered about the garden dazed and distracted, smiling softly. Then suddenly he would stop and speak aloud to no one. Gazing at the moon, he proclaimed its luster to be far inferior to the pale perfection of a lovely skin. Stopping by a shrub, he would pick a blossom and declare the softness of its petals to be as coarse as grinding stone beside that of a tiny hand upon his wrist.

Yet the young master seemed deaf to his retainer's urgings, so the boy was sent into the night to fetch the doctor. But the doctor said he could not come till morning. He sent a powder to be disguised in a pot of warm wine to make the young man sleep, but they could not induce him to take it. In desperation, the old housekeeper herself went into the next lane to the house of a midwife and roused her from sleep to come look at Wei K'e-yung. The midwife stood in the shadow of the veranda and observed him carefully as he wandered about. When she left she said: "You must give him the powder even if you force it into him, and send for the doctor again at dawn. I fear he is under a fairy enchantment and will not live many days if not properly treated."

Terrified by her words, the old couple heated the wine again, but they were afraid to try and force him and angry to discover that the boy had run off and hidden himself for fear they would require *him* to do it. In the end the old woman tricked him, saying: "This is the finest wine in the countryside. Taste it and see how it compares with the sweetness of a kiss."

Soon he was asleep beneath a tree in the little garden, but he did not sleep long and awoke at dawn only minutes after the boy had again gone for the doctor. He seemed amazingly vigorous and called for a huge breakfast, which he shared with the doctor when he arrived. While they ate, the doctor asked many questions and observed his behavior closely. At last he expressed his diagnosis.

"I agree that you are suffering from an enchantment, but it is not one the fairies have cast. This is a very mortal illness and the only cure I know for it is marriage—and the sooner the better or your health will suffer. If there are no candidates, I can recommend the services of a fine matchmaker who has served my own family well."

When her master only smiled, the old woman said, "I believe he has already been approached on that subject and has even seen his prospective bride."

"Ah," said the doctor. "A most foolish youth. This must, indeed, be the cause of the affliction. He should not have set eyes upon her till all was arranged. It is well known that such indiscretions can cause fevers of the brain. I would consult a geomancer at once for an auspicious date before more foolishness compounds his illness."

In the afternoon Madam Feng came again and accepted the commission on behalf of Wei K'e'-yung to arrange an acceptable wedding date and see to the traditional exchange of gifts, even though Mistress Ku had no family. In the evening he received word by messenger that the date had been set. The geomancer was much distressed and had cast the bones six times while Madam Feng sat by nodding and watching each throw intently, but the results were consistent. The wedding must take place in four days. All the signs for the next two

years pointed to a disastrous union. So short a betrothal was
barely within the bounds of civilized behavior and, had there
been families involved, would have been wholly unacceptable,
but Wei K'e-yung was delirious with joy. Especially since the
lady of his yearnings had no objections either.

On the eve of the wedding, Ku-She sat in the courtyard of a
small, plain house she had taken under the name of Madam
Feng, while Yin Whun once more dressed her hair, combing
out the matron's coiled bun. The girl prattled as she worked
and Ku-She watched the sun-colored sky fade, and the lantern
light tint the night air of the veranda.

"It will not be long now, Mistress. They are within your
reach and very soon you will possess them again. Then we will
return to Hibiscus Village and all will be right with the world
once more. The Lung Wang will forgive you, and the Jade
Emperor will reward you and all Hibiscus Village will be
honored. . . ."

Ku-She bowed her head behind her fan and did not reply.

"Please forgive your stupid servant, Mistress, but I still do
not understand why you must actually *marry* this worthless
mortal. I know it has not been sanctioned by the Emperor of
Heaven, and thus you cannot be bound to it, and I know I am
too stupid and ugly to have played this part on your behalf, but
when the matchmaker's queries failed to uncover what you
sought, was there not some other way? Some way that would
not have required you to suffer this creature for even one
night?"

"No," Ku-She said softly, the fluttering fan hiding her face
in the flickering shadows of the lantern light. "I shall not be
with him long. I will have the Golden Chopsticks again, but
the price of my honor is great and I shall mourn this loss with
every snowflake that falls."

Then Ku-She fell silent and would discuss it no more, and
the maid fell silent also and put crystal snowflakes into the
velvet-black hair with silver pins.

The wedding was simple, as was proper for a woman's
second marriage. At dawn the groom's sister met the bride at

the gate to the go-between's house and escorted her on foot to the temple. Even with her wealth, a sedan chair would not have been seemly for a widow, and though the Snow Fairy had never been married it was necessary to disown her pride and play the part. After the brief ceremony the groom rode off on horseback to prepare the house, making the proper offerings to the Door God and Kitchen God and his ancestors while his sister and new wife followed on foot. But halfway home the women were met by a fine sedan chair decked in red wedding banners. The correct gestures having been made in an already unorthodox union, Wei K'e-yung was determined that his beloved bride should have all the honors he could give her.

Much to the amused tittering of the household and the chagrin of the lady's personal maid, the newlyweds were not seen outside their room for three days, and then only Wei K'e-yung emerged. He went to his study briefly and reappeared with the apron of his blue robe filled with books and small objects, ink slab and brush, and his lute over his shoulder. Yin Whun slipped into the room as soon as she noticed him below, but she found her mistress sleeping, her hair a wild tangle and a beauty upon her face the likes of which the maid had never seen before. Her smile was subtle, and her skin pale and cool in the summer heat. There was a tint of rose on her temples and cheeks and lips and the swell of her breasts. To look upon her sleeping so made the girl hesitate in her intent, and before she could wake her mistress the young husband returned, the same rosy blush upon him, and she had to leave them.

The food and wine left at the door was brought in regularly now, and twice more Wei K'e-yung reemerged to run to his study and return at once with small boxes and other objects in his sleeves and apron. Yin Whun merely waited, for it was clear that her lady was about her business. But the day passed and another, and again Wei K'e-yung was in and out of the room several times.

Finally, on the night of the fifth day, the housekeeper summoned the maid from her evening rice saying: "Your mistress requires you. Hurry."

There was a brusqueness and indignation in the old woman that Yin Whun had not seen before, and she ran to Ku-She's room as fast as she could. On the way she found Wei K'e-yung sitting in the garden. His head was in his hands and there was such an air of despair about him that, for once, Yin Whun felt a tug of tenderness for him, but she hurried on to Ku-She, her heart beating wildly. What awaited her in the darkened bedroom, however, was not at all what she had been prepared to find.

Ku-She sat on the bed, her face in her hands lost beneath the unkempt fall of black hair shrouding the head and shoulders and gathering in her lap like a dark pool. Her slender body heaved with the heavy sobs of her crying and the room possessed a distinct chill. The maid ran to her mistress and hovered about her, not knowing what to do, not daring to touch her. Finally she abandoned caution and embraced Ku-She fiercely, crying: "Oh, my most cherished Mistress, what has he done to you? The foul mortal! If he has injured you I will tear his limbs from his body and scatter the pieces to the four pillars of the world!"

"NO!" Ku-She cried, throwing herself from Yin Whun's embrace onto the bed.

"Lady, please tell me what has happened. Unworthy as I am, there might still be some service I can do you. How may I console your grief?"

Ku-She did not reply at once, and only sobbed on for a few moments more, but gradually her crying lessened and the chill in the room grew, until she sat upright on the bed again and pushed the hair from her face. Her skin was pale as a winter moon, and the blush was gone from her. Her eyes were swollen from the tears and dark as the mountain caves.

"We are lost," she said at last. "I am lost. It is I who have failed. Chou Ch'ung-i and the Jade Emperor can find no fault with you. But I am *doomed*. I can never be forgiven. The fault is too great. The failure unredeemable. . . ."

"The chopsticks," the maid whispered. "Oh, Mistress, does this mean the mortal does not *have* them?"

"No," Ku-She murmured. "He does not have them. The foul pestilence of a monk did indeed make him a gift fit for an earthly emperor, but it was a treasure only mortals would regard for its age and history—a scroll of poetry by a scholar of great learning in a past dynasty . . . but not my precious chopsticks."

Yin Whun sat beside Ku-She in a quiet daze. All the spirit

had gone from her mistress and her own energy seemed to have fled as well. She thought of Wei K'e-yung and her moment of pity for him, thinking his sadness to be over the loss of his treasure and his new wife both at once. Now she felt only anger toward him for having sidetracked them for the long days and interminable nights through which her mistress had had to suffer his use of her.

"We will find him yet," she said quickly.

"No," Ku-She said. "We will never find him. He must surely know we are in search of him, and will continue to stay beyond our reach. It is hopeless, and I do not have the strength to continue."

"Perhaps the judges in the Court of the Dead will snare him this time," Yin Whun said.

"Perhaps, but he has evaded them for many lifetimes. I can not rely upon his capture, nor would it relieve me of my failure and my guilt."

"But, mistress—"

"*Enough.* It is done now. I cannot go back without them and I can search no longer. When Chou Ch'ung-i reports my failure, as she eventually must, all of Heaven will be alert for him. Perhaps such an effort would have been advisable from the beginning, and we were *all* foolish to believe I would have proved adequate to this task. But the full of the moon is past and I can do no more. It is beyond me."

"Then what will you do, Madam?" Yin Whun asked in a small voice.

"I will stay here with my husband. In the mortal world. I will live as one of them, keep to this house, forgo my magic and tell him I have lost my wealth. I will call no attention to myself, and if he is to rise in society it will be through his own merit without my power to beguile, for I would eventually be found by the use of it. I will be a good and honorable wife to him, and when the time comes, I will follow him to the Land of the Dead as a mortal woman.

"The Emperor of Heaven will find a way to correct this difficulty in time. No purpose would be served by my returning. If I have failed I might as well stay here and make this one man happy. That much good I can still do."

The little maid twisted her small hands in her apron and

stared at her mistress with large, dark eyes, and a wondering confusion upon her brow.

"Do you care for this mortal, then, as a true husband, My Lady?"

"Yes," Ku-She murmured, and the blush slowly rose upon her temples once more. "I love him as dearly as anything I have ever known, and will gladly follow him into the Land of the Dead when the time comes. He captured my heart the moment I saw him. His manner filled me with admiration, and his beauty filled me with desire. It was the grief of my very soul that I knew I would have to leave him when I took the chopsticks, just as it is now the grief of my soul that I will never again see Hibiscus Village, nor attend to my heavenly duty. There is no happiness for me either way, but my love for him may at least make my short mortal existence contented."

"But there is no fault in you, child. You may return to Hibiscus Village and the service of my Sister Tung Shuang-Ch'eng."

"No, Madam. I will stay with you. It would be necessary for me to reveal your whereabouts, and I will never betray you. If you choose to remain here a mortal span, I will remain also, and return to the fairy realm when you have followed your husband into the Other World. I desire no service but yours, and will be as faithful as my miserable, worthless soul permits."

Ku-She was grateful, for the burden of her secret would be great over the years. She bade her maid help her dress and arrange her hair and make her appearance fit, and as the girl set about the familiar tasks, Ku-She began to feel some of the burden lift ever so slightly.

In the garden the old housekeeper plied her young master with tea and wine and cakes, but he would have none of it. The old man brought his books and his lute but he would not look at them. He bade them leave him and sat beneath the tree in silence.

"That witch!" the old woman said. "Not five days married and she has already rejected him. It was an unholy match in the beginning. If she were truly a respectable woman she would have remained faithful to her first husband. . . ."

"She had a shrine set up to his ancestors, didn't she?" the old man muttered at his wife.

"A simple thing to do. It means nothing to one such as that. Look how short the betrothal was. She has married him for sport and nothing more. She beguiled him and rejected him just to see him suffer. He has not pleased her in bed and she will find a way to be rid of him soon enough, I'll wager. Or she will stay and twist him about her wrist, tease him and reject him and make him miserable, until the day he becomes a man of note in the Imperial Court and then tell everyone that she has made him so with her love. She will demand gifts and clothing and jewelry and not let him near that fine fortune she claims for herself, and he will suffer her torments because she has bewitched him."

"Hush," the old man said. "Lovers often quarrel. He will soon see the error of his ways in letting her get too much power over him, and he will correct the situation. If he is careful how he lets her manage his household, and is firm with her when she tries to manipulate him, they will have as good a marriage as can be hoped for. And if she learns her lessons well, she could even make him happy."

"He is obsessed," the old woman muttered. "And men obsessed are fools when it comes to managing their wives. I wager she will not let him take concubines. Not even that maid of hers. She is the jealous sort, I can tell. As long as she cares to possess him she will not allow another near him."

"Enough," said the old man. "He will hear you, and no good can come of that."

In the garden Wei K'e-yung sat beneath his tree and felt the weight of his despair. For days he had shown her all his prized possessions, displayed his skills and his learning, sung her his poems and composed verses to her beauty. These things had pleased her and he had gloried in her quiet praise. She had rewarded his verses with the pleasures of the very body he had praised, and he had never known greater desire nor greater satisfaction. He had shown her all his small treasures, and finally the gift of his uncle Pan Ch'ao, his greatest treasure. But here she had amazed him. At first she had begged to see more. But there was nothing more. She had accused him of holding back secrets, until he had finally admitted there was one treasure he held more dear than the scroll. She had begged him to show it to her, and he had teased and refused till he had won more favors from her. When finally he could tease her no more, he had brought a mirror to the bed and held it before her saying *she* was the greatest of his treasures, his own beloved bride, but amazingly this had not pleased her at all. She had railed at him with wild and frantic eyes and again accused him of keeping secret possessions, until his protestations had finally convinced her. Then she flew into a fit of weeping and would not let him touch her or console her or entice her. She cried out that she had been cheated and deceived and that all was lost, and cried uncontrollably. He could not understand her rejection. She had known he was not wealthy, yet she had clearly expected something of greater material value from him than he could give her. He had thought she loved him, but now he knew only that she would not let him near her and he was in despair.

Gradually, so slowly that he did not really notice it, the hot, late summer air grew cooler. When he finally became aware, it was the gentle liquid whisper of silk that aroused him and the quiet scuffle of feet behind his tree. Looking up, he saw his bride and her maid approaching slowly. The maid stood at the edge of the path and his new wife came to him, kneeling by his side and placing her forehead upon the stones. The cool breezes surrounded her and played with the edges of her silk gown. Even bowed to the ground, her beauty was hypnotic. He was enthralled, and could think of no reproach to say to her. She begged his forgiveness for her wicked and thoughtless behavior, and swore she would never again cause him so much as a moment's unhappiness. He knew she had said this, though he could not recall the exact words. He had often found himself wondering at this lately, for at all other times he was remarkably clear about whatever was said to him by others. Now, however, he knew only that there was no crime she could ever commit for which he could not grant immediate forgiveness. Her presence made his happiness complete, and in his heart the quarrel had never happened.

Ku-She rejoiced in her husband's forgiveness, but her heart was still troubled. She longed to tell him the truth, but in fact her first act as his wife, and the manager of his household, was to deceive him further. She forged a document in the form of an official notice that her late husband had offended the Imperial Court, and that a judgement had been sent down that his lands and all his personal wealth be confiscated on behalf of the emperor. It further implied he should count himself lucky he was already dead. Then Ku-She sent her maid out to the marketplace with the document hidden in her sleeve, instructing her to find a messenger to deliver the item to the house three days hence.

When the messenger came at last, she fell into a fit of weeping and would not eat for two days. She begged her husband not to abandon her now that she was poor and had nothing to give him but her love and possibly children some day. There was no doubt, of course, he was as bewitched as ever.

The servants scoffed. The old man said now she would learn to be a proper wife. The old woman said she had grown used to wealth and would leave him soon enough for another rich old man, and when she had his fortune as well, she would again seek a young and handsome plaything. The lady's maid and the old housekeeper bristled like a pair of fighting birds. But Wei K'e-yung had only grown to love his wife more deeply, and the more he loved her, the more her beauty seemed to increase. He longed to show her to his friends, to display her as a jewel upon his breast. He called her Pao Shih, his precious jewel, his glorious gem. But she had grown shy and would not be seen. When men came to the house she would keep to her rooms and not even speak to them from behind the screen in the reception hall, nor allow herself to be glimpsed passing in the halls. If men came to the house when her husband was away, she would have the old man receive them and the boy wait upon them if it was necessary but under no circumstances would she enter their presence. In this regard her behavior was impeccable, and the servants grew to respect her irreproachable propriety. She did not invite the other women of the neighborhood in, and her husband's sister, Liu Ch'ing, was her only outside companion, and that infrequently, as Liu Ch'ing was soon to be delivered of her first child and was not strong. Ku-She explained her reluctance to entertain by saying that her husband's wealth was not great, and her own means were now lost, and all their resources were needed to support Wei K'e-yung's studies, for books and tutors; it would be unwise to entertain frivolously.

Wei K'e-yung could not argue with this, and he was glad to have found someone so conscientious and perfect in her duty, but he could not help but wish that just once in a while she would allow a moment's harmless lapse.

The month turned into the harvest season and the crop was poor. The summer rains had been sparse, the lakes low, the rivers sluggish. The monsoons would replenish the coast, but inland things did not look hopeful, unless the winter snowfall was heavy.

As autumn set in, the scholar's house, which had been a haven of coolness in the summer heat, took on a decided chill.

As winter came Wei K'e-yung applied himself more and more deeply to study—of both his books and his beautiful wife. He spent as much time in the bedchamber as he did in the study, and often his wife visited the study as well, endlessly embroidering silver snowflakes on a white linen canopy for their bed. Her needlework was exceptional, and Wei K'e-yung convinced her to sell it to help in their support. Reluctantly, she agreed, but would not work the snowflakes, which were her finest patterns. She embroidered girdles and aprons and pillows with birds and flowers, which fetched a high price, but in the end of the Twelfth Month, she once again began to work the snowflakes onto fine lengths of swaddling clothes.

Wei K'e-yung was overjoyed. He no longer pressed her to appear in public, and waited out her pregnancy with her in blissful seclusion.

That winter proved the coldest in the city of Wuchang's memory. Though not a flake of snow fell, the temperatures were bitter and the house, which the previous year had proved sound even against the worst winter storms, could barely be kept warm. Wei K'e-yung spent a good deal of his income on fuel and extra clothing for, oddly enough, it often seemed colder in the house than in the street. Concerned for his child, Wei K'e-yung kept his wife even more bundled up than the rest of the household, and insisted a brazier be kept near her at all times; but neither she nor her maid seemed much affected by the cold. Often he would see her wandering about the little garden, lightly dressed and not at all uncomfortable. He admonished her for this, but she said that as a child she had been brought up in the mountains, where the winters were far worse than this, and if he would not deny her these walks their child would be born with a similar tolerance for the cold. Reluctantly, he let her have her way, for he could not deny he would have given much for a similar sympathy with nature that winter.

The spring was late, and the early buds pushed their way relentlessly through hard-packed earth, but finally, slowly, the winter died and gave over to a cool planting season. The streams were dust and the rivers and ponds little more than puddles, but the crop was set in and water carried from wherever it could be taken—even kitchen wells and household cisterns. In the city of Wuchang things looked easier at first. Flowers bloomed and trees greened. The summer heat did not afflict them the way the winter cold had, and once again Wei K'e-yung's little house was an oasis of cool and gentle breezes. Like many others, it had its own well, but as the summer passed, prices in the marketplace grew steadily higher and the quality of goods poorer, and finally rice and produce became scarce.

Wei K'e-yung's kitchen garden did well enough with the help of his well, but anything they could not grow put an increasingly heavy burden upon his means, and he began to fear for the next year if things did not improve soon.

And he worried about his family. With the coming of spring, much of the joy had left his wife, and as her time drew nearer, her mood deepened into real sadness. The midwife came from time to time and scolded him for not cheering his wife. It endangered the child, she said. The mood of the mother during the waiting time determined the child's personality and could even influence gender. This melancholy outlook would no doubt produce a petulant, unhappy girl whom they would have trouble marrying off.

Wei K'e-yung tried everything he could think of and somewhat more than he could afford. He proposed a trip to the countryside, but she refused to leave the house, even in a closed chair, and he could not really blame her. On the few occasions when he himself had to venture outside of Wuchang's ancient walls he had found the countryside in a desperate plight. Much of the spring planting had refused to grow, and by midsummer what remained was parched and dying. The fields looked burned; the trees and bamboo groves bore withered yellow leaves and rattled like bundles of dry kindling in the scorching breezes. The soil was dust and blew entire fields away, and the rivers were trickles of sludge; the ponds and lakes were bogs. Only the mosquitoes thrived in the slow stagnations, and before long there would not be enough water even for them.

After such trips Wei K'e-yung would return home full of stories. He would make extra sacrifices to the dragon protecting his well and to his ancestors to intervene on his behalf, and he would give his garden an extra measure of water as well, but even in the city the drought was making its presence felt. The streets, like the fields, were dust that crept into all the houses, and the large trees beyond Wei K'e-yung's garden wall were already shedding their leaves. He pulled them from his well with each bucket for the garden or the household, and his wife's sadness grew deeper. She did not sit with him as often now, and rarely walked in the courtyard.

Throughout the summer Ku-She kept mainly to her own rooms and kept company only with her maid. Her melancholy was deeper than anyone could know, for it was a true grief and a true guilt.

"It is not your fault," Yin Whun would say. "It is that cursed taoist magician who has done this."

And though Ku-She would nod and not argue, she knew whose fault it *really* was, and she wept often and could not be cheered.

The child was born on the third day of the seventh month, and much to the midwife's amazement was a loud, robust, healthy boy with bright black eyes and a quick smile.

Wei K'e-yung was overcome with joy, and his love for his wife grew a hundredfold. He sent word to his sister and her family, his neighbors and teachers and everyone he knew, that on the third day of the eighth month there would be the traditional one-month-old celebration for his firstborn son. But still the sorrow hung upon his wife, and this hurt him deeply.

"You should have joy in our child," he said.

"I do," she replied earnestly, nursing her son in her cradling arms. "Besides you, my beloved husband, he is the greatest blessing of my life."

"Then why do you sigh when he smiles at you? Why do you weep when he laughs?"

More than ever, Ku-She longed to tell Wei K'e-yung everything, but there was no answer she could give him.

In the evening, while her husband studied and the child was laid to sleep and the servants busied themselves with preparations for the coming celebration, Ku-She sat apart with her maid and mourned the fate of the world and her small family.

"I thought I could hide here and be happy with him. I thought the Jade Emperor of Heaven would find a way to repair the damage my failure has done, but I see that it is not so. The world is dying. Without the rain there is no hope, and without the snow there can be no more rain. It is bad enough to be at fault for allowing my chopsticks to be stolen, but to be responsible for this. . . .

"For the love of this man I hid from my duty and I have not been happy this long year, though I love him more each day. And now I have given him a son. I have borne a child into a dying world, but I cannot refuse to love him. I am doomed to watch my two most cherished ones wither as the grass and trees around us do even now, and turn to dust like the streets outside. And when all the world lies dying but you and me, my beloved husband will look at me and know why I survive. He will know what I am and that I have caused this, and he will hate me where he dwells in the Land of the Dead until the end of time.

"How could I have been foolish enough to believe I could live a mortal's existence and die a mortal's death simply because I wished it? How could I have been blind enough to believe the Judges of the Court of the Dead would not have barred me from their realm and sent me directly to the Jade Emperor if I *had* discovered a way to follow Wei K'e-yung?"

Yin Whun soothed her, but she would not be comforted.

"He asks why I weep but how can I not? My child! His every smile cuts into my heart. His little life so short, he would have been better off not to have been born, and yet I cannot wish that. He would also hate me if he were old enough to know. But he never will be. . . ."

Ku-She went to the window and looked into the night, full of cold, hard stars.

"In five days this house will be filled with people for the first time since our marriage. It is unavoidable. This time I cannot refuse. It is the child's right, and my husband deserves this much happiness. I will appear as required, even though Heaven's spies may take notice and discover me."

She turned from the window, and tears stained her cheeks and a passionate despair burned in her eyes. "Then I must return to Heaven. I will confess my fault, throw myself upon the emperor's mercy, do whatever he wishes, suffer eternal tortures if only he will spare these people!"

"Forgive me, Mistress," Yin Whun said, "but the Jade Emperor has surely done all he can and only time will finish whatever great work he has set in motion. It does not seem likely that he would cause all the Earth to perish just to get even with one lowly, elemental fairy."

At once Yin Whun fell to her knees and knocked her head against the floor, exclaiming that so foul a mouth as hers should instantly be filled with ashes or her tongue cut from her head. But Ku-She only sat upon the bed and bade her maid rise, for she knew the girl was right.

On the morning of the celebration Ku-She rose early and supervised the servants in their final preparations. She had made up her mind to confess all to her husband that evening, spend one last night with him if he still wished it, and return to Heaven. Thus resolved, though the choice had been hard and ached within her even now, she felt better than she had since the loss of her precious treasure. As she worked about the house she discovered a growing joy—for the event, for the child. She had always loved the banquets in Hibiscus Village heralding the beginning and end of seasons and this, though smaller and simpler, was an event of the utmost importance to her. She would make it as grand and gay as she could. When she went upstairs to dress she had Yin Whun do her hair in the grand fashion and put the crystal and silver snowflakes in its coils.

Wei K'e-yung was, without doubt, a man bursting with pride. Pride in his new son, but also pride in his wife. Lean as his budget was, poor as the items available in the market had been, she had set before them a banquet fit for an Imperial Prince.

Everyone in the neighborhood had come, many he supposed, out of curiosity about his mysterious wife, and some folks had come from great distances. She received them all graciously and with perfect correctness. Everywhere she went, the sun shone and cool breezes played. Everything she touched seemed grander for having been at her hand. Even the gifts seemed finer when they passed from her hand to the little red-and-gold-covered table, and no one went away humbled or embarrassed by the meanness of his circumstances, for each guest found that he had selected the most perfect item of its kind available. Of all the eyes that witnessed this wonderful event all were pleased by what they saw but only two pairs recognized it for what it was. One belonged to the lady's maid. The other belonged to the monk, Wei Pan Ch'ao.

Even before her husband presented him to her she knew him. The faint glow of magic, like infant dragon fire, hung about his person and flickered slightly as it mingled with the shadows of great age. Yet he was a man not at all past his prime, and vigorous with a careless smile and a quick, sharp tongue. His hair was graying, but only slightly, and his form was straight and wiry and his movements youthful. He had known her as well immediately upon entering the scholar's gate, for her fairy aspect was full about her, and though her magic masked much from mortal eyes, his were no longer entirely mortal.

"He is among us," Ku-She had whispered hastily to Yin Whun. "What am I to do? I cannot let him slip away, and yet I cannot reveal myself before all these people. He knows who I am, I am sure of it. He will evade me once more unless something is done quickly."

"I will help in any way I can, Madam. You have only to command me," Yin Whun said.

"I have a thought," said Ku-She. "But do I dare to call upon the aid of my sister fairies? The Jade Emperor's spies will surely know if I do, and yet I have little choice. Stay close to me, Little One. I will require you the moment there is a chance to slip away."

It was not long before her chance came. While her husband and his uncle were engaged in happy conversation, Ku-She and Yin Whun fled to a storage room on the second floor in the farthest corner of the house.

While Yin Whun watched the door, Ku-She knelt upon a mat and raised her voice to Heaven.

Sisters, hear me. I require your aid. All the fairies in the Jade Emperor's service may suffer unless I succeed in this, and to that end I beg your assistance."

A long moment passed in silence and Ku-She, with a sinking heart and trembling hands pressed to her bosom, cried out: "Help me, Sisters! *Please!*"

Wei K'e-yung had searched the ground floor of the house for his wife, and no one had seen her. She was not in her chamber, but when he emerged he found her descending the stairs, looking pale and tired and sadder than he had seen her in days. His heart turned at the sight of her beautiful, melancholy face, for he had believed the sorrow gone and now he knew that the joy of the day had been only temporary. But she smiled again when she saw him and he took her hand and they descended into the garden once more.

After a brief time, Wei Pan Ch'ao came to pay his respects and depart. His nephew was amazed that he did not intend to stay longer and accept the hospitality of his home for the night, as he usually did when in Wuchang. Wei K'e-yung had cherished the visits of this eccentric and learned uncle since childhood, and his affection was mixed with more than a little awe. But the monk insisted he had to be on his way.

As they stood beside the garden wall, unnoticed by any of the guests or the young man at his side, a small white spider dropped onto Wei Pan Ch'ao's shoulder and hid itself in the collar of his robe.

Ku-She watched him go with a feeling of desperation. It was still early in the afternoon and the taoist could go far before the guests left and her husband retired and she was free to slip away to search for him.

In a quiet shrine by the northern city wall, Wei Pan Ch'ao stopped and paid his respects to the priest, lit incense before the altar, took tea and sat in the shade of a sickly mulberry tree in the garden. The shrine was to a minor local god and was kept by one old man and his young novice, so it was not long before Wei Pan Ch'ao was alone, apparently dozing beneath the tree. Therefore it was surprising when he spoke aloud in a soft voice, though no one had approached, and his eyes were still closed.

"You may come out now, my child," he said.

There was no response but this was to be expected.

"Come now," he said. "I am not a foolish old man, though I may seem so at times . . . when I choose to. You may look like a spider and hide in my robe, but I know you for what you are. You are the fairy maid of my nephew's wife, Pao Shih . . . but that is not her name. She called upon the Fairy of One Hundred Insects, who enchanted you and made you into a white spider so you could follow me and later lead your mistress to me. Magic knows when other magic is present, and the fairy aspect is on you even in this form. I did not hear her call, but I felt the magic gathering in the upper corner of the house and realized what it must be, for I knew her at once. Come out, child. I will not harm you or your mistress. We have much to talk about."

Slowly the little spider emerged from a fold of cloth at the back of his shoulder, and scurried down his arm to the ground, where he saw her as a tiny glow in the dry grass.

"Can you assume your normal form at will or do you have to wait for the fairy to unbind you?"

"No," said the girl kneeling on the ground before him, "I can restore myself, as you see. But I cannot regain the spider form."

"You trust me," he said.

"I am the lowliest of fairies in the realm of Heaven," she said. "I can do little but serve others, but I can tell a lie from the truth and, though I cannot call you an honest man, I do not see deception in you now."

The monk looked her squarely in the eye but she did not avert her gaze. "You are bold on your mistress's behalf."

"I am her humble slave and would follow her to the four corners of the Great Bowl of the World. I would place myself before her, and any harm due her I would take upon myself if possible."

"What is her name?" the monk asked. "Is it the Fairy of Ku-She or Tung Shuang-Ch'eng you serve?"

"My lady is the Fairy of Ku-She," Yin Whun replied.

"Your loyalty is commendable, child. I shall tell her so. And you may serve her by conveying the message that I wish to meet with her most urgently. I have been searching for her since the turn of the year. I will be in my nephew's garden by the kitchen wall at midnight. If she will come to me, we have much damage to repair."

The maid hurried back to the scholar's house and slipped in by the kitchen garden. Ku-She was surprised to see her so soon. It was barely dusk and many of the guests were still about, the men drinking and gambling in the main hall, the women in the garden examining Ku-She's embroidery.

"He will come to you," Yin Whun said. "In the garden at midnight."

"How can he be trusted?" Ku-She exclaimed. "You should not have revealed yourself. You have failed me, and now he will vanish again."

"Forgive your stupid slave, Madam," the maid said, bowing to the floor. "But his magic is strong. He knew me from the moment my spider form touched his shoulder. He knew when you called to your sisters. And, though he is not a noble man, he has seen the error of his ways. His last encounter with the Judges of the Court of the Dead was but narrowly escaped. This drought is killing the world, and no matter how powerful his magic, it cannot place him beyond that ultimate fate. He has cheated death for many lifetimes and he does not wish to face it now because of a bad joke."

Ku-She understood the truth when she heard it too, and her anger subsided. "Then he will come," she said.

"Yes, Madam, I am sure of it."

Ku-She patted the maid's hand with a sigh. "It was well done, Little One. And it is nearly over." She looked into the garden from the shelter of the kitchen porch and saw her husband searching for her among the women. "Farewell, My Love," she whispered. "Have great joy today, for tonight you will surely lose me. I can no longer reveal the truth to you as I had planned, but you and our son will live and I will watch over you from the fairy realm as best I can."

Then she went out to him in the garden with her most beautiful smile and all the warmth of her love in her eyes.

Wei Pan Ch'ao felt the cool breeze of her approach before she appeared at the far end of the courtyard; and she could see him, though to other eyes he would have been but a shadow upon the wall by the kitchen corner.

"At last," she said politely bowing her head. "The thief. The instrument of my shame. Why do you come to me, jackal? You should simply return the chopsticks to Heaven and make my failure all the more miserable. Surely that would please a jester such as you—a mean joke upon a lowly fairy. Yet you cause your people and your own kin great suffering and then you come to me. Why?"

"By the time I knew I had lost you I was far from here, and did not know where you had fallen from my path. I did not intend this to go so far, but I cannot return them without your help. I can no longer enter Hibiscus Village as I used to. Heaven is too alert, and I cannot go before the Jade Emperor's court free of risk. At his most merciful, your exalted ruler would grant me a home in the Land of the Dead, rather than require me to suffer an eternity of his pleasure. It is unlikely, however, that even the return of the Golden Chopsticks would persuade him to be even *that* lenient. So, as I have no wish to walk into the den of the hungry tiger, it is wiser that *you* return them, thereby fulfilling your assigned task, though somewhat belatedly."

"If I am to be punished for *your* jest, it seems only right that you should be also," Ku-She said angrily.

"I completely agree," Wei Pan Ch'ao said. "But I am concerned about my life, Mistress Fairy, not about what is right. Until I have your word not to reveal me to Heaven or the Judges of the Court of the Dead, you will not have your chopsticks."

"I agree," said Ku-She, furious, "because I have pity for these creatures and that leaves me no choice."

"And because you love my nephew and your son," Wei Pan Ch'ao smiled.

Her reply was an icy glare the monk felt to the marrow of his bones.

"Your promise, Madam?"

"You have my word," Ku-She said slowly and deliberately, "that I will not reveal you to any heavenly agency in return for the safe return of my Golden Chopsticks. *Now give them to me.*"

"Ah," the monk smiled. "I do not have them."

Ku-She was rigid with fury. "You *vermin*! You *tricked* me!"

"No, I never said I still had them. But I know where they are and we may retrieve them without difficulty. Not long after I took them, I grew tired of carrying them with me; the hunt was more interesting to me than the bait. I gave them to an old farmer in exchange for a few nights' hospitality. They were the grandest things he had ever possessed, though he did not know the extent of that truth, and swore before his ancestors that he would never part with them."

"And where does this old man dwell?"

"In the Szechwan Province. In a village about twenty li beyond the city of Chung'king."

Ku-She frowned in thought. "My sister fairies wish me well and can be trusted, but it is dangerous for me to call upon them. I risk discovery and they risk the wrath of Heaven, but this is worth such a risk. I shall call upon the Fairy of One Hundred Birds to give us the form of hawks so we may fly far and fast without fear of being preyed upon. And if we keep our wits about us, men can be avoided."

"Then make haste, Small Fairy. Your goal is nearly in reach."

"Tomorrow at noon," she said. "I will meet you outside the Western Gate. I will bear the appearance of a straw gatherer, but you will know me. I will have this final time with my loved ones, for I shall very likely never see them again. Now go. I do not want you here."

Ku-She turned and crossed the garden and sat down on the broad, moonlit sill of her husband's study window and began to weep. From inside Yin Whun heard her and laid open the shutters and sat on the sill also.

"There is one last thing I would require of you, Little One," Ku-She said at last when her tears had ceased. "Then your service to me will be at an end, and you may go where you will. It would not be unwise, I think, if you did not return to Heaven. Though they can find no fault with you for *my* failure, they may lay blame upon you for your loyalty to me in not revealing my whereabouts to them. Therefore, I will not take you with me when I leave tomorrow."

"Madam, No!" the maid cried. "I am your slave forever and will follow you always! I only wish to serve you."

"And you shall serve me. You are brave and clever and trustworthy and patient, and I will need all of that if I am to succeed in this last deception. I know that you hold no love for Wei K'e-yung and he has taken no interest at all in concubines, but if you love *me* as your mistress, you will perform this last task with a glad heart. Assume my form and take my place in his household. Make him happy as I have failed to do of late, and be mother to my son. Give him sons of your own if you can, but do not ever tell him that I am gone, nor what I was, nor what has become of me. This task is the greatest trust I have ever laid upon anyone, and though you do not care for him, perhaps you will one day love him for my sake and come to cherish the child also."

"You must stay a mortal lifespan, but at its end you may go where you will. I do not care to wonder where I shall be then."

Yin Whun leaned forward and whispered eagerly, "But, Madam, if the Emperor of Heaven is *pleased* by the return of the Golden Chopsticks, and the monk given over to the Judges of the Other World he may see fit to *reward* you. He could easily make your husband an immortal if he so chose, and your son is half-fairy and may be so already!"

"Do not give me false hope!" Ku-She said angrily. "It is hard enough to leave him. Do not expect me to think of more. Only do as I say, and care for them as you would for me. Keep my secret, and a great burden will be lifted from me."

"My dearest Lady," the maid whispered. "I will do all I can."

"I will go up to him now. Tomorrow at noon go with me to the Western Gate. When you return through it again you will wear my likeness. I have promised the monk immunity for this, but you are free to do what you please. You may account to the household for your own disappearance as you see fit."

At the beating of the noon drum Wei Pan Ch'ao passed onto the road outside the Western Gate of the city and found two women selling straw beneath a dying tree. As the entire world was turning to straw, they were having no apparent success but to the monk's eye they glowed softly with the fairy magic that transformed them into withered peasants, and he knew them immediately. As he approached, one of the women stood and walked toward the gate, and as she passed beneath it he saw Ku-She walking away from him. But the glow of magic was still upon her, and he turned back to the tree where the old woman hailed him and bade him examine her goods.

"The other was my maid," she said when he drew near.

"You have set her to deceive your husband," he said, and there was anger in his eyes.

"She is trustworthy and I have set my greatest treasure in her care. I will not reveal you as you ask, if you will keep my secret from Wei K'e-yung and my son. Swear this as I have sworn to you, and we will depart."

Wei Pan Ch'ao swore and they set off together along the road, leaving the straw beneath the tree. Another four li and they approached a dense bamboo grove which Wei Pan Ch'ao did not recall seeing before. They entered the grove and emerged a short time later in upward flight through the dry yellow leaves—a pair of brown hunting hawks.

Even on wing with few stops for hunting and rest, the journey required many days. The longer and farther they flew, the angrier Ku-She became, for it was clear that she had pursued the thief the entire summer without cause, and had only gotten farther from the treasure the closer she came to *him*. It was possible he had even left them behind before she discovered their loss. Indeed, when the hawk that was Wei Pan Ch'ao finally began to circle a village, it was in a district she had not seen, for the monk was well past it when the Judges of the Dead had set her on the path.

The farm was two li beyond the village and even from the air, miserable as the drought had made all the land, it was clear the farm had been abandoned before the spring planting, for there was no sign of cultivation at all.

"What has happened?" Ku-She demanded as they flew low over the abandoned cottage.

"I do not know," Wei Pan Ch'ao replied. "I must go into the village and enquire."

"If we abandon the bird forms, we cannot take them on

again without my sister's aid, and I dare not call her again so soon. If we have farther to go we must do it on foot once more."

"Then let us fly into the village and listen and watch. If night comes and we have learned nothing, I will try to trick someone into telling me what I want to know. If there is still no success by morning, I fear we will have no choice."

Together they flew into the little town and sat beneath the eaves of shops and cottages, but there was no gossip about the farmer, nor could Wei Pan Ch'ao find him anywhere in the village. At nightfall they perched together beneath the porch roof of a wineshop, and shortly after the second watch was sounded a man emerged who had clearly had more than his fill. Seeing their chance, the two hawks flew after him into the darkness. Outside the village he headed for a small farmhouse not far away, and when he had gotten about halfway there, Wei Pan Ch'ao flew at him out of the darkness, striking him hard from behind and knocking him to the ground, where he sprawled facedown. At once the two birds landed on his back, and Wei Pan Ch'ao ordered him to stop screaming or he would feel their talons in his spine. When the man continued to squirm, the monk pricked him through his shirt with one razor-sharp clawed foot, and the farmer lay still, moaning quietly.

Then Wei Pan Ch'ao questioned him about his missing neighbor. The old man, it seemed, died shortly after the taoist had left him, and his son, much to his amazement, had inherited a magnificent pair of golden chopsticks along with the wretched farm. He had sold the land and gone off to the city to find someone with sufficient means to purchase the treasure. With the money, he planned to set himself up in business and grow rich and fat.

Without a word, the two birds took wing and flew east into the night toward Chung'king. They arrived well before dawn, and the gates were still barred. There would be no place to lodge now, so they flew into the heart of Chung'king and took a thorough look about, learning the pattern and character of the town and its condition. There would be no simple tricks upon drunken farmers here, and Ku-She and her companion had no choice but to abandon their bird forms. Ku-She assumed the guise of a fortune teller in the marketplace, and Wei Pan Ch'ao went about openly looking for the man. But Chung'king was a major trade center full of merchants and peddlers and peasants escaping the ruined land. The place was crowded and foul and bewildering. It took seven days to find someone who knew the farmer's son, and Wei Pan Ch'ao learned only that the man was in prison for his debts. He had purchased a rice distributing firm the previous summer, but as the crop failed in the spring, he had fallen into ruin and had finally been thrown into prison.

That night at a poor inn over broth and eggs he told Ku-She what he had learned.

"He has sold them, of course, but I cannot learn to whom."

"Then you must find him in prison and learn the man's name. I have seen you slip through walls in my own garden," she said. "You will find a way to him."

That night as the prisoners slept and the guards within grew lax, Wei Pan Ch'ao entered quietly by a shadowy corner of the east wall and began methodically searching the pens of wretched, sleeping bodies littering the floors. Here and there the remnant of a rich brocade or a gilt collar showed through the grime and tatters, proclaiming the wearer to be a man fallen from a considerable height. For the most part, however, the floors were strewn with folk garbed in the peasant styles of farmers and street peddlers. Some were so wretched it was difficult to tell if they were male or female. All were starving. Some were dead.

Wei Pan Ch'ao searched through the night but did not visit all the pens, for there were a great many faces to be examined closely in the dark and he did not dare summon even a small fox fire. Privately, he began to wonder if he would know the farmer's son if he found him, for some of the starvelings were barely recognizable as human. . . . And what if he were already dead? The man had no relatives in the city to bring him food even in the best of circumstances, and there would be little or nothing to steal from others here. He did not say this to Ku-She the next morning, however, and resumed his search the following night.

Shortly after the sounding of the third watch Wei Pan Ch'ao approached Ku-She where she sat in a dark corner near the rear wall of an inn.

"I have found him at last," the thief said, "but he demands payment for his information. We must secure his release and ensure his continued physical comfort and he will tell us what we require."

"Very well," she said. "I will see to it. Be at the prison gate at noon tomorrow, and when he is released to you bring him to this inn where I shall be waiting."

Early the next morning an old woman entered the local magistrate's office and found a clerk responsible for the rolls of debtors in the prison. From her wicker bag she produced a cloth-wrapped object, which the clerk accepted, scrupulously checking the scrolls and declaring that, indeed, one tael of fine silver was precisely enough to pay her grandson's fines. The bar of metal was accepted and noted in the records, and a bailiff sent off to release the man. At noon Wei Pan Ch'ao brought the man, leaning heavily upon a stick, to the private room the fairy had secured. There they found a bath and new clothes of sturdy homespun. When the man was presentable Wei Pan Ch'ao led him into the next room, where Ku-She sat in regal beauty. Her fairy aura was upon her, and the poor man could not be entirely sure of what he saw. But he knew she was beautiful and he was enchanted. She spoke to him softly and drew from her girdle a small, brown bag which looked to be quite empty.

"Reach in," she said, and when he did he drew forth a steaming meat bun, which he devoured greedily. When he reached in again there was a second, but the third time there was nothing. The wretched soul looked imploringly at the strange and beautiful vision before him. The room, he realized, had grown cold and there was a frosty glow about the air.

"We have given you what you asked," she said. "You are free, and twice a day you may withdraw two buns from the pouch; it will serve you faithfully for a year. In return you must give us the name of the man to whom you sold the golden chopsticks. If you deal falsely with us, the bag will give you nothing more to eat and you will starve once more."

The man fell to his knees and pressed his forehead to the floor. "I sold them to an agent for the Provincial Governor of Szechwan, Cho Wing Mah, for twenty taels of silver and fifty strings of cash. They are in the treasury at the capital in Cheng'tu by now, for I sold them at the end of the harvest season last year. This I swear to be the truth. I do not know the agent's name but His Honor the Governor can easily be found. I will . . ."

The chill was suddenly gone from the room, and when the farmer looked up he found he was alone in a shabby upstairs tearoom and a small table stood before him loaded with rice and vegetables and hot tea.

At the close of the day the clerks did their usual accounting of the gold and silver and copper cash collected in fines. To everyone's amazement, there was found among the bars of silver one common brick of packed, red clay and the tally was short by one tael of silver.

The provincial capital was a week-long walk. Ku-She did not dare call upon her sisters again so soon, and the oxcarts that normally carried goods across the trade routes were few these days, but the land of the Szechwan basin, though ringed by mountains, was a vast plain and easy walking.

It was now the middle of the ninth month. The harvest here would have been in full progress, for the province was normally blessed with a long growing period, and two harvests a year were not uncommon, but there was little to gather and the weather was once more turning cool. The autumn airs, however, did nothing to lessen the suffering of the land. It lay open in jagged cracks like the crazing of a glazed vase, and was hard as brick beneath their feet. The branches of dead trees rattled like the bones in the geomancer's bags, and most of the grass had vanished. White mourning banners fluttered like ghosts in the streets of the villages they passed, and funerals were a daily sight.

When they reached the capital, it became clear that the Provincial Treasury was not as sound as it might be. Wei Pan Ch'ao had no trouble slipping inside after nightfall, but the chopsticks were nowhere to be found. It would be necessary to seek them in the governor's own household. So to this end, Wei Pan Ch'ao approached one of the governor's agents and offered to sell the man his only daughter for a serving maid. The girl, he said, was of rare and astonishing beauty and unless some such arrangement were made they would both starve.

The agent refused, for both the treasury and the governor's own means were in strained circumstances, and a great many parents were eager to strike such bargains these days. But when he saw Ku-She he could not resist her. Enchanted, he approached his master, who was not pleased by the recommendation, but the following day the agent had arranged for Ku-She to present a petition to the court and the governor fell under the fairy enchantment as well.

He installed her in his household and lavished his attentions upon her, but she coyly did not submit to his urgings and toyed with him, keeping his pleasure sufficiently satisfied that three days and nights passed without undue difficulty. He would not discuss his affairs, however, so while he was at court she spent her days questioning the other servants as closely as she could. At last she learned from one of the maids to his First Wife that the master had fallen far short on the tax levies, and had found it expedient to pay a bribe to his superior in order to retain his position. She had overheard him describe the goods to his wife and among the rare books and silks there had been a pair of golden chopsticks.

Above the Provincial Governors were the lower ranks of the Imperial Bureaucracy, and for this it would be necessary to travel to the Imperial Capital at Peking, which surrounded the Imperial City like a tea cozy, and the Forbidden City deep within that. It was a journey of 2,550 li and a month's travel by foot over largely mountainous terrain, and the weather was turning cold. Once more Ku-She decided to risk contact with her sisters and beg for wings. It would be a long and dangerous flight, but it would cut the time by more than half. But when she called, there was no reply. The monk urged her to try again the next day and pressed her hard when she refused. At last she agreed if he would wait two more days, but again it was to no avail and she would hear no more of his urgings.

"I *dare* not," she said angrily. "I cannot know why they do not answer, and each time I call to Heaven I risk being heard by those whom we seek to avoid. Especially you. I have promised not to betray you but you would give us both away."

After that he was silent on the subject and they began to walk.

Ku-She would have traveled day and night, but Wei Pan

Ch'ao, his magic notwithstanding, was still human enough that he required sleep, and food, and shelter when the nights grew too cold. They took refuge where they could in deserted cottages and in roadside temples and shrines. The peasants in the villagers were not hospitable, and generally harried strangers from their neighborhoods with hoes and clubs and stones. They foraged where they could, and relied upon Wei Pan Ch'ao's magic to steal what they could not otherwise obtain fairly. Ku-She still possessed the enchanted basket and the teapot, but was loath to use them, for somewhere in Heaven the fairy magic would be felt.

The cold deepened and Wei Pan Ch'ao's pace began to falther. "It is not only my magic that keeps me alive," he said. "I have always taken pains to care for myself. It would be foolish to waste what I have gone to such lengths to achieve. I avoid foul weather and extreme exertion whenever I can. I have eaten well, and if I cannot winter in the south I have sought shelter in the most secure temples."

Once more he urged her to call upon the Fairy of One Hundred Birds, but Ku-She would not, and urged him instead to quicken his pace and spend some of the energy he had been conserving for so long. For several days he managed to do as she asked, for her patience was waning and they needed each other. But these efforts did not last. He trudged on doggedly, but seemed to make less and less progress for the increase in effort, and the terrain as they approached the range of the Lu-liang Shan in Shansi grew more treacherous and difficult than it had been for several days.

One afternoon when they had stopped to rest, far too early to suit Ku-She, in the shelter of a tiny cave above a dry stream bed, she became dismayed, then alarmed, to discover that she could not rouse him. He burned with fever and presently began to mutter through clenched teeth, for the heat of his fever was not enough to keep him from shivering violently.

Hastily, Ku-She gathered wood and dry grass, clearing a large area before the cave with her bare hands for fear the fire would ignite everything in sight. The fire she built was nearly smokeless, for everything was bone dry, but there was also little heat, and Ku-She resorted to the fairy magic of her pot to keep him full of warm tea and broth, but the broth would not stay with him. She covered him with evergreen boughs and packed earth and kept her own distance, touching him only when necessary, for cold was her own most natural condition.

His fever warmed the little oven she had built about him and the tea was brewed with wild healing herbs, but there was nothing more she could do than watch him and tend the fire.

Days passed and his ravings sometimes ceased as he, in the nature of mortals, struggled with the ebb and flow of life. Once in a while something would return to the look in his eyes, and he would lie still, gaze fixed upon the rock close above his head, and the faint glow of magic would hang about him briefly. But for the most part he had neither the strength nor wit for magic, and sustaining spells were not the same as healing.

There was nothing to do but watch and listen to his ravings. She could not abandon him, though she feared he might not live, and despite her already burdensome load of grief and guilt over the state of the world, she felt a sharp and singular guilt now over this *particular* death. He aged rapidly before her eyes, even as he struggled for life, and though it was his own folly that had set all this in motion, she felt herself at fault for placing such immediate peril upon a life so fiercely held for so long.

She dozed from time to time, for there was little else to do. On the fifth day of his fever, however, she was startled awake by his murmuring. There was a quality to his voice that was urgent and lucid, and she drew near to hear him.

"Flee. . . ." he said. "Flee this place, Little Fairy."

"You are not well enough," she said, no longer thinking him clearheaded.

"Nor may I ever be. I expect I shall die here."

"You surely will if I go."

"Nonetheless, you must. I have been very close and the Judges of the Dead must already know where I lie. If they come for me they will find you, too. Flee. You have no time now. Call upon your Sister of the Birds and fly to the capital. You are at no greater risk to do so than to remain near me."

"But, Uncle . . ."

"I repent my wickedness and my folly. Not only has it brought great harm to the world, which is often as wicked and foolish as I, but it has put at risk the only things I hold dear in all this long life."

"Uncle," she said. "I have a duty, but as long as you live I have a duty to you as well."

"Then observe your duty . . . Niece! As the elder of your husband's line you owe your duty to *me* and I require you to go. Quickly. You cannot refuse this."

Reluctantly, Ku-She knelt and bowed her head to the stone three times.

"In truth, Uncle, you have been a sly and crafty adversary and I have long held no liking for you. Had we met under other circumstances I would have gladly offered you up to the Judges of the Dead. But I do regret this parting now, and only for the sake of our love for your nephew and *his* son do I abandon you. I will leave you what little I have, so you may eat and drink as you have strength, but once my purpose is achieved and I have possession of the chopsticks once more I will not be able to return for you, for Heaven will have its way with me.

"Farewell, Uncle."

For days the brown hawk flew north and east to the fringes of the capital of the earthly emperor, and at last into the heart of the city. The man she sought was a bureaucrat of moderate success, and would live near the walls of the Imperial City within Peking itself. But his station was not high enough for him to own a villa within those walls. Nonetheless, once the district of his residence was located, word of the man himself was not hard to come by. His name was still on many lips, for only six days before his daughter had wed the eldest son of a high Imperial Minister, and it took the fairy no time at all to learn the further fate of her Golden Chopsticks. They had become part of the girl's dowry and were now housed within the Imperial City itself, in the keeping of the Minister Fong Wen Wah.

Ku-She grew reckless with desperation, for it was rumored that Fong had a treasure of imcomparable worth to present to the emperor. With the monk gone, she had no thief to spirit his way through the walls, and now speed was even more imperative. It was said, and not untruly, that even to the touch of Heaven, the most remote and deepest depth of the world was more accessible than the Forbidden City. The Imperial City surrounding it would be difficult enough for her to breach without the use of magic. She would call upon her sisters one more time, and soon, but first she had to locate her destination, and she could not waste this precious aid on trifles like flying over the wall as a sparrow or tunneling under them as a mole. With the help of the priest she had sold herself to gain access to one foolish household, but not again, and never here. Those this close to the emperor could not afford the slightest hint of imprudence. Austerity was the public image of the Ming Court and its officers, and their private lives were too public to be anything less than impeccable. Even the city of Peking suffered visibly and the plight of the countryside was the highest order of every minister's day. There would be no foolishness here.

She wished she could assume the form of a man, if only to slip in at dawn with the porters when the gates were unbarred. But all the workers, servants, merchants and whatever goods they carried were examined thoroughly by the guards. Even the residents did not enter and leave the Imperial City without examination of some sort. She longed for Wei Pan Ch'ao's ability to walk through walls, for that was a gift she did not possess, even with all her fairy powers intact and the full freedom to use them.

In the end she resorted to her own fairy magic, the ability to beguile the eye, and hoped fervently that it would be enough, and that it would not give her away now that she was so close.

At the last moment of the day, as the drums in all the gate towers signaled the first watch of the night, Ku-She slipped quickly through the final, diminishing space between the massive ironclad wings of the Western Gate of the Imperial City.

The final rays of sunlight slanting across the rooftops struck the top of the city wall and the drum towers like molten gold, and suddenly the world about the Western Gate was transformed. The wall was edged with fire and the shadows were dazzling in the purity of their darkness, black as midnight skies, deep and vast, then shimmering and glossy as obsidian, and again impenetrable and dull as the iron binding the gates, which had itself turned to silver.

And yet it was the gate. Only that. The same as it ever was. It was only a moment and the images were fleeting. It changed and changed and changed, and was still only the gate, so that the men could not be certain of what they saw. Confused, they hesitated, casting furtive glances at the wall and each other, and in that hesitation between one step and the next, something slipped through the gate. It, too, bedazzled and confounded the eye and no one could be quite sure of what he saw or if he saw anything at all. It seemed a slim, dark shadow, a piece of the flickering, newly-lighted torches; it looked to be a beautiful young girl; it was an ancient, pale wraith of an old woman; it was a sparkling, shimmering ice-bright swirl. It darted through the gate and into the park beyond the broad road, quick as a thought. The blur of motion sank into the shadows like a drop of water into a pool and the glamour died.

The sunlight faded from the top of the wall as the solid closure of the gates halted the guards' motion. Each looked about quickly, thinking the vision had been his alone, and said nothing to his companions. It had seemed but the blink of an eye, and yet that instant had been *filled* with images and strange beauty. They barred the great gates in silence, not daring to speak of it, and already the memory was fading, and with it the certainty that anything had happened at all.

In the shelter of a small shrine within the park, Ku-She waited for the activity about the gate to subside, as the first night watch took their stations, and relieved the men Ku-She had so thoroughly beguiled. The last of the evening traffic would soon be out of the streets, and she would then set about her search for the villa of Fong Wen Wah. She had entered the Western Gate because it was the one nearest the place she sought, but she had only been able to gain a rough idea of the lay of the streets, and she did not know how far it would actually be from where she now sat hidden.

As she waited she watched the sky, clear and crisp and bright with stars. Yes. There in the south. She waited, and it was there again. And in the west now too. Soon enough it would come from the other quarters as well, but it was far away and there was still time.

Again the vague, flickering glow of dragon fire appeared on the southern horizon, and Ku-She watched the streets to see how much activity was still about.

Heaven had found her by her magic at last. Without the aid of the great storm clouds, the dragons would be slow to arrive, but others might well reach her before then, and the Imperial City was not a close, confusing, sheltered jumble like the outer city of Peking itself. It was a place of broad parks and ornamental lakes and carefully placed woodlands and grand, spacious villas and estates and districts of huge, sprawling warehouses and great temples and tiny shrines. Though she could move about with little fear of mortal eyes, Heaven's scrutiny would be of a far different kind. There was yet time if it did not take her too long to locate Fong Wen Wah. So taking her bearing from the Western Gate, Ku-She slipped quickly and silently into the deepening winter night.

Fong Wen Wah lit the braziers in his study himself, adjusted several chucks of charcoal and began to grind inks with warmed water he had brought into the room with him. He examined the parchment before him with great dissatisfaction. The morning's effort. The hand itself was superb, one of his finest examples of gossamer script, but wasted on the content. The form and the verse were not in harmony. It disturbed him that recently his thoughts had not been worthy of his hand.

Dismissing his last effort, he paused with loaded brush above a fresh parchment. The poetry commending such a magnificent gift as his to the Son of Heaven whom he served should be a work of the highest order, and gossamer script required inspiration to capture the entirety of the thought in one single, fluid, utterly graceful line. But the poised brush never touched the parchment.

"Your Honor," the old woman said. "I beg your forgiveness for this inexcusable breach of protocol, but I must see you most urgently."

Startled, Fong Wen Wah leapt up with a cry, brush poised like a weapon, his face darkened with rage.

"How dare you enter my house! I will have you driven out and thrashed till there is nothing left of you!"

Putting down his brush he reached for the gong mallet but the old woman did not move.

"It is true," she said. "You have the right, but you will have to do so yourself. You have but one servant in the house tonight and he sleeps in the kitchen in a drunken stupor . . . with my assistance. The gardener and gatekeeper are too far away to hear the gong, and those maidservants who did not go south with your two wives have gone to their own families for the night. Your household is sparse. That is why I have chosen this time to speak to you."

"You threaten me?" he said, amused now, for she was not only old, she was also small and light of bone. "I could crush you with this mallet if I chose."

"There is no threat," she said mildly, her head politely bowed.

"Then what do you want?"

"Only that which is mine."

"I have *nothing* of yours," he said, his voice full of contempt for the mere idea.

"Ah, but you do, though you do not know it."

"And what proof have you?"

"You will find me convincing enough, My Lord."

Minister Fong laughed. "Speak. Claim your possessions and convince me."

The old woman smiled. "Through the good fortune of your son's recent marriage you have come into possession of a pair of golden chopsticks."

The indulgent smile left the minister's face.

"The handles are inlaid with tiny perfect snowflakes of silver and ivory and mother of pearl and each is capped with a snow-white moonstone. They were stolen from me and I will have them back."

"You presume too much on my good humor, hag," he said, features once more grim. "How would a creature as low and miserable as you rightfully possess a treasure fit for an emperor?"

"How did *you* come by them, My Lord? From a man of lesser station than yourself, to be sure. And how did *he* come by them? From a country magistrate who acquired them from a peasant-turned-merchant. Each knowing the treasure too grand for his own station found use in passing it on to higher and higher ranks, but never so high as from whence it came. I have followed the chopsticks across the land for a long time, for in the beginning they were mine and even so, I was but their custodian."

"You would claim much for yourself, though I cannot say precisely what."

"I am not what I seem."

"Nor am I," the minister said angrily. "For I am not a fool! Nor one to be spoken to so boldly. You tempt me to violence, hag. You dishonor my name and call me a thief. . . ."

"Not a thief, though only you can undo the theft."

"You have convinced me only that at some time you have seen the chopsticks. No more than that."

"And that I know, as you do, what they are."

Fong Wen Wah regarded her silently.

"They are objects of great beauty and exquisite workmanship, but that is not what makes them worthy gifts for your emperor. You have taken them from their box as the others never did. They looked and saw a rare treasure. The lowly felt unworthy to touch them. The more astute preferred to keep them pristine. But you took them into your hands and felt the fairy magic tingle in your fingers. *This* is the gift you felt to be worthy of your emperor. A prize stolen from Heaven."

"Yes," he said. "There is fairy magic there. And all the more reason they would never befit the likes of you."

"Ahhh," she breathed, bowing slightly. "But I have told you I am not what I seem."

She turned away from him and crossed the room to the garden doors, and as she passed a deep chill fell upon the room. Though the braziers hissed and burned brightly, all their warmth had vanished in an instant, and Fong Wen Wah watched her with a growing dread as frigid as the room. When she turned and regarded him from the door, she looked half her former age and as fair as any woman he had ever seen. She smiled and invited him into the garden.

The moon was full and it cast a brilliant white glow on the courtyard. Had he cared to, Fong could have read a book by it.

The old woman had vanished, as had the handsome woman at the door. In the cold moonlight stood a young woman of little more than twenty, possessed of the most perfect beauty the minister had ever seen, though her exact image seemed to elude him. The shimmer of her fairy aura enfolded her and he knew she beguiled him, yet he also knew her beauty was true and it pained him to look at her. She was clad head to foot in a shimmering white gown, ropes of pearls and white jade about her neck, and her hair done up with jeweled silver chips and silver pins with snowflakes falling from them.

"Do you know me, Mortal?" she said. But Fong Wen Wah was silent with wonder.

"The world is dying, Man. Do you know why? Has it not occurred to you to wonder?"

Quietly Ku-She called to her sisters, and slowly the frozen winter garden began to warm about him. Crocuses and hyacinths and azaleas put forth buds and bloomed, and the fruit trees blossomed as well. The air grew soft and the night sky lightened, for in another season at this hour it was barely dusk. The trees greened and the grass grew long. Catalpa and dogwood threw open their flowers and all the plants about the path bloomed riotously. The air was heavy with dry, itching heat and the minister found himself tugging open his quilted gown. The greens became dark and robust, and apples and cherries and loquat ripened and fell from the trees as cooler breezes ruffled leaves beginning to blush with color, then fade to brown and fall. The grass grew dry and rustled in the cold wind, and the minister clutched his robe about him once more, mute with wonder.

Had he really seen an entire year flee across the face of his garden with the speed of the hand flinging forth that inspired verse he had longed for . . . only a moment ago? He felt as though a lifetime had passed in those moments, not just one year.

He looked at Ku-She. Her beauty no longer pained him. "Who are you?" he asked.

"I am the Fairy of Ku-She, and I have come to claim what is mine."

There was ice in her voice, but not the daggers of icicles hanging from the rooftree. Rather the delicate, fernlike patterns of the first glaze on a shallow pond—fragile and brittle. "Do you require more proof, Mortal?" she asked.

In reply he threw himself at her feet and pressed his forehead to the paving stones. Then he went into the house and quickly returned with a simple ivory box. No sooner had he delivered it into the fairy's hand than a tall, pale form appeared and moved toward him across the garden. It was another strange and beautiful woman upon a white mule. In her hands she held a crystal vase, pale and translucent with a glow and flutter of movement inside.

Minister Fong Wen Wah was transfixed.

"Much evil has befallen the world for lack of these," said the fairy upon the mule. "We thank you for their safe return."

"Forgive me!" Fong Wen Wah cried. "I should have understood at once!"

"Perhaps your mortal emperor would have had you give them into his care. You were at least wiser than to cherish them too closely for your own sake," Ku-She said.

Then she turned and mounted the White Mule beside Tung Shuang-Ch'eng, and as the creature turned away, they vanished.

Still numb with wonder, the Imperial Minister Fong Wen Wah stood mute in his garden. He roused himself presently for it had begun to snow. He returned to his study, securing the doors, and once more seated himself at his writing desk, brush loaded and poised above the snowy parchment, and when the moment came, with a single remarkable stroke, he wrote the finest poem of his era.

When the Season's End festivities were over and Hibiscus Village was quiet once more, the Fairy of Ku-She and Chou Ch'ung-i were summoned before the Jade Emperor of Heaven himself.

The world was again growing green and lush and Ku-She had word from her Sister of One Hundred Flowers, whose agents filled Wei K'e-yung's garden with color, that her son was strong and healthy and her husband was content. Knowing this, Ku-She presented herself willingly to hear the emperor's decree. Chou Ch'ung-i had petitioned the Heavenly Court on Ku-She's behalf, but the Jade Emperor was not impressed.

The fairies knelt before him on a floor paved with turquoise and sky-blue jade. The emperor's throne was made of clouds and he sat upon the curled back of a sleeping golden dragon. Rising behind him, rooted in the misty cloud, was a willow tree of alabaster, and its tiny, gold leaves hung like the fringe of a canopy before him and tinkled gently in the breeze. When he spoke his voice could not be heard, but the thunder of it vibrated within the bones of the little fairy, and his whisper touched her soft as silk.

"We are not pleased with you, Child," he said. "Though you cannot be blamed for the theft, nor accused of failure to fulfill your duty, your conduct in pursuit of that fulfillment can be greatly criticized. You *set aside your duty* for your own pleasure and caused great suffering by so doing. You married *without the consent of Heaven*. You took a *mortal* to spouse and brought forth a child who is half of our realm and half of theirs. This flaunting of our authority cannot be taken lightly, and requires that you be punished severely. Yet all things must be considered. Chou Ch'ung-i declares that you have always been faithful and conscientious, that you have taken great joy in the fulfillment of your duty to your season, and that your artistry is unparalleled. It has also been noted that you sacrificed your worldly pleasures when your duty was once more placed before you, and in the end you succeeded. These facts temper our judgement, but do not prompt us to forgive you. Do you admit your fault, Fairy?"

Lying facedown upon the tiles, Ku-She acknowledged her guilt.

"And do you repent your wickedness and accept whatever punishment shall please me to serve upon you?"

"Oh Highest Master of All That Is," Ku-She said meekly. "I can never repent my love for my mortal husband, though I do admit it was wrong to act upon it, and I do greatly repent and regret the evil which befell the world as a result of my selfishness in love's name. I was weak and unfaithful. I was not fit for the task my duty required of me, even if there had been no love to deter me. I am the most wretched being that could exist and am deserving of the harshest punishment you can inflict."

The Jade Emperor was silent in consideration for a long time. The two fairies dared not move and lay still as death upon the tiles.

At last the emperor spoke again.

"Do you love Heaven?"

"Yes, Lord," Ku-She answered simply. "Hibiscus Village is all I know of the glory of your realm, but simple as it is its splendor is greater than anything in the mortal world, and I cherish it and my sisters who dwell there as surely as you yourself do."

"Where is the monk Wei Pan Ch'ao? Tell us this and I may be tempted to greater leniency."

A small smile escaped onto Ku-She's lips and she was grateful for her prostrate position. "Oh Most Excellent and Exalted Ruler of Heaven and Earth," she said. "I truly cannot say. I gave the monk my word I would not reveal him in exchange for his assistance, but when I left him he was dying and I honestly do not know what became of him if the Judges of the Dead do not have him."

The emperor's voice beat like a gong upon her ear. "And would you tell us if you *did* know, Fairy?"

"In all honesty, Lord, I could not. Would you wish to compromise the word of Heaven? Even so small an oath given by so puny and miserable a fairy? No, my most Excellent Master, I could not say even if I knew, but I would not deceive you in this, and in truth I do *not* know."

Again the emperor was silent for a long time. By Ku-She's reckoning a day and night might have passed, for such time meant nothing to the Master of the Universe. Such things were important only to those such as she, who watched the seasons pass. But she lay still and waited.

"You are banished," the emperor said at last. "But your child interests us, so in your exile you will serve us still . . . for a time. You will return to the Earth and resume your married life, but as a mortal. You will be stripped of all your fairy power and magic. You will suffer all the ills and failings of the flesh of mortals, and in time you will grow old and die as they do, but you will not be allowed to follow your husband into the Land of the Dead, and once he has passed there you will be granted no further news of him, even after your own return to Heaven. Once he passes those gates he will be lost to you forever. In life you will have no influence upon his fortunes or fate and you must follow him however those fortunes fall, for you will not be allowed to leave him while he lives, nor will you be allowed to die before him . . . and you will bear no more children.

"I cannot deny your child immortality, for it may be that he possesses it already. He will, however, be exempt from all physical harm or possibility of death until he is twelve years old. At his twelfth birthday he will be sent for and examined, and if he is mortal he will be returned to you, and he too will be denied to you upon his death. But if he is fairy and immortal he will be kept here and raised as we see fit.

"Upon your own death you will return to Hibiscus Village and regain your stewardship of the Golden Chopsticks. You will never be allowed to venture into the mortal world again, and you will never speak of this time of banishment or these mortals to anyone."

The little fairy was stunned. Never for a moment had she imagined the Jade Emperor of Heaven would return her to Earth and her family. To be mortal and share her husband's lot . . . but never to be able to help him. . . . It was not the heaviest burden she could have been forced to bear. Even to be denied all knowledge of them after death was less harsh given this small sojourn into mortality, for she had expected no less of the emperor and had, in fact, feared she had seen the last of her beloved husband in this life or the other already.

Ku-She was ordered to place her affairs in order at once, and her belongings in the hands of Madam Chou, who would see to the temporary guardianship of the Golden Chopsticks; then she was dismissed from the emperor's presence. The audience hall immediately vanished, and the two fairies were kneeling upon the paving stones of Madam Chou's own courtyard in Hibiscus Village with her attendants all about.

The maids helped Chou Ch'ung-i to her feet and Ku-She remained prostrate till she was given permission to rise.

"The Most Merciful Ruler of the Universe was extremely lenient with you, Little Fairy," she said to Ku-She, as she seated herself in the shade of a willow tree. "I had not hoped for so much, since my petitions on your behalf were largely ignored."

Ku-She was once again on her knees at Chou Ch'ung-i's feet.

"Oh, Madam, your most miserable and unworthy slave thanks you with all her worthless soul for what you have done."

"I have done little enough and succeeded hardly at all at that. Get up, child, and pay heed to me."

Ku-She kissed the fairy's feet once quickly before doing as she was told, and faced Madam Chou with a bright and smiling face. The Mistress of Hibiscus Village did not look pleased.

"Do not take this lightly," she said. "I have no doubt you will learn the true harshness of this punishment in time. But you must know and understand that it is your son who is the sole reason for what the Heavenly Jade Emperor has granted you. If there is not already a plan for this child, there may well be by the time he reaches his twelfth year . . . be he immortal or not. Do not think the Jade Emperor has forgiven you by granting what seems a boon, even a limited one, when you expected disaster. Heaven's memory is long and its judgements are often harsh. This small lifetime in exile may not rid the court of its prejudice against you, and when you return you may find your place here less happy than it was. And if your child is here . . . I cannot speculate upon that."

"Would they turn him against me?" Ku-She asked, shocked.

"It is not possible to know the Jade Emperor's mind. It is only possible to say that Heaven does not forgive its own kind easily, and there are far fewer forms of punishment available in this realm than in the mortal one. Heaven will employ whatever is available to it.

"You will be returned to your husband's house tomorrow. I give you my blessing, and my hope that this mortal life will not deal too harshly with you, for I would not want to see you return to your duty bitter and resentful. Go now and see to your affairs. There is little time."

In the cave above Hibiscus Village, Ku-She found many of her sisters waiting to say farewell. Some had brought tokens wrapped in red silk, but these were laid away in a small ivory box belonging to Tung Shuang-Ch'eng, for Ku-She could take nothing into the mortal world with her. The White Mule stood by patiently and allowed new spring leaves and flowers to be plaited into its mane, while the fairy women sang and played the lute and helped Ku-She pack her belongings. The Fairy of One Hundred Flowers scattered gardenia petals among the silks as she packed, and the Fairy of One Hundred Herbs laid lavender atop each chest before it was closed and sealed with fine beeswax and marked with Chou Ch'ung-i's seal.

Before dawn the young men came, tall and willowy and dressed in the new greens and yellows and pale blues of spring. They collected the trunks and were gone, quickly and silently. And one by one Ku-She's sisters kissed her and touched the hem of her sleeve in farewell and raised their fans before their faces as they left her. Only Tung Shuang-Ch'eng and the White Mule remained in the cave.

Ku-She was dressed in a simple, pale-blue gown of light silk which Madam Chou had sent with the porters. It bore no sign of her station or function, and looked curiously like one Ku-She had owned in Wuchang. It was all she would have to remind her of Heaven, and it was humble and plain and utterly unremarkable.

As the dawn broke Ku-She sought her Sister Tung Shuang-Ch'eng, for she had agreed to walk to the edge of Hibiscus Village with her, but she found Tung Shuang-Ch'eng asleep on her couch and, try as she might, she could not wake her.

Outside the cave the air was fresh and clean with spring and new life, but there was not a sign of anything stirring, not a bird song nor a touch of spring breeze, nor the smallest of her Sisters' charges nestling in the grass. In spite of the great joy and anticipation she felt at the thought of her beloved Wei K'e-yung, the sudden desolation and loneliness tugged at her. It was as though she were already forgotten. Her Sisters could not be blamed. They had spent the night with her because they would not be allowed this parting, but it was cruel to forbid her Tung Shuang-Ch'eng's company on this last journey to the village gates. They were more truly sisters than any of the other fairies or elementals. They had been created together and had served the same season together for longer than the counting of time. Of all the things in Heaven she would miss, it would be Tung Shuang-Ch'eng she would miss the most.

She stopped to unlatch their gate and paused for one last look into the darkness of the cave. She knew every vein and crevice in the stone, every vine upon the rocky wall, every pebble in the path beneath her feet, but she looked at it all carefully one last time, trying to see it perfectly and to remember it as long as she possibly could.

Turning back to the gate she paused once more and, quickly, bent down and scooped a small blue-and-grey-speckled-pebble into her hand. Clutching it tightly in her fist, she closed the gate and followed the path down the mountainside and through the village. The gate stood open, but there were no young men to guard it. She passed beneath the carved beams with their hundreds of birds and animals and plants . . . and high up, ringing the top of the left supporting column, a garland of snowflakes. Twenty paces on, at the turning of the path, she looked back and found the gates closed. Another dozen paces and again she looked back but the gate looked ordinary and dull. There was no brightly painted carving, only old, weathered, ironbound planks set in a grey brick wall. The path before her had become overgrown and another two dozen paces further was lost entirely.

When she looked back this time, though the wall should have been clearly visible at this distance, only a low morning haze lay across the land and there was no sign of the path behind her. Slowly the mist drifted and seemed to move away from her, dispersing in the rising morning light. When she opened her hand where she had clutched the pebble from her front path she found only a shard of common shale and at last, quietly, she began to cry.

Book Two

In the garden of the Governor of Honan Province at Kaifeng, there was a small pavilion called The Breeze Among the Willows at Dawn. It sat on the edge of an ornamental pool and the long, delicate branches of the willows hung around it and the water lapped gently at its steps. It was a simple structure of carved wooden columns and open, deep-seated windows without shutters. On the beams overhead the phoenix led flocks of painted birds through the clouds, and in the summer four wooden cages hung from the rafters filled with small, brightly-colored song birds. The curtain of willow branches surrounding the pavilion sheltered it in a dappled, emerald shade, and the path to the gate was lined with soft moss and paved with blue and grey flagstones. On the opposite side three stone steps led down to the water's edge, but there was no little boat tied there anymore. The pool was filled with water lilies, and tall bullrushes stood proudly near the banks flanking the little building. In the summer breezes the sound of their motion lent a different note to the whisper and rustle of the willows.

Across the pool were beds of white and golden-orange lilies. An orchard rambled away to the left and beyond that, partially hidden by the trees, was the house of the governor, with its whitewashed wall and the moon gate which let into a courtyard near the governor's private study.

Beyond the house and the walls of the private compound were the long, low, sprawling buildings of the Provincial Office with its clerks and treasuries and audience halls.

The little pavilion was part of the park surrounding all this

73

and the park itself was surrounded by a high stone wall with a great ceremonial gate in the east, which faced the heart of the city of Kaifeng.

Beyond the gate the street was teeming with bustle and noisy commerce. Street vendors sold hot rice cakes and quail eggs in vinegar and fried grasshoppers and lichee. The streets were lined with teahouses and wineshops and silk merchants and goldsmiths, and all manner of goods and services could be found easily. The market squares were abundant with produce, and the wares of the countryside, and the sounds of men and women haggling over prices rose and fell on the summer breezes. Young men on horseback called to each other and hailed their friends sitting on wineshop porches. In the teahouses and restaurants the hum of voices bartering for goods buzzed like the summer bees, and children ran through the streets carrying messages for their employers or crying the wares of the wandering vendors they served.

But in the little pavilion called The Breeze Among the Willows at Dawn the streets were far away and there was only the sound of the birds, and the lapping of the pool upon the stone steps and the gentle voices of the serving girls as they set out tea for their ladies.

Madam Ku Pao Shih sat upon a couch of carved sandalwood and pale yellow brocade and watched the little boy playing at the water's edge, while the maids laid out tea cakes in lacquer boxes and warmed the tea on a small brazier on a window seat. The little boy had a large collection of pebbles in a basket by his side, and he was tossing them purposefully into the pool after taking careful aim at the large carp sliding in and out of view among the lily pads. He was newly arrived at ten years of age, and a child of considerable beauty.

His mother loved him past reason. He was her joy and her greatest pleasure after her adored husband, but she was melancholy as she watched him playing at the pool's edge and she was afraid for him.

Pao Shih heard the tapping of tiny feet on the flagstones at her back as the governor's Second Wife approached the pavilion. Yin Whun seated herself on a fat, green cushion at Pao Shih's feet and clucked to the baby in her arms. At once the maids fluttered about her reaching for the child, but the young mother preferred to keep her and they returned to their other duties.

Pao Shih said nothing. Her fan worked busily in the summer heat and she continued to watch her son playing by the water. Her gown was the lightest gauze available; almost indecently sheer, for she suffered greatly in the summer heat. She spent much of her time in the pavilion by the pool, for its shade and cooling breezes rising from the water.

Only the spring and autumn were tolerable. In the winter she suffered even more than in the summer heat, and rarely left the house. The maids were careful to keep braziers lit near her favorite chairs, with pots of hot tea nestled on the coals and stones warming in the oven for her feet, and she would snuggle deep in quilted coats even in the house while ice glazed the little pond. It had been like this for nearly nine years, and long ago her husband had stopped wondering at the change in her. All during the winter of her pregnancy, the coldest winter in anyone's memory in the little city of Wuchang, she had strolled about the garden without a coat and paid no mind to the braziers making a futile attempt to warm the study. She said she had been raised in the mountain provinces and was used to the cold—indeed, her prediction that it would not affect their son seemed to have proved true, but shortly after the child's first year Wei K'e-yung had noticed the change in his wife. That winter she was continually ill from the cold, and since then could not abide the winters. But the summer was no comfort to her either, and quite soon she had ceased to take pleasure in the turning of the seasons. Though she rarely spoke of her discomfort, the entire household did its best to relieve her in any way it could. In the summer there was little they could do.

When the service was ready Madam Ku dismissed the maids, who retired to the orchard across the pond to work their embroidery and wait. Yin Whun placed her daughter in a willow basket hung from the rafters and settled on the green cushion again. While Yin Whun sipped tea and Pao Shih nibbled a tea cake, they continued to watch the little boy by the pool.

"Have you noticed anything more?" Pao Shih said at last.

"No," Yin Whun replied. "Nothing lately, but I think there is evidence enough already. They will take him, Madam. I have no doubt of it."

"Hush!" Pao Shih hissed. "Quietly when the boy is near. . . ."

Yin Whun sighed and put down her cup. "How much longer will you wait? Surely you would not have him go to the examination unaware."

"No, of course not, and I fear I cannot wait much longer. He is ten years old. Old enough to begin acquiring many of the concerns of an adult. Already his father is thinking of his eventual marriage and the kind of bride he will choose."

"Ah?"

"He has not made any formal overtures, but a betrothal within the next two years would not be unseemly, and lately he has had his secretary enquire discreetly about eligible daughters in the households of several of His Imperial Highness's retainers."

"The years have been good to our husband," Yin Whun agreed. "It would not be unthinkable for T'ai-Tsung to marry a degree above our present station."

"K'e-yung-ah, will rise quickly enough in any event, but an advantageous marriage could not hurt. I have had my own thoughts on this subject for some time, but lately I have had to set them farther and farther away. . . ." Pao Shih stopped talking, as a flutter of motion approached the bank of the pond. The little maid Ai Lian called out that the tutors had finished their tea and Wei T'ai-Tsung was once again required in the study.

Without hesitation the child took formal leave of his mothers and ran happily off to the house.

"He is so like his father in that," Pao Shih said warmly. "His love of study would have made him a scholar of great standing . . . but for this.

"The time here has been good to me. Perhaps overly so. My son is a bright and studious child with all the makings of a fine life virtually laid at his feet. My husband has risen quickly in the Imperial Service and his path to even higher achievements is clear and straight before him. All of this has come about without the slightest unnatural assistance. Had I had it to give I do not think I could have done better for either of them, and in that I am grateful, for it has helped me to see how rare and precious my loved ones truly *are*. But it has also been too easy to forget what The Jade Emperor and Chou Ch'ung-i both said—that this is my *punishment*. And now I find the old fears returning—the ones that plagued me so upon my return. What will they do to my child if they should take him? He is only a fairy after all. Nothing to be counted too highly in the Jade Emperor's Court." She reached out and stroked Yin Whun's hair. "I would count him fortunate to be placed in service as you were. There are far worse things he could be put to. And I must remember that his fate is not only *part* of my punishment but, considering the ease of the last ten years, most likely the *focus* of it."

"You still have many friends in Hibiscus Village. Madam Chou herself . . ."

"Has little influence in this. We can expect no help in what we must do. He will not only go to the examinations aware, he will go *prepared*."

"Perhaps it is *well* that he is only a fairy," Yin Whun said. "They will not expect much of him and we will not have to teach him to hide such great magics."

Pao Shih rose from the couch and walked to the water's edge, her gauze gown floating about her in the light air. The birds trilled and fluttered in their cages and her fan fluttered in her hand.

"We have two years to teach him what he must know. Heaven has all the time it needs to undo him. We must teach him well and we must teach him caution, for he may have to find his way alone at the end. What worries me most immediately, however, is not how the child will take this news. First we must tell his father . . . and this I dread more than anything. To confess to ten years of deception. To have to reveal my guilt and his part in all that happened so long ago. . . . I do not know what he will do . . . how he will feel. The Jade Emperor said I may not be parted from him as long as he lives, but what must I do if he sends me away?"

"Need we tell him so soon? Is it possible . . . ?"

"No. He must know now if we are to have any chance at all. We have much to accomplish if we are to be certain of our success. To place so much of a young boy's education in the hands of women would be improper. Our husband's cooperation is necessary to arrange the tutors in such a way that this time is not evident."

Pao Shih turned and found Yin Whun standing by the willow basket gently rocking her baby.

"Do not fear too much, Madam. How can he turn us out? Will he give up his son so easily? Without us the boy is surely lost. He will know this. I cannot say how our husband will feel toward us, but he is a practical man when all is done. He cannot afford to send us away and he would not *dare* tell anyone. What can he do? Your reputation is irreproachable. He has no excuse to divorce you . . . or none that can be publicly stated."

Pao Shih lowered her fan and looked out across the pool and the lily gardens to the house. "I have nothing to lose but his love," she said. "And I must risk that now, for if I do not it will surely be lost when T'ai-Tsung is taken to be tested."

Yin Whun led Pao Shih back to the couch and arranged the damp gauze about her feet, then sat on the cushion again and began to fan her with her own fan. The water was cool on Pao Shih's legs, but it was small relief.

"It is possible, Pao Shih," Yin Whun said, "that he may love you still. In spite of everything. He has been a good and proper husband these ten years."

"But I have not been a good and proper wife. He would be right to despise me."

"Then we must think of a way to tell him that he will understand and accept. For all our sakes let us consider this most carefully."

Pao Shih looked down and plucked the sleeve of Yin Whun's gown, winding the soft silk about her fingers. "You advise me well, Little One. You have always been my wisest counsel, and I did far better than I knew when I brought you with me. We will do this thing together then. I only wish there were someone in Heaven to whom I could make prayers or offerings for success in this." She smiled sadly and her fan began to flutter again. "It is silly that I should care, but I am the only mortal on Earth to whom *all* of Heaven is deaf."

Wei K'e-yung was a young man for the rank he held. At the age of thirty-two he had been Governor of Honan for nearly a year, after a three-year tenure as Prefect and Chief Magistrate of the Kaifeng District. In that time the province had been prosperous and well managed; its judges and both city and village officials were honest, its taxes were paid on time and its roads were well kept and as safe as could be expected in a province of such size and prosperity. And the governor enjoyed considerable prosperity himself. His business affairs were as well managed as his Imperial Post, and he owned considerable land in his home province of Hukwang, where the harvests of kaoliang and soybeans and winter wheat had been exceptionally good in recent years. In Kaifeng he owned a lucrative brokerage in fine quality rice papers, which supplied the Imperial City and the offices of the Imperial Court in Peking, and another which dealt in the finest quality inks and pigments for watercolors; and in his hometown of Wuchang he had, the previous year, constructed a kiln yard with seven ovens for the manufacture of glazed paving tiles. His secretary, Loy Quan Dong, had seen to the hiring of trustworthy managers who reported directly to him, and he in turn kept the governor amply supplied with reports of his various holdings and affairs, for Wei K'e-yung's first concern was his career. His affections, however, were reserved entirely for scholarship and his family.

The first years of his marriage, however, had been something of a strain on him. He had loved his new wife with a passion a man of culture and discipline had been raised to consider vulgar, but she was the most delicate and beautiful creature he had ever seen, and her reserve and propriety were so perfect he could not consider any response to her to be unworthy. He was enchanted and inspired in his study and completely happy. However, with the winter and her pregnancy she had fallen into a deep melancholy which had not lifted with the birth of their son, and when she had sent her maid home to nurse a dying father for nearly a year, a reluctance had settled upon her which he had only with patience and great care managed to overcome. When Yin Whun had returned, his wife's eagerness for him seemed to be renewed as well, but with that spring her melancholy had changed also and she seemed almost fearful.

But when he received his first appointment as First Secretary to the District Magistrate at Hangchow her moods lightened, and two years later, when he was appointed Deputy Magistrate of Yingtien, she had become a wholly other person. Her beauty still astonished him when he awoke beside her in the morning, and she was still the passion of his life. The melancholy of those years had lifted and seemed to have left no mark upon her. Even Yin Whun had begun to warm to him with time, and when his circumstances were such that he could begin to think of a Second Wife he found no reason to look outside his own household.

If Pao Shih was the passion of his life, however, his son was his joy and his pride. The boy was all a man of Wei K'e-yung's scholarly bent could ask—bright and quick at his studies and as much a lover of learning as his father had been. It was the one sadness left in their lives that, try as they did, Pao Shih could never give him any more children, and he had begun to worry, even after taking Yin Whun formally into his bed, until his Second Wife had finally given him a child. A girl to be sure, but at least the failure to produce children could not be laid at *his* feet, and with time Yin Whun could possibly give him more sons.

On the whole a reasonable man could not be happier and yet, for the last six months, he had been given to vague feelings that all was not well. He had noticed in Pao Shih subtle but disturbing reflections of her old sadnesses. Not often, but from time to time. Ten years ago they had been poor and the general state of the world was desperate from drought and crop failure. All of life looked bleak. But now he was prosperous, their life was easy and the world was full of abundance as it had rarely been; the household was settled and well run and functioning in enviable fashion. It worried him that he was too busy to properly take note of the moods of his household, but his career and his duty to the Imperial Service demanded a great deal of his attention. It worried him, too, that his beloved Pao Shih might find him lacking in his attentions as a husband or that Yin Whun's new baby might have reminded his First Wife of her failure to give him more children. He knew of no way to reassure her that his love for her did not depend upon such things, and that their son was all any man could have asked of a woman.

Yet, duty called and he would find himself still in his office or his private study as the city beyond his walls sounded the second or third watch of the night, and he would realize that days had passed, or an entire month, and he had done nothing.

Occasionally he would speak of this to his First Secretary. Loy Quan Dong was a man to be trusted for his discretion and loyalty. Wei K'e-yung knew nothing he said of his private affairs would pass beyond the study doors. In business and the affairs of his office Loy was astute and careful and very thorough but, in spite of his age and station, he was not married and his advice on women was rarely useful. It tended to fall along the lines of ". . . such are their ways . . ." and ". . . who can ever hope to understand them . . ."

"Is it truly a problem, My Lord?" the secretary had asked him. "Has it kept her from your bed?"

"No," Wei K'e-yung had said. "It is not like that. It is only sometimes that I notice it, but it reminds me of the old days. I cannot help but worry."

"All women have such moods," Loy Quan Dong said reassuringly. "It is nothing to concern yourself with. You must charge your Second Wife with the improvement of her mistress's mood. Such is her duty. If she fails in this I recommend she be punished, but only another woman can be expected to understand such things . . . or a physician. Perhaps the geomancers."

At such times he thanked Loy Quan Dong politely but knew the value of the counsel.

Still, Wei K'e-yung had felt the need to do *something*, so he had charged one of the kitchen maids to carry offerings once a week to the shrines of the Weaving Maid and the Lady of the Moon. He had no idea if it did any good, but at least Pao Shih's occasional melancholies did not deepen or grow more frequent, so he allowed himself to believe that it did.

In the pavilion called The Breeze Among the Willows at Dawn the lady Pao Shih sat at dusk alone with her husband's Second Wife, who was her only trusted companion. Across the ornamental pool her son chased fireflies, which he caught and placed in a paper lantern carried by the gardener's son.

It was the evening of the twelfth day of the Eighth Month and the moon was nearly full. The air was soft and hinted that the deeper coolness of autumn would soon be upon the garden, and Pao Shih was truly comfortable for the first time in months. The birds were taken into the house in the evenings now, and though the insects were still active, the lady's fan had ceased its usual constant fluttering and lay on the couch beside her.

Yin Whun carefully combed out her mistress's long, black hair with an ivory-and-silver comb and dressed it in elaborate coils. She appeared to be totally absorbed in her task, but a small corner of her attention was always upon the boy in the garden.

"Beginnings are elusive and delicate things," Pao Shih said, "but I cannot believe I have deceived myself in this."

"You have not. We have witnessed these things together and you know I have no power to share your dreams."

"Still . . . the Moon Festival is in three days. That will mark precisely a month since I last thought something unnatural had passed. Even then I was not sure of what I saw."

Yin Whun moved around the couch to the cushion at Pao Shih's feet. "What will you tell Wei K'e-yung?" she asked plainly.

Pao Shih sighed and folded her hands in her lap. "I can think of nothing. With my fairy powers gone, I have no way of convincing him. He will merely think me mad and send me away or confine me. Either way, he will not believe me."

"Use me, Madam. I have *some* small abilities."

Pao Shih smiled and patted the girl's hand. "With the touch of your hand you can clear his mind when he has had too much wine or help him to sleep when he is too little at ease. You can calm a fever in illness, though you cannot cure the ill. All things you set your hand to are perfect and perfectly done. Your skills are those meant for service, Little One. They are difficult to demonstrate."

"Yet there may be something. . . . Please, let me think a while. There *must* be something."

Across the garden Pao Shih saw Yan Ping hurrying toward them with a lantern on a willow pole, and the gently, late-summer air carried the sound of the evening gong.

"There may yet be something indeed," Pao Shih said, rising from the couch. "Speak to me again tomorrow. We must find a way to convince him soon. There is too little time."

There were many things that ruled the lives of Imperial Officials in the service of the Ming. Whereas a man of wealth and station attained solely through the pursuit of private business might, after a time and the amassing of sufficient money, become a man of leisure, this was not so for those who chose to serve their emperor. The emperor and all who carried out his business stood as models of correct moral behavior and proper work habits. Their lives were ruled by duty, and the disposal of their time was rarely left to their own management. Even the Governor of Honan began his day at dawn when his staff assembled in the courtyard before the large audience hall, and the day was long and strictly regulated.

Audiences began and ended promptly at such and such an hour. There was so much time in the morning dedicated to reviewing the reports his secretaries had prepared on the business of the day ahead; and so much time given to looking over official documents sent down from the bureaucracy in Peking; and so much time for the practice of law in affairs not conclusively handled by his District Magistrates; and so much time for drafting and reviewing his own documents for the government offices in Peking; and so much time for reviewing petitions too important for his staff to abstract; and the guiding of the administration of his province, roads, taxes, the conditions in the districts, and business in the cities . . . and beyond all that a man of his position was expected to maintain his own scholarship, for such was the nature of the Imperial Service that the learned were more favored than those who were merely efficient.

This well-ordered time was marked in a variety of ways. The beating of the drums in the towers dividing the day and night into the various watches; the locking and reopening of the city gates at dusk and dawn; the burning of candles or a quantity of oil in a marked vessel; the creeping shadow of the sundial or a shaft of light along a knotted rope or the measured dripping of a water clock; from the gross to the fine moments, time in the service of the Ming was measured and sorted and assigned and watched, and whatever was left belonged to a man's family.

Therefore, from the time Wei T'ao-Tsung was eight years old, every tenth day, no matter how it fell within the calendar, the Governor of Honan left his office at the prescribed time for the noon meal and spent the afternoon with his son, teaching him his place within the family and how a gentleman of his station was expected to behave. It was in this way that he began to notice an occasional odd thing. This merely intrigued him at first, but lately it had begun to disturb him even more than his wife's moods.

This afternoon he had chosen to give Wei T'ai-Tsung a riding lesson. As was his usual habit when riding out into the country unescorted, he took one of the dogs from the kennel, a young hunting dog trained to the horses but somewhat lacking in experience. The dogs needed to be worked; his son needed to learn to handle them. There was too little time and far too much a father needed and wanted to do for his son.

They rode out of the city gates in high spirits, Wei K'e-yung quoting examples of his favorite classic poets and the boy finishing the final verses and naming the authors.

Kaifeng resided at a reasonable ride from the banks of the Hwang Ho River, and Wei K'e-yung took that road for it was a lovely, balmy day and he had always found the river extremely beautiful at this time of year. It was broad and deep here, and the late-summer light sparkled across the surface like stars in a dark-blue sky. Together they sat on the bank and Wei K'e-yung told his son the story of how the river came to be called the "Yellow River." The dog chased birds and field mice along the river bank and Wei T'ai-Tsung tossed pebbles into the swift current to see their ripples distorted and carried off in an instant; and then they began to speak of the dragons.

The afternoon sun slanted in hazy, golden shafts between great puffy clouds sailing low overhead and touched the surface of the river like the silken summer bed hangings of his mothers room. From time to time a distant shaft many li downstream would shift and shimmer on the air or vanish entirely.

"The dragons are very active today," Wei K'e-yung said to his son. "They ride the rising vapors to the clouds and each time you see a flicker of light . . . like so . . . there . . . a dragon has passed along the 'bridge.'"

"There must be many dragons here today Father," the boy said. "Or are they playing? Do they slide *down* the 'bridge' so they can be carried up again?"

Wei K'e-yung was pleased by this.

"It is possible. It is also possible that we sit at the limits of many territories. *Or* . . . perhaps we see the dragon's children. Just as you and I ride and talk, so the dragon instructs his own sons."

"Someday *I* will have such power," the boy said, smiling, his black eyes sparkling like the dark river.

Wei K'e-yung was vaguely disturbed and asked why Wei T'ai-Tsung said this.

"Master Wing says I am an excellent student and if I study hard, one day I may be a very powerful man. I would *like* to ride on the clouds, Father, and I would take you up with me and we could see all the land in the Great Bowl."

Wei K'e-yung smiled with some relief. "You are a man and the son of a man. Only the gods and immortal heroes have such power. A mere mortal may never hope for so much unless the Jade Emperor of Heaven grants it, and only the greatest heroes of history have ever been strong enough or clever enough to merit such favor. Besides, Heaven has no need of heroes now. There is no discord and no danger that is not fit and natural to the world. It requires a *great event* for even the most special of men to earn such powers."

The boy looked crestfallen.

"Be content, child. Master Wing was quite correct, but he was speaking of a purely mortal realm. There is much ahead for you in life if you apply yourself. And what may be achieved here on Earth is no small thing, for Heaven relies upon us to conduct ourselves in such a way that the Jade Emperor need not concern himself with our doings. In this way we are the greatest of all creatures, for nothing else on Earth possesses so much power in the management of its own affairs."

But the boy was not appeased.

"No," he said, and there was anger in his voice. "One day I *will* ride upon the clouds!"

Wei K'e-yung sighed and got to his feet. "It is not impossible that within your lifetime an event will arise to challenge Heaven and Earth and you—if you are properly schooled and skilled—could earn Heaven's gratitude. It is wise to be prepared for all possibilities, but it is *unwise* to set your heart too firmly upon such goals. Come, we must ride back to the city."

But Wei T'ai-Tsung remained seated on the riverbank, petulant and angry. The boy was not often given to fits of temper, but when his mood grew stubborn, Wei K'e-yung's own patience became short. He called to the dog and turned toward the grove of trees where the horses were tied. When his son did not move to follow, Wei K'e-yung demanded that he do so.

"I wish to stay with the dragons," Wei T'ai-Tsung said.

"What you wish is not at issue. I will tolerate no more of your temper," his father said. His tone was uncompromising. "You will do as you are told."

"I want to stay with the dragons," the boy said again, slowly and firmly.

The dog, of course was completely heedless of the growing discord, and chose to exercise its high spirits and its lungs by dashing back and forth between father and son, barking loudly like an agent attempting the reconciliation of two feuding houses . . . and finding no success or cooperation at either gate.

Annoyed, Wei K'e-yung kicked the animal—an ineffectual blow that glanced off its hindquarters and sent it bounding away, baying and pouncing and dashing in circles.

"I am a reasonable man," Wei K'e-yung said, getting a hold on his temper. "But there is only so much disrespect I will ignore. If you return with me now without further comment or disagreeable behavior, I will not think of this incident again. If you hesitate even a moment longer you will be punished, and the severity of the punishment will depend upon how long you continue thus."

Wei T'ai-Tsung sat stiff as a post, his arms folded across his chest, but he turned and gave his father a petulant look. His mouth was silent, but his eyes inquired angrily.

The dog began running circles about the boy and dashed up to lick his face. Wei T'ai-Tsung pushed the animal away, and when it persisted he grabbed a stick and got to his feet, hurling it at the dog, which ducked away again, then dove for the stick with its mouth.

Father and son stood staring at each other and the dog ran circles about the boy again.

"Mount your pony immediately," Wei K'e-yung said in a low, stern voice, "or your archery will be forbidden to you for the next five days. If you persist, I will instruct Master Wing not to attend you for the rest of the month, and there will be no calligraphy and composition."

For a moment Wei K'e-yung thought he saw his son's chin begin to tremble as though the boy might cry, but as quickly as he had seen it, the child's face was controlled once more. He turned his gaze from his father and headed toward the grove with the dog still dashing around him. It rushed in and nipped at his sleeve playfully, then bounded away when the boy struck at it with his hand. Wei K'e-yung called to the dog, but the animal was overexcited and its play was becoming frantic. It rushed the boy again and this time he shoved it hard in the ribs, tumbling it onto the grass.

"Stop it!" he shouted. "Leave me alone!"

It came up, its forequarters low to the ground, its hind legs braced, muscles tensed for the next dash, barking frantically. The child glared at it. Wei K'e-yung looked about for a stick to discipline the dog and spied a reasonably stout one, but as he bent for it, the dog rushed the boy once more.

"I said *stop it*!" Wei T'ai-Tsung shrieked, hunching his shoulders and balling his fists. His young face looked like a demon mask, knotted and hot with anger and frustration. His eyes were squeezed shut and his mouth was a hard line. Then he spun abruptly about and went to the horses.

The dog was gone.

On the grass where it had stood an instant ago was a large red-and-grey rock which had not been there before.

For a long moment Wei K'e-yung did not move; he barely dared to breathe. His son took no notice. The boy stalked deliberately past his father, a scowl upon his young face, and headed for the grove. Wei K'e-yung looked after him, then looked back at the riverbank. The stone was still there.

Slowly, he approached the grove himself. Wei T'ai-Tsung was working with the girth on his pony's saddle and made a great show of ignoring his father. The child did not appear to realize what he had done. Or at least he did not seem to recognize its import. Like a man with a hunting hound he did not fully trust, Wei K'e-yung decided he could not let Wei T'ai-Tsung see that this event had unsettled him. He quickly adjusted his own saddle and mounted, ordering his son to do the same. The boy obeyed without further comment and guided his pony into the road beside his father, who set a brisk pace back to Kaifeng.

Within a half-dozen li the child had forgotten the quarrel and his good humor had returned. He sang and told his father stories from his tutor, Master Po's, seemingly endless fund of fairy tales and ghost stories. Then he told his father about his morning's lessons.

"Someday," he said brightly, "I will write a great book and it will become one of the classics of literature, and all the scholars will study it."

Wei K'e-yung smiled, for the edge was wearing off what he had seen by the river and the memory was becoming duller.

"A commendable goal," he said. "But first you must make yourself capable and then you must make yourself worthy. I have no doubt that the former circumstance will come easily to you. The latter you must discover for yourself and there your tutors will be of no use to you. Who can say how inspiration is attained? Have Master Po or Master Quan, in your history studies, taught you the circumstances of the lives of the scholars you particularly admire?"

"I know the life of Po Chu-i," the boy said eagerly and began to recite his history.

His son was no different than he ever was. His rare flashes of temper were quickly forgotten; his mind easily and profitably engaged in other, worthier matters. Wei K'e-yung breathed deeply of the fresh, fragrant early autumn air and tried to clear his own mind of fanciful and troubling thoughts. The bright cool day, this was real. The sound of the peasants in the fields, the smell of animals and the feel of his horse's motion beneath him, these things were real. But as he rode toward the gates of Kaifeng he could not rid himself of the knowledge that what he had seen by the river was also real and no matter how he tried he would not be able to persuade himself that he had imagined it.

Alone in his study that night, with the darkness close about his windows and the oil lamps casting shadows that shifted and lapped at the corners of the room like the ripples of a dark, silent pool, he found he could not force his mind from the scene at the river, even with the press of necessary work. The things that trouble the mind by day assume a new and greater dimension at night, and Wei K'e-yung's disquiet grew till he could no longer deny that he was afraid.

The following day was the fifteenth of the Eighth Month and this was the Moon Festival, which marked the turning of the year toward autumn and winter.

Though the public offices were closed, Wei K'e-yung still had a great many official functions to perform. There were prayers for the harvest and the planting of winter crops; the dedication of the newly completed Memorial Gate; ceremonial visits to countless shrines; the official tour of the prison, and in the afternoon he was to visit the university and hear the reading of six memorials to the emperor and choose one to be forwarded with his recommendation. Yet, busy as he was, the memory of what he had seen the day before lay in wait for him at every quiet moment. He did not dare discuss it with his secretary. Though the man was his most trusted aid and counsellor, he was also a loyal public servant, and Wei K'e-yung knew such talk could put his career in serious jeopardy. The rule of the Ming was aggressive and pragmatic and the men who served such emperors were expected to embody these ideals. Wei K'e-yung was not foolish enough to think that even a man who believed wholeheartedly in his gods would willingly accept the idea that the supernatural had actually visited his neighbor's household. Perhaps the peasants in the fields would cherish such a notion and even credit it, but men of the governor's station would require somewhat more in the way of evidence before *they* would accept such things. And the only proof he could offer was his own son, whom he would *never* risk to save his own reputation. He had no choice but to remain silent, but the memory haunted him.

In the evening there was a banquet in honor of the emperor who was represented by two of his highest ministers. Honan was an important province and the emperor's emissaries were always men of the first order. It was no less than Honan's due but no imperial honor could ever be taken lightly, so the banquet was lavish and Wei K'e-yung devoted nearly all of his attention to the dignitaries. Through it all, however, his son remained constantly at the fringes of his thoughts.

The banquet and its entertainments lasted well past the turning of the night and Wei K'e-yung returned home to a silent house, exhausted and ill at ease. The women were asleep and he could not bring himself to disturb them. But he knew he must speak with Pao Shih . . . and soon. As he had ridden home it had come to him that one day, one of his son's tutors might well see what *he* had seen, and he dared not risk that. The problem was how to continue with Wei T'ai-Tsung's education otherwise. If he had been a rich merchant with his affairs safely in the hands of trusted managers, he could have seen to the boy's education himself, for he was renowned for his own scholarship. But he barely had time for the least part of a father's duty once every tenth day.

He needed Pao Shih's counsel. In domestic matters, particularly where they concerned her child, she was as efficient and practical as he was at the emperor's business.

Unfortunately, he had no idea how to make her believe him.

The following day Wei K'e-yung left word that his son's tutors were to await him in his private study as soon as the noon meal was over.

The workings of the Imperial Governor's office were their usual model of efficiency, but the Imperial Governor himself was not. His staff politely assigned the cause to the success of the previous night's banquet and thought no more about it, but Wei K'e-yung sat in his office and brooded most of the morning.

When he returned to his house later in the day he found the men waiting patiently, if curiously, as he had requested. Wei T'ai-Tsung was in the pavilion with his mothers waiting to be called.

The governor examined the men closely on his son's progress and their plans for his further education and was quite pleased by what he heard, or would ordinarily have been, but for the burden on his mind. Then he explained that it had been brought to his attention by the women of the household that his son had been somewhat listless in the evenings and his appetite had fallen off, but in all other respects he appeared to be well enough. He enquired, choosing his words with the utmost care, if the three scholars had seen anything . . . odd or unusual in the boy's behavior.

Master Po, who taught the classics, was quick to say no, nothing appeared amiss to him. Master Wing and Master Quan, however, thought for a moment before answering, but they too reported nothing amiss and Wei K'e-yung, who watched them closely as they answered, was inclined to believe them. He dismissed them, saying he wished his son to rest a bit and they were free for the afternoon. Then he sat a while in his study, relieved but concerned. He was not sure how much longer it would be before one of them *did* witness something. Then he could only hope the man would come to him and be discreet enough to say nothing to anyone else. He could also only hope the incident, whenever it might occur, would be minor enough not to arouse too much astonishment.

Before returning to his office, Wei K'e-yung sent for one of Pao Shih's maids and told her to inform her mistress that he would visit her in private that evening. He was to join the emperor's ministers for dinner but he would come to her after that and he did not wish her ladies to serve them. She would see to their needs herself. Then Wei K'e-yung went back to work and accomplished little more than he had in the morning.

In the garden pavilion Yan Ping delivered her master's message, giggling and fluttering, for she was still young and filled with romantic notions about the very apparent passion the governor and his wife shared. Pao Shih admonished the silly child to be more decorous, but it did little good.

With the afternoon free Wei T'ai-Tsung begged to be allowed to practice his archery, so the gardener's son was sent for and the targets set up in the orchard across the pond and the boys ran off happily to their sport. The maids were dismissed and Pao Shih and Yin Whun had their privacy again.

"What can he want?" Pao Shih mused. "It has been years since he wanted such privacy that he sent the little ones away before we were ready for the bed."

"I cannot guess," Yin Whun said. "But it is, perhaps, a small sign. It is time he learned this secret."

"Yes, it *must* be tonight. The opportunity is too perfect to waste. It is by his request that he will be so alone . . . but I still do not know what we must say."

"He has asked to see you alone," Yin Whun said.

"You will be there nonetheless," Pao Shih said firmly. "You will wait in the inner chamber till I call for you; there may yet be use for your small magics."

The maids returned and the rest of the afternoon was spent deciding upon the proper wardrobe for the evening, and the fitting up of the rooms. Pao Shih told her maids to see to it there were sufficient coals in the stove and that tea and wine were set out to warm along with bowls of lichees, oranges and autumn nuts were ready. Yan Ping begged to be allowed to gather flowers petals for the bed and Pao Shih indulged her and also told her to set out bowls of rosewater instead of incense in the inner chamber.

When the maids had rushed off to prepare the lady's chambers, Yin Whun smiled and said "We must find that one a husband before long. She is fourteen and would be wasted without a man to please her."

"Perhaps when she is sixteen," Pao Shih said, "but I would not free her. She is young and frivolous, but she is also intelligent and loyal. You did well when you bought her, and Ai Lian also. I would not be parted from such servants, especially now when we will have need of so much secrecy. We must find a young man in service who pleases her and buy him for her. Perhaps in the spring I will charge the housekeeper to begin discreet inquiries. It may take some time but I would have the girl choose for herself as long as he is in service. To maintain such loyalty is a delicate thing, but it is worth the effort."

Yin Whun smiled. "Yes, Lady, I have always loved you for that reason."

The Imperial Ministers, Tsou Yuan-piao and Kao Ch'i-yu, were gentlemen of the highest moral standards, as well as gentlemen of great intellect and social propriety. Short of being a monk, however, this did not mean such men were not allowed to indulge in most of the ordinary pastimes of the common men of the day. Wine, rich food, gambling, fine clothing and the pleasures of women were not forbidden. Even occasional overindulgence was tolerable, as long as it did not become a habit and a matter of public display. They were human after all, and it was a fact that only the emperor, who was the Son of Heaven, was *more* than that. It was not surprising then, that Wei K'e-yung returned home somewhat less than completely sober, a condition he augmented even more in the privacy of his own study, because he still had no idea how to tell his wife what he knew he must.

In the scented rooms of her private chambers, Pao Shih began to wonder what kept her husband. The housemaid who had been set to watch the gate had come hurrying to fetch the lady's chambermaids as soon as Wei K'e-yung had dismounted from his sedan chair. At once Yin Whun slipped into the bedchamber and Pao Shih had set the tea and wine to warm on the stove with her own hand. Then she picked up a book of poems her husband had composed for her years ago, and settled in to read. But he had not come. There was no sound of him in the women's wing of the house, and now she had no attendants to send in search of him. She did not know if she should go to seek him herself and risk his displeasure if he should arrive and find her gone, or wait and risk losing the opportunity she had steeled herself for all day.

It was very late but that was not unusual when Wei K'e-yung was required to entertain in this manner. She hoped he had not exhausted himself, forgotten her and retired to his own bed, but she felt there was nothing to be done but wait, for if that were the case there was nothing she would gain by disturbing him.

Eventually she heard the soft scuff of feet in the corridor, and before he even entered the room she knew his condition. She found herself disturbed more than disappointed, however, for his request to see her in absolute privacy hinted at something other than the quenching of a flame, and she began to suspect what it might be.

As there was no longer a need to be artful she removed the wine pot from the coals and met him at the door.

"Husband, you honor my chamber."

She made to bow down but he stopped her with an arm about her shoulders. Small as she was, she took some of his weight upon her and guided him to his favorite chair.

"Forgive me," he said. "I do not often come to you like this. I had not intended to tonight."

She brought him tea and lichees and loosened his robe. He had already left his girdle and shoes somewhere.

"Husband, I do not criticize. It only saddens me to think that the emperor's emissaries have not brought you good news."

"No, no," he said. "They have said nothing disturbing. There was no news of consequence at all, in fact."

"Then was it sport that brought you home so overused?"

She moved to pour tea for herself and he reached and caught briefly at the hem of her wide sleeve. She poured her cup and returned to his side and he took hold of her arm and drew her down to sit on the low stool at his side. She was small and pale and still very beautiful and he dreaded what he had to tell her.

"My gem, my beautiful jewel. Do not make light of me." His speech was slow and halting and his words were occasionally unclear. "How often have you seen me so far into the wine? I apologize, for it is not the action of a responsible husband but . . ."

Pao Shih waited, but he did not continue. He seemed to have become intently interested in the pearls in her hair.

"Yes, Husband?" she said.

"You have always been remarkably beautiful. Do you know that? I had thought it might fade with time but it has not. You are not the young girl any longer but it is not . . . that has made no difference. I had thought 'she will grow plain with age, but it will not matter because she is the most perfect, precious woman on Earth. Only Heaven could claim finer. But my Pao Shih is still my lovely jewel and she is still splendid.'"

"Your tea grows cold, My Love," she murmured.

He laughed quietly. "Forgive me. My tea was already cold when I finally got to your room." Then he frowned briefly, a perplexed look. "But I did not come for that tonight . . . though I did not . . . *not* come for it. I . . ."

She took the tea from his hand, for he was paying it no heed at all and seemed in danger of dropping it. She returned to his side and stood over him.

"Wei K'e-yung, Husband."

He looked up at her. "My Jewel," he whispered.

"Husband, you had something you wished to tell me."

"Help me," he said in a strained voice. "I must lie down." He sat forward as though to rise, but could not get to his feet. Pao Shih tried to help him and managed to get him to stand, but she could not support him well enough to get him into the bedchamber. She called to Yin Whun who had been listening at the door, and together they helped him into the other room and onto the bed.

"Ah," Yin Whun said, shaking her head and clucking her tongue. "He is very drunk."

Wei K'e-yung, who seemed oblivious to her presence even with his arm about her, suddenly took notice of his Second Wife and sat up on the bed. For an instant he seemed more clear.

"Ah," he said reaching out. "Have I slept so long?"

"No, Husband," Yin Whun said. "Not long."

He sighed and lay back on the bed again. Pao Shih sat beside him and Yin Whun remained standing at the bedside.

"Wei K'e-yung," Pao Shih said in a stronger voice. "You came here to tell me something . . . ," she looked to Yin Whun and continued carefully ". . . about my son. Please, Husband, I *must* know what it is."

Suddenly Wei K'e-yung sat upright again and seemed nearly sober. He was fighting the wine and he was very determined. He looked at Yin Whun and told her firmly that she was dismissed.

"It is all right," Pao Shih said. "She may stay. We have no secrets from each other."

"No! This is for no ears but yours and by all the dragons in Heaven I would not tell it to *you* except that he is your *son*, Madam!"

"Go, Little One," Pao Shih said, but she shook her head gently as she spoke. Yin Whun withdrew to the door and again waited to be called.

Wei K'e-yung seemed to be getting control of himself, but it took great effort.

"What did I tell you before I slept? Ah! I feel as though I had *not* slept. I am no clearer for it. What did I tell you?"

Again Pao Shih took a small chance. "That you had seen something," she said.

He closed his eyes, his face knotted as though he were in pain, and lay back on the bed. "It was the day before the Moon Festival. We rode to the river and something happened there which I cannot explain."

Slowly, struggling through the fog of his wine stupor, Wei K'e-yung told his wife of the conversation on the riverbank; of the child's unaccountable anger and his stubborn fit of temper and finally what he had seen Wei T'ai-Tsung do. This last was delivered sitting on the edge of the bed with Pao Shih standing some distance off, for as he related the events he had grown stern and almost angry. He sounded much like he did in court when he was required to admonish a subordinate who had not executed the duties of his office honorably.

There was a considerable silence then, and Wei K'e-yung

fixed his stern but fuzzy gaze firmly upon his wife. At his word, Pao Shih returned to his side, the calm and dutiful wife, but Wei K'e-yung seemed ill at ease and confused by her.

"You do not seem particularly disturbed by this, Madam," he said.

"Have you never witnessed its like before?" she asked. "Even in small things?"

"Of course not!" he said, annoyed. "What do you mean? What small things? What have you seen?"

Pao Shih remained calm in spite of her husband's sudden firm grip on her arm and the deepening frown upon his brow.

"Forgive me," she said. "I am only a silly woman, but our son does spend most of his leisure time in my company. When he is with the tutors his activities are limited and strictly defined, which is proper, but when he is at play or at his sport he must necessarily exercise his own particular . . . talents. From what you have told me I would say these likely have little to do with his scholarly activities.

"Have you never noticed, Husband, that he holds an unusual attraction for animals? No horse in the stable has ever been too nervous around him, not even that ill-tempered bay the District Magistrate at Chengchow sent you last spring. The dogs in the kennels are eager at his approach—even the bear hound that loves nothing but the hunt. You have seen him in the evenings making firefly lamps with the gardener's son. Have you never noticed that Lin Yi's lamp may hold only a dozen, but your son's will glow with the flickering of ten times that number? The wild birds in the garden do not fly from him. When he is at the pond the fish gather near the bank where he stands.

"And this is so in spite of the fact that he is no kinder to these animals than any other boy his age. He delights in throwing stones at the fish, yet they do not move deeper into the pool. In the spring he brought a bird's nest to show me from which he had discarded the eggs. They lay broken beneath the tree; an act of thoughtlessness but cruel nonetheless. Yet the little bird he had so robbed flew about his head singing and settled upon the nest when he set it on the pavilion steps beside him. She took crumbs from his hand without a care. Small things, but unusual."

Wei K'e-yung was frowning still but it had grown thoughtful. "Yes," he said. "I suppose I have seen such things, but it had not occurred to me to notice them. Yet you noticed them and said nothing to me!"

"Forgive me, Husband," Pao Shih said. "But such little things by themselves could hardly seem worth mentioning. Would you have been at all concerned if I had told you your son was loved by the bear hound or that he caught more fireflies than Lin Yi? It is only in perspective that these things become significant."

Wei K'e-yung released her arm and tried to rise but found his legs unequal to the task. As his position shifted, however, he caught a glimpse of something beyond the door. Yin Whun's left sleeve. It did not register at once but when it did Wei K'e-yung was furious.

"Here, Husband," Yin Whun said, stepping into the room at Wei K'e-yung's angry bellow.

In his official capacity, Wei K'e-yung was a stern governor; fair and impartial but dedicated to the strict letter of the law. At home he was far less conservative and in private most informal. He generally did not require his wives to abase themselves when first entering his presence unless the formality of the occasion required it. But Yin Whun did not even make the most perfunctory bow and tonight this infuriated him.

"How dare you disobey my order?" he raged. "I could have you beaten for less! I will have the proper respect."

But Yin Whun stood her ground. "Most humble pardon, Husband, but you told me to leave the room. I did so. You did not say how far."

"Do you dispute with me?"

"On the contrary," Yin Whun said gently. "I merely point out that I was faithful to the exact extent of your command."

"Ah," Wei K'e-yung said, apparently somewhat mollified in his drunkenness. Then; "I do not remember what I said. But I do know, madam, that you have spied upon this conversation."

Pao Shih intervened. "Husband, it does not matter. I told you we have no secrets, she and I. She is the one person with whom I am most constantly in company. She has seen what I have seen. She knows what I know. She is . . . what I once was."

"Riddles," Wei K'e-yung snapped. "You do not seem to

appreciate the gravity of my news. This is not one hundred fireflies in a paper lamp, nor a knack for calming horses. This is a thing of unnatural proportion. A thing the likes of which only Heaven may contrive and there are demons enough there who sport with men's lives that I fear our son has fallen prey to one of them."

Wei K'e-yung staggered up from his wife's bed and stood shakily, clinging to the frame of the canopy.

"Tea," Pao Shih said and Yin Whun slipped quickly into the next room to fetch the cup.

"What god may I have offended? What must we have done? What must I have done . . . ?"

Yin Whun offered the tea but he did not seem to notice her now.

"Nothing," he said resolutely. "It cannot be that Heaven is angry with me. I have given no cause. Therefore it is surely the prank of some malevolent spirit."

"It is all the same," Pao Shih said. "The fireflies, the fish, the horses and now the dog; there is no difference. But what you have seen is not the will of Heaven. Had Heaven anything to do with it the boy would never have been born, let alone as he is."

"What then?" Wei K'e-yung demanded, clinging to the bedframe. He was growing angry again. "Do not give me more riddles, woman. What is it you know?"

Pao Shih was silent for a time. Yin Whun stood beside her and slightly behind, as a servant might and there was something profoundly disturbing about the posture even to Wei K'e-yung's wine muddled mind. They were aloof and strange in their silence. Wei K'e-yung wondered fleetingly if he had ever really noticed how perfect Yin Whun's beauty was. She was like a small, flawless pearl beside Pao Shih's glorious gemlike magnificence.

"I am not well," Wei K'e-yung said and sat back upon the bed, though he still held onto the frame. It did no good, however. His wives were still disquieting.

"Forgive me, Husband. I am not what I have claimed to be all these years. More riddles for a bit I fear. At this moment I am what you see before you: a wretched woman, your wife, human and more than a little sick at heart for I have deceived you for a long time.

"I have not always been as I am. When we were married it was not a human woman you took into your bed . . . and it was not a human woman who bore your son. You ask how you have angered Heaven and conclude that, since you have given no cause for offense, this can not be the case. But I assure you, it is the case. Only, Heaven is angry with me, not you. It is I who have offended, but it is both of us who must suffer.

"What you have seen, however, is not our punishment. Rather it is because of what our child is that we may yet suffer."

"I do not understand," Wei K'e-yung said, frowning and shaking his head, desperate for clarity.

"My first offense was marrying you. I am a subject of the Jade Emperor of Heaven and may not marry without his consent, and a mortal would be utterly out of the question. My second offense was abandoning my duty to Heaven to live with you and my third was to bear you a child. As punishment I was stripped of my immortality and my power and sent here to live out a mortal existence and raise the boy until such time as Heaven could determine if he was mortal or immortal. For nine years I have watched and for the last six months I have seen the signs of his heritage slowly emerging. You have only just discovered it."

Pao Shih bowed her head but remained standing. "Forgive me, Husband. I had hoped this confession would never be necessary. I had no wish to deceive you, only to live out my life as your devoted wife."

Wei K'e-yung's laughter had a slightly hysterical quality to it, but it was short lived. The anger returned suddenly and he tried to rise but staggered against the bedframe again and held on there.

"I do not dispute you, K'e-yung-ah. You have seen what you have seen. I have no doubt of it, for I have also seen its like. Only do not doubt me, Husband, for my story is no less true than yours."

"I wish . . . this farce . . . to end! You! My Second Wife . . . her loyal friend, how long have you known this fancy of hers? Why did you never tell me my wife was not fit?"

"I have always known," Yin Whun said. She was distant and cool where she stood in Pao Shih's shadow. "I have known her secret longer than man has walked the Earth. I have known it even when it was not a secret at all."

"No," he said, sitting back on the bed yet again. "I am not well. I can not trust what I hear. I am too drunk . . ."

"Do you wish to be sober?" Yin Whun asked. "It is a small thing of which I am most capable. I have done it for you before, but you have rarely been as drunk as this. You merely thought your tolerance for wine was exceptional."

"Do so," Pao Shih said shortly. "He can not be reasoned with in this condition."

Yin Whun stepped around her and walked to the bed. She reached out her right hand for her husband's forehead but, more quickly than he had believed himself capable of moving, he snatched her wrist and attempted to throw her aside. To his astonishment he found he could not move her from her course and at the same moment her left hand stroked his head: cool, gentle fingers upon his brow, one caress and then a second.

Suddenly Wei K'e-yung gasped and released Yin Whun's wrist, drawing himself away from her across the bed as quickly as he could move. In an instant the wine had left him and he was alert and sound and, he thought, possibly more sober than he had ever been in his life. Yet the memory of the drunkenness of the moment before was clear in his head. The contrast was shocking and he could not delude himself that it had not been so.

He was terrified.

"Tea," Pao Shih said again, and Yin Whun left the bedside and returned with the pot and three cups on a tray. She poured him a cup but he would not take it from her hand so she placed it on the bed and withdrew to serve Pao Shih who had seated herself in a chair.

"You said your powers had been taken from you," he said carefully.

"Mine have," his wife said. "Yin Whun's have not."

"What are you? Fox spirits? Serpent spirits? I had never much credited the stories peasants tell of such women. I fear I must revise my opinions."

"Indeed," Pao Shih said, pleasantly, "you must, for such things are more common than mortals know. But it is not the case with us. I was an elemental spirit. A fairy. Once I was called the Fairy of Ku-She and my duty, along with my Sister Tung Shuang-Ch'eng was the care of . . ."

"Of the snow," Wei K'e-yung said.

"Most specifically of the Golden Chopsticks, without which there could be no snowfall. Think, Husband. Remember the summer of our first love. Ten years ago. Do you recall how cool your garden was when all else stank of the heat. Do you recall how miserable your house was that winter when you could not keep warm enough and I, pregnant with our son, walked about the garden in light clothing. Do you recall how you scolded me then? It was Ku-She who lived under your roof that year. Who hid in your house, not out of shy propriety but out of fear, for already Heaven was angry with me."

And so it was that Pao Shih told Wei K'e-yung the story of his uncle's theft of her Golden Chopsticks and all that had occurred until they were returned to Heaven at last. Wei K'e-yung listened without comment and Pao Shih was at a loss to understand how it affected him. When the first blush of dawn began to fade the candle light in the bedchamber, her tale had come to the Court of the Heavenly Jade Emperor and the sentence he had placed upon her and upon their son, and then to the things she had lately seen, and her fears of Heaven.

"If he had been mortal after all it would never have been necessary for me to tell you this. But he is not. It is impossible to say so soon what his power will ultimately be. I was only a fairy, which perhaps is not an insignificant thing in the world of men, but in Heaven it is barely more than the station of that simple apothecary on Yellow Lotus Street who grinds the herbs for the gardener's wife. As the Servants of Heaven are reckoned only Yin Whun occupies a lowlier station and at the moment she is far greater than I, for she is still a fairy and I am, for this lifetime, entirely mortal."

At the conclusion of her story there was a considerable silence. Wei K'e-yung's face did not for a moment betray his thoughts except for his certain lack of joy. At last he rose from the bed and composed his robes about him in a more respectable manner.

"Does the boy know of this?" he asked.

"No," Pao Shih said. "Nor do I think he suspects that anything he does is not wholly natural, but he must be told soon. If we are to keep him from the Court of Heaven we must begin his education at once."

"I will dismiss his tutors until I have made a decision," he said, pausing in the doorway. "You will say nothing to anyone and you will remain in this wing of the house until I send word to you. I will prepare some special projects for the boy which he will work on in my private study. You will not see him in the meantime."

Pao Shih stood and glared at her husband.

"What decision is there to be made?" she said angrily. "We have no choice in this unless you wish to lose your son, and if that is the case we may as well send him now . . ."

"I will inform you of my decision," he said sharply. "Until then you will say nothing more. I will send your women to you. They will see to your needs and I will inform the kitchen staff that you will be dining in your chambers. Do not test me in this."

Then without a word of parting Wei K'e-yung turned and strode quickly from his wife's chambers.

Pao Shih sat heavily back into her chair. The anger had gone out of her and had been replaced by a look of despair. Her shoulders drooped and her hands rested limply in her lap. Yin Whun sat on a low stool at her feet. Neither of them spoke a word.

Presently they heard the sound of the chambermaids scurrying down the corridor toward Pao Shih's rooms and Yin Whun rose and went out to them. The girls were quiet in the next room. Yin Whun took Pao Shih's combs and pins from her long, dark hair and began to work the coils free with her expert fingers. Then she dressed it loosely for sleeping and urged Pao Shih gently from her chair. "Sleep now," she said. "I will help you undress. You have been up all night and the day before was long. I will take Yan Ping to my own chambers with me. Ai Lian is more suitable to your needs just now. You can do nothing more till he calls for you and I doubt it will be today."

Pao Shih rose and allowed herself to be prepared for bed but she did not think she could sleep. "My mind is vastly troubled, Little One. I feared this would happen. He has lost all faith in us. But we can not be content to allow Heaven to take my son. Something must be done to persuade our husband to trust us."

"When dinner is served we will send the maids to the kitchen for their own meal and we will discuss it then. But you can not think clearly in such a state. So to bed and to sleep. I will help you." Yin Whun smiled. "I am better than the opium."

"Indeed you are. You are better than many things, Little One and I am grateful for your company."

When Pao Shih had settled into bed Yin Whun placed her hand upon her lady's temple and stroked her hair gently back to the nape of the neck. When she lifted her hand away Pao Shih was already falling into a deep and peaceful sleep. Though the day was warming considerably, Yin Whun drew the shutters closed and the curtains about the bed and retired to her own chambers and her own bed. But her need for sleep was considerably less than that of mortals and while her maid believed her mistress slept Yin Whun lay awake and considered their dilemma.

It was not until after the evening meal that Wei K'e-yung finally came to some sort of terms with the sudden alteration of everything he thought he once knew about his life.

When he left his wives that morning he had gone directly to his rooms where he found his robes laid out waiting for him as usual. It was well past dawn and he was late. As he left the gate of the private compound he met a young page whom his secretary had sent to enquire after him.

It took Loy Quan Dong only a moment to realize that the governor was in a dangerous mood, and within the hour he had rearranged the day's audiences, postponing anything of a delicate nature to the following day. He then sent pages with the news to those gentlemen who might thus have been inconvenienced. Reviewing the day's schedule, Loy was relieved to note there were no matters of law passed on to the court by the District Magistrates, for Wei K'e-yung was in no mood to deal impartially with men's lives and fortunes.

None the less, in spite of his best efforts and stern admonitions to the staff to avoid anything that might inconvenience or annoy the governor, it was a long and difficult day. Rather than the absent minded distraction of the day before, this day the governor was intensely attentive to everything that crossed his path and it was impossible to please him. Even Loy Quan Dong's subtle and polite inquiry into the nature of the governor's displeasure brought an immediate eruption of angry words but no information.

At the end of the day, when the staff had been dismissed and most of the doors secured, the governor remained, sitting alone in his office; and Loy Quan Dong remained, sitting in a courtyard garden, watching and waiting.

At last, well after dark, Wei K'e-yung went home. Loy followed him out the gate at a discreet distance and bade the gatekeeper lock up anything that remained open. Then Loy himself went home, perplexed and troubled.

Dinner was waiting but Wei K'e-yung declined any food, requesting only a pot of tea. He gave the staff leave to take dinner to the ladies in their chambers and to feed his son in the kitchen. When the tea was brought to him he took the pot himself and retired to his study.

It was only then, when there were no more distractions strong enough to compel his attention, that he allowed himself to think about how totally his life had disintegrated.

Seated at his writing desk he wrapped the comfortable familiarity of his study about him like a winter shawl. No matter where he had had the fortune to reside over the years his study had always been laid out in precisely the same way. Only the acquisition of new books disturbed the pattern and allowance had been made for that from the beginning.

His lute hung on a peg by the door. His calligraphy brushes and inkslabs were kept in lacquered boxes on a particular shelf behind his desk. Against the wall directly before him was a carved chest, the first piece of fine furniture he had purchased when he began his career in earnest. On the right it held his fine rice and mulberry papers, inks and watercolors, and his own finished landscape paintings. On the left was his collection of the brushwork of scholars renowned for their artistry. The room was full of memories and mementos. The desk and chair had been a gift from his own father when he first entered the university, and though his parents death had caused him to return home to manage the remainder of his family affairs, the desk had stayed with him; a symbol of his father's pride and faith.

Now these things were all he could depend upon in his life to be true.

From moment to moment he felt angry, afraid, betrayed, and lost. He saw his career in ruins about him. He was suddenly a man without family and heirs; he felt utterly insignificant, like a playing tile in a game he could not even see, for the board was greater than the limits of his imagination.

The women at the other end of his house had betrayed him, lied to him, deceived him in every possible way. How much of his life had been his own and how much illusion was the result of their scheming and magic? And they were not really women. The thought of what he had loved, caressed and held in his arms terrified him. Had he ever seen their true form? And what had they given him for children?

Confusion . . . and anger . . . and the fear.

For it was not merely the deception now, that was bad enough, but the fact that Heaven would soon be directly involved; that for all these years his household had existed in two realms at once and he had been totally blind to it.

What was to be done? It was not a secret he could keep forever. Pao Shih . . . could he even call her that anymore? . . . would not have told him if she had not felt they were on the verge of being undone. The Imperial Court would be correct in finding fault with him and having no further faith in him. His position in the Imperial Service was too delicate for such a circumstance to be ignored. His career, of course, would be over. Dismissal from the service of the emperor was certain and the confiscation of his wealth was likely, for the Ming could be harsh when they felt their trust had been betrayed. He had been no less harsh himself on the court's behalf, and in matters he now considered trivial by comparison.

In fact, he was no longer sure in which emperor's service he had really been all these years. Heaven had certainly not seen fit to inform him of his agency, and yet he had been it's agent. He had raised the child, albeit unknowingly, for a post no man could aspire to . . . or a vengeance no man could imagine.

In spite of everything, when he thought of the boy the pride and love of a father filled him.

Yet the boy was not the son he had thought he knew. He was a creature like his mother . . . difficult to contemplate, and fearful to imagine.

The tea sat untouched and cold in the pot when Wei K'e-yung roused himself from his distraction. He could not find an answer and the questions became more complex as he thought about them. His life had never been simple, but it had been orderly. This was chaos.

He struck the gong on his desk and a young man appeared at his door almost at once. He sent the tea away and ordered a pot of warm wine, but when it arrived he did not want that either. He remembered too clearly the drunkenness of the night before and what had come of it. The touch of Yin Whun's hand was still crystal clear in his mind . . . and all that had come after. Instead, he sent the wine away again and told the boy to fetch a draft of opium from the housekeeper and bring it to his room.

He shuttered the study windows himself and paused at the door into the courtyard. The stars were hard and bright in a night gone cool with autumn. It reminded him of the feel of his house the first summer of his marriage, and he shivered. If he had known then, what would he have done, he wondered. Would he have dared to touch her, knowing what she was? Would he ever dare touch her again? Or Yin Whun? She had said she was now entirely human, but he did not know if he could believe this. Her story and the Heavenly Emperor's need to punish her would make it likely, but even if it was true, she was no longer the woman he had loved for ten years. She had always been a lie. The woman he had cherished had been born and married and widowed and had never for a day been anything but mortal. He had not married the Fairy of Ku-She, but a tiny, beautiful girl of irreproachable honor. With a word that woman had died and turned to dust in his heart. Worse, she had never been and only the cold, hard lie, like a lump of iron rested there.

Ku-She.

It echoed and echoed and would not be still in his mind. He could not grasp it.

From beyond the low wall that separated his courtyard from the women's compound, he heard the high, clear ripple of a woman's laughter. It angered him suddenly; that they should be laughing at this bottomless pit of dilemma into which they had cast him.

Quickly he shuttered and bolted the door and went to his bedchamber where he found the opium waiting. The sleep was quick, and deep and oblivious.

In the women's quarters, Pao Shih sat silently at her dressing table, hands loose in her lap, her expression distant while Yin Whun dressed her hair for bed. From the verandah that gave onto the little courtyard serving her quarters and Yin Whun's she heard the gentle laughter of one of the chambermaids as the girls sat gossiping about the news the kitchenmaids had brought in from the street that day.

"Tell them to take their silly twitterings to bed," Pao Shih said sharply. "I can not abide it."

"They mean no offense," Yin Whun said. "They are just young girls."

"I am not in the mood for such humor. They can chatter all they want somewhere where I do not have to listen to it."

Yin Whun went out and sent the girls away. When she returned she found Pao Shih standing at the window looking into the night sky.

"Let me finish your hair, Lady," she said from the doorway. "Then you should try to rest."

"It is sufficient," Pao Shih replied. "You may retire, Little One."

It had been a long time since there had been cause for it, but Yin Whun remembered the sound of tears in her mistress voice.

"I would not leave you alone tonight," she said.

"Please do. I have no real hope he will come to me tonight, but if he does not, I want no other company."

There was a long silence during which neither moved. At last Yin Whun was convinced Pao Shih would not change her mind, but as she was about to take her leave her lady turned her head and looked back over her shoulder. Her dark eyes were lustrous with tears and her cheeks damp.

"I have done this so very badly. It shall never be repaired."

"There was no other way. The thing was too far out of hand, what with his drunkenness and suspicions. You could not control that."

"I should have told him sooner. Much sooner."

"It has only been six months since T'ai-Tsung's powers began to emerge and even then we ourselves were not immediately certain of what we saw. A day, a week, a month . . . I doubt it would have made much difference."

"I was thinking of ten years ago," Pao Shih said. She turned her face to the window again. "Good night, Little One."

The following morning the governor was at his office punctually and his behavior was a model of studied impartiality and reason. He looked less haggard than he had in days, but Loy Quan Dong thought he detected the last lingering traces of an opium-induced sleep about the governor's movements and the look of his eyes. None the less, Wei K'e-yung seemed as unperturbed today as he had been irrational the day before, and though things progressed smoothly, Loy Quan Dong found this day nearly as trying as the others, for he did not fully trust that this change would last.

He set a page at the governor's side with instructions to alert him instantly if Wei K'e-yung began to act oddly in any way. The day ran on smoothly, however, and the only lapse of note was that the governor declined to return home for his midday meal as was his usual habit. Instead, he sent to the kitchen for the same soup and rice and salted fish the clerks and pages were fed, and ate alone in his office.

"I must see him at once," Pao Shih said firmly, pacing the veranda by her courtyard. "This can go on no longer. We *must* settle it now."

"Forgive me, my worthless opinion . . ." Yin Whun began patiently.

Pao Shih was sharp, in her voice and her movements. "Your opinion is *never* worthless. Even when it is not required."

"Shall I be blunt with you then?"

"You usually are, even when you kowtow and beg my mercy."

"Our husband has barely had time to consider the matter, to decide how he should feel, and therefore how he should behave. Knowing *him* we also know that *he* must know these things before he can decide what must be done. Even in his career he has always been inclined to studied consideration rather than immediate action.

"I believe he can come to no possible conclusion but the one we already hold, but he will require time to find his way to it.

Give him that time, Pao Shih. In my humble opinion it is unwise to do anything else. He will simply take it further amiss than he already has, and the conclusion will be reached no more quickly.

"When she went for the morning tea, Ai Lian said the housekeeper told her she had supplied a draft of opium early last night. We both know how uncommon it is for him to employ that remedy. He is greatly troubled by this. . . ."

"And the opium has given him refuge from it. A precious night was lost." Pao Shih paced the room in uneven patterns, her shawl clutched tightly about her shoulders. "I cannot wait. I do not know if my son will take this news any better than his father did, but I am the one who must tell him. Wei K'e-yung may never completely understand. The child himself may already suspect something. I cannot depend upon our husband's decision to be either favorable or prompt and, as I have no power of my own any longer, I must act when there is opportunity. He is away in court all day. Who in this house would dare stop me from seeing my child?"

"You would go against him in this?" Yin Whun asked.

"No, but I would have this thing done with."

"And force a decision. This may only serve to anger him more."

"It is a measure of how little he understands the situation that he believes his rights as husband are sufficient to hold us in this isolation and keep my son from me."

"Please, Pao Shih," Yin Whun said. "I beg you not to act in such haste. One more day could not hurt. It would be so much better if he came to this without coercion. Why this sudden haste?"

Pao Shih stopped her pacing and faced Yin Whun directly. "Because I must do this while I can. He will be in the court tomorrow and again the next day, I know . . . but I cannot say where my courage will be by then. It was my cowardice that has brought this difficulty to such a pass. I cannot let that happen with the child. The news will be no better or worse then than it is now, but my *heart* may fail me."

"You have more courage than you think, Madam. I have seen it."

"Perhaps, but it is a hateful business and I would have it over with."

"Please," Yin Whun pleaded earnestly now. "For all our sakes, do not press him so. Give him *one* more day. Only that."

"One more day," Pao Shih said softly. "Very well, one more. But just one. More than that I fear I could not endure."

That night Wei K'e-yung sat alone in his study well into the third watch of the night. More and more his mind traveled to his losses rather than to the treachery he had invested in his wives' motives; his career in ruin, his fortune gone, his family destroyed. He mourned his ruined future, and the more despair he felt the more he thought of all he had to lose; and the more the list ran through his mind the more often he discovered his wives and son headed the list.

But mostly it was Pao Shih he could not get from his mind; the knowledge that she had never been what he had thought her to be and yet whoever . . . whatever . . . he had lived with for ten years had been a joy to him and worthy of his love. At least he had felt so at the time.

As he sat at his desk brooding over his tea, from time to time he would look about the room, reassuring himself with its familiar comfort. At one such time his gaze came to rest upon a small landscape which hung on the wall across from his desk. There were only three pictures hanging in this room. One was his own, one his father's and this one.

As a young man he had purchased it from an agent who dealt in antiques, and particularly the works of ancient scholarly painters. Though the signature had been defaced and some of the characters which coincided with the personal name of an earlier emperor of the Ming had been removed, as was the law, the date and title were intact and that, along with the style, had caused it to be attributed to the great landscape painter Ts'ao Chih-po of the late Yuan Dynasty. It was an exquisite little painting, delicately brushed and tinted, with fine, clear details and perfect visual balance. Wei K'e-yung had loved it at once and had paid more for it than he could really afford, but such a prize was not commonly found by one of his youth, and he proudly took it home.

His father had been impressed by its artistry, but doubtful of

the attribution, and more than a little appalled at the price for
so dubious a work, but Wei K'e-yung had hung it with pride
above his desk, and took it with him when he left for the
university. It was there that he was thoroughly stripped of his
illusions about it by a master whose specialty was the paintings
of Chinese scholars under the Mongol rule. The man had
criticized if favorably for its technique but an examination of
other, *real* works by Ts'ao Chih-po quickly revealed the
deception. The master suggest Wei K'e-yung hang the picture
anyway as a reminder and a lesson about hasty decisions and,
thoroughly humbled and resolved to educate himself properly,
he did so.

Over the years his collection had grown, and grown quite
impressive as well, and when he had advanced somewhat in his
career he felt it no longer wise to display this reminder of his
foolishness. But much to his surprise he discovered he could
not bring himself to take it down. He had loved it the moment
he saw it, and he had had nothing but pleasure whenever he
looked at it, and it was then that he came to realize that he had
really purchased it for its beauty rather than its name, and that
ultimately it had been worth every copper of the price. So he
took it and hung it in his study where he could look at it with
pride and never concern himself with what others thought of its
poor credits.

Looking at the painting now as he thought about Pao Shih,
Wei K'e-yung remembered all this and was ashamed, for his
wife was still as precious to him as she had been when he first
took her into his house. Perhaps more so, for he had grown
attached to her and her ways day by day over the years, and he
could not bear the thought of losing her.

Yin Whun laid down her needlework and left her seat on the
veranda as Yan Ping burst into her chambers, flushed and out
of breath from running. She had been calling as she ran and
Yin Whun had heard her coming. She delivered a few sharp
words on such indecorous behavior as the little maid struggled
for breath, but at last the girl merely caught her mistress by the
hand and gasped "Come!" as she tugged her toward the door.

"Child," Yin Whun said. "What has upset you?"

"It is Big Wife," the girl gasped. "Little Wife, please . . . you must come at once!"

Ah, foolish, foolish, Pao Shih, Yin Whun thought as she followed the girl through the house. *What have you done? Why need you have been so hasty?*

As they hurried along Yin Whun noted with some small confusion that they had passed the boy's rooms without pause and were, in fact, heading for the servants' quarters. These were a series of small rooms with individual doors letting out onto a veranda running the length of two sides of the kitchen yard. The gardener and his family had a small cottage near the compound gate and the housekeeper and her husband the stablemaster had a modest suite of rooms in the servants' wing, with a doorway that let directly into the house. The other servants, including the ladies' chambermaids, were required to enter the house through the kitchen. So when Yan Ping turned left before reaching the kitchen door, Yin Whun knew precisely where they were going. They passed the shuttered cupboards and storeroom doors and a flurry of housemaids startled back to business by the sudden appearance of the Second Wife. At the end of the corridor Yin Whun heard the sounds of weeping, the loud crash of breaking crockery and a scream.

There was thunder in her eyes as she brusquely ordered the servants back to work and set Yan Ping in the corridor to see that they obeyed. Then she entered the housekeeper's quarters.

The room was a shambles. Crockery, teapots, rice bowls and a painted vase lay in shards about the floor. There was a huge, wet splatter on one wall where something had struck and broken. The bedclothes were in a tumble on the floor and several items of furniture were overturned. In the midst of this disarray Mistress Hsieh, the housekeeper, huddled against the foot of her bed trying to cover herself with a corner of her bedding. Her hair was wild and her gown disheveled and torn in places. She was weeping bitterly into the bed sheet in her hands. Pao Shih stood over her, one of the stablemaster's short riding crops held tightly in her hand. Her face was nearly colorless, but her eyes were wild and dark with rage, and she gripped the crop so tightly her little fist looked carved from stone.

As Yin Whun entered the room Pao Shih raised the whip and

struck the woman again, and cried aloud herself as the blow fell and the poor woman on the floor gasped into her sheets.

"Where is he?" she hissed, her voice grating and raw from overuse. "Where?"

The housekeeper ducked another blow, this one aimed at her head and saw Yin Whun standing in the doorway looking stunned.

"Little Wife!" she cried, rising to her knees and reaching out toward Yin Whun. "Please save me! She will kill me and I have done nothing."

Pao Shih, seemingly blind to all but her immediate purpose, took aim at the back thus exposed to her and landed a heavy blow that sent the woman sprawling facedown onto the floor with a scream of pain. Then Pao Shih threw the whip down and went for the woman with her hands as Yin Whun rushed forward to stop her.

"Where is my *child*?" she screamed, hoarse and hysterical as her hands found the woman's hair. *"Tell me! Tell me where he is!"*

With difficulty and the help of the housekeeper's youngest daughter who had been cowering in a far corner, Yin Whun managed to pull Pao Shih off the now equally hysterical Mistress Hsieh. The three of them tumbled together onto the floor and Pao Shih fell weeping into Yin Whun's arms.

The governor's First Wife was not one for beating the servants. She had rarely found it necessary, and those few who had been so incorrigible as to require it from time to time, she had sold off. Yin Whun could not recall *ever* having seen her in such a passionate frenzy. It took some time and gentle coaxing interspersed with occasional stern words for Yin Whun to discover what had distressed her lady so. But once it was clear, she did not wonder at it.

When Pao Shih had gone to her son's room after breakfast, she had not found him there. Thinking him in his father's study at work on some lesson she had gone there, but the boy was not there either. T'ai-Tsung had been forbidden to play in the park unaccompanied. The gardener and his son could be seen from the study window pruning the shrubs in Wei K'e-yung's garden just inside the moon gate. She called to them, but the gardener said he had not seen the boy all morning. Annoyed, Pao Shih had gone to the kitchens, thinking perhaps her son had lingered there over breakfast, but the kitchen maids told her they had not given him breakfast that morning, and the cook said she had not prepared dinner for him either. She had, however, sent the stablemaster off with a considerable picnic in a willow hamper the afternoon before at Wei K'e-yung's order.

A vague dread had filled her with that news, and she had gone straight to the housekeeper's little apartment, where she found the woman inspecting the seamstress's mending. When Pao Shih had demanded to know where her son was, Mistress Hsieh had seemed dismayed and said that, of course the boy had gone fishing.

Pao Shih was not at all satisfied with the answer and pressed the woman further. Mistress Hsieh said Wei T'ai-Tsung had ridden out with her husband and two young grooms directly after the noon meal the day before, as Wei K'e-yung had instructed. She had packed the boy's clothes herself and her husband had seen to the fishing tackle. The master had instructed her to provide for the boy's needs for "several days," but had not specified precisely how many. Pao Shih's agitation had blossomed into rage and violence, however, when the poor woman was unable to say precisely where the party had gone.

Yin Whun stroked Pao Shih's hair and she grew calmer. Then the Second Wife rose and turned to the housekeeper, who was still sitting on the floor attempting to arrange herself more presentably. As Yin Whun stood, her face was stern and cold and the woman prostrated herself at once, knocking her head upon the floor. At Yin Whun's word she sat back on her knees but kept her head bowed.

"I thank you most humbly, Madam. This miserable and worthless creature would surely have died but for your intervention."

"Speak to me plainly and tell me the truth or I will beat you myself," Yin Whun said. "Where has your husband taken the boy and why?"

"I know only what I have said to my master's most honored First Wife. He came to me yesterday in the morning and said he had charged Hsieh Tzu-ang to take Wei T'ai-Tsung on a fishing trip; that the boy had been slow at his studies of late and the change of air would benefit his concentration. He had spoken to the cook, who was preparing a hamper, and to my husband, who already knew his instructions. I prepared the boy's things myself and took them into the stable yard, where the pack animals were already being fitted out. The grooms knew nothing and Hsieh Tzu-ang was at the governor's offices receiving money for the journey. It then became necessary for me to settle a dispute among some of the housemaids, and they departed without my husband saying so much as a word to me. You may ask the first cook. She knows how little we like to be separated, and she gave me tea to improve my mood when I found him gone like that.

"I swear upon my ancestral shrine, upon my very life, that I do not know where the master chose to send them. He said nothing of it to me. It never occurred to me that he would not have spoken of it to Big Wife."

"You know they have not been cordial for several days," Yin Whun said pointedly.

"This is true," Mistress Hsieh said, her head still bowed. "But the master has not been himself. Twice he has sent for opium and more often for warmed wine; more than is usual for him. I thought it some slight infirmity aggravated by annoyances in his work. I thought him merely out of sorts and the disagreement no more than what most husbands and wives are used to."

Yin Whun called to Yan Ping, who entered the room with Ai Lian close at her side, their eyes wide with amazement at the condition of the room. Together they helped Pao Shih to her feet.

"I am satisfied," Yin Whun said. "She has told the truth. Now you must go to your room and rest. I will be there momentarily."

Pao Shih nodded silently and allowed her maids to help her from the room. Mistress Hsieh still knelt upon the floor, trembling slightly.

"You are not at fault," Yin Whun said. "Do not concern yourself. I will send in the maids with a bath for you, and you may do as you please with the rest of the day. The household will report to the first cook as necessary. Do you have another suitable gown?"

"Yes, Lady," she said, breathing easily for the first time since Pao Shih entered her room.

"Good. I will have the seamstress repair this one and send a new one as well. But tell me, had you known where Wei T'ai-Tsung had gone would you have told us?"

Mistress Hsieh bowed to the floor again and said, "Much as I love both you and the Honored First Wife, my duty is to the Governor of Honan. Had he told me to be silent I would have been, even if it had been necessary to cut out my untrustworthy tongue to do so. I have been in the household of the Governors of Honan for twenty-four years, since my mother sold me as a kitchen maid at the age of ten. I have been the housekeeper for eight years. I have seen many governors in this time and learned many things, and I do not hold this station lightly. Forgive me, Madam, but it must be clear to you that I cannot dare to risk a careless word, even to you, or the governor would be quite right to have me buried alive."

"The governor was correct not to tell you. Clearly he recognizes the value of your loyalty and prefers not to waste it by requiring such extreme measures of you."

"In my experience, Madam," the housekeeper said, "it is not every man who can trust his wives as fearlessly as the governor can trust you."

With her forehead still pressed to the floor, Mistress Hsieh did not see Yin Whun's brief but bitter smile as she turned away and left the servants' quarters.

Shortly before the midday meal, Wei K'e-yung received a boy in his office who had come from the house with a message.

He knew what was wrong, of course, but once again he chose to take his noon meal in his office. He did not expect this interview with his First Wife to be brief, and he preferred not to have to explain his tardiness to the court or terminate their meeting in the midst of this unpleasantness, which he would then have to carry back to his office. He sent back a brief note with the boy to be delivered to either of his wives, inviting Pao Shih to see him in his private study after the evening meal. Then he did his best to put it out of his mind.

At dusk, when the gates of the city had been closed and barred and the drum towers had sounded the first watch of the night, Wei K'e-yung was at last resigned to the fact that he could put it off no longer. As he crossed to the private compound he was annoyed to see, at the fringes of his vision, the figure of Loy Quan Dong once more following him out the gate at a not quite sufficient distance to remain unnoticed. The man was his most trusted retainer and he had to admit his own behavior had been questionable of late, but he did not like being spied upon, and now was the *worst* of all possible times. He had no doubt the man was free of suspicions, for few men would have entertained the idea that Wei K'e-yung was slowly accepting as reality. But it was inconvenient for his secretary to be so concerned just now, and Wei K'e-yung decided something must be done to distract Loy Quan Dong onto the path of a false explanation.

He took his evening meal, though he ate little of it and did not touch the wine he had requested. Then he braced himself for the battle and went to his study. Once there, he took a moment to remove the more fragile of his treasures from reach, having had a full account of the condition of the housekeeper's rooms. Upon his return to the house he had left strict orders that the servants were to retire immediately after dinner, but still he felt the need to shutter the windows against the night and bolt the garden doors. When he turned from this last task he was startled to find his wife kneeling on the floor behind him, her forehead pressed to the rug, waiting to be acknowledged. To have entered so silently was possibly the most disturbing thing she could have done just then, short of appearing before his eyes out of the thin air, and though he had no doubt been distracted by the sounds of his own activity, the surprise of it put him off. He was curt in his acknowledgement of her and when she stood, her tiny hands clasped over her apron, her face pale and expressionless, he found he could not look directly at her. He took a half-dozen unshelved volumes from his desk and began fitting them back onto their shelves with his back to her.

"Where is Yin Whun?" he asked.

Pao Shih's voice was small and quiet. He could not read the emotion in it, but it seemed to come from a great distance and with effort. "She has remained in her chambers," Pao Shih said. "She would have come with me but I forbade it. She was most displeased, but she will not interrupt us."

"It is clear you have more power over her behavior than her

own husband does," he said. "Though all things considered, this should not surprise me."

Pao Shih had not replied and he fitted the last book into place in the lengthening silence. Yet he still could not turn and look at her. "You asked to see me, Madam," he said.

"Will you be so false as to ask why?" she said.

He braced himself, but there was no more and her voice remained small. He could stand there facing his books no longer without looking ridiculous or cowardly, so he turned away and made a greater business of seating himself at the desk than was necessary.

"No," he said, looking at her now, but avoiding her face. "I did what I considered necessary until this thing is resolved. It is awkward enough with the household about and my duties to the office. And as you have apparently proven I could not trust you to keep your word and not try to see him . . . even if you possibly did not intend to say anything to him," he added with a somewhat conciliatory tone of voice. He looked up then, prepared to face her anger or at least the indignation he would have felt at such a comment, but his heart almost stopped at the sight of her face. She looked so frail and so much younger than her years; her face was ghostly pale, and her eyes looked unnaturally large and very dark in the lamplight. They shone and glittered like black gems, but it was not anger or cunning, but tears, that caught the flickering light of his lamp. The rose of her lips was unusually warm and soft, her whole face softened from the tears moistening her cheeks and that full little mouth. Her head, bowed ever so slightly, rose as his gaze met hers at last, and caught there. He felt drawn into it, as though his soul were lifted out of his body while it remained solid and heavy in his chair.

Magic. Was it magic? He did not think so. He knew it was by his own choice that he did not turn away from her, did not want to. But when she spoke he was shocked back into place with a shudder.

"What have you done with my child?" she whispered, her lips trembling and damp with tears.

"He is safe," Wei K'e-yung said, astonished. It had never occurred to him that anyone would think otherwise. "I have sent him on a holiday. Hsieh Tzu-ang has taken him upriver to the ford to fish for a few days. I thought it best he not see this discord between us until we had settled matters. What did you *think*?"

"I knew only that you had taken him from me in secret. That you had sent him away and that I might never see him again." Her quiet tears resolved into open weeping, and she clasped her hands against her breast and her body began to tremble. "You are all I have—my life—my husband and my child. I could not live without you and yet I cannot die until Heaven has given me leave. What a miserable creature I will be then, for Heaven will surely take my child and you have learned to hate me . . . and your son too."

Having said this she sank down onto the rug and began to cry bitterly. There was nothing more she could say to him. She had thought to plead if necessary, to beg his forgiveness and swear to endure any punishment that might please him, to regain her child if only for the short time till Heaven sent for him. But she found herself totally without thoughts or words or the power of speech. Her grief overcame her, and she was no longer capable of anything. That Heaven had meant to punish her was abundantly clear now, and the Jade Emperor had chosen his revenge with perfection.

Wei K'e-yung was far from unaffected. He felt as though his heart would tear at the sight of her, and in spite of everything he found himself kneeling at her side, his arms about her, rocking her gently as he had watched her do when their son was very small and had come to them with some imagined fright. She grew calmer in his arms until at last her sobs were mere sniffles and he helped her to her feet.

"My Jewel," he said.

"What will you do, Husband?" she asked, her voice steadier, but still full of emotion.

"Go to your room and rest," he said. "We will talk in the morning. I will put off my business until we have resolved this. I fear I have waited overlong already."

"And T'ai-Tsung?"

"Hsieh will return home in four days unless I inform him otherwise. I see no reason to alter that plan. He was so happy to be going out alone and he will have burden enough to come home to."

Alone in her chambers, Yin Whun cursed the layout of the house that did not permit her to hear even as far as Pao Shih's own rooms. She at least consoled herself with the knowledge that he could not kill her, even in a rage. The Jade Emperor had precluded that possibility. Given her behavior this morning, however, Yin Whun *was* more than a little concerned for her husband's life. If he were to die, however, both Pao Shih and the boy would be taken immediately into Heaven and her fears of separation would no longer hold sway. No doubt other consequences would accrue, but Yin Whun tried not to think of such things. For once she wished her magic to soothe and induce sleep could be used upon her own self, but there was no magic for her, not even in the opium the mortals employed. Instead, she paced her rooms and waited and tried not to be afraid.

At dawn, when the first stirrings of the house had begun, Yin Whun carefully left her quarters and slipped into Pao Shih's chambers. She was relieved to find her lady's robes of the night before laid upon a chair, undamaged and carefully folded. Within the moment, Ai Lian appeared with the morning tea and Yin Whun took it from her, preferring to rouse Pao Shih herself, for there was no telling what mood she would be in. She set the pot on the dressing table and went to unshutter the windows, but stopped before she was halfway there, and left the room at once, closing the door firmly behind her.

She was smiling broadly and her voice was light when she sent the girl off to tell the servants their master was in his lady's bechamber and they need not worry themselves with searching.

"He will think me a fool," Wei K'e-yung said, recalling to his wives the conversation on the riverbank when Wei T'ai-Tsung had vowed he would ride with the dragons.

Pao Shih made a reassuring little smile. "It is unlikely he would ever mingle with the Great Dragons. At least not on such a level. He is only half-fairy, after all, and it is entirely possible he has reached the limits of his power already.''

"But what *is* this power? What I saw by the river was horrifying.''

"It is difficult to say. Over time we may learn it better. What you have seen him do is not the power, it is but a result of it. I believe it is the dog, and not the stone, that is significant; this attraction he has for all animals is our clue, I believe. Has anyone been to the river to see if the stone is still there?''

"No,'' Wei K'e-yung replied. "I would have to go myself. It would be too difficult to explain. Is this important?''

"Perhaps,'' Pao Shih said. "It will tell us if his magic holds.'' She slipped her shawl about her shoulders, for the autumn evenings in the pavilion were growing distinctly cool, though the days were now the most pleasant time of the year for her. She did not mind the coolness. A light shawl was a pleasure which would soon enough give over to the misery of winter again.

In the west, beyond the treetops of the orchard, the sky was rose and lavender and above the deepening blue of evening was turning gradually to indigo. The first stars were winking into sight, hard and white—tiny flaws in the canopy of Heaven which the Jade Emperor had seen fit to preserve.

"Is it an attractive stone?'' Yin Whun asked, studying her fan in the warming glow of lantern light.

"It is odd, as I recall,'' Wei K'e-yung said, thinking back. "It does not look at all like a dog. Its shape is rather unusual. I do not think I stopped to consider if it was attractive. I found the moment too unnerving for such considerations.''

"But as you recall it now,'' she said. "Might it be considered oddly attractive? Or at least interesting or curious?''

Wei K'e-yung looked perplexed and a bit put off. "I . . . suspect it *might*. In a gruesome sort of way.''

"No, Husband,'' Yin Whun said patiently. "I mean to one who had no notion what it was.''

Again he looked perplexed and thought a while. "I would not consider it a great aesthetic delight, but yes, I suppose it could be considered attractive enough from certain angles.''

"Fine,'' Yin Whun said. "I want it for my garden in the courtyard. I have wished for an object for contemplation for some time now, and I believe this particular rock, which you have described so eloquently, has struck my fancy. Would you care to make me a present of it, Husband?"

For a moment he stared at her, then smiled and laughed. "As you wish, Little Wife. But only on the condition you share its . . . unique qualities . . . with your sister-wife. I am sure Pao Shih would find it as intriguing as you do."

"Our gardens are forever at each other's disposal," Yin Whun said, bowing behind her fan.

"My Little One is always most clever," Pao Shih said, smiling softly. "I would be honored to share in our husband's gift to you."

"What will you do with it?" Wei K'e-yung asked, sobriety returning to his voice.

"I cannot say yet," Pao Shih said. "We must see it first. Perhaps nothing. Perhaps it will show something to Yin Whun. She must be my eyes and ears and hands in this, for I have been blind and deaf to that world for ten years. Some things my intellect and instincts may still tell me, but my fairy senses, my ability to even recognize the presence of magic, are useless to me. They are as dead as this womb which will bear you no more children. But as long as my memory and reason are intact, I am not wholly ineffectual." Pao Shih smiled again. "And my Little One is *very* clever."

Wei K'e-yung looked thoughtful again. "Can he retrieve the dog?"

"We will see," Pao Shih said. "Expectations of any sort, however, would be unwise just now."

"Yes," he said. "I agree."

The darkness had closed about them like shutters, and the amber lanternlight within the pavilion seemed to define the entirety of the real world. Since Wei K'e-yung had abandoned himself to the strangeness of what he knew his wives to be, he had felt unexpectedly at peace with it. The stewardship of this most profound secret had given him a sense of intimacy with them which was wholly different from anything he had the power to imagine. Even though his deep and passionate love for Pao Shih and his trust in her to manage his affairs as a proper Principal Wife, warmed his heart and gave him cause for pride, he realized they were only such things as the world of men might recognize. He felt now as though he had been let into a greater world through a secret and well-hidden door. All was the same and yet nothing would ever be *precisely* the same again, and the intimacy of his love, though still real and true, had grown far greater by the intimacy of this new realm.

Yet though he was at peace with it, he was not happy. The prospects it brought with it were distressing, and the boy was at its center.

"T'ai-Tsung is due back tomorrow evening," Wei K'e-yung said, "and I still do not know what we must do."

"One thing at a time," Pao Shih said. "I agree he must be told as soon as possible, but first I wish to see this thing he has done and then I would watch him for a day or two. In light of his comment to you about the dragons, he may suspect something already. I would have you question Hsieh and his grooms most carefully about all that they saw while in his company."

"I warned Hsieh as strongly but subtly as I could not to anger him or contradict him if he seemed adamant on a point, no matter how silly it might seem. In this way I hoped to avoid any further displays that might arouse suspicion, but I do not know how long we can indulge this without ruining the child or simply encountering the unexpected."

"A day or two," Pao Shih said. "No more. I do not yet know if it would be better done in your presence or in private."

"I would be there," Wei K'e-yung said.

"It may be so, but I ask you to trust me in this, Husband. My confession to you was not well done, I know this. The child, however, will be more carefully treated. I promise. I will do only what I consider best, and I will try to frighten him as little as possible."

Wei K'e-yung looked grim. "That might not be possible at all."

Wei T'ai-Tsung was ecstatic. The strangeness of the idea did not frighten him in the least, and while his parents were all amazed, Pao Shih was relieved while her husband was somewhat appalled and Yin Whun was quietly disturbed. It required an act of physical restraint on his father's part to prevent him from running into the garden to tell Lin Yi.

"But Lin Yi is my greatest friend!" the boy protested. "May I tell *no one*?"

"No one," Pao Shih said firmly.

The child drew himself up, despite his father's restraining arms, and looked at his two mothers indignantly. "You have told Father," he said, childish self-righteousness heavy in his voice.

"Only now," Pao Shih said. "And only because the times have become desperate . . . and only because he *is* your father."

The boy looked petulant, but remained silent.

"When you marry we will discuss whether or not to tell your wife. It is a great secret to carry alone, Tsung-ah. When she is chosen we will have to consider not only her rank and reputation, but her trustworthiness. Since she will be young also, we may have to wait some time to determine this last quality. But apart from such a one, my son, you must guard this secret as closely as the most costly treasure. You must not reveal it to *anyone*. Not *ever*."

Wei T'ai-Tsung was confused. "Why?" he said. "If I have this power, what could any man ever do to harm me?"

Pao Shih sat very erect upon the carved couch in the Pavilion of the Breeze Among the Willows at Dawn. She had acquired that disturbing dignity that Wei K'e-yung had seen on her the night she had revealed her secret to him, and once again it affected him. It affected the boy as well. Wei T'ai-Tsung could feel a slight tremble run through him as he stood in his father's embrace. Pao Shih held out her hands and Wei K'e-yung released the boy, who went to her slowly and stood before her with his hands in hers.

She was very quiet but her words were clear and firm.

"Do you wish to live in this world . . . with your father and the Little Mother and me . . . among your friends and among men?"

The boy looked troubled. "Yes, Mother, of course I do." He looked quickly at Yin Whun and then at his father and back at his mother again. A small frown knit his brow. "Would you send me away?"

"No, child, not for anything. That is the reason we are telling you all this now. We do not know precisely what power you have or what it may someday become. I cannot say *what* men might be able to do to you . . . or you to them."

"I'm sorry about the dog," the boy said quickly. "I would never do that to a person. I didn't *mean* to do it to the dog. I'll be very careful. I promise."

"Yes, you *must* be very careful. You must never let anyone see this but the Little Mother and me, and then only when we ask. It is not that we fear you would be unwise in its use. It is a fairy magic, after all, and not likely to amount to much as the powers of Heaven go, and you are a fine and intelligent young man. I know you would educate yourself in the use of this power as you educate yourself in the classics and arts. A scholar is wise in many things and you would be wise in one thing more. But men would fear you and, though it is unlikely they could hurt you, your life would not be pleasant.

"It is not the injury of men that concerns me, however. There is *another* agency that could very easily hurt you if it chose.

"Though I do not think this is what they would do, for through your power you are of interest to them. They would take you from the world of men forever . . ."

"*NO!*" Wei T'ai-Tsung cried, tugging at his mother's hands. "I would not go. I would fight. I would stay here where I belong."

Pao Shih gently, but firmly, pulled the boy close to sit beside her on the couch.

"Listen to me, my child," she said solemnly. "You will go there one day, no matter what. But I would have you go on your own, when you are ready and in your own chosen time; when you have learned your powers, however small they may be, and know their value and their use. You will be a man and you will know your own mind. They will have to deal with you correctly then, and not as a child who may be shaped and twisted as they see fit."

"But, Mother," Wei T'ai-Tsung said, "*must* I go? Even then?"

Pao Shih smiled. "Yes, child. You will want to. You are immortal and Heaven is the only fit place for you. As your father serves the Son of Heaven so you will one day serve the Jade Emperor himself. There is no greater post a scholar could aspire to, and you will be the greatest scholar of all. This duty will one day fall upon you, but I would not have it nipped in the bud . . ."

She paused, at a loss for more words, and the child studied her face intently.

"Heaven is not happy with me, Tsung-ah. In their eyes I have been most wicked, and my mortal life here is part of my punishment . . . but there is more. They would take you from me while you are still young and raise you in the Court of Heaven, in what manner and to what ends I could not even dare to guess."

"Would they harm me?" the boy whispered.

"No," she said. "That they would not do. But they could teach you to hate me. . . ."

"Never!"

". . . and they could charge you with an eternal duty of menial servitude in which your fine, young mind and hunger for learning would be bound, as in a prison. For you to go to them in your own time, mature in your power and in your wisdom and your scholarship, they would then have to acknowledge your true worth."

The boy held her hands tightly and leaned toward her, his young face earnest and intense. "I will tell no one, Mother, I promise, and I will learn whatever you and the Little Mother require of me."

She patted his hand and smiled, but though it was a fond smile, it was not a happy one.

"There is one thing more, Tsung-ah. And it is the most important of all." There was a long and awkward silence while Pao Shih collected her thoughts and her courage. The boy waited without a sound but she could see the worry collecting in his dark eyes.

"Your existence is known to Heaven already."

Wei T'ai-Tsung gave a start of surprise, and a shadow of real fear passed over his face for the first time.

"Your birth is one of the reasons Heaven has found fault with me. When the Heavenly Jade Emperor stripped me of my fairy powers and sent me into exile, it was to raise you and watch after you until your twelfth year. On your natal day you will be summoned to the Court of Heaven. There is no way this event may be avoided, for it is written in the scrolls of the court and is therefore as inexorable a fact as the existence of the moon. All things that are written in Heaven must come to pass. There, you will be examined on the subject of your immortali-

ty, for in your infancy there was no hint of it. If you are found
to be mortal you will be returned here at once. . . . If they
see even the slightest hint of your power, however, you will
never leave the court. . . . not even to bid your family
farewell.

"This is why you must learn to be very careful. Not merely
to hide your secret from men, but to learn to hide it from the
Jade Emperor's examiners. We have barely two years to
accomplish this, and if we are successful you must be very
careful all your earthly life. . . . until you are ready to
present *yourself* to the Court of Heaven. Do you understand,
T'ai-Tsung? I do not tell you this to frighten you, but so you
will understand what we must do and you must never speak of
it."

"I understand, Mother," Wei T'ai-Tsung said.

"Excellent. Once we have fooled the emperor's examiners,
the Little Mother and I will begin to teach you the use of your
power. For now, however, we must first teach you to conceal it.
These lessons will not be easy, but I have no doubt that you will
master them as fully as those your tutors set you to."

"May I have my other studies as well?" the boy asked,
somewhat doubtfully.

"Of course," Wei K'e-yung said. "You will have all your
old lessons, but not quite as before, for time must be given
each day to your mothers and that subject. You will say nothing
of this to your masters. They will be told that your health is not
of its former quality and the physicians have recommended
shorter hours. You must remember this if they enquire of you,
and you must be very careful what you say to them from now
on."

"Yes, Father."

"Good. I will send for them in the morning."

Wei K'e-yung picked up his son's bow and arrows, which
the boy had laid aside when he entered the pavilion, and held
them out to him.

"You may go to your archery now. Lin Yi is waiting."

Wei T'ai-Tsung rose from his mother's side and took the
bow, reluctantly it seemed. "I think I would prefer to go to my
room and read," he said solemnly.

"Nonsense," Wei K'e-yung said. "You must behave as
usual. It is not just a matter of what you hide, it is also what
you show."

Wei T'ai-Tsung made an obedient bow and took up the arrows. "Yes, Father," he said quietly. He looked out across the park to where the small, distant figure of Lin Yi stood patiently by the targets. "As you say, Father."

"Go, now. And shoot well."

"Yes, Father."

In the matter of defining his fairy power, it quickly became clear that the child himself would be of little direct help. He had never thought his rapport with animals an unusual thing. It surprised him somewhat that it was even a subject for consideration. He did not believe that he actually *did* anything to achieve this. The fireflies were simply there to be gathered into his lamps; that the fish might not cluster about anyone curious enough to look into the pool had never occurred to him.

He was very sorry about the dog. He had never done anything like that before, but he did not really know *what* he had done. He remembered only that he had been angry. There had been no thought of rocks that he could recall. And, sorry as he was, he had no idea how to change the rock back into a dog.

Pao Shih asked him to think about this for several days as though it were an exercise his tutors might give him; to go to the garden and view the rock as often as he pleased if this would help, but it did no good. He had no idea at all.

Then one evening she and Yin Whun took him to the pavilion, where Pao Shih had acquired a cage of six small rats. Each evening for six days they met beneath the willows, but the child was unable to transform any of the little rodents into rocks or anything else simply by willing that it be so. Perhaps the anger was necessary, but Pao Shih did not want to risk that.

Wei K'e-yung was pleased. It seemed to him that this would make the thing easier to hide, if even the child himself could not uncover it at will, but his wives were not so encouraged. Such things did not occur haphazardly. This was an aspect of his true powers and it was troublesome that he could not now repeat it. But his talents were still emerging. It was possible that the anger had called upon something unfinished, something which would reappear in its true form in time. So once a month Pao Shih acquired a small animal, and Wei T'ai-Tsung attempted to exercise his will upon it, but to no avail. With time even his mothers became certain the event with the dog had been an accident—a corruption of some other of his abilities. Called too soon into use it had gone wrong, and the dog had been irretrievably transformed.

Other things were occurring, however.

Pao Shih had lately come to realize that her son's first true sign of his fairy heritage had been his immunity to the cold. He had inherited this from her, and though he did not carry the cold with him as she had, making the hot summer days cool for all in his presence, there was a seasonlessness about him. He had been so since infancy, and she cursed herself for having paid it so little heed. She would have to wait and watch through the coming summer, for her own misery in the heat was so great she had paid no attention to its effect upon her son, except to the extent that he had never complained of it. As winter came on she took note of his habit of dressing lightly, even outside in the park, and she instructed him to adopt the habit of dressing more warmly. He insisted he did not feel the cold and would not know what to wear, so she told him to watch what those around him wore and dress as they did. She purchased a new servant for him. He was old enough now to have a young man of his own and, having no knowledge of his new master's habits, he would help Wei T'ai-Tsung naturally in all these things without realizing it.

Yin Whun set to the task of finding a suitable servant. Her fairy talent for knowing the truth, and the carefully constructed examination she employed, had proved valuable over the years in choosing such of the household servants as the two women required for their own security. When Pao Shih and Wei K'e-yung first married he had an elderly couple in his employ who were loyal only to him and had cared little for his new bride, and even less for her personal maid. Upon Wei K'e-yung's first appointment, Pao Shih had seen to their dismissal by selling them off with the old house in Wuchang, and from then on Yin Whun had been in charge of staffing the household. As Wei K'e-yung rose in rank, more and more of the staff had come permanently attached to the office and the dwelling provided with it, but the women had always managed to keep a loyal, trustworthy, if uninformed core of servants in their most immediate and personal service.

Yin Whun applied herself diligently, and within a month purchased a young man of sixteen named Zhao Min, and his sister, Jing Shu, who was eighteen, from a wealthy silk merchant in the city. Yin Whun was greatly pleased with herself over this and, though only the young man had been required, Jing Shu entered the ladies' service at once for Yin Whun felt her to be a perfect complement to Ai Lian and Yan Ping, and Pao Shih agreed that it was wise to place as much distance between themselves and the household as possible. It was also noted with some satisfaction that little Yan Ping began to blush rosily at the mere mention of Zhao Min's name and she eagerly volunteered for any errand that might send her into the young man's wing of the house.

Wei T'ai-Tsung, however, was reserved in his new servant's presence, but Zhao Min himself was greatly taken with his young master and did all he could to please him.

"He has never had a man of his own before," Yin Whun said to Pao Shih, who would have preferred her son put more faith in his Second Mother's judgement. "Besides, his secret is also new to him. In time he will learn to live comfortably with both."

"Has the secret ever been comfortable for you or me?" Pao Shih said.

"As he comes to understand more, he will at least learn what faith can be placed in those who are loyal. In this young man is a gift beyond price, but he may still be too young to see it."

As the months passed, however, the boy's reticence did not diminish and, in fact, a distance began to grow between Wei T'ai-Tsung and his former friend Lin Yi, which all too soon became unbridgable. Though the boys had continued to share each other's leisure company, from the day of his parents' revelation to him, he no longer seemed to find any joy in the association. He no longer trusted himself to be casual in his conversation with Lin Yi. The laughter and easy banter stopped and the winter, with its diminished outdoor activities, provided an excuse to avoid the older boy's company almost entirely.

Pao Shih was saddened by this, for the friendship had grown spontaneously and it had been genuine and close. Wei T'ai-Tsung had few friends outside the household, preferring his study to the frivolous sport of most of the other boys his age whose families were of proper station to be acceptable companions. Lin Yi was a servant and the son of a servant, but history was full of men of humble lineage who had risen in life as the faithful lieutenants of great men. It was a different thing from the likes of Zhao Min, for Wei T'ai-Tsung and Lin Yi were *true friends* and the boy listened to Lin's advice, which was generally sound and levelheaded, if sometimes unimaginative or grounded in peasant pragmatism and superstitition.

Lin Yi's father went to Wei K'e-yung after a while and asked how his son had offended Wei T'ai-Tsung, that he no longer cared for his company. He assured the governor that he and his son would do all in their power to repair the unintentional error, but Wei K'e-yung assured him that they were blameless. The boy had simply grown more attentive to his studies of late, and was beginning to concern himself with the possibilities of entering a university. He felt certain that with the spring and a renewed desire for outdoor sport, all would be as it had been. In the meantime the gardner and his son went about their work, but Lin Yi rarely set eyes on his former friend and by spring Wei T'ai-Tsung seemed completely indifferent to the idea of Lin Yi's company in any capacity. Thus rebuffed, the gardener's son soon found his own reasons to avoid the governor's son, even in his work, and the disaffection was complete.

His parents' urgings to develop other friendships or interests outside the household fell on deaf ears, and Wei T'ai-Tsung spent more and more of his time in contemplation of his slowly emerging gifts and in his studies.

He spent long hours in Yin Whun's garden in contemplation of the Dog-Rock. His masters were pleased that, at his early age, he had found an object which so inspired him to meditation and a contemplation of nature, but they were a little disappointed in his taste. Long past the time his mothers had freed him of the exercise, Wei T'ai-Tsung continued to visit the rock and consider what he had done and how he might have accomplished it, but the poor dog remained forever changed.

Pao Shih and Yin Whun kept careful watch of everything that occurred around the boy, and spent much of their time educating him in the ways of Heaven and Hibiscus Village and their relationship to the Earth and men. Pao Shih told him of her own fairy powers; what they had been and how long it had taken her to learn to live without them for, even in tiny ways, they affected everything she had done. She recalled how difficult the first year of her marriage had been, trying not to do so small a thing as enhance the taste of their meager meals or brighten the light from her husband's oil lamp, when studying late into the night had wearied his eyes and times were too hard to justify the cost of a second lamp in the room. And she told him of the difficulties of the years after her return, mortal and feeling blind and deaf, for a whole level of awareness had been stripped away. The visual world seemed flatter and greyer; sounds were duller, less resonant, as though half the orchestra had stopped playing; trees and flowers and all the elements of the natural world which had seemed so alive to her looked artificial; the world became like a painted screen, for she could no longer see the flickering, lively presence of her Sisters' agents in these things.

She asked him how *he* saw things, and relied upon Yin Whun's still-present senses for guidance, but the boy as yet seemed to have little but a mortal's eye for the world.

It was one day in early spring that Yin Whun came to Pao Shih, who was collecting blossoms from the fruit trees in the orchard with Jing Shu, with a worried look upon her face. Pao Shih sent the maid into the house with their basket and Yin Whun told her that she had finally seen the faintest glow of fairy magic hovering about the boy as he sat in the shade of the veranda near the Dog-Rock, lost in the study of it. A time or two before she had thought some small light of it might be hovering there, but it could have been a trick of the sun or lamplight. This time it was unmistakable. It was faint and unsteady and did not last long, but it hung about him like infant dragon fire. Then his tutors had called him to his studies and the light had faded completely. She had remained hidden discreetly behind an audience screen watching the boy at his lessons for some time, and no hint of it had returned while he worked. But she felt certain that, now that it had begun to manifest itself when he thought hard about the magic things, it would come to him more frequently and eventually be with him at all times, as it was with her and Wei K'e-yung's uncle, the Taoist magician Wei Pon Ch'ao. Though no mortal could see it, it would be the first thing they must teach him to hide from the emperor's examiners. It was still faint and infrequent. With luck it would not grow out of hand too quickly for them to control.

Three days later Jing Shu approached her lady Pao Shih saying her brother had been sent by his young master, who respectfully begged the Principal Mother to see him at once. He had been at the preparation of his lessons for the next day, but when he had called Zhao Min to him, Wei T'ai-Tsung had seemed distressed for no reason the young servant could discover.

Pao Shih sent for her son at once and summoned Yin Whun as well, and retired to the little pavilion. This had become her private place, and her son now knew well enough to leave his servants in the garden across the pool when his mother called him there. When he arrived he was calmer than she had thought from Jing Shu's description, but he was clearly unhappy about something. Over the winter he had begun to resort more and more to proprieties when he was troubled, and when he entered the pavilion he made a formal greeting and stood by the couch awaiting his mother's leave to speak. But when she enquired, he seemed at a loss as to what to say.

"I have *done* something," Wei T'ai-Tsung said at last. "This time I *know* I have done something magic . . . but I don't know how important a thing it is."

"And what is it you have done?" Yin Whun enquired, drawing him to the couch to sit beside Pao Shih. She kept her voice light and pleasant, for the boy's tendency to become too grim was another thing that would have to be corrected.

"I have summoned something," he said, frowning thoughtfully. He told the story slowly and carefully and his mothers did not find it surprising, though they still did not quite know how to define the nature of his power by it.

Wei T'ai-Tsung told them how he had been reading his history when he heard the fussing of a bird outside his window. It had not been important, but the bird kept at it and, curious, he looked out to see what it was. It appeared to be hunting something he could not see among the garden rocks and he sat watching it, fascinated. Wondering what it was, he remembered clearly thinking that, if the bird was at all polite, it should come to his window and show it to him. It was merely a bit of humor, but it had been phrased in his head as a request and a moment later, much to his surprise, the bird had fluttered onto his windowsill and deposited a large, shiny black beetle there. The beetle at once began to scuttle away, but the bird had imprisoned it beneath a taloned foot, and stood starring at Wei T'ai-Tsung, cocking its head from side to side with nervous little jerks, while its black eyes seemed to look into his own enquiringly.

He had been stunned, but the bird did not move to leave. Finally he had complimented it on its catch and thanked it for showing it to him and, with a trill and a ruffling of wings, it had snapped the beetle up in its beak and flown off.

"At first I thought this was very fine but also very strange. Then I began to think as you have instructed me to about any odd event, and I was sure it must be the magic but I had to be very certain . . . so I called the bird back. Pao Shih noticed for the first time, before he moved to show it to her, that he held something in his hand.

"And the bird came to you I presume," Yin Whun said.

"Yes, Little Mother," he said. Then he produced a small fold of paper which he laid upon the couch and carefully unwrapped. It contained a crushed black beetle, its shiny carapace snapped nearly in two in the middle.

"When it came back it had already eaten the beetle," Wei T'ai-Tsung said. "So I told it to catch another one, and this time when I summoned it, as soon as it laid down the beetle I sent it away." He shifted the paper and looked down at the thing he had brought. "This one isn't as nice as the other one," he said very quietly.

"Would you do this thing once more? For us?" Pao Shih asked.

"Yes, Mother," he said, but not happily.

"Think of the voice you would speak with," she said. "To exercise this magic too much will only make it stronger, so you must not *shout*. Rather, think of speaking to me or your Second Mother and when you call to it *speak* quietly."

"Yes, Mother," he said and sat silently for what seemed a long time . . . but nothing happened. "It came to me!" he said earnestly. "It truly did."

"I have no doubt of that," Pao Shih replied. "Did it fly from the garden when you dismissed it?"

"Yes," Wei T'ai-Tsung said.

"Then it may well be too far away to *hear* you," she said. "We will try another bird. That one. See it in the willow tree, there?"

"Yes, I see it," he said, and fell silent, and in the next moment the bird flew into the pavilion and landed on the back of the couch. For a moment there was a gleam in Wei T'ai-Tsung's eyes, and a smile lit his face briefly. He offered the beetle to the bird, which took it from the paper he held and waited, poised on the couch back, till it was dismissed. But when he turned back to his mothers the joy quickly died.

"It is well done," Pao Shih said. "You are learning to recognize your new talents. And it is also well that you found joy in it. Ah, my young man, you must not be so grim. It is a secret, but it is a *wonderful* secret. It is a good feeling when the magic happens, nothing can change that. Only do not be angry with yourself . . . please. It is a thing that will be with you forever, and once we have fooled the Jade Emperor's examiners, you will learn how wonderful it feels to work with it, even with such caution as we must exercise at first."

"Will you do this for us again?" Yin Whun asked. "I would see if it is effective on things other than birds."

Pao Shih agreed and reluctantly Wei T'ai-Tsung summoned a small, brown mouse from the willows, which scurried into the pavilion through a carved lattice near the tea-warming table.

"I wonder," Yin Whun mused. "Could he summon the fish from the water if he wanted to?"

"I do *not* want to," the boy said resolutely.

"No," Yin Whun said. "I would not ask it of you."

They sat in the shade of the pavilion and the willows for some time longer, and the afternoon sun began to cast long shadows and the evening chill could be felt in the cool spring air. They discussed ways to train the mind into habits of thought so he would not have to be constantly on guard against every idea that entered his head, and as they talked Pao Shih became aware that Wei T'ai-Tsung was watching Yin Whun more and more fixedly by the moment.

"Do you see something more worthy of your attention than the subject at hand?" she asked him at last.

"Forgive me, Mother," he said, "but . . . I do not know what it is. There seems to be a shadow . . . no it is like a light but it is not . . ."

"About Yin Whun?"

"Yes," he said. Then a soft intake of breath, "*It is very beautiful.*"

"It is her fairy aura. It is the mantle of her magic," Pao Shih said.

"Do you look like that?"

"No, child. But I did once."

"Why have I not seen it before?" he asked, amazed.

"It is that sight that mortals do not have," Pao Shih said. "It is that sight which I lost so long ago, only now beginning to blossom in you. I can no longer see her that way, but I remember the look of it and, yes, it is very beautiful."

"Will I look like that?" he asked.

"Yes, some day you will. You do already from time to time."

"When you called the bird and when you called the mouse . . . it was upon you then. Not bright and not at all steady, but there. Your sight will come and go as your aura does, but one day both will be with you fully and they will remain so forever."

Suddenly all the excitement and newfound pleasure fled from the boy's face and he turned away from them. "I must learn to conceal this, too, mustn't I?"

"For now. But it is only on you when you are working the magic; as you learn to control the magic you will conceal the aura as well."

"Mother!" he said suddenly, leaning toward her across the couch. "I am afraid. There is so much to learn and it is so strange. What if I fail?"

"You will not fail, my son. We have only just begun. As we learn more of what you can do we will know better what *we* must do. There is still time, and you are an exceptional student. I have faith in you."

"Yes, Mother," Wei T'ai-Tsung said.

Despite his mothers' efforts, however, the boy had ideas of his own on how best to control matters he did not wish to face. He began avoiding as much contact with animals as possible. He stayed away from the kennels and stables and would not ride the pony unless compelled to by necessity. He kept to the house as much as possible, often shuttering his windows against the sights and sounds of the garden—going out when he was summoned to the pavilion but never by choice.

Pao Shih was forcibly reminded of the first year of her marriage, when she had hidden from the wrath of Heaven by secluding herself in her husband's house, but it had solved nothing then and it would solve nothing now. She gave him exercises requiring him to spend a portion of each day in the presence of some of the household animals: "You cannot control what you merely avoid," she said, and slowly, through the course of the summer, Wei T'ai-Tsung began to understand a little of what he did and how to keep thoughts of such dangerous things from his mind. Little by little he began to grow more comfortable with the tasks and more confident, and his reclusive behavior gave way to a more normal existence, but he still kept himself at a distance from Lin Yi and seemed not to trust Zhao Min at all.

Pao Shih and Yin Whun were still perplexed as to the exact nature of Wei T'ai-Tsung's gift. It cut across territories they would normally have considered unbridgable. There was his attraction for the fish, which were under the control of the Great Dragons; the birds were the province of the Phoenix; the dogs and horses belonged to the realm of the Chi Ling. In midsummer Wei T'ai-Tsung had forced the ripening of loquat, which were still green on the orchard trees; and in autumn he had caused the spring-blooming lilies to give bud and blossom.

Though none of these things was an act of great consequence, it was the diversity which confounded them. It was necessary that in some way there be a constancy to the essential nature of all things under a fairy's control, but as yet it was impossible for them to discover what the thread was.

Throughout the winter they worked steadily, carefully testing him from time to time, but his own satisfaction with his progress was hampered by the occasional frustration of discovering yet one more small thing that needed to be hidden. But by the Fifth Month of the new year three lunar cycles had passed since anything new had occurred, and longer than that since Pao Shih or Yin Whun had seen so much as a flicker of the fairy aura, even when in the presence of Yin Whun's own magic.

As the third day of the Seventh Month drew nearer—the day of Wei T'ai-Tsung's twelfth birthday and the day of his testing—the boy grew restless and fretful. He would wander aimlessly through the house, picking up small objects and putting them down again or carrying them about for no apparent reason. Wei K'e-yung gave him leave to accompany him on his official duties from time to time and the boy did so, a silent shadow in his father's wake, never in the way, but never far off. Then there would be days when he could not be taken from his books for any reason, even to eat. He practiced his calligraphy by writing poems for his mother and a small essay on filial piety and the love of a son for his parents beyond the bounds of propriety.

Though the servants and his tutors found his behavior erratic and confusing, Wei K'e-yung and Pao Shih knew he was afraid. Wei K'e-yung dismissed the tutors, giving them leave to take ten days at their own leisure, and attempted to spend as much of his own small free time with his son as possible.

"Have confidence, T'ai-Tsung," he said as often as he could. "Your mothers have taught you well. There is no need for concern."

Pao Shih and Yin Whun were pleased with him and their confidence helped keep the fear under control, but privately Pao Shih was as frightened as her son, and Yin Whun was often required to help her sleep at night so the fatigue and strain would not show and cause her son more worry.

On the eve of the second day of the Seventh Month, Pao Shih ordered the kitchen staff to prepare a special meal, not as elaborate as the one they planned for the next day, which was the young master's birthday, but one Pao Shih knew would please her son more than a true feast, for all his favorite dishes were not of banquet quality.

Pao Shih had made careful selection of her son's attire for the day of examination, and had ordered a new sash with gold tassels and new shoes of embroidered blue silk which Zhao Min had already laid out in his dressing room with Wei T'ai-Tsung's best clothes. She had also carefully selected her own gown and coat, and Yin Whun had promised to arrange her hair.

"When will they come for us, Mother? And how will we travel?" Wei T'ai-Tsung asked at the evening meal.

"I cannot say for sure," Pao Shih replied. "The Jade Emperor of Heaven has many concerns besides those of a lowly fairy, and the Court of Heaven has an imprecise measure of time as mortals know it, since it is of little importance to them. But you may be certain that before the day is out, we will be summoned. As to our mode of travel, do not expect anything too grand.''

"I had hoped for a dragon," he said.

It was imperative, Pao Shih said, that they be prepared to depart at dawn, no matter how long they eventually had to wait, and to that end, they would be well advised to retire early. Wei T'ai-Tsung protested that he could not sleep in any event and Yin Whun offered her assistance, but the family lingered in each other's company later and later into the night, not wishing to be parted. At last, seated on the veranda about the main courtyard in the amber glow of lanternlight, there came the faint and distant sound of the drum towers signaling the passing of midnight. The day had begun.

Wei K'e-yung laid his lute aside and for a moment there was no sound; even the crickets and night birds seemed to have taken leave of their voices. Pao Shih stepped into the garden and looked up at the stars. The night was pleasantly warm and very clear and the stars seemed a very great ways away. Somewhere within her, within the stillness she had so carefully laid like a blanket over the fear, there was a tiny spark of anticipation, the smallest flickering of joy, like a little flame in an uncertain wind. For the first time in eleven years she would see Heaven again.

She turned back to her family and held out her hands to her son, who left his father's side and went to her.

"Do not be afraid," she said, smiling beautifully. "We are only going home."

The boy smiled too, but uncertainly, and between one heartbeat and the next, they were gone.

Wei K'e-yung sat in his study, brush poised over parchment, the ink drying in the bristles. It was the fourth time he had cleaned and dipped it, trying to make the first of a few simple corrections to a routine document his secretary had prepared for publication. But the thoughts would not come. His mind was not on the document or his hand; it was not in the study or the house or even the physical world at all.

He was very tired.

He had been up all night, fooling no one into thinking that he was working, least of all Yin Whun and her maids, who followed her about as she endlessly paced the house and garden.

He did not know what he had expected—a formal request that he present his family to the emissary of Heaven? Some token regard for his status as head of his household and an official in the Imperial Government? Something! But there had been nothing. Heaven had plucked them from him with no more thought than he gave the trees in his orchard when he plucked a peach. He was a Provincial Governor, a man of wealth and substance and standing, an official of note. He was nothing, and he felt the magnitude of his mortal insignificance in these events. His wives were but fairies, the lowliest of the Jade Emperor's subjects. They were next to nothing and *they* had more significance than he. This was a small matter to the court—a minor bureaucratic annoyance.

The night-long blossoming sense of his own insignificance was fertile ground for a similarly blossoming sense of futility. He had begun to entertain the idea some hours earlier that he actually might never see his wife and son again, that the deed had been done, that they had been snatched from him and it was all over.

The brush clattered onto the desk and his gaze refocused. Outside the window the false dawn was fading. The next light would be true sunrise and he would no longer be able to avoid the day and the need to carry on as though nothing had happened.

He slowly began to recognize the outlines of trees and colors and finally an awareness of a distant commotion . . . coming from the direction of the pavilion by the pond—the high, frantic sound of women's voices.

Wei K'e-yung gathered his robe about his hips like a farmer and ran through the garden toward the pond with no care to his dignity. At the edge of the orchard he found the three serving maids huddled together, fretting softly, and several paces beyond, Yin Whun, who knelt in the path. Her hands were clasped in her lap and the set of her shoulders was tense, her face turned away to the pond where a tiny, slender figure wandered a slow, aimless pattern among the lily beds.

As Wei K'e-yung approached Yin Whun turned to him. Her face was tear streaked and she reached for him and clutched the folds of his gown.

"Ah, Husband," she sobbed in a husky voice, "she does not know me. She does not hear me. She does not even seem to see me."

"Has the Jade Emperor kept her then, and sent back only the body? And what of my son?"

Yin Whun turned back to the lake and sobbed.

Wei K'e-yung reached down and took her by the shoulders, lifting her to her feet. He bent forward, his face close to hers but she still looked away.

"What of my son?" he demanded, giving her a firm shake.

Yin Whun did not look at him. "He is not here," she murmured.

Abruptly he released her and stepped across the path toward the pond and his First Wife.

Yin Whun's hands flew at his sleeve. "Husband, wait! *Please* wait! Do not blame her. She did what she could." She followed him for several paces, clinging to his sleeve, then firmly took his arm and pulled him about. But the grief on his face stopped her anger. He took her hands from his sleeve and pressed them to her bosom.

"Be quiet," he said. "I must speak to my First Wife."

Pao Shih took no notice of his approach. She wandered a serpentine course along the bank. Her expression was vague and bewildered, and she made no response when he spoke to her. When he stepped in front of her she looked at him with as much recognition as if he had been a tree, stepped past him and continued her rambling.

"Pao Shih . . ."

Nothing.

He shouted at her then—her fairy name, never used in public—and she paused, but only for an instant, and once more began to wander.

"*Wife!*" he said, catching her arm and pulling her to a stop. She looked up at him but he could not tell if she knew him.

"They have taken my son," she said. "They have taken away my child and thrown me back here and I do not know what they will do. . . ."

"Why?" he said. "What was missed?"

"The anger," she said miserably. "The anger . . . the one thing we avoided because it was so dangerous and unpredictable. They baited him, and when his temper could stand no more, it was there . . . the fairy glow. . . ."

Then the small light of reason went out of her eyes and she seemed to wilt; like a tree shedding its leaves in autumn she suddenly looked bleak and barren and hopeless. When Wei K'e-yung touched her this time there was no response. Nor when he put his arms around her and led her back to Yin Whun and the house. She merely drifted along at his side, going where he moved her. She felt nearly weightless in the crook of his arm.

Yin Whun stood on the path, tiny hands covering her mouth, eyes large and dark and intense. When they drew near she reached for Pao Shih, and Wei K'e-yung guided her gently into Yin Whun's arms. His face had acquired a harder expression.

"Take her to her rooms. Do not leave her alone. If she will not sleep or rest quietly, do whatever you do. I must see to my office."

"What will *you* do?"

"I have no idea."

"Let in only your secretary and lock the gates to the private compound," Yin Whun said, holding Pao Shih close to her. "Give no audience today. Consider only written petitions that can be placed in the hands of your clerks. We must talk, Husband. We must find a way to keep our secret."

"See to her," he said, waving to the maids to come assist their mistress. "Then come to me in my study."

In the sanctuary of his study Wei K'e-yung hastily finished the document he had spent all night on and wrote a series of instructions for his secretary, which would keep his staff busy, if confused, for the next day.

As he approached the offices, Wei K'e-yung saw several of the clerks sitting outside the kitchen with their morning rice and soup. It was some time longer, however, before his secretary arrived.

The junior clerks were set to the task of receiving written complaints and petitions from the irate citizens gathered at the gate, and a scribe was sent out to assist those who could not write. The senior clerks were set to the task of evaluating the petitions and submitting written comments to the secretaries who were trusted with the responsibility of deciding which complaints were to be handled by the two young Deputy Ministers, and which must be saved for Wei K'e-yung when he would be free to deal with them.

Even so, the first watch of the morning was completely gone before Loy Quan Dong approached him with his deepest condolences. He commended Wei K'e-yung's faithful adherence to his duty even in such a terrible time, and assured him the staff could carry on adequately in his absence. He felt it only proper that Wei K'e-yung be at home to comfort his family.

Wei K'e-yung was a bit confused but tried not to show it. Discreetly, Loy Quan Dong had not asked any embarrassing questions, so rather than risk enquiry from less careful quarters, Wei K'e-yung gratefully placed everything in his secretary's hands and left the office.

As he turned toward the residence compound he discovered the source of this solicitous behavior. The gate was decked with the white banners of a household in mourning for the dead, an unmistakable statement to all who passed by. Wei K'e-yung was furious and hurried to the house in search of Yin Whun.

He found his Second Wife waiting in the garden outside his study. She entered at once, leaving the doors and windows open and crossing the room, reopened the door he had just closed.

"We must have privacy," she said, striking the small gong by his desk. "If the doors are closed we cannot know who may listen behind them."

In a moment Zhao Min appeared and Yin Whun sent him to sit at the head of the corridor and allow no one to pass.

"Husband," she said. "You need not trouble yourself with details. I have taken care of everything."

But Wei K'e-yung was angry in his grief. "What is the meaning of those banners? No one is dead! It will not do. You should have consulted me. Now we must explain things and we cannot!"

"I have not been idle, Husband," Yin Whun said patiently.

"Yesterday while I was at the silk merchant's I overheard the servants comforting the cook, whose grandson had died the night before. I had seen the boy in the shop from time to time and he sometimes delivered our orders here to the house. He was a year younger than Wei T'ai-Tsung but they were about the same size.

"The old woman's lament was partially due to the extreme nature of her son's poverty and the fact that they would not be able to provide a proper funeral for the child—not even adequate offerings to the temple on his spirit's behalf.

"As soon as Pao Shih was settled in her rooms I set all the women to watching her, dressed myself as one of the kitchen maids and slipped out to the poor man's house. At first they were reluctant to sell, but they have four other sons, all younger, and no daughters to sell into service and they can barely feed the remaining children. I promised the child would be buried with honor and two taels of silver would feed and clothe his wife and sons for a long time if properly managed. I also promised to provide a portion of ricecake and wine as offerings for his soul once a month and to say prayers on his behalf at whatever temple they desired on the proper days.

"They do not know who I am or on whose behalf I have made this bargain, but they are satisfied. The child's body lies in your son's room already. I was careful not to be followed.

"I will tend the body myself; beyond that it is necessary only that a physician be present when the City Magistrate pronounces the death official. You could do it yourself but that would not look proper. Appropriately dressed and viewed briefly from a distance the boy will serve our needs."

When he heard her story, Wei K'e-yung's rage was such that it took all his will to keep from striking her. Instead he lurched from the sill and began pacing a tight oval before the window in long, heavy strides.

"*Woman!*" he raged through clenched teeth. "What can have possessed your mind? This is *impossible!* I cannot bury this child as my son!"

"Husband, you must. There is no other way. T'ai-Tsung's absence will be noticed."

"YES!" he cried. "He must be ill. He must be away . . . for his health. But he cannot be dead! If we bury that child how will we explain my son's presence when he returns? You are a foolish woman to act so quickly. The banners must be removed and some explanation given for the mistake."

"K'e-yung-ah . . . Husband," Yin Whun said gently. "Your son will not be returned."

He spun about and glared at her. "Then we must find a way to rescue him!"

The look on Yin Whun's face stopped him cold. Suddenly his mind was flooded with ten-year-old memories. He saw clearly the little maidservant who had entered his house with his wife. The contempt she had held him in then was barely concealed. She had looked upon him with scorn and sometimes even loathing that first year. Her love and loyalty to her mistress were absolute, and in her eyes he had been less than worthless.

Pao Shih was his beautiful flower, gentle dove, his jewel. Pao Shih, brave and resourceful when the need had been at hand. But in some ways Yin Whun's intellect was more formidable. It was hard and sharp like a knife, quick and practical. Her courage was of the uncompromising sort that would set her firmly between what she loved and certain destruction if necessary. In the years since he had taken her for his Second Wife, life had been relatively docile. The side of her nature that was the loyal and loving serving girl had held sway. The knife had been sheathed for a long time and he had forgotten. And in the long, soothing comfort of familiarity he had allowed himself to forget what *she* was.

"Do not prove yourself a fool, Mortal," she said with frigid contempt. "Who do you think you are . . . *what* do you think you are to believe you have any power over this matter? There is no recourse from such a decision from Heaven. There will be no rescue. We thought you understood that. Why do you think Pao Shih grieves as she does? The Heavenly Jade Emperor will never release him, and there is no means on Earth to steal him back and hide him safely. Fooling the judges was our *only* hope. It has failed and I must bear the burden of responsibility as much as Pao Shih, but it is irrevocable.

"You *know* this is so, Husband. All that is left is to safeguard your own career in the mortal world. Think of him as dead. He is no longer your son. Mourn him, for he *is* lost to this world and you will never see him again. Not even in the Land of the Dead."

Wei K'e-yung sat heavily upon another sill.

"But he *is* alive," he said sorrowfully. "He is immortal and somewhere he walks about and speaks and . . ."

Yin Whun stood and crossed to his side, laying a tiny hand on his shoulder.

"He belongs to Heaven, just as the dead do. For you, there is no longer any difference."

Wei K'e-yung looked away into the garden and though he said nothing Yin Whun saw the resignation settle upon him. "Come," she said gently. "The child must be prepared."

"I do not want to see him."

"Very well . . ."

"Can they be trusted?"

Yin Whun stopped halfway to the door. "My fairy powers are minor, but among them I have an instinct for the truth," she said. "If I had not believed them to be honest, I would have thought of something else."

"Men change," said Wei K'e-yung bitterly. "I see this passing before me daily as I sit in judgement of such men. When the silver is gone and they are again at starvation's door, who is to say they will not come asking for more. Once the death is publicly announced it would take little imagination to guess who has the means to purchase a body."

The hard edge glinted in Yin Whun's eyes. "And for what *reason* would the governor need to make such a bizarre purchase? They can prove nothing, and to whom would they complain? You are the authority. They can hardly go to your office with their suspicions. Within a few months even the body itself will prove nothing but that it wore your son's clothing.

"Trust me, Husband. They were grateful simply to be given the chance to honor their son's memory properly. But I will keep discreet eyes on them from time to time. Perhaps an occasional, anonymous gift would not be uncalled for."

"I cannot think," he said.

"Never mind. I will take care of everything. That the honesty of your grief may be seen is enough for now. Only send me your secretary, Loy Quan Dong. I will make the proper arrangements through him and the housekeeper as is fitting.

"But you *must* go to the funeral, Husband. And you must do what you can to comfort your wife. Her grief may not be reasoned with just now. You must go to her as her beloved husband, for besides her child, you are the greatest treasure of her existence. She will respond to no other."

"I will do what I can," Wei K'e-yung said.

"You will do more than that," Yin Whun said sharply. "Remember that it is for your sake that all this has come about in the first place. She has sacrificed much for you. I have given you two daughters; perhaps in time I can give you another son. But for her there is nothing but you, and you must give her all you can now that she is in need."

Word was given out that the governor's son, who had been forbidden to fish in the ornamental pond, had sneaked out in the middle of the night as a childish prank and had fallen in and drowned. His First Wife, who often walked in the garden early in the morning, had found her son there and was suffering from prostration due to shock and grief.

Yin Whun went about her business and the care she had taken in the selection of the family's most personal servants was repaid a hundredfold. They would believe what they were told.

In the afternoon a fine coffin arrived, and the child was placed in it at once. Though the lid was not sealed, no one would have thought to dishonor the family by looking into it.

The Court of the Jade Emperor of Heaven was the most splendid and terrifying place imaginable. Far more so than could be dreamt of by a young boy. In spite of his mothers' best efforts to describe such a place, it was beyond the capacity of mere words to convey the magnificence and the strangeness. There was no sense of the passage of time in the halls and rooms of the great palace and Wei T'ai-Tsung had no idea how long he had actually been there; an eternity might have elapsed or mere moments since that horrible instant when, humiliated by the examiners demeaning and insulting remarks about his father's mortal status and his unfitness as a spouse for even a lowly fairy, he could take no more and his anger had begun to burn in him.

His judges grew quiet, and it was then that he realized what else about him had begun to burn.

They had wearied him with questions and tests, all of which he had managed to sidestep as his mothers had shown him, but in the end it had been so easily done. He wondered if they had needed to spend so much time on him, or if they had known all along what they would do and only wished to tire him sufficiently that he could not avoid being provoked.

Horrified at what he had done, he had humiliated himself further when he began to cry, but he felt helpless and hopeless and miserably stupid and very much afraid. The judges were kind to him then. Madam Chou Ch'ung-i was one of the judges and she assured him that this deception would not be passed on to the Jade Emperor. All those who had tested him were inclined to be lenient with her, for the Fairy Ku-She had been well liked and her misery at having to return to Earth without him, and the necessity of facing her husband with the news, would be punishment enough.

But they would not let him see her, even to say good-bye. Instead, he had been taken to this room, where he sat on a brocade couch and awaited the Jade Emperor's pleasure. The room was filled with sunlight, though there were no windows to be seen and he could not quite determine its true size. It seemed at once both vast and confining. The walls were white or pale blue—so light it was nearly the same. The couch upon which he sat was carved of aromatic sandalwood and the brocade was the deepest green he could imagine. It was the only thing in the chamber besides himself, so he sat and waited and tried not to be too frightened.

At last a young man came to him, though the boy could not say how he entered the room. He was quite tall and beautiful, as Yin Whun was beautiful with her fairy aura about her. He did not precisely see it now, but he knew it was there. He wore a light armor of sky-blue and foam-green scale edged in gold and a coat made of the pastel hues of dawn. He told Wei T'ai-Tsung that he was a page in the Emperor's Hall and that he had been sent to accompany the boy to his new post.

As he followed the youth through corridors dappled and scented of forest—though they were as insubstantial as a dream—he knew what it was to be a common household slave. To be set to any task the master or mistress might fancy without the opportunity to prove yourself worthy or fit for better things.

As they moved through the palace he felt the dream shifting about him and he had the idea that they walked a narrow passage between the high, grey stone walls of a ravine. There was darkness for a while, though he had no difficulty seeing his guide, and there was a cold, icy plain where the light shimmered off the frozen ground in waves of rainbow color, but pale and vague as though seen through a gauze curtain. Yet at all these times he never lost his certain knowledge that these were the corridors and passageways of the palace and he tried to memorize his route so that he could help as much as possible when they came for him.

At a turning in the passage the young man entered a broad meadow flanked by low, rolling hills, bright green in the morning sunlight. Some distance away he could hear the sound of gulls and the breaking of waves upon the shore and he could smell the sea. He knew for certain they were no longer in the palace, though he had no idea when, or how, they had left it. Yet, much as this looked like the countryside of Earth, he knew they were still in Heaven. A mild panic seized him, for he knew he was lost and he did not know how they would ever find him.

Ahead between two low, round hillocks was a great, brightly-painted Memorial Gate, and beyond it the air shimmered like the heat rising from a brazier. As they drew nearer, the landscape beyond was clearly visible—fields and peasant cottages and, in the distance, a small, walled city. There were people moving about. It looked no different than any earthly countryside, and yet the boy knew beyond doubt that it was the Land of the Dead they approached, and he was filled with dread.

His companion seemed to sense this and turned to him and smiled for the first time since their journey began. Though not a word was spoken, Wei T'ai-Tsung found the gesture reassuring, and was calmed at once. Yet he also knew it was the fairy mind that had calmed him and though he felt much better, he reserved a small measure of distrust.

The Land of the Dead was a double-walled compound and within the shadow of the Memorial Gate was a great fortress of grey stone, much vaster in dimension than the distance between the walls would at first appear to accommodate. As with everything in this place, Wei T'ai-Tsung did not trust what his eyes saw, but the place was large and dark and the stone was rough under his hand and his footsteps rang in the halls, and all in all it seemed more substantial than anything he had seen here.

In this place, his guide said, he would begin his apprenticeship in the Jade Emperor's service. He would be a page to the Judges of the Court of the Dead and he would study here, for there were tutors available from among the greatest scholars in history. They resided just beyond the shimmering "gateway" and Wei T'ai-Tsung would be expected to see to his scholarship as well as to the discovery of his own abilities so that the Jade Emperor might know how best to employ him.

Wei T'ai-Tsung found himself alone in a small, grey room. There was a cold, dim light issuing from a high window and the room was furnished roughly and simply as a monk's cubicle, with a narrow bed, a table and chair, an oil lamp, two pegs upon which hung his new clothes of somber grey and brown, and a low bench which was furnished with a few simple, basic toilet utensils. The room had no door and he could not recall how he had entered it, but he knew that he would leave it without difficulty when he was summoned.

Thus resigned, Wei T'ai-Tsung lay down on the hard cot, utterly miserable and suddenly more exhausted than he had imagined, and fell asleep dreaming of his father and mothers and how they would rescue him if he only had the tact to be careful of his new lords, and the patience to wait for them without falling into despair.

Since the boy was still a child, a lavish funeral would have been considered inappropriate. But being the only son of the Provincial Governor, what was considered of small consequence was equal to what most families would have been grateful to do for the head of the household. The governor was expected to bury his son according to his means. To do less would have been insulting to the child's spirit, not to mention the eager citizens of Kaifeng for whom funerals, rich or poor, were a form of public spectacle and, therefore, entertainment.

Condolences arrived at the gate constantly, and it was impossible for Wei K'e-yung and Yin Whun to mourn privately. Only Pao Shih, who sat mute and solemn in her darkened chamber, was spared the scrutiny. If she could not cry and carry on in the prescribed manner of lavish, ritualized grief, it was better to say she was overcome. In the main reception hall memorial scrolls hung on the walls. The air was lavender with the burning of incense, and all the women of the household went about on their knees, wailing and rending their garments. Wei K'e-yung and Yin Whun put on the coarse white robes of official mourning and great quantities of paper effigies were burned; money, horses, dogs and servants all of rice paper, as well as the child's favorite toys and clothing, and the books he would need to complete his education in the afterlife. The bonfires burned for three days, at the end of which time it was customary for one of as little significance as a child to be removed from the house to the burial site. But the geomancers could not locate a suitable direction, nor could they name an auspicious date or hour.

"It is as though the child is not dead," they all said, but in the summer heat, the evidence issuing from the coffin could not be mistaken.

Wei K'e-yung was at a loss. When Pao Shih had married him she had used her fairy magic to influence the geomancer's bones to achieve the wedding date she desired. But Pao Shih was no longer possessed of her fairy powers and such influence was not among Yin Whun's small skills. Perseverance and pragmatism were, however, and she once again disguised herself as a kitchen maid and slipped out of the compound. Locating a geomancer who had not been consulted by the governor's agent was easy, since there were a great many to be found in a city the size of Kaifeng. She answered his questions in a manner proper to the child whose body they actually sought to bury. Then in the privacy of Wei K'e-yung's study they altered the documents to make them appear to have been prepared for Wei T'ai-Tsung. That afternoon the appropriate land was procured, and at dawn the next day a small procession carried the little coffin to its grave.

Once inside the gates to the family compound the deed was at last done and a respectable period of mourning shrouded the family and its secret in safety. But eldest and most-beloved son or not, Wei T'ai-Tsung had been merely a child, and the next day Wei K'e-yung appeared in court, impeccable and correct in his official robes. Yin Whun dressed simply in sober colors and went about the business of running the household, but Pao Shih could not be persuaded to put off her white hemp. Nor could she be enticed from her rooms.

Among his first duties as page to the Judges of the Dead, Wei T'ai-Tsung was required to enter the names and ages of all the deceased who passed through the gates on a given day. It was a tedious chore, but he applied himself diligently and the bailiff only cuffed him on the ear once for an inaccurate entry.

Nonetheless, he was grateful when they relieved him of that task and set him to another. It proved to be no better, however. Along with dozens of other scribes, he was required to make a careful accounting of all offerings burned at the funerals and sacrifices made in the temples on behalf of various souls. The accounts were scrupulously kept with tallies for offerings at the ancestral shrines, tallies of temple offerings and sacrifices, tallies of prayers said at grave sides on the proper days, and especially those items burned on paper which constituted a newly-arrived soul's wealth in his new home, since nothing could be acquired that was not sent to him in the flames.

The bailiffs in this section were strict, for it would not do for these efforts to go astray or accrue to the wrong accounts. If anything, this work was more tedious than the other had been, except where the accounts of the newly dead were concerned. Mainly, it was a matter of sorting and careful entry in the vast ledgers of the court record. The task of setting up a new account, however, was at once simpler and more difficult. There was a great deal to enter as quickly and carefully as possible, and if the deceased was wealthy it could be a monumental job, but it was simplified by the fact that it all belonged to one name and did not need to be sorted and cross-checked to avoid errors.

Wei T'ai-Tsung proved so diligent at the ledger entry, that the judges gave him as assistant to one of the clerks in charge of setting up an account for a young man who had died three days earlier in Kaifeng. The clerk was greatly vexed. It was a funeral of significant proportions, especially for a child of the age in question. Yet things were greatly amiss, for the name of the deceased did not appear on the rolls of the newly dead, yet the paper offerings and prayers accumulated at a great rate.

The Earth-time passed steadily below, and the scribes entered what they were given without question; but their curiosity was growing and the clerk was becoming more irritated.

When he was sent to his study and his rest, Wei T'ai-Tsung promised himself that when he returned he would look at the name, for Kaifeng had been his home and he was most curious of all.

Five days passed in the mortal world before Wei T'ai-Tsung was once more set to the task of accounting, and because the mysterious ledger was still not right, he was again given to the same clerk. He looked for a chance to see the name on the boards between which all these lists would eventually be bound, but before the opportunity came, a great oath was heard from the clerk and in short order from the secretary to whom he reported as well. The boys whispered the news down the line until it reached Wei T'ai-Tsung. The date and direction had at last been determined, and the name of the soul to whom they applied was indeed on the rolls, but the account to which all this wealth accrued was not the same as that of the dead boy. This boy was a poor silk merchant's son while the account was in the name of the son of the Governor of Kaifeng.

Stunned, Wei T'ai-Tsung stood at his desk, and his ink slab and water jar fell to the floor and shattered. At once, the bailiff was behind him and laid a heavy blow to the side of his head. Wei T'ai-Tsung howled and turned to the man, striking him squarely in the chest with his fist, but the blow fell as on a wall of stone, and the boy found himself lifted bodily from his place at the table and hauled off to the secretary of the section for discipline.

Kneeling face down on the tiles at the secretary's feet, Wei T'ai-Tsung told him the name on the ledger was his and that there was a great mistake for, clearly, he was not dead. The secretary was intrigued and questioned him further. When Wei T'ai-Tsung had explained who he was and how he had come to be there, the secretary took him firmly but gently by the arm and led him before the Chief Judge of the Court of the Dead, repeating the story and adding his own comments about the dilemma over the account and the true name of the deceased.

The Chief Judge was far kinder than Wei T'ai-Tsung had dared expect. He dismissed the secretary and took Wei T'ai-Tsung to a balcony, high up on the fortress wall.

"Look below," he said. "Do you see the funeral procession gathering beneath that willow? There."

The boy looked and saw a familiar piece of land on the road to the Yellow River outside the Kaifeng city walls. It was a lovely spot and a substantial funeral party was indeed gathering on the gently sloping hillside.

"Do you recognize anyone?" the judge asked.

A slow nod was all the boy could manage. He stood transfixed and the judge did not grant him leave to turn away. He stood on the fortress balcony and watched his family lay a coffin in the grave. He watched the mourners and saw the grief on his father's face. His mother was nearly in collapse. All this he saw, and in the days that followed he entered the prayers and offerings at the family shrine into the list that bore his name, for the court could do nothing but keep accounts.

He had no hope now, and when he went to his rest he could not even make himself dream of rescue. They had abandoned him, buried him . . . as thoroughly as the body of the silk merchant's son who would never enjoy any of the things burned at his funeral. That they had chosen this means to explain his absence was all Wei T'ai-Tsung needed to know they would not even try to free him, and he lay on his cot and cried bitterly till at last, exhausted, he slept.

On the evening following the funeral, Wei K'e-yung entered Yin Whun's private chambers and sent her maids away.

"She will not see me," he said.

"Has she said so?" Yin Whun asked, alert, since Pao Shih had not said a dozen words to anyone since she was found in the garden.

"No," he said with a sigh. "I have gone to her rooms and waited at the door while her maids announced my presence. She does not respond. I could see her plainly. She does not *refuse* me entry, but she does not so much as look away from her window. I am no comfort to her. She does not want to see me."

"You must not believe that."

"How can I believe else?" he said.

Yin Whun ached for him. "Even after all these years of

marriage, K'e-yung-ah, you do not know her as I do. This child is an uncommon event among fairies. She does not mourn his loss as you do. Not for a dead son . . . no, she fears for what Heaven may do to him to revenge itself against her. This is, after all, a part of her punishment. The Jade Emperor, though just and wise, is often cruel as well. The pain this loss would cause her was well known, and that is why they have chosen to treat the situation so. You are her only solace. . . ."

"Then I am nothing," he said bitterly, "for I am no comfort to her."

"Do not despair, Husband," Yin Whun said patiently. "It will need time but she will come to you again. Only do not desert her now. Go to her room again. Sit with her. Say nothing for a while. Tomorrow night take a pot of tea to share with her, even if she does not take any. Eventually she will. Then bring her wine."

But Wei K'e-yung was looking away through the window into the night.

"Is her grief so much greater than mine? I will never see him again. That is true for the rest of my mortal life and I must live with it for that long. She is immortal and one day, when I am gone and she and I are separated forever, you two will return to Heaven and he will be there. It is well to say I should not abandon her in her time of need, but her grief has more remedy than mine."

"Then the two of you must seek what remedy there is in the present together and let the future take care of itself."

"You have always counselled me wisely, Little Wife. I will trust you in this as well."

Yin Whun took up the embroidery she had set aside when her husband entered the room. "You will see," she said. "All will be well in time."

Wei K'e-yung paused in the doorway and turned back to her. "And what of you, Little One?"

"Go and be a dutiful husband. I will be here in my proper place."

Once again Wei K'e-yung returned to his First Wife's rooms, but this time he refused to be denied by Yan Ping and Jing Shu. Angrily, he sent the women into the hall and entered Pao Shih's room alone.

She still sat at the window, gazing fixedly into the darkened garden. The moon was high and nearly full and the fireflies flashed and dazzled the eye in great abundance in the shadows beneath the fruit trees.

Saying nothing, Wei K'e-yung drew a chair up to the window beside her—near enough to touch but not so close that one would not have to reach to do so. He drew up a small table with an oil lamp on it and contented himself to read silently from a book of essays on court etiquette and the proper comportment of a judge.

He awoke in the morning, stiff and aching from having slept the night slumped forward in the chair. The book was still in his lap and the oil lamp was just beginning to gutter in the fresh dawn breeze. Pao Shih was not beside him.

He sat up, and a silk shawl fell away from his shoulders. It was embroidered with the snowflake patterns she so loved to contrive and he folded it carefully as he rose and went into the sleeping chamber, but she was not there either. Nor were any of her maidservants about.

Disturbed, he stepped into the hall, where he found two of the girls asleep on the floor. The third would doubtless be with Yin Whun. He woke them and sent them into the garden to look for their mistress and went himself to Yin Whun's rooms but she was not there either.

A dread he did not dare examine seized him, and he tried to make his way calmly to the front of the house, but found he was hurrying before he even passed out of the corridor. At the veranda of the inner courtyard he stopped, not sure where he was rushing to and feeling mild panic at his indecision. *She is merely taking the air,* he told himself. *This is a good thing. She has not stirred for over a week. There is no cause for worry . . . but where has she gone at this hour?*

He did not want to think about the fish pond, and walked to the other side of the courtyard toward his study. What had she told him the Jade Emperor had said? That she would not be allowed to die before him? That she would not be *allowed* to die before him. It was curious how little comfort there was in that decree in light of how drastically Heaven had dealt with his family of late.

Entering the west wing of the house from the veranda he saw Yin Whun standing by the door to the audience hall with the girl Ai Lian beside her. As he approached, the little maid tugged gently at her mistress's sleeve and Yin Whun turned to him with a gesture of silence. Through the doorway he saw, at the far end of the hall, the alcove housing the tables of the family shrine . . . and Pao Shih, with her back to them and unaware of any presence. The lacquer on the table was bright, and the brass glowed with the luster of its newness. Before her was a steaming cup of tea and bowls of hot, freshly prepared food. The little brazier was alight and Pao Shih fitted one bit of paper after another into the glowing coals as they watched. Each flared briefly and curled away to ash. It was impossible to tell what offerings or prayers they held, but the brush and ink slab on the mat beside her stated plainly that, whatever they were, she had prepared them herself; just as she had prepared the sacrificial meal and seen to its service in the privacy of grey dawn. Now she knelt on the mat, watching the pale, trans- lucent waverings of the air above the brazier, as though in that shimmer her offerings were still visible as they ascended to Heaven. Wei K'e-yung moved beside Yin Whun, but she put her hand upon his sleeve and restrained him.

"Do not speak to her," she whispered. "Only watch and wait. I do not know what she is likely to do now."

"Her women are in the garden searching for her," Wei K'e-yung said to Ai Lian. "Fetch them in, girl, and wait in her chambers. We will send for you if there is need."

The maid bowed and ran off and Yin Whun held to her husband's arm. "You must prepare yourself for work. You have slept in your robes and are much in need of your toilet. Now that we know she is safe you must not trouble yourself. I will watch here as long as is necessary."

"You are still in your dressing gown," he said without looking away from Pao Shih. "Have your maids see to your own needs first. I will stay with her until you are prepared, and then I will see to my robes and my business. Go. I would be alone with her for a little while."

She had done the correct thing, he thought, though they both must know it could have no *real* meaning or effect. No . . . he too must think of the child as dead. It was more than a show of propriety. In time the grief would subside, as with any death, and the performance of the rituals would help them forget that it was not all that it appeared to be. He fingered the snowflake shawl and watched her rise and address the altar one last time. *Yes, beloved*, he thought, *you have done more than what is correct. You have done what is wise.*

At last Pao Shih turned from the altar and made her way back through the audience hall. She seemed not to see Wei K'e-yung, though he had put himself plainly in view in the doorway. Her face had the same faraway look of distraction it had held for days, and his heart sank. He had hoped this had been a sign that she was rousing; it was so in character with her old ways of thinking in the face of adversity that he had hoped this had been a deliberate and reasoned act. He had hoped she would recognize him again. But she did not stop. She walked slowly and carefully across the room like one unsure of her footing on an icy path, and paid him no more heed than if he had been the gardener's boy.

But as she passed through the doorway he put a hand on her sleeve, barely a touch, and said her name so softly even he barely heard it . . . and she stopped. He put the shawl about her shoulders and for a moment her hand covered his where he had paused to adjust the folds at her collar. She turned her head and looked up at him but did not speak and looked away again, making her slow, careful progress toward her rooms once more. He followed at a distance until he saw her young women rush to her across the courtyard. Perhaps, he thought, he should go to Yin Whun and tell her Pao Shih had returned to her rooms, but he did not feel like seeing anyone just then so, rather than go to his own quarters to dress for court, he went to his study, took out his brushes and inks and practiced his hand copying poetry, until Loy Quan Dong came from the court to fetch him.

That night after dinner, Wei K'e-yung took a pot of chrysanthemum tea, two porcelain cups and a book of poetry Pao Shih had given him shortly after her return from Heaven (though he had not understood that at the time), and went to her private chamber, where he sat beside her and read while she watched the fireflies and the moonlit night. At the sound of the second watch he bid her good night and sent in her women to prepare her for bed and retired to his own bedchamber alone.

The next morning he rose at dawn and went to the ancestral shrine without bothering to look into Pao Shih's rooms. He found her there as before, placing the bowls and incense as he had expected, and he watched from the doorway until the ritual was complete. She stopped beside him at the door as she left and stood silently a moment, then went away to her rooms.

In the Court of the Dead Wei T'ai-Tsung took up his post on the ledger accounts regularly. It had become his accustomed position, and the clerks found him a diligent and gifted, if somewhat grim, scribe. The boy never smiled and never joked with the others when sent to his brief intervals of leisure during the work period. There was only one lapse he had ever committed in his entries, but when it had been reported early on, the Chief Judge had replied that it was of no consequence and he should not be admonished for it in future. And so from that time on, no further prayers were registered on behalf of Wei T'ai-Tsung and the boy grew bitter and angry.

He was a diligent student, however, and applied himself with a grim and brilliant determination to his scholarship. His tutors were greatly impressed with the acuteness of his mind, but they also were perplexed by the nature of his fairy power, for it followed no pattern or form they could define.

It was the one joy in Wei T'ai-Tsung's young life and the only credit he did not deny his mother—that she had taught him well how to mask his talents from the eyes of Heaven, even in his anger, for it had become his constant condition and no longer betrayed him to his enemies.

Book Three

The dragons were angry.

And there was rain. An endless springtime of rain—cold and
stinging. The sky was grey as slate for days upon days—dark,
gloomy afternoons—and often it was difficult to know precisely when the sun had risen in the mornings. The thunder
growled and rumbled, a sound so constant that after a while it
ceased to be noticed, until it would suddenly explode in great
crashing, ear-shattering clashes and the lightning would tear
into the earth.

The dragons were angry indeed. They sought something . . . something of their own. For when those towering,
twisted lances of fire fell from the sky, scorching and shattering
whatever they struck, the cause was well known to men. The
Lung Wang was enraged and sought to punish the object of his
displeasure. That the lives and property of men often fell
victim to his vengeful rages was of no consequence to him, for
the Great Dragons were all but oblivious to the doings and
concerns of men. They ruled the waters and the rain, all the
scaled creatures that moved upon the Earth and all that lived in
the waters. And when the storms broke so violently and the
rains lasted so long this early in the year, it was not merely
the peasants and common men who believed such things. Even
the pragmatic, skeptical, learned men of the Imperial Government had to give credit to such thoughts . . . and worry.

There was flooding, from the spring thaw and the runoff of
so much rain. Even the fields too high to fear the rivers and
ponds were drenched, soaked so a man could not walk across

them. There was no planting in such ground . . . in such weather. Carts stood mired to their hubs, oxen and horses sank past their knees in sodden pastures and, if they could not be pulled free, died where they stood. Mud ran ankle-deep through the doorways, covering the floors of peasant cottages, which often leaked from untiled roofs when the endless days of rain soaked through the thatch. The homes of the more prosperous were somewhat better off, but the cold wetness was bone deep and the driving rain battered the shuttered windows and sometimes sleet rattled on the tiled roofs . . . and everywhere the lightning fell, shattering trees, gouging roads and fields and smashing homes and city walls . . . and sometimes people died, in ruined buildings or mud slides, or occasionally where the lightning found them on the roads.

It had begun to rain early in the Second Month, in the northeast provinces of Chingshu and Shantung and the northern finger of Honan. By the Third Month the rains had spread to the eastern provinces—Nanking, Chekiang, the remainder of Honan and the northeast wing of Hukwang, which included the city of Wuchang and the many lakes and rivers of the Wuhan District. For these two months it rained without pity, and a dozen days into the Fourth Month as well, but by then the violence of the weather had diminished to an occasional brief assault of lightning. Mainly it rained. Not in torrents anymore, but a steady, grey drizzle which kept the fields mired in uselessness, rotted the wood of house frames and roof beams, and made the people miserable.

And most miserable of all in such weather was the First Wife of the Governor of Honan. Though she bundled herself continually against the cold as had been her winter habit for nearly eighteen years, there was no relief. Everything was damp, and the cold clung to the wet cloth like a cruel lover. Wood for the stoves and for making charcoal was scarce, and had to be imported from the west and south at great cost, and the wicks for the oil lamps had to be dried in the ovens before they would burn.

Her husband had his own concerns and they were formidable. His province, along with Hukwang and Nanking, formed the heart of the great Central Plain of China and it was already far too late for the spring crops to be anything but a dismal failure. Occasionally there were brief respites in the relentless rain and, even more rarely, a break in the clouds. The sun would pour down through these rifts in glorious, golden shafts, lighting brief shimmers of rainbows across the sky, or the evening sun would color the horizon a dull, but discernible, rose and purple. But just as hope of an end began to rise, these small gifts would be withdrawn and the drizzle would come again.

Wei K'e-yung and his fellow officials knew if the end was not in sight soon, and the ground did not dry out quickly after the rain was gone, there would be no planting at all this season, not even a miserable one. The winter wheat and other early harvest crops were lost. Unless relief came soon, there would be no autumn harvest to speak of either. The produce of the south and west would not be enough to sustain the entire nation, and it would be costly beyond imagining and limited, for nearly all the rice and most of the other staple grains and produce came from the central plain . . . not to mention the silk and cotton and tea.

The Governor of Honan looked to his commerce and looked to his taxes and saw an economic disaster that could threaten his career.

Toward the end of the Fourth Month the rain gave way to more open, sunny skies, but great banks and islands of clouds continued to hang low and nearly motionless overhead. The Dragon Kings had not found what they wanted, and their minions kept watch.

Memi K'ai-Hua walked a slow, tottering path from the moon gate at the rear of her father's garden to the little structure called the Pavilion of Eight Fragrant Blossoms, which nestled among the fruit trees in the orchard behind the house. Peach, cherry, loquat, persimmon, apple, lichee, plum and nectarine lent their perfumes to the spring air and the name of the modest structure sheltering in their midst. The grounds of the park surrounding the offices and home of the Governor of Honan were still mired with soft, sucking mud, even five days after the last of the rain and plank pathways had been laid down to make it possible to reach several necessary parts of the estate without difficulty and discomfort. The men and boys of the household trotted along these plankways with a firm, brisk tread, seeming to revel in the bouncy, uncertain footing as the muddy ground oozed and shifted under their weight. But little Memi, her small feet encased in delicately embroidered satin slippers, was anything but confident of this journey. She carefully negotiated her way along the precarious plankway with a tea basket clutched between her hands, and her eyes fixed firmly on the path ahead. Yin Whun had been careful in her eldest daughter's education, for she knew far better than any mortal the kinds of service rank required, particularly of the young.

The pavilion itself was an octagonal structure set on a foundation of fitted stone blocks. Vines of climbing ivy and honeysuckle wound around its pillars, and the floor was paved with blue and green flagstones. Three low rosewood couches stood about the place, and the beams and ceiling were painted with patterns of clouds and birds on a bright-blue sky. The caged songbirds hung here now, rather than in the Pavilion of the Breeze Among the Willows at Dawn, for the Lady Pao Shih had not set foot there since the death of her son six years ago. The ornamental pond and its little shelter remained, but the bullrushes had been allowed to take over the bank so that the sight of them was nearly obscured from the house.

But Pao Shih still suffered from the summer heat, so the Governor had had a new pavilion constructed in the shade of the orchard, so his wife could find some comfort where she could not see the pond and the pavilion where she and Yin Whun and the boy—of whom she never spoke any more—had spent so much of their time. He had had it built as a gift the summer after their bereavement, for he knew there was little enough she could do to endure the summers and he needed a way to *demonstrate* his affection, for his companionship seemed to have little effect upon her melancholy that year. He was gratified to find that the pavilion roused her spirits enough that she no longer clung so persistently to the seclusion of her rooms. And though she seemed at first merely to have traded one refuge for another, this one at least was not as confining.

She began to speak to people again, and resumed most of her functions as First Wife and the responsibilities of managing the household. But she was not the same.

With a small sigh of relief and a silent blessing to the gods of

province, Memi K'ai Hua climbed the three broad stone steps
to the pavilion and set the wicker tea basket on a low table. She
removed the cover and took the cups from their nesting places
about the pot, then she poured two cups of lichee flavored tea.
She presented the first to her Principal Mother and the second
to her Paternal Aunt, Liu Ch'ing, with a little bow and the
proper courtesies.

Liu Ch'ing was pleased with the child, and gave her leave to
pour tea for herself and sit with them.

"Thank you, Ku'Mu," the girl said politely, a perfect model
of decorum, but her hand shook ever so slightly as she poured
the tea into her own cup. She was nine years old, and this was
the first time she had been allowed to serve the two most
important women in her father's family. Now her heart raced
with excitement because she had not only been found acceptable, but she had been invited to stay and listen to their talk.
The only thing that could possibly have been better would have
been for her own mother to have been there too, but, though
Pao Shih and Yin Whun were cordial enough, there was a
reserve between them.

This, Memi accepted as natural to the order of any
household—that the Second Wife would always stand aside in
deference to the First—but the servants said it had not always
been so. There had been a time when the two women had been
virtually inseparable. It was said that Yin Whun had entered
the household as the First Wife's personal maid, and that the
two women had loved each other as sisters, so much so that
Pao Shih had persuaded her husband to marry the maid so she
would enjoy an equal status with her former mistress. There
was no one in service to the family, however, who remembered
those days firsthand, and Memi herself did not recall any time
in her own life when they had been more than politely cordial.
She wondered, though, for from time to time she would see her
mother watching Pao Shih from a distance as she sat alone in
the Pavilion of Eight Fragrant Blossoms, and there was
something in her eyes the young girl could not identify.

She would have liked to ask her aunt about it, but it was
unlikely she would ever have a chance to be alone with her,
and when the women tired of her company she would be sent
back to her tutors and the nurse and her little sisters until the
adults sent for her again.

She saw her own mother often enough, and her father too, though less than she would have liked. But to be allowed into the presence of these two ladies was a rare treat to be treasured by a young girl on the skirts of womanhood. It was usually Liu Ch'ing's oldest daughter, Zou Ming, who was fifteen and newly betrothed, who waited on them when they came to visit. But Zou Ming had not come calling this time and Memi felt very grown-up.

The conversation was formal and dealt largely with Liu Ch'ing's recent widowhood and the plans for Zou Ming's future marriage. The governor's brother-in-law had not been a wealthy man, though he had fared well enough for a merchant of his station. His father had died some years earlier, leaving little but the care of his mother as his estate. This duty had fallen upon Liu Ch'ing in her own widowhood and her brother, Wei K'e-yung, though he had no formal responsibility for his sister as long as her mother-in-law lived, had given her a small house in Kaifeng and a modest support for her and the old lady, who was quite incapable, and Liu Ch'ing's three children.

His motives were not entirely unselfish. In Wuchang his sister had been his newlywed wife's principal companion besides Yin Whun, and they had a deep affection for each other. He had hoped her company would improve Pao Shih's state of mind and that his three daughters by his Second Wife would benefit from the company of their cousins, for he recalled how little his son had known his own family and how few friends the boy had had.

Memi did not remember her brother. She had been three when he died, and she took it on faith that he had ever actually existed. She was too young to attend to the family shrine, but she had seen the offering bowls there which would have been his, and, though her parents never spoke of him, the servants had told her of the drowning and how the First Wife had fallen into a mourning from which she had never fully recovered. The housekeeper, Mistress Hsieh, said that was when the women had drifted apart, for in her melancholy Pao Shih had not properly tended to her husband's needs, while Yin Whun had consoled him in his grief and given him two more children, after the First Wife had lost the only child she had ever been able to bear. They said there had been great passion between the governor and his First Wife and that had been lost as well with time and the tragedy.

Memi and her sisters and her cousins thought Pao Shih was the grandest lady they could imagine. Her regal beauty was still flawless in their eyes, even though the ebony hair was lightly streaked with grey, and the delicate frame possessed a more matronly bearing than it must once have had. Memi's own mother was so young by comparison, she found it difficult to credit the histories gathered from the household.

"Where is Yin Whun?" Liu Ch'ing asked when the conversation turned from Zou Ming's education as a bride. "I did not see her about the house when I arrived."

"She has escorted Yan Ping to the midwife," Pao Shih said. "The baby is due any moment and her husband is on your brother's personal business in Chengchow. He is not due back for two days and the silly girl is early. She was so upset by Zhao Min's absence, Yin Whun did not dare send her off alone."

"What of the housemaids?" Liu Ch'ing asked, incredulous.

"I do not disapprove," Pao Shih said. "We have always taken great care in the selection of our personal women and they are worth the cost to keep them well and happy. Yan Ping may have the disposition of a giddy peasant girl, but I would trust her with my life and I would not lose her."

Liu Ch'ing knew better than to dispute the wisdom of this attitude. She had seen where it had gotten Yin Whun.

"There is talk," she said, shifting the subject to safer ground, "that the dragons are not the only Heavenly agents who are vexed of late."

"Oh," Pao Shih said, an unusual sharpness in her look. "How is that?"

"Since I am alone and my mother-in-law is of no use I have had to make the sacrifices and temple offerings myself. Such places abound with gossip; even the priests are not above it. Lately I have found it an amusing diversion to go about collecting such tales."

"And with what do they credit the dragons' displeasure?"

"A theft," Liu Ch'ing fairly giggled.

"Of what?" Pao Shih asked, curious now.

"Oh, I hardly know. It depends upon who you listen to. Some say the Lung Wang has lost the Great Pearl governing his direction. Others say one of his daughters was kidnapped by a demigod with pretensions to a higher station. There are other notions equally silly. I do not think a man can actually know what has given Heaven cause for anger. But the speculations are amusing."

"And who is angry besides the dragons?" Pao Shih asked, an edge of disinterest once more creeping into her voice.

"They say . . ." and Liu Ch'ing giggled behind her fan. ". . . that someone has opened the gates to the Land of the Dead and set the souls to wandering."

"Ah," Pao Shih said irritably. "That is preposterous. We would surely know if *that* were the case."

"Why so?" Liu Ch'ing said, excited by the idea. "Everyone knows you cannot tell a ghost by sight. You must do something to make them reveal themselves or test them in some way. But can you *imagine*? What would you do if your first husband walked in to claim you? Would you have to submit to him? Would your marriage to Wei K'e-yung still be valid?"

"Free or not, he would still be dead," Pao shih said. "The circumstance would change nothing. What would you do, Hsiao'ku, if *your* husband returned?"

Pao Shih had struck a nerve and regretted it. Liu Ch'ing's eyes suddenly grew damp but she kept her control behind her quickly moving fan.

"I do not think it is worth crediting," Pao Shih said. "The world would be a very crowded place with all those extra people wandering about."

"Perhaps it is a long walk," Liu Ch'ing said quietly "and they have not yet arrived."

There seemed little else to say after that and Memi was sent back to the house with the tea cozy to send a servant to fetch Liu Ch'ing's two sons, and two young men to assist the ladies back along the plank-paved walk.

In the days following the floods and torrential rains, while the people of Honan Province were struggling to salvage whatever they could of their farms and businesses and lives, an increasing number of disturbing reports began filtering into the offices of the Provincial Governor. Uncommon events. Things not connected with law or economics or the management of affairs of state. Things which many of the clerks felt properly belonged in the hands of the priests, or even the taoists. But because they were events with lasting physical results and because they had happened in his province, it was up to Wei K'e-yung to record them and have them looked into officially and decide if a remedy or course of action by the Imperial Government was appropriate, or even possible.

By and large there was nothing to be done but read the documents arriving from the District Magistrates and wonder, for the things they described were as inexplicable as the two months of rain had been. The most disconcerting thing about them, however, was the widespread pattern of the problems. Similar events were occurring in scattered locations all over his province, and the frequency of the reports was escalating rapidly.

In eleven districts, few of them even adjacent, there were reports of dead fish and eels washing up on the banks of rivers and ponds in great numbers, and snakes and small reptiles of all sorts littering the fields. The first report by an hysterical woman in Lintsing to the north—that her long dead father had returned and abducted her elderly mother to return with him to the village fifty li to the south where they had lived twenty years ago—was not taken at all seriously. The clerks attributed it to the man having run off years ago and his family thinking him a murder victim rather than the deserter he was. But the District Magistrate provided proof of the death and burial, so the clerks concluded it was merely a man who looked like the woman's vague recollection of her father.

Closer to home, however, came reports from the growers of silkworms that all the mulberry trees in their orchards were dying, shedding their leaves as though autumn was at hand. The damage from the floods had already taken its toll and there was no sign of disease. What silkworms they had salvaged would starve when they hatched and that harvest would be lost too.

When eight more people in five districts reported seeing dead friends and relatives, and the fish continued to die in great numbers, and other strange, unnatural happenings began to fill the reports which appeared daily now, the clerks in the Provincial Offices stopped laughing and many began to whisper of demons. This atmosphere of hushed fear did not improve the governor's disposition. Nor was he reassured by the fact that he was not alone in this mystery, for reports of similar disorders were coming to him from other provinces as well. Only those places where the rains had been fierce were affected by the mounting piles of stinking, rotting fish, but from all over came reports of ghosts and other odd things.

The central and southern regions of Hukwang Province were dotted with lakes and small ponds and mazes of rivers and streams. It was an area that had suffered badly from the spring flooding, but it possessed in exceptional capacity for rapid runoff, being used to some degree of minor flooding every spring, and its recovery was rapid. The roads from Wuchang to Shangsha and Nanching and Hangchow were opened quickly, but the roads northward to Kaifeng and beyond were slower to become passable. In spite of the lateness of the season a planting was going into the ground as fast as the peasants could work, but they were dreadfully hampered without the aid of their animals. Nonetheless, the land was growing lush again, the wild things flourishing in the enrichment from the over-flowing rivers, and the willows in particular were thriving.

Though the farmyards and villages still looked abused, the wild places of the countryside were extraordinarily beautiful. Nestled among the clusters of small lakes and ponds of the Yi'yang District was one particular little pool which, though not extraordinary in most respects, proclaimed its special nature clearly to properly trained and knowing eyes. The little streams flowing to and from it moved swiftly, but the pool itself was very calm, for it was a well of great depth, silent and cool. Its banks were crowded with tall grasses, which swept about its curve in a lush green crescent. On the open bank was a single, perfect willow which leaned yearningly toward the pool, its delicate branches caressing the water with the barest whisper of a touch. And beneath the tree was a wide depression, not deep, but very definite.

A young man sat beneath the tree, his back against the trunk and a lute in his hands. He was extraordinarily beautiful with a fine-boned, aristocratic face and a slender, graceful form. There was strength in the tall, sleek frame. More so than that accounted for merely by his youth. His was a well-trained body and the eye was keen and quick and evidenced an intelligent, well-schooled, and perceptive mind. He reclined beneath the willow with long legs stretched before him, crossed at the ankles, his shoulders braced by the tree. His strong, nimble fingers plucked the lute strings and he sang a love song. It was a very sad love song. Before him, amid the ever-weeping branches of the willow, hung a large, irregular drop of amber suspended from a golden chain which he had entwined about a branch. His eyes were soft with the emotion of the song, but his mouth smiled as he sang the words.

At last he rose from the hollow and placed his lute upon the grass. Reaching deep into his sleeve, he withdrew a small carved rose quartz vial with a silver stopper tethered by a silk cord to the bottle's neck. With a small tug he pulled the stopper free, and with an elegant sweep sent the precious little object arcing into the center of the pool. It plunged into the dark water with barely a ripple and sank rapidly. All was quiet in the pool.

The young man smiled a satisfied, almost affectionate smile and turned from the bank back into the shade of the tree. "Come, my love," he said freeing the amber from its branch and tucking it carefully into his sash. Then he bent and picked up his lute and turned once more to the pool, where he bent in a long, graceful bow.

"Farewell, Tsu-fu," he said. "Sleep deeply and well . . . forever."

Then he walked from the dragon's pool and headed north.

Pao Shih received her midday meal in her private chambers as had been her habit for several years. Yan Ping served her and stayed to attend her, for the lady had been gracious enough to allow her to bring in her new baby to nurse. She had had some small worries about its effect on her mistress's disposition, as Pao Shih was not famous for her affection for young infants since the death of her only child. Her inability to bear more children had been like a raw wound for a long time and all the household was careful still not to do anything that would reopen that wound or remind her of the scar. Even Yin Whun's second daughter, Yun-chih Te-Hsing, had been forbidden to enter her presence until she was five years old, and little Li-Wu Tien-t'ang had only this spring been formally introduced to her Principal Mother for the first time.

Infants, after all, are infants, and gender is an invisible thing beneath the swaddling clothes. But a five-year-old girl has little chance of reminding a grieving mother of a twelve-year-old-son, and so the children had entered into the First Wife's good graces, if not the heart of her affections. She was pleased with them and did her proper part to educate them as ladies . . . and there was no doubt that she was fond of them, even so.

Yan Ping was happy today, for Lady Pao Shih had clucked and cooed over her little one quite cheerfully with not a sign of the old pain, and seemed most content in the infant's presence.

It was a fair and pleasant day and, as was her usual habit after the meal, Pao Shih retired to the Pavilion of Eight Fragrant Blossoms. She took several books of poetry and carried her embroidery basket herself and bade the girl bring her baby and attend her.

Though still soft, the ground had firmed to a reasonable consistency and the planks had been taken up, but the women still picked their way carefully along the path to the pavilion. By this slowed progress they were still some distance away when Yan Ping spotted the governor's Second Wife sitting in the pavilion reading. Pao Shih's step slowed ever so slightly, but the maid had no doubt her mistress had seen her too.

Though the pavilion was as public a place as anything in the park, it was largely considered by the household to be the First Wife's private domain, and Yin Whun rarely visited there anymore without a polite enquiry and Pao Shih's leave. The rift between the women was not a strain so much as a distance which had grown wider with the passing of time. They never argued and rarely took exception with each other, but they were formal in their politenesses and did not *seek* each other's company anymore.

Yin Whun did not look up as they approached, and at the steps of the pavilion Pao Shih dismissed Yan Ping to return her baby to the house and bring them a pot of lichee tea. Apprehensive, the maid rushed off, wishing to return as soon as possible. Yin Whun laid down her book and made a formal salutation as Pao Shih seated herself and returned the greeting.

"Madam," she said. "I see the fine weather has flushed us both from the house. It is hardly curious after so much rain."

"You look well."

"Thank you," Yin Whun said politely. Such meaningless references to her health always vaguely annoyed her, since Pao Shih knew it was impossible for her to fall ill. "You look fit yourself."

When she was certain Yan Ping was out of hearing Yin Whun turned to Pao Shih and began earnestly: "Madam . . ."

"Tell me," Pao Shih said, examining her embroidery. "What brings you to me today? This is the fourth time in as many days that you have sought my company . . . by the shrine, in the courtyard garden and again last night. Such devotion has become unfamiliar."

Yin Whun seemed on the verge of saying something but was at a loss for words.

"Has he abandoned you then?" Pao Shih said. "There have been many cares of late I have no doubt, and I know his habits of working. Though he no longer confides in me, even in our intimacy, I still know him very well. You are more used to his confidences lately, it is a precious thing and not cheerfully lost. How long has it been since he came to you?"

"Madam, it is not that. . . ." Yin Whun said.

"Your usual directness has been in need of exercise lately. Even *I* can see that you are vexed by something. If not our man then what?"

"I am troubled," Yin Whun admitted, "and I wish to consult with you."

"Ah," Pao Shih said, laying her embroidery aside and pointedly picking up a book. "Do you?"

In the house, Yan Ping hurried with her chores as best she could, but the baby fussed at being left with the nurse and the kitchen was in a high state of disorganization and the preparation of the tea took a seemingly interminable time. Being the personal maid to the governor's wives gave her a substantial degree of prestige within the household, and she exercised her advantage, giving orders and making demands, but things were still slow.

With the pot and cups at last nestled in the warmer Yan Ping made her way quickly back to the orchard and the storm she was certain was brewing in the pavilion. But what met her eyes there, as she scurried along the path, was curious and hardly what she expected. Yin Whun was on her knees before the First Wife, her forehead pressed to the lady's feet. The girl stopped where she was and waited on the path till she was summoned, the tea cozy nestled in her arms. From the distance she heard only snatches of the conversation, mostly Pao Shih, for Yin Whun's words were lost on the pavilion floor.

"Why should any of this concern *me*?" Pao Shih said. ". . . what have I to thank them for? . . ." And something to do with the Court of the Jade Emperor? No, that could not have been right. Then clearly, "I would sooner languish in the Land of the Dead than return to that place."

"If the Land of the Dead still exists," Yin Whun said clearly, sitting back on her heels.

Yan Ping froze. As Yin Whun had sat back, Pao Shih had looked directly at the maid waiting on the path. At Pao Shih's signal she hurried forward and placed the tea basket upon the steps, performing her obeisances before both women, for Yin Whun was standing now.

"Forgive, please, this wretched creature for taking so long with the tea," she said, honestly frightened for the first time in her memory. There was storm in Pao Shih's eyes and Yin Whun was none too pleased either. "When I saw that you and Little Wife were in conversation of some importance I felt it most prudent to remain where I was and wait to be called."

From the corner of her eye she saw Pao Shih look to Yin Whun and then nod and turn her attention back to the girl.

"What did you hear?" Pao Shih asked bluntly.

"Nothing," she said, her nose still to the floor. Again she saw the look and she hurriedly added ". . . except that I did hear the Small Wife say there may no longer be a Land of the Dead. . . ." Again the look and again the nod.

"Get up, child," she said. "Serve us the tea before it has grown cold."

"Then you may leave us," Yin Whun said. "I will see to Big Wife's service myself."

Yan Ping paused in her ministrations.

"As you are told, child," Pao Shih said.

When the maid had gone Yin Whun took up her tea and began to pace the space before the couches.

"I have heard the rumors," Pao Shih said. "I am not entirely as isolated as you seem to believe I have made myself. And I know about the animals—that it was not just our own. But if you do not know what it means, Madam, then why should I? And why should I care? If death is abolished then what of the Jade Emperor's curse upon me? It makes no difference. I will merely remain here . . . as I am . . . for as long as fate or fortune dictate."

"Death has not been abolished," Yin Whun said. "Merely the dwelling place of the dead. They have begun to return to us but they are no less dead. And the stableboy is no less dead for his spirit having nowhere to go."

"You know this for a fact?" Pao Shih said, a hint of sarcasm in her voice.

"I cannot say how it feels, Lady. But my tie to that other realm . . . it hums like a lute string, cruelly struck. The vision burns and dims. It is greatly disturbed. And though the tellers of these tales speak neither truth nor lies to their own knowledge, I seem to know which of the rumors is more true than the others."

"Your *gift*," she said heavily, "is of little use it seems. And why should any of this matter to me? I am mortal and must deal with these events. It is of no importance how or why they occur. I am powerless and one rumor is as good as the next or even the truth."

"But, Madam . . ."

"I do not *care* what happens to Heaven!" Pao Shih all but shouted. "I only care what happens on the Earth, and little enough of that. I must live out this miserable life with a man who hates me . . . though I cannot help but still care for him. That, too, is my fate."

Yin Whun sat carefully on the end of Pao Shih's couch. "Sister," she said gently and quietly, "he does not hate you."

"No. I know he does not. But he no longer cares. I have driven him away."

"In all truth, Pao Shih, you have done that," Yin Whun said. "When he was in need as deeply as you were, you kept him away, gave him no comfort. And when he tried his best to comfort *you* and show you his love, you gave him no reason to hope you would ever care for *him* again. You were selfish, Pao Shih, and now you must live with the result."

"I am still selfish," she confessed. "Though there has been no passion between us for years now I still love him . . . and I have never kept him from my bed. Without the passion or the promise of children, however, he has found little need of me lately. And I suspect even less want. He always was a . . . dutiful husband."

"He is not completely lost, Lady," Yin Whun said. "But he can no longer come to you. He has been so often rebuffed, he no longer has the spirit for it."

Pao Shih looked enquiringly at Yin Whun. There was sadness and a touch of disbelief in that look.

"Since . . . the boy . . . died . . . you have been his preferred companion; his confidant. Would you hand him back to me?"

Yin Whun smiled. "I have been your surrogate before, Madam. The first time was by your request. This second has been longer and did not require me to wear your image, but nonetheless . . ."

Pao Shih reached out and patted Yin Whun's hand where it rested upon the cushions near her. "Our tea is cold, Little One," she said. "Would you do the honors?"

Yin Whun rose and went to the teapot, which was no longer any warmer than the contents of their cups, but when she put her hand to it and lifted it from the tray a fine, pale steam began to rise from the spout, and what she poured into the cups was piping hot.

The women passed the afternoon in the little pavilion, content in each other's company. Yin Whun performed the duties of a maid and the pot of tea seemed never to grow cold or empty, till the evening shadows began to grow long and the sunlight turned amber. She sang poems of the snow and the fairies while she dressed Pao Shih's hair and told her lady stories which only they knew were remembrances of true events. When Ai Lian and Yan Ping came to fetch them to dinner they were distressed to see the tears upon Pao Shih's lovely cheeks, but the sadness was not the old melancholy, deep and numbing. It seemed a sharper thing and there was a clarity in her eyes that they had not seen for so long they barely remembered having ever seen her so.

"Has he come to you again?" Yin Whun asked, suppressing a giggle and attempting to remain decorous in front of the maids.

Pao Shih bent and picked a lily which she placed in Jing Shu's basket with the others.

"We passed a pleasant evening in each other's company," Pao Shih said. Her face and voice gave nothing away. "He brought cassia-scented wine and his lute. Yan Ping would have been delighted. It's a pity she spends her nights with her husband now, though I suppose he leaves her no reason to fill her head with silly fancies about my husband and me."

Behind her the maids carrying the flower baskets drew their broad sleeves before their faces and giggled.

"Off with you," Yin Whun said sharply all of a sudden. "Take these into the house and then see to our rooms. Big Wife and I will dine in my chambers, but we will come in our own time. Wait for us there."

Pao Shih was taken aback by Yin Whun's sudden peremptory behavior and took exception to it. "I have not gathered all I wish to," she said archly.

"Forgive me," Yin Whun said with a deferential bow. "But in my humble opinion there is nothing more worth gathering just now. I think a walk would be most pleasant, however. I will attend to whatever needs you may have myself."

Pao Shih was annoyed in the extreme but she sent the maids off, for she had sharp words for Yin Whun that she did not wish to say in front of the girls. Before she could speak, however, Yin Whun placed a hand upon her sleeve. Her head was bowed and her eyes closed in the attitude of one listening to a sound a great distance away.

"Forgive me," Yin Whun whispered. "It was clumsy but it was necessary."

"Little One, what is wrong?" Pao Shih asked, concerned now.

When Yin Whun looked up there was the briefest flicker of pity in her eyes but it was quickly replaced by a look of urgency.

"There is one here who would speak with you," she said. "Have they gone?"

"They are out of hearing," Pao Shih replied, glancing over Yin Whun's shoulder. "What have you to say?"

"Not I . . . your Sister. . . ."

Suddenly the garden began to shift about them. There was no physical motion, but everything seemed transformed. Pao Shih gasped, for it was as close to the fairy sight as she had been in eighteen years and, though it was merely a mortal's view of its effect, it shocked Pao Shih so she cried out.

All about the plants seemed to possess a vague, faintly glowing double image, for each existed in two realms at once. She had forgotten how intensely *real*, how much fuller and richer and rounder the world was. She had grown used to seeing only half of it, but suddenly the dimension had returned, and she felt a dizziness, like vertigo. Things sparkled and shifted and did not remain still and she could not be certain of precisely what she saw. Or of what she heard.

"Sister," the voice said, and it was like a scent on the wind—barely even words. "The Flower greets the Snow."

At once Pao Shih was on her knees in the grass, bending toward a short, profusely-blossoming fuchsia from which the voice seemed to issue.

"Who addresses me so?" she cried, anguish and yearning in her voice. "Is it truly you . . . my Sister of Flowers?"

"Indeed it is," the fairy replied, and beneath the bush appeared a tiny, exquisitely perfect miniature of the Fairy of One Hundred Flowers. "Do not cry, Ku-She," the fairy said. She placed a delicate, small hand upon Pao Shih's where it rested on her knee. The touch was light as spidersilk and the hand barely spanned a finger.

At her touch, however, the tears which had merely moistened her cheeks gave way to real, heartfelt sobs, and Pao Shih threw herself onto the lawn and cried. Yin Whun knelt beside her and stroked her hair, working the calming magic of her hands, and the Fairy of One Hundred Flowers ran from the shelter of the shrub and threw her arms about Pao Shih's shoulder. She barely had to bend at all to kiss her cheek and as Pao Shih began to respond to Yin Whun's caress she pushed herself up to a sitting position and the fairy retreated beneath the shrub.

"I do humbly beg your pardon," Pao Shih said earnestly in a trembling little voice. "But I had thought never to see any of my beloved Sisters again until this sentence had come to an end. In fact, I had made myself put you all from my mind. . . . I had forgotten how much I loved you."

"It is well that you did," the fairy said. "We are all of us under the emperor's command to have nothing to do with you as long as you are on Earth. But, though we are constrained not to speak to you, you must know we could never wholly abandon you. Have you not noticed that this park has always flourished, no matter what the conditions elsewhere? We have watched over you, though such as we could do is far too little to matter."

"Then why have you come to me now, Sister? If you are under the Jade Emperor's edict, then this is a most dangerous thing you have done."

"We have all consulted on this and agreed it is worth the risk. Even Madam Chou, who officially knows nothing and would be powerless to help me if I am caught. I have news of your son."

Pao Shih gasped and drew back. The pain in her eyes was terrible and the little fairy felt a twinge of guilt, but there was an imperative upon her to continue regardless of the pain it caused.

"No," Pao Shih said, vehemently, turning away. "I do not wish to hear this. If I had to know what the Jade Emperor has done to him, what punishment or humiliation has been placed upon him, I do not know how I would be able to endure the rest of this lifetime."

She turned back slowly and looked at the fairy. "I had thought this mortal span such a puny and insignificant thing— so brief and fleeting, like a candle flicker. But when you must live within the years, waiting, waiting, with no meaning, no purpose but to endure another season, then the time becomes a wholly other thing. Time to a mortal is much like the fairy senses to . . . to us. It possesses dimensions and complex- ities and subtleties the immortals do not know, just as no mortal truly sees the fullness of the physical world a fairy knows.

"I have grown attached to a particular notion that makes the time endurable. The child had such great promise as a scholar; on Earth his career in the Ming court would have been brilliant. I have fancied that in the Court of Heaven his existence has followed a similar, possibly even more brilliant, path. Must you disabuse me of this dream?"

"It is not inaccurate," the fairy said. "The Jade Emperor quickly noticed the boy's potential and set him to study with the greatest scholars of antiquity, who reside in the Land of the Dead. He has kept the boy at court and set him at the side of all the important deities that he might learn the ways of Heaven and be of great use to the Jade Emperor in time."

Pao Shih was nearly faint with relief. "Oh infinite blessings on the Wisest of All Beings. I should never have doubted. Of course he would know and he would hardly venture to *waste* such a precious gift."

"Ku-She, please," the fairy pleaded. "I have very little time and much to tell you, for all is *not* well with your son, though Heaven has done its best for him."

"What is wrong?" she asked.

"Though he has had all the best that Heaven could offer him, he has grown bitter, resentful and filled with hate. Though it is clear to anyone that you were powerless in this, he felt himself abandoned when he was taken into Heaven. He must have harbored hopes of rescue for some time, but though *we* know that was impossible, a child would not believe so. Yet you never came. I do not know if the Jade Emperor encouraged him to turn his heart against you—it is possible. I can only say that his anger and hatred are turned against *all* both in Heaven and on Earth. The Jade Emperor has escaped the boy's loathing no more than you.

"There is also the matter of his power, which is far greater than anyone imagined from the issue of a fairy and a mortal. But it has defied description or definition all this time. He has successfully hidden both its nature and its extent, and very little is actually *known* about it."

"Oh, Heaven, what have I done?" she said, drawing her sleeve across her face.

"There was nothing you *could* do," the fairy said.

Miserable, Pao Shih got slowly to her feet and turned away from the azalea. "Why have you told me this, Sister? Of what use is it but to make me more unhappy?"

"I bring you a warning," said the Flower. "You should look to the safety of your family and your household, though how you may accomplish this I cannot truly say. You and your husband are in grave danger."

Pao Shih turned a perplexed look back to the fairy.

"Wei T'ai-Tsung has left Heaven and he has left much damage in his wake. For a long time he had made suit for the hand of the youngest daughter of the Guardian of the Hearth, and became enraged when it was denied by both her father and the Jade Emperor. In vengeance he has stolen the poor girl, and it is said he keeps her a prisoner in a lump of amber hung about his neck. As a prank he has set the foxes to run through the halls of the Palace of Heaven itself.

"These are but *examples* of his pranks, but there is much worse and these things bear upon the mortal world as well. He entered Hibiscus Village and kidnapped the Spirit of the Mulberry Trees from the retinue of the Fairy of One Hundred Trees for his Second Wife. As the trees die so too die the silkworms. He has stolen the Golden Ax of the God of War and with it he has broken the gates to the Land of the Dead and set the souls to wandering, the harmless and the evil alike. He has stolen the pearls from beneath the chins of the Great Dragons of the Northeast and East and I fear now the Southeast too. Those dragons already in the clouds in early spring were not terribly affected by this but those still in their pools have been trapped there, and Wei T'ai-Tsung has systematically sought them out and has begun to poison the pools one by one."

"The dead fish," Pao Smith gasped.

"Yes, as the dragon dies so too do all the scaled things within his territory."

"Ah, *foul!*" Yin Whun cried. "To murder a *dragon* so!"

"There are other things as well. Some small matters, some not. He has vowed to gather all the Dragon Pearls and thus hold power over all the dragons, be they on land or in the clouds. I do not know what he will do with them once he has hold of them."

Pao Shih sat on the lawn again and looked bleak. "My child," she whispered. "How can it be so? How *can* it be?"

"He is but a fairy?" the Flower said. "This is true, but he is strong and most of all he is clever. It is his mortal heritage that has made him more than anyone expected. Your choice of a husband was fortuitous. If the child had not turned bitter and vengeful, he would have been greatly respected and highly honored in Heaven."

"What will they do?"

"Whatever they can. He is nimble and quick of wit. It is one thing to punish him, but first they must catch him. He knows Heaven well. His various apprenticeships taught him all he needed to know of comings and goings and where and what and whom. There is little our Sisters and I, or even Madam Chou can do, but stay alert and guard what is ours, for there is no knowing where he will choose to strike next.

"This is why I have come to you. Even more than the Jade Emperor himself Wei T'ai-Tsung hates you and your husband. There is no doubt that in some way, at some time, he will attempt to avenge himself upon you. I cannot tell you how you may protect yourselves, for I do not even know how I will protect my own realm."

"I must find him," Pao Shih said, rising to her feet once more.

"That will be difficult."

"Then help me. . . ."

"I cannot, Ku-She. I must guard my own as must all your Sisters. But even so, the Great Dragons have sought him high and low without success. The storms and floods. Surely you must have realized the dragons were angry. If they have had no success—if the God of War and Yang Oerlang and their minions and all whom the Jade Emperor has set in search have not yet found him—what could *I* do to aid you? What could *you* do?"

"Possibly nothing. But I must try. It is often true as the philosophers have said, that we hate most what we love and cannot have. Though he hates me now, there may still be some small love left for me. I must try to persuade him to abandon this course. *I must try!*"

She knelt on the grass before the shrub sheltering the tiny fairy. "Help me, Sister, please."

"I cannot, Ku-She. Do not press me so, I beg you."

"One small favor, then," she pleaded. "Find me the monk Wei Pan Ch'ao. I would wager all the Province of Honan is worth that he still lives. Find him and send him to me."

The fairy bowed her head. "We will try. I can promise that much. But now I must be gone. I have stayed overlong. This was to be a brief errand but I am loath to leave your company, Sister. You have been sorely missed. Farewell. . . ."

And with that the garden once more began to shift and shimmer. The bedazzlement was gone and the colors grew grey, the morning light faded and lost its brilliant clarity and with a sigh, Pao Shih fell back upon the grass and began to weep.

Alone among the gods, Chang-O felt secure and safe from the wicked tricks of Wei T'ai-Tsung, for she was the Lady of the Moon and lived apart from Heaven. Her home was a splendid palace of ivory, white jade and crystal, and sat alone on the orb of the moon amid willows and white birch trees.

At night, as her palace traveled through the sky, she wandered the white sand pathways of her garden or sat beneath the birches surrounded by her ladies, whose soft voices sang love poems to the gentle plucking of their lutes or the reedy pipings of a flute. Just before dawn the lists of children to be born that day were burned by her own hand in an iron brazier, so their little spirits would be set free and their tiny bodies could enter the world to claim them.

The exact numbers of her retinue were known to no mortal man, nor were they constant; they grew and diminished as the moon waxed and waned. At the full of the month her house was crowded and bright with laughter; at the dark of the month she was alone in the cold and empty rooms.

Chang-O was beautiful beyond comparison, but it was a cold and distant beauty—pale and stark. The tides yearned for her. Men and women blessed their love in her light and their children in her name. The geomancers and astrologers praised her wisdom and Wei T'ai-Tsung desired her.

One night, in the dark of the moon, Wei T'ai-Tsung stood on the tallest peak of the Western Mountains and summoned all the crows for one thousand li in each direction. He bade them form a bridge into the sky and they obeyed at once, flying into the dark sky, row upon row, forming a broad black roadway with their backs and beating wings. Wei T-ai-Tsung mounted and began to walk, and the road formed before him as quickly as it vanished behind.

At last he set foot in the darkened garden of the Lady of the Moon herself. Nothing stirred. The stillness was as deep as the night, and he could not see the palace or even the trees around him.

Then in the distance a tiny glimmer of light caught his eye. It was like a star, but very low to the ground. Cautiously he began to move toward it and at last, free of the trees, he saw

the palace, for all around the stars were burning brightly except
for the spot where the palace stood. It was a great, black hulk
against the spangled brightness, blotting out the stars—all but
one, which shone alone at the center of that darkness.

Wei T'ai-Tsung smiled, for he knew it must be the brazier in
which the morning lists would be burned. He had but to be
patient and soon the lady would come to him.

Thus satisfied to wait, he crossed the broad marble porch
past the brazier, and settled himself in the curve of one of the
two moon gates flanking the palace entrance. But his patience
was rewarded far sooner than he had hoped. In the stillness he
heard the quiet, unhurried steps of tiny feet wandering the
cold, stone corridors. As she came nearer he caught the scent
of gardenia and heard the tinkle of her hairpins and finally he
saw the gentle glow of her garments as she emerged from the
dark, deserted house onto the porch, where she stopped by the
brazier and fed it several fresh lumps of charcoal with a pair of
silver chopsticks.

Wei T'ai-Tsung's longing for her became acute and he rose
from his hiding place and stepped forward.

Chang-O turned suddenly and stared at him, but he could not
tell if it was fear or anger that sent her pose rigid and made her
clutch the chopsticks tightly in her pale hand. Her face was
smooth and white, her eyes like the night sky between the
stars, her hair coiled in the old style of a great lady and dressed
with a net of silver, and all about her was an air of cold and
distance.

"Lady," he said, stepping forward with a courtly salutation;
then with common familiarity, "Chang-O."

Her posture and her manner remained unchanged and she
did not return his greeting.

He smiled and approached more closely. "My name is Wei
T'ai-Tsung and I am your new lord."

"How dare you speak to me so?" she said, drawing back in
disgust. "One such as you would hardly be fit to clean this
brazier. Presumptuous *child*! You are the get of a simple fairy
and a mere mortal and not one tenth my equal."

"I am, however, your master in power and soon I will be
your master in the bedchamber, for I intend to take you for my
wife."

"I am married already," she said, "and to a far better husband than you."

"Ah," he said with a cold smile and a bow of his head. "The archer Yi. He who was once an immortal but was banished and who died because you, in your greed, condemned him to mortality by drinking all the magic elixir he had procured for *both* of you. An act as cold and heartless as this place you dwell in . . . and one I can well approve of, for I have similar plans for all those in Heaven and on Earth."

"It is a deed I have repented for all eternity, but though he is no longer a living man, nor an immortal one, he has been honored in the Land of the Dead and is now one of the high officials governing that place . . . and he is still my husband, for I have taken a vow of eternal constancy."

"Then your honored Yi is homeless like the rest of the ghosts I have cast out of the Land of the Dead and condemned to wander helplessly . . . trying to contain them with no hope of success.

"As for your vow, it is without force or consequence. I said I would *take* you for my wife and that I shall. Your consent is not needed . . . nor even necessarily desired."

Stepping forward quickly Wei T'ai-Tsung seized Chang-O by the wrist, but the chopsticks in her free hand were sharp and flashed a bright silver arc through the night to slash across the hand that gripped her. With an oath, he drew back his wounded hand but lunged for her immediately as she began to move away from him.

Slashing the chopsticks wildly at his face, she dodged his encircling arms and fled into the dark cavern of the palace, but he was close behind her. Her garments fluttered about her as she ran, like a cloud of moths about a flame, and he caught at the hem of her overdress several times before grabbing it firmly, but it was not with his good hand and she pulled free before he could capture her completely.

As she ran she screamed for help, but Wei T'ai-Tsung only laughed. "You are alone, Madam," he said, slowing his pursuit. "My education in the High Emperor's Court was very thorough. There is none here to help you."

Still she ran from him. He pursued her through the corridors and halls and she overturned furniture and toppled statuary in his path, but gained no distance and did little to disturb his progress. At last, in the corner of her east courtyard, he trapped her in a corner between the high garden wall and the stone well. She trembled with exhaustion and anger. The chopsticks had fallen from her hand in a distant corridor and there was nothing at hand she could use as a weapon. Her gaze darted to the well, but she was tired and did not move quickly enough. Even as she turned Wei T'ai-Tsung had her about the waist and began tearing at her garments as he pressed her against the wall.

Screaming her husband's name like a curse at her assailant she fought and kicked, scratched and beat Wei T'ai-Tsung about the head with her one free hand. But he was young and tall and broad-shouldered and very strong . . . and very determined. Chang-O, however, had no intention of having him achieve his ends undamaged. Her power, however, was not of her person, but wholly bound to the moon and those things held in its sway. She could inflict no injury upon him except as a woman fighting a man, and so fight she did—as fiercely as her strength allowed.

Though her resistance had amused him at first, Wei T'ai-Tsung began to tire of the struggle, for she was not relenting. Annoyed, he forced her against the wall again and drew back his hand, striking her across the face. She screamed and twisted with the blow, but he had loosed his grip in order to strike her, and both her hands were now free. As he pulled her to him again she clawed at his eyes with her left hand while her right went to the ornamental silver pins in her hair. Pulling free one long, sharp silver spike she drove it at his face, but he pushed her away as her arm descended and the pin sank deep into his left shoulder. Before she could withdraw it and attack again, he howled in pain and flung her so hard against the wall that she slid to the ground dazed. As she fainted, Wei T'ai-Tsung flung a curse at her and at the base of the wall where the lady should have lain, there was only a large, black lump of coal.

In the lady's own bedchamber he dressed the wounded shoulder with wine from her bedside and silk from one of her gowns. Then, still fully dressed in boots and all, he lay upon her bed and slept through the day and into the next night. He ate his fill from her kitchen, overturned the brazier onto the marble porch, scattered the dust and cold cinders into the doorway, and once more made his way into the garden where the crows waited in the treetops. As they carried him back to Earth on their backs he noticed that the moon was still fully dark; not even the tiniest sliver of light dared brave its outer edge.

A smile played briefly across his face, then it returned to the cold, hard-eyed expression he had come to wear most often when contemplating his new career. The moon was dark and would remain dark as long as its lady was imprisoned. And as long as it was dark there would be none to attend her and find where she lay. He was satisfied. Perhaps someday he would remove her to another place and have what he desired before returning her to her dark prison, but that could prove dangerous, and for now he was content to keep her as she was.

At the first light of dawn, Wei Pan Ch'ao rose from his narrow bed and began to systematically sort his few possessions, setting some to the left and some to the right. By the time he was finished, the collection of items on the left was twice the size of that on the right. From beneath his bed he took a basket woven of reeds and broad banana leaves with two straps so it could be slung upon his back. This he put beside the items on the right. Everything fit neatly into place with room leftover.

He laid his few spare clothes upon his blanket and rolled it tightly, tying it to the bottom of his pack. Then he gathered the pile on the left into his apron and carried it down the hall past cell after cell, the exact image of his own. By a doorway into the inner courtyard he found an empty basket, into which he deposited the items in his apron, then continued a little farther along the hall to a particular door, where he left the basket and returned to his own room.

He picked up the pack and carried it across the courtyard to the kitchen. There, he filled one small bag with rice, another with millet, another with dried mushrooms and dried shrimp and the last with dried fruit. He took a bundle of leeks and a small brick of tea, two new apples and two oranges. From a rafter he took two mesh-strung gourds, which he filled with water from the kitchen well. With these items stowed safely in his pack, Wei Pan Ch'ao went to the shrine, where he stopped briefly to light incense and say a prayer or two for the speed and safety of his journey.

On his way out he took a sturdy walking staff from the pile by the shrine porch and struck off into the forest without a backward glance. He did not think anyone had seen him leave, but it was a matter of no concern. The population of monks at the monastery changed almost daily and though he had been there for seven years, this was the general and accepted way of leaving—to simply be gone one morning.

As he walked north through the dense growth and occasional shafts of morning sunlight, a large green parrot with red, yellow and blue underwings flashed by close over his head, heralding his progress with a raucous voice. A short time later another flew by and settled on the branch of a tree ahead of him, regarding him steadily as he approached. He stopped a short distance away and studied it in return.

"You see," he said. "I am on my way. And if you yourself are not the fairy, you may relate this fact to your mistress for me."

Then he passed it by.

A moment later the parrot flew over his head once more with a loud screech and he did not see it again.

That night he camped at sunset beside a little brook. He gathered fruit and roasted tubers which he dug from the bank. Then he lay down to sleep, wondering what his dreams would be.

The night before his sudden departure his dreams had hosted a vision. It had been a very ordinary dream at first; nothing prophetic, just a quiet little reminiscence of a time in his life— he could not really remember when—but a time spent in a tranquil little hut by a glacial lake in the mountains of the northwest. Something significant had been learned there, a key to his longevity . . . but quite abruptly the dream had changed. A large green parrot flew through a window and perched on the back of a chair, facing him. The room suddenly grew dark and transformed itself into his cell in the forest shrine. He looked about, thinking the bird had awakened him and that he was actually where he appeared to be, but he was not in his bed. He was seated at his little writing table as he had been in the hut at that moment in the dream, and the cell's ceiling was lost in darkness, vast and deep, in which he thought he saw the occasional glimmer of a star.

Mortal, said the bird, ruffling its wings. It spoke in a soft and melodic voice, neither male nor female and with none of the harsh screech of the parrot.

I know you, it said. *You were briefly a hawk at my pleasure. You sought my aid through the Fairy of Ku-She. I now seek yours on her behalf. Go to her. She requires your magic.*

At once Wei Pan Ch'ao moved from his seat, kneeling before the bird and knocking his head upon the floor. Then he sat back on his heels and regarded it respectfully.

"Lady Fairy," he said. "I remember your kindness well. It was one of the most impressive experiences of my life. How may I serve you now?"

I have done all I can in finding you and charging you to go to my Sister of Ku-She. She has been banished from Heaven and lives still with your nephew who is Governor of Honan at Kaifeng. You must reach her as quickly as you can. I dare not aid you further in this for I am already in violation of Heaven's judgement and I risk much.

There is great trouble in Heaven and we must all look diligently to the safety of our own. The ills of the Earth follow, as all things must, the patterns set in Heaven. Yet mortal as you are, you may still be of some service if you reach Ku-She in time.

More than this I cannot tell you. She must do that, but as you journey observe your world carefully. It will teach you much about the nature of this evil.

Then the bird flew up into the starry void where the ceiling should have been, vanishing almost at once, and the darkness descended and Wei Pan Ch'ao spent the rest of the night in a profound and dreamless sleep.

But neither the parrot nor the Fairy of One Hundred Birds visited his sleep on his journey north.

He lived off the land as much as possible, conserving his small stores, and as he traveled he talked to people in the villages and in the fields and at the roadside shrines. Slowly the nature and complexity of the world's ills became apparent to him, but he was at a loss to explain their cause or even their relationship to one another. He was appalled at what he learned but he was equally appalled at himself—that the world could have come to such a state of disorder and that it should have escaped his notice for so long.

The disastrous prank with the Golden Chopsticks and his narrow escape from the arms of death had sobered him considerably. When the snow had finally begun to fall he had humbled himself as he had never done in all his long life.

Then he had once again set out into the world to wander as he had for more years than he could keep track of, but it was not the same. The world held no adventure for him anymore. Its lessons seemed redundant and small, and his own pranks and entertainments seemed petty. Avoiding the Court of the Dead remained his only worthwhile challenge, but the prospect of running eternally *from* death with nowhere to run *to* began to look as tedious and burdensome as the life of drudgery of the lowliest menial slave.

For three years he traveled aimlessly in this way. It did not for a moment occur to him to concede to the Judges of Death, but his life was no longer a pleasure to him.

What has happened to me? he wondered. *Why is everything so meaningless?* And in that question he found the germ of his answer. His quest turned inward. He continued to wander only until he found a suitable refuge for study, and there he retired from his travels.

It had been thirteen years since that decision had settled upon him when the green parrot flew through his window and into his dream. Wei Pan Ch'ao had lived and studied in that cell in the forests of the southern mountains for the last seven of them, his first two havens having proved insufficient to his needs. He had learned much from the treasured writings of the monks and scholars who had honed their minds and sharpened their wits on the concepts of the universe for centuries— through study and contemplation, thought and experiment, discipline and practice and the perfection of some particular art. He had become a wiser man. He had also become a more powerful magician. But through his isolation and dedication to study he had become blind to the world, both Heaven and Earth, and now it was all too clear that much was dreadfully amiss.

After ten days on the road he was into the Central Plain and approaching the Yangtze River, and his years of sedentary study at the monastery were taking their toll. He had forgotten how far things were and how long it took to walk them. How much time was required to get as far as Kaifeng by foot? He had known these sorts of things once with a precise clarity, but he was not sure anymore.

He crossed the Yangtze near Wuchang and ten li farther on he stopped in a small village for the night, where he stole a horse by bartering the farmer a barrel of water magically transformed into wine in exchange for a night's lodging. While the family slept, sated on the wine, Wei Pan Ch'ao and the farmer's best horse headed for Honan at a furious pace.

The Monkey King was thrilled with Wei T'ai-Tsung's pranks, for he had long been regarded as the patron of devilment and an alliance was precisely to his liking. The youth was clever and resourceful and the Monkey King had followers to place at the young man's command. But Wei T'ai-Tsung was too somber a fellow, taking his pranks too seriously, to entirely please the Monkey and so he began to scheme—as was his wont, being loyal to no one—of ways to play pranks of his own upon Wei T'ai-Tsung.

In the pavilion once called The Breeze Among the Willows at Dawn but lately whispered of, only by the servants, as That Place in the Garden, a shadow passed briefly between the pillars of the gateway. It was early evening and the shadows were deep in the little building, for the willows hung about it in robust profusion and the tall bullrushes had been allowed to grow about it like the leaves of a folding screen. The shadow took form for a moment, then faded back into the cool, dappled green shade . . . and waited.

At the moon gate Ai Lian waited, but far from patiently. She had been left there by her lady without apparent cause and she was concerned, both for the unusual impropriety and for her mistress's destination.

"Come away," Yin Whun said sharply as she emerged from her own suite onto the veranda.

"But I fear for her," the young woman said. "She never goes there anymore. Not for years."

"I will attend to her myself," Yin Whun said, wrapping a light shawl about her slender shoulders as she passed by the maid at the gate. "If she requires attention, I am the better judge of that."

"But . . ."

"Enough. You will see to her rooms and await us there. Send for Yan Ping and Jing Shu as well. Not another word. You are dismissed."

Yin Whun made certain the maid had entered the rooms before she moved away from the moon gate to follow Pao Shih across the park to the Pavilion of the Breeze Among the Willows at Dawn.

In the pavilion there was not a sound but the rustle of the willows and the quiet lapping of the pool upon the moss-grown stone steps. Pao Shih sat at the water's edge and watched the carp sliding lazily about beneath the lily pads. The water rippled and distorted, but where the breeze moved the tree branches so they cast shadows, her face was clearly reflected in the watery mirror.

She knew him at once. Though the years had changed her, streaking her hair and dimming her youthful beauty to that of an unusually handsome matron, he appeared not to have changed at all. In appearance they now looked to be nearly the same age. In fact, at forty her husband bore so striking a resemblance to his uncle that, given other circumstances, her eye might briefly have been fooled.

He had made no sound at his approach. He had simply been there, his image reflected in the water behind her own.

On the bank across the pool Yin Whun stood waiting. A long-forgotten memory stirred and a brief flash of hatred. . . forgotten, remembered, put aside. He would be a useful tool, and this, at least, was not his fault; except that it could be traced directly back to his theft and all the events and sorrows that stupid stunt had fostered. She was not feeling charitable today, but she managed to put that thought aside too. They would need whatever allies they could get, and the monk, no matter how detestable, was far from insignificant.

"Uncle," Wei K'e-yung said with a properly respectful bow, "you honor my house." But it was clear from his manner and his voice that he was far from pleased to see him after so long. "The years have been good to you. I had hardly expected to see you in such perfect health."

"I dare say you had hardly expected to see me at all after eighteen years. But those years have been profitably spent in study and contemplation and in that time I have learned a thing or two about the universe."

"Indeed it would seem so," Wei K'e-yung said, coolly polite. "You look hardly at moment older than when I last saw you."

"Ah, Nephew," the monk smiled. "That is a very *old* trick. I am sure your wives have acquainted you to some degree with my skills and accomplishments, but I would welcome the chance to talk of such things with you myself. Perhaps this visit will be an instructive one for both of us."

Wei K'e-yung bowed his most courtly bow, the kind he reserved for dignitaries he could not afford to offend, no matter how little he liked them personally, and instructed the servants to show his uncle to his rooms.

"It is good to see you again, Nephew," Wei Pan Ch'ao said before following his meager baggage into the house. "I am most pleased and proud to see how well you have advanced yourself."

When the servants were well out of earshot Wei K'e-yung stood looking after them, a deep frown on his face, his wife beside him. "Why has he come *now*?" he wondered, expecting no real reply. ". . . after all these years. I had honestly thought him dead. Why? Just when things are growing so *strange. . . .*"

"He is here because I sent for him," Pao Shih said simply.

Wei K'e-yung looked at her uncomprehendingly for a moment. "You have known his whereabouts all this time?"

"No," she said. "It was necessary to locate him."

There was the threat of storms building in the dark of Wei K'e-yung's eyes, but Pao Shih had gained much over the years in determination and a kind of cold reserve, and she did not turn away from him.

"Once again you have kept secrets from me," he said.

"I am guilty of this, Husband, that is true. Nor will I defend myself by saying that you will forgive me when you hear the reason. Possibly you will, but that does not greatly concern me. This is not a sin of omission so much as one of delay for, though it was never possible that we would not discuss it, I saw no point in speaking of this until I knew whether or not I would have the monk at my disposal."

"You aggravate me beyond measure with this scheming, Woman. What have you done?"

"Nothing . . . yet."

"How did you find him, and why?"

"He is necessary," she said. "As to how . . . the fairies helped me."

A small shudder ran through Wei K'e-yung and his eyes briefly reflected a flicker of fear, then went dark and angry again.

"Is there no end to it?" Wei K'e-yung said heavily, turning from his wife. "What have you and my uncle plotted between you that I cannot even suspect?"

"At the moment he knows no more than you, though he understands things about the world and what happens in it that you do not, and so I imagine he suspects more than you do.

"I have no love for this man, Husband, though I cannot deny him a fair portion of respect. He is far from anything you ever imagined and is no longer entirely human. There are few things in this fine house, even among your antiques, that are as old as he is. And even as a fairy, with my power full upon me, there are ways in which he was more powerful than I. But he is also responsible for all that has caused us both to suffer, and, indirectly, he is not without his portion of blame for the current ills of the world. . . ."

Wei K'e-yung swore darkly, a thing he rarely did, even in jest, and turned in the direction his uncle had gone.

". . . nor are *we*!" Pao Shih said in a firm, clear voice.

Wei K'e-yung glared at her.

"The noon meal is past and you are due at audience," she said simply. "Tonight, after the evening meal, I would have us all assemble in the Pavilion of the Breeze Among the Willows at Dawn; Yin Whun too. It will be time to answer what cannot be discussed here and now with the ears of the house all about."

Wei K'e-yung nodded curtly. "Madam," he said stiffly. "I will see you at dinner."

As dusk came on Wei K'e-yung himself began to light the paper lanterns hung from the rafters of the little pavilion by the pool. He was slow and methodical about the task. The spirit had gone out of him, and he needed something familiar to do to remind him that, no matter how poorly, life went on around him. Lighting the lamps was a very necessary thing just then.

Wei K'e-yung was greatly disturbed by his uncle's presence. Once he had loved this man; he was fascinated by his stories, most of which the boy had assumed to be fiction made personal. But Pao Shih had acquainted him with exactly what his uncle was when she gave her account of the search for the Golden Chopsticks. He had felt a sense of betrayal then. Now he mainly felt anger . . . and fear.

He had been furious at the news of his son. He refused to believe it. But his wives and uncle brought too much testimony to bear. He was a governor, a magistrate and a judge, and all his years of training eventually weighed upon him and made the evidence undismissible. And the evidence of their own responsibility was clearly implied, though none of them spoke of it openly. What was *not* clear was the remedy.

Wei Pan Ch'ao had been in the world. He had seen the state of affairs, in many places far worse than in the immediate vicinity of Kaifeng. He did not think this was by plan. It smacked of a certain haphazard approach to this reign of vengeance which simultaneously made Wei T'ai-Tsung difficult to predict, but also less than efficient in the achievement of his goals.

"He has made mistakes already," the monk said. "His reported alliance with the Monkey King was hardly an act of good judgement, for the Monkey may turn on him, and the Monkey is as powerful and as unpredictable as the boy."

Try as he could, however, argue as hard as he knew how, Wei K'e-yung was unable to persuade his wife not to accompany the monk on the search for their son.

"It is not *I* who shall accompany *him*," she had said. "*He* will accompany *me*. This search is mine and only I can have any effect, but without my magic I can have little chance. *He* will be my magic. You have duties here. You must do all you can to keep the province in good order despite the assaults our son has hurled upon it. I am of no use in that, and I cannot sit by idly and watch him destroy the world and wait for him to come to destroy me as well."

The arguments raged late into the night, but it eventually became clear to the governor that his wife would not relent, nor could he persuade them that he would be of more use on the hunt than in his office. Their arguments were strong and irrefutable, and eventually he could argue no more.

The next day was spent in preparation for the journey. The household was buzzing with confusion. Pao Shih could not work her small deception of transformation and substitution to hide her absence this time, and the lies were inconsistent and thin. Pao Shih planned to travel by horseback dressed as a man and the clothes and provisions they packed were unmistakable. The housekeeper was outraged, but Wei K'e-yung told her firmly to keep her place or he would have to deal with her harshly and most unpleasantly. The staff was similarly admonished to keep silent. These were strange and dire times and it was not always easy to explain why one did what was necessary.

The household also buzzed about the monk, whom their master called Uncle, but who looked more like a brother.

Unexpectedly, Wei K'e-yung did not return to his office after the noon meal. He sent for Loy Quan Dong and had him rearrange his calendar, and then spent as much time as possible in Pao Shih's company. The danger of their situation—whether she stayed or went with the monk—had not escaped his mind.

That night after dinner they sat alone in the orchard pavilion—the one he had built for her—while he played his lute and sang his poetry for her. Summer was full upon them and the heat was oppresive, but they sat close together, sipping wine and talking, and he shared her bed till morning.

He arose at dawn and went to his office as usual, for he could not bear to bid her farewell. Knowing she would be gone when he returned was pain enough.

As she herself dressed for the journey in a suit of boy's clothing, Yin Whun came to her room. Pao Shih was amazed to see her and then angry, for she too was dressed for the road and in disguise.

"You cannot leave me behind this time," she said. "I have followed you and served you all of my life. What would I do here if you were not to return? I can no longer return to Heaven on my own, even if your son had not turned it on its side, and I have long cherished the thought of that place. I have missed it. How can I stay here? I do not age as you do. Even the servants have begun to notice. I will not grow old and die as he will. What else *is* there for me but to follow you?"

"The monk will never agree to it," Pao Shih said.

"It is not his decision," Yin Whun replied bluntly. "But do not think me too selfless in this, Madam. You know me better than that by now I think. Even my loyalties tend to be somewhat pragmatic. If we succeed in this, perhaps the Jade Emperor will see fit to reward me. I would give anything to be granted the status of a full fairy. But think, too, that ineffectual as I am, in some ways I am still better suited to this task than you or the monk, for I am still a small fairy and in touch with that realm. I can be your eyes and hands still. And with more reason than ever."

Pao Shih could not argue with this, and secretly did not want to. She did not cherish the thought of so much time spent alone in the monk's company. And though necessity had shown her, years ago, that there was a man there worthy of respect, she still could not say she liked him.

But he surprised them both by making no argument, and shortly before the drums sounded the midday watch, the three rode out of the compound gates, each with a pack on their back and two horses in tow.

In the far east, beyond the limits of the ocean waters, beyond the farthest reach of the Great Dragons, at the very rim of the Great Bowl of the World there stands a tall, steep mountain. It rises from the sea, higher than anything upon the land, even the great peaks of the western ranges and no man could possibly scale it. But no man has ever seen it for, like the Land of the Dead and Hibiscus Village where the fairies dwell, it has no direct path or precise location in the mortal world.

At its summit is a great place of red carnelian and amber. The gates are bound with bands of gold, and a wide river of molten lava flows past them. There is no bridge across this smoking, bubbling river, for the house is not entered from the world but by way of Heaven, for this is the domicile of the God of Fire who keeps the lamp from which the Sun God lights the torches of his chariot each morning. It is a fearful journey through the corridors of the Palace of Heaven to reach this gate, and only the greatest lords of the Jade Emperor's realm attempt the trip without qualms.

But the King of the Monkeys is a brazen and fearless scoundrel who has, since the beginning of time, tempted fate most severely, simply for the sake of a good joke. And so the God of Fire had no doubt of what he heard when the chittering laughter rattled down his halls. He was sorely annoyed, for the Monkey was welcome in no one's house, and his courtesy calls were famous for their lack of that attribute.

"Well met, Cousin!" the Monkey cried, giggling and chattering as he swung from the painted beams overhead. His red sash fluttered like a banner, and his staff rattled against the ceiling tiles. "I bring you greeting and I bring you news."

"Be gone from here, Scoundrel," the Firelord bellowed. "You are no kin of mine, nor I of yours!"

"Ah! Cousin-brother-uncle, we are all one family . . . the children of the Most Holy Jade Emperor of Heaven. And so, Grandfather, I bring you a word of warning."

"Fool! Get from my hall. I will have none of your nonsense."

But the Monkey King scampered closer and cocked his red cap as he wrapped his tail about a beam and swung free. Chattering with laughter, he poked at the Fire King's tall hat with his staff and set it askew upon his head.

With an angry oath he reached up and batted the Monkey's staff aside, and at once the thing caught fire all along its length. The Monkey howled and dropped it, petulance in his voice as he complained of the evil treatment.

"I bring you important news and you torture me! I have a mind to leave you to your fate. You would at least have the company of many of your Brothers who have been robbed by that upstart half-fairy."

"Your ally!" the God of Fire raged. "I should fry you even as you hang there."

"Then you would never know where he is," the Monkey chided, scampering back up onto its beam.

"And why should you tell me?" the Fire asked.

"Because he is not a man of honor. I gave him my good friendship and he turned on me, the ingrate. So, being an honorable creature myself, I felt it only polite to return the favor."

This the God of Fire could well believe, for the Monkey King was not noted for his loyalty or the longevity of his alliances, and it was completely within his nature to dissolve them by betrayal.

"What do you know?" the Fire God asked.

"Ah, now you would have me in *your* coatsleeve," chattered the Monkey. "Shall we haggle over it? Barter for it? What will you give me?"

The God of Fire said nothing, but sent a dark and smoldering look the Monkey King's way, and suddenly the beam he clung to began to burn. The Monkey screamed and retreated to a higher perch, scolding and cuddling his scorched tail.

"All right, then," he said peevishly. "For nothing, and I hope you are too late to make use of it. I would look to the Flame of the Sun if I were you. A clever thief could do much damage with that."

"It is well guarded," the Firelord said. But he rose from his seat and stared up at the Monkey.

"Are you certain, Cousin? When did you last check?" Then shrieking with laughter, the Monkey King swung about, leapt across the burning beam and disappeared into the halls of the Palace of Heaven. Immediately the God of Fire called to his men at arms and fled through his palace to the room where the Lamp of the Sun was kept burning.

In the still of the abandoned great hall, a slim, silent figure slipped gracefully as a shadow from behind a pillar and darted quickly past the throne of the Fire God and through a doorway in the far wall. Beyond it, a dark corridor twisted downward into the living rock of the mountain. At last he came to a vast cavern in the mountainside which opened out over the sea. Set into the walls of the cave were great aviaries; iron-barred cages which contained the Fire-crows of the God of Conflagration. The birds were large and shiny black and each burned with a dark fire, like dragon light, which hovered about its body.

In his sash, Wei T'ai-Tsung still carried the Golden Ax of the God of War, but he did not need it. With a touch of his hand, the iron latches crumbled and fell to dust. The doors swung to and the cages stood open. Within moments there was not a bird in sight, but a great, dark cloud, shot through with ominous firelike flickerings, rushed across the water toward the distant shore.

With a wicked chuckle and barely a backward glance, Wei T'ai-Tsung quickly returned the way he had come, before the enraged God of Fire had had time to return from his fruitless journey to the lamp.

The birds flew on, covering great distance with unbelievable speed, and once ashore they spread far and wide, lighting in trees and on rooftops and in the eaves of temples and houses. And everywhere they came to roost fires broke out.

Through the heart of the summer Wei Pan Ch'ao and his two companions traveled across the Great Plain of China, following whatever leads they could find. The poisoning of the wells had followed a somewhat erratic but noticeable pattern at first, but eventually word came to them of dead fish and lizards beginning to appear in Yunnan and Kweichow and it was clear that Wei T'ai-Tsung had acquired yet another pearl. There was no way of telling how many dragons had been trapped in their pools in the regions he had already captured, but it was at least possible that he had committed all the murders he could there, and had turned his attention to the new territory. So the three travelers turned that way also.

They did not expect to find him in residence there, for from the nature of his pranks and the ills they brought to the Earth, it was clear that he slipped in and out of Heaven as he chose. And from Heaven it was possible to return directly to any place on Earth he desired. But if his harassment of the dragons held true, they would have more chance of finding him there than anywhere else.

Yin Whun was of considerable service in locating the pools

and deep river wells of the local dragons, but most were uninhabited, the great saurians having taken heed of the dangers attendant upon such residence. They were not yet in the provinces under the stewardship of the Lung Wang of the Southwest, yet even here Wei Pan Ch'ao discovered an occasional poisoned pool.

"Why?" Yin Whun had asked, baffled and appalled.

"Because he has not yet acquired the pearl for this direction," the monk mused. "Nonetheless, he has exercised some power over it. The dragons must know he has located their homes, and in the winter when those left aloft *must* take refuge beneath the water . . . where will they dare go?"

"Into the sea, most likely," Pao Shih said.

"Where they may all be eliminated at once . . . or controlled perhaps. I do not speculate upon what he has in mind, but if he does not actually have all the pearls by autumn he has left a dilemma for those remaining."

They continued their progress southeastward, and as they went they saw more and more of the results of Wei T'ai-Tsung's handiwork. The Fire-crows in particular had taken a large toll and wherever they passed, Wei Pan Ch'ao advised the people to build cages of iron to have ready. For many of the magical elements of Heaven, including the Great Dragons, iron is an impassable barrier. It is irrefutably of the Earth, with no counterpart or elemental intermediary in Heaven. The dragons cannot abide it. Its presence is painful to the dead and, as with the Fire-crows, it is capable of binding absolutely whatever is surrounded by it. So Wei Pan Ch'ao counseled the peasants and local magistrates to forfeit whatever tools and utensils they could; to melt them down and forge iron bars to trap the crows if they should come; to bait the traps with gold, the purity of which would attract their eye, or with swallows, for like the dragons, the crows could not resist them. Then he instructed them to bind the cages with five-colored silk and bury them beneath the ground till the God of Fire could reclaim what was his.

If all the birds were captured, there would be no forge or hearth fires till the Firelord reclaimed them. The winter would be terrible without fires, but even one Fire-crow loose in the world could be a dangerous thing. The fields and villages they had visited already were proof enough of that.

Yin Whun made occasional furtive forays into the fairy realm, taking great care lest she be caught. But as servants often do, she knew the shortcuts and back ways of that small corner of the Heavenly Realm more thoroughly than most of her betters. She eavesdropped and whispered with the serving maids of the other High Fairies, who were surprised to see her and whom no one would ever think to question, considering them too stupid and insignificant to know anything. But again, as is the way of servants, they knew everything that went on in Hibiscus Village and even some news of the concerns of the higher immortals.

He had been here . . . he had been there. No one knew precisely what he wanted. And no one knew precisely what he could do. He had been clever and cunning in his apprenticeships, an eager student, learning much but revealing so little that the true nature and extent of his powers were not known even to the Jade Emperor. There was anger in Heaven, but there was also fear, for the youth had already demonstrated he was more powerful than any would have suspected possible for a fairy. He moved about quickly and easily and even the Lady of the Moon had not been safe from him.

With as much care and subtlety as she could, Yin Whun tried to relieve a little of the misery of the sick and injured and those women whom the dark of the moon had left arrested in their pregnancies, unable to give birth. But there was little she could do to relieve Pao Shih's suffering in the summer heat. The masculine clothing was uncomfortable to her and the horses they rode steamed and sweated, making her condition even less bearable, but she did not once complain.

Wei Pan Ch'ao was put heavily in mind of their last sojourn together; on foot, walking into the winter mountains of the north and his own non-stop complaints, far from groundless but embarrassing in retrospect. This journey was in many ways far easier. They had mounts and provisions and enough money for any contingency, and it had been a very long time since the prospect of brigands had bothered him. What did bother him, and Yin Whun too when they occasionally had the privacy to speak of it, was their concern that Pao Shih had thoroughly unrealistic expectations.

The monk had few illusions that the mind capable of conceiving the vengeance being practiced upon Heaven would be amenable to reason, or that the spirit would welcome the return of a mother's love; especially a love that had not progressed past what a twelve-year-old would understand and was hopelessly mired in guilt.

"What if he must be destroyed?" Wei Pan Ch'ao asked.

"I cannot say, though I doubt she would accept it. She has said she will do whatever is necessary, but I know her heart and I do not think she allows that idea to be a part of necessity. Still in all, what does it matter? How could *we* accomplish what Heaven cannot?"

"I am not without some skill," the monk said casually. "But do not discount what Heaven could do to him if it caught him. That kind of thinking is what serves him best. Heaven has only failed to destroy him because it cannot *catch him*. In this regard I believe we have an advantage. He may yet come to *us*. I have taken pains to leave a clear enough trail if he should care to look."

Yin Whun was caustic in her reply. "And my lady is the bait?"

"As are we all," he said.

By the end of the Seventh Month they were well into the low mountain ranges of the province of Yunnan, where the Yangtze River made its most southern dip before heading northward again into the Szechwan basin. They had passed numerous farms and villages abandoned in the hopes of refuge in the south and east, for things were very bad here, and the poor peasants and merchants of the district had no notion of how dire things were elsewhere. The Fire-crows had not yet arrived here, but that would merely be one more misery heaped on the others.

Pao Shih and her companions discovered many poisoned pools, and poor Yin Whun could barely approach them, for here there were murdered dragons aplenty. With her fairy senses she could not help but see what lay at the bottom of the wells and ponds, and she was upset and bitterly angered.

Pao Shih felt pity for the great creatures and remorse for what her son had done, but she had been human too long. Her anger and sorrow were of another sort.

One evening they took their rest in a village of greater than usual size. It had a wall and three gates, though none that could be barred at night, and it verged on being a small city. In the spring, before things had begun to come apart around them, the magistrate had begun the construction of a drum tower near the market square and the town boasted several respectable inns. But the farmlands still snuggled close about its walls and there was even some cultivation within them.

It had regularly been their practice to enquire after a young man of Wei K'e-yung's description wherever they went, and from time to time they had found traces of him. The people of this locale had seen someone similar quite recently within the month, and one particular innkeeper believed he had lodged with him, so they chose to stay there for the night also, hoping to discover someone in the wineshop downstairs who could be of more help. They took a room on the second floor which was humble and only just adequate to their needs, but had the advantage of being quite private, for it was isolated from the other rooms by the stairwell and looked out over the street.

As they sat at their evening meal and discussed the next day's possibilities, however, Pao Shih and the monk became gradually aware of a certain distraction in Yin Whun. Pao Shih recognized the posture; that look of one listening to something far off.

"What is it?" she asked quietly, but Yin Whun did not respond at once.

"Something . . . is close at hand," she murmured at last.

"What?" Wei Pan Ch'ao asked, suddenly alert.

"Nothing. . . . It is a thing that is . . . searching. . . . Something will happen."

But even before she finished speaking the dogs began to bark and the sound of screaming horses rose from the stableyard.

By midday there was not a dog left alive in the town. They lay heaped in great piles outside the town wall. The ghostly flutterings of white banners marked the houses of those in mourning. But it was not only the dogs. What man had assumed from time past memory to be the natural order of things had suddenly turned deadly. There was not a domestic beast in all the town, or anywhere in the surrounding territory, that had not turned wild. The dogs, however, had been the

worst, suddenly turning feral and attacking the sheep and goats
they herded and the masters at whose feet they slept. Small
children had been killed as they tried to quiet a creature they
had never had reason to fear, and grown men and women were
dragged down by the animals as they began to run in hunting
packs. The oxen and the horses seemed to grow calm again
when the dogs had been dealt with but it was a false hope, for
they remained so only as long as they were not approached by
men, and the beasts in the innkeeper's stable had to be
blindfolded and snubbed to the fenceposts to keep them under
control.

Throughout the day the monk and the two women remained
in their room while the chaos was calmed and in the evening
they went down to the yard to see to their horses. The animals
were utterly intractable and when Yin Whun placed her hand
on one in an attempt to work her calming magic, she drew it
back suddenly with a gasp, as though burned.

"What is it, Little One?" Pao Shih whispered.

"There is nothing there I can reach," she said. "Only evil.
The demons are free in these creatures."

Late that night while the monk visited the stableyard, Yin
Whun slipped into the fairy realm once more. Pao Shih
warmed wine and waited but it was not for long.

"There is no change," Wei Pan Ch'ao said, returning to the
room only moments before Yin Whun did.

"Nor will there be," she said, accepting wine and seating
herself at Pao Shih's feet. "For Wei T'ai-Tsung has committed
yet another murder. He has killed the Hawk and the Hound of
Yang Oerlang, and though mankind is still under his protec-
tion, the birds and beasts are open to possession by demons. It
was what I felt in the room last night. Demonkind passed
through here looking for whatever it might find unprotected."

"And so we are here, far from home and afoot. So be it. We
will leave here tomorrow I think. We must plan how to travel
light, for a cart will not do in these mountains."

"Where will we go?" Yin Whun asked. "He has been in
Heaven again. Is he likely to come here so soon?"

"We will follow the river for a time, north toward
Szechwan. If winter finds us before he does, I would prefer to
spend it in the Red Basin than here in these mountains. And
without horses our mobility has become severely hampered."

In the morning they sorted their belongings and bartered what they were leaving behind with the innkeeper for their lodgings to help conserve their money. Then, about midday, they set out northward following the twisting, turning, often difficult course of the Yangtze River.

Wei K'e-yung did his best not to worry. It was difficult and he was largely unsuccessful, but he did succeed in showing it very little. As there was no acceptable explanation for his wives' departure in that fashion, nor for their having left the three girls behind, he simply forbade anyone to discuss or even mention it. In the main that kept the household quiet, but his clerks and secretaries were another matter, and he wondered how long it would be before an enquiry was made by the bureaucracy in Peking. Quite a while he imagined, for they no doubt had their hands full with significantly more important matters just now, and as long as he ran his public affairs as efficiently as he always had any irregularities in his private life could wait.

In spite of the possibility of censure, however, his superiors did see fit to answer his request for more staff by sending three young men. Their experience was not great, but any help with the tangled mess of administration that had emerged from that bizarre summer was more than welcome. One of the young men was the nephew of a high court official with whom Wei K'e-yung was vaguely acquainted and in whose good graces he would not mind resting. One other was the son of the Provincial Governor of Yunnan, a man known to Wei K'e-yung only by his reputation and some recently-published examples of his scholarship, regarding which Wei K'e-yung could merely be polite. The third was a youth who reminded Wei K'e-yung strongly of himself at an earlier age; of small means but great ambition and considerable talent. Out of courtesy for his colleague and respect for the possible court connection, and because his house had been too empty of congenial company of late, Wei K'e-yung invited the three young men to his home for the evening meal. Loy Quan Dong did not approve and said so, but the governor sent a page to his kitchen to tell them to make ready and invited Loy along also. The secretary accepted and, thus appeased, Wei K'e-yung had no further worry of bad report.

The evening was pleasant enough and the men spent much of their time examining Wei K'e-yung's collection of antique calligraphy and his wine. But he did not feel all that much better for the company. Still, the hour grew quite late before he felt compelled to send his guests home. The servants had retired except for two kitchen maids, so he accompanied his guests to the street to procure litters to take them home, since there was not a horse or ox in the city anymore.

At the gate the young man who was nephew to the Imperial Counsellor begged Wei K'e-yung's indulgence on a private matter which he needed to discuss. As he had not mentioned this earlier and it was already late, Wei k'e-yung put him off more politely than he felt, but agreed to give him some time in the morning in the privacy of his office.

The youth seemed satisfied and when his litter came, bade the Governor good night.

"Come inside with me a moment," Wei K'e-yung said to the secretary when the young men had gone. "I have had an odd feeling all evening and I cannot quite account for it."

"In what way odd, My Lord?" Loy Quan Dong asked.

"Something about them disturbs me vaguely, but I cannot say precisely what or which one. Have you examined their papers?"

"Of course, Sir."

"Of course," Wei K'e-yung smiled, turning back into the park. They walked in silence to the private compound and Wei K'e-yung bade the gatekeeper bar the gate and retire. The house was quiet and there was no one about to prepare tea or warm the wine, so they took what was cold from the table and went to his study to talk.

"What disturbs you, Lord?" Loy Quan Dong enquired, seating himself at Wei K'e-yung's invitation. "For myself I found them as shallow and overaffected as most young men in their position."

"Yes, yes, of course. I truly cannot put my finger on it." He sat at his desk and fiddled with the gong mallet thoughtfully. "That fellow, Zao . . ."

"Zao Feng Min," Loy said. "From Peking."

"And an uncle at court . . ." he mused. "Why do you suppose he could not get a better post than this?"

"Times are hard. Any post would be difficult just now."

"Precisely. He has wealth, family position, and not a great burning ambition as far as our conversation tonight indicated. Why take a post at all just now?"

"Perhaps, My Lord, his uncle is out of sorts with him."

Wei K'e-yung smiled. "Yes, perhaps so. I am being foolish no doubt, but the feeling was so strong."

"Feeling?"

Wei K'e-yung thumped the mallet on the desk and made a wide gesture of dismay. "I don't know . . . disquiet."

"Will you see him tomorrow?"

"No doubt. I hardly think I can avoid it. And I do wonder what he wants. Ah! This is foolish!"

"Sir?"

"They have gone their way and I am still feeling off."

"Then perhaps it is time . . ."

"No, my friend, at least help me finish the wine. And if it grows late enough, stay the night. I have robes you can have for the morning."

"Very well," Loy Quan Dong said, settling back with a cordial smile. A rare thing for him. "Perhaps a change of subject will improve your spirits, Sir."

"Whatever strikes your fancy," Wei K'e-yung said, tracing the pattern in the clay of the winepot with his mallet handle.

"I trust your wives are well?"

Wei K'e-yung glared at him, but thought better of it. It was only the wine and his largess prompting that indiscretion.

"No doubt," Wei K'e-yung said noncommittally.

"Ah, I am glad to hear it. They have long appeared to be such fine and admirable ladies, I would hate to think anything amiss."

Wei K'e-yung frowned. "*Appeared* to be? What do you say?"

"Only that outward appearances can sometimes be deceiving. That a person can seem well when indeed he is not so. That someone, like the youth from Peking, can appear to be wealthy and advantaged when in fact he may be in disgrace with his family." He paused and looked Wei K'e-yung squarely in the eye. "That one can appear to be human . . . and in reality be something entirely other."

Wei K'e-yung clutched the mallet handle so tightly his knuckles went white.

"How dare you . . ."

"With considerable ease, *My Lord*," Loy said sarcastically. "A fairy wife would be an advantage to any man . . . as long as no one were to know. But two!"

"What do you want?" Wei K'e-yung said in a very quiet, very deadly voice.

"A favor. A small boon such as a fairy might grant. A word or two only." Loy Quan Dong's manner had become smooth and ingratiating in a most threatening way. "I grant you it is late, but if you would wake them so that we may speak *now* it would likely save you considerable embarrassment later."

Wei K'e-yung's eyes were like thunderstorms and his frown deepened. "They are not here. You know . . ."

Of course he knew. Wei K'e-yung stopped suddenly in mid-sentence. The disturbing feeling had not left him with the departure of the young men, but he had thought that was simply because it was on his mind. Now he knew it was because it had been Loy who had disturbed him all along. He suddenly surged from his chair, the mallet poised to strike. "*What is this?*" he bellowed.

But Loy Quan Dong was on his own feet in an instant and grabbed Wei K'e-yung's wrist. He was unbelievably strong and, try as he might, Wei K'e-yung could not prevent the mallet from being torn from his grip. For a moment the two men wrestled each other across the desk. Then to his astonishment Wei K'e-yung felt himself lifted off his feet with as little effort as he would have needed to heft a puppy. He tumbled across the desk and landed on his knees on the floor before Loy Quan Dong, whose right hand was now on his throat. He began to feel dizzy . . . unbelievably dizzy. The room began to sparkle and shift. It seemed deeper and broader. The shadows were black as onyx and the lamplight flared and shot showers of golden sparks into the shimmering air, but it was the man standing before him who was the most amazing sight. He was tall and beautiful, in that strange perfect way that Yin Whun was beautiful, while somehow being less so than Pao Shih in her mortal state. It was the magic. The beguile-ment. He wore that strange glow that Pao Shih and Yin Whun had called an aura, the mantle of the immortal and of the magic. Yet Wei K'e-yung knew the youth's beauty was as real as Pao Shih's, even without the fairy-fire.

"Most Honorable Father," the youth said with a courtly bow and his most gracious smile, never loosening his grip on Wei K'e-yung's throat. "I humbly beg your forgiveness for not performing a proper obeisance, but I think we both agree that would be foolish of me."

Wei K'e-yung could just breathe but the stranglehold was too tight to allow him to talk. He tried to remain calm, but he knew this would not turn out well no matter what he did. His son's touch, however, had a somewhat paralyzing effect and he found resistance impossible as Wei T'ai-Tsung lifted him to his feet and guided him backward into the chair in which the image of Loy Quan Dong had lately sat.

"Be comfortable, Father," he said. "I would have a word with you." Then he released the choke-hold on Wei K'e-yung's throat but remained bent forward over the chair, his hands on the arms, preventing any hope of escape.

Wei K'e-yung cleared his bruised throat but kept his hands in his lap. He stared up at his son with a dark look of resolute defiance and said nothing.

"So you say they are not here. It would be easy enough for me to inspect the house, splinter by splinter . . . but I believe you. I think they are *not* here. The question remains, then. Where *are* they?"

Wei K'e-yung cleared his throat again. "Is he dead?" he said hoarsely.

"Who? Your secretary? Of course. It was the simplest way to keep him from being inconvenient. Now, Most Honorable Father, if you would kindly answer my one simple question. . . . Where have you hidden them?"

But Wei K'e-yung would say nothing. Though eloquently polite at first, his son's patience was limited and soon he began to rave, though he never raised his voice loud enough to be heard by the household. Wei K'e-yung thought to call out, but he dreaded what would happen if anyone heard him and came to his aid.

Wei T'ai-Tsung raged at him, heaping upon his father all the bitterness of his years in Heaven, how cruelly they had abandoned him, the scorn he had suffered in his servitude because of his half-mortal heritage, and his vows of revenge.

Slowly Wei K'e-yung became numb to the abuse and even the guilt. The youth interspersed his vitriolic ravings with gleeful accounts of his "small vengeances" upon Heaven, but always he returned to the question.

"You are everything the fairies said of you," Wei K'e-yung said bitterly. "I am ashamed to have sired you."

Wei T'ai-Tsung struck him then and the force of the blow hurled the chair against the desk. It struck, and the back shattered, dumping a dazed and bleeding Wei-K'e-yung onto the floor.

"You *should* be ashamed! But of worse things than that!" Wei T'ai-Tsung cried. He hauled his father to his feet but the man could no longer stand on his own. Something had been broken. "You will tell me what I want to know. You will, Father. I promise you."

But he did not. Eventually Wei T'ai-Tsung realized there was no more use in asking. He left the body on the study floor and went out through the open doors into the garden. Beyond the low wall were the women's quarters and, in spite of the fact that he knew they were not there, Wei T'ai-Tsung was drawn to them.

He sat in the little garden, contemplating for a long time the stone Yin Whun had brought back from the riverbank, until the first birds began to twitter and the dawn glowed faintly beyond the wall. Then he got up and walked away. But at the moon gate he stopped and turned back, uttering a single quiet word.

At once a young hound appeared where the stone had been. It hurtled forward in mid-leap, tongue lolling, eyes bright and gleeful. It pounced and bounded, barking frantically and then gathered itself and galloped full tilt across the garden. As it swung to nip at him in passing Wei T'ai-Tsung reached out and grabbed it. With a single quick move he broke the dog's neck and left it lying in the gateway.

As the glow of dawn rose in the east so another, eerier glow rose also, but this one from the south, as the crows of the Firelord entered the city of Kaifeng.

It was the trees who had seen and heard.

Thus it was the Sisters of the Trees and the Herbs who came

together to break the news to Pao Shih that her beloved Wei K'e-yung was dead. The garden door and windows had been open and all that had passed had been witnessed, but the tree spirits were powerless and by the time they had alerted the fairies it was too late. The God of Fire had reclaimed some of his flock before too much damage had been done and the dragons made a rare concession and granted rain. The agents of the Jade Emperor had arrived before the sun had cleared the horizon but the culprit was not to be found. The fairies were commended for their vigilance, but not a word was said of Pao Shih or the reason the villain had visited this place and done this deed.

They had camped on the riverbank that night, being a distance from even a small village. Her Sisters chose to visit her in a dream, that being the safest and gentlest way they could approach her. Heaven had not given them leave to speak to her but they could not let this pass, so they once more risked the Jade Emperor's wrath for their Sister's sake. The Fairy of One Hundred Birds and the Fairy of One Hundred Fruits spoke to Yin Whun and the monk as well, so that when Pao Shih awoke she would not have to bear the pain of relating the event, and there would be no doubt as to the truth of her vision.

There was nothing to be done, so the monk left the grieving women at their campsite and walked along the river for a while to compose himself and contemplate their failure. Toward dusk he returned to find Yin Whun asleep beneath a tree and Pao Shih sitting on the riverbank in a daze. He picked up the wineskin from their packs and went to sit beside her, but she did not want any.

"Yin Whun would soothe me better than that, but the poor thing has nothing left. She is nearly as drained as I am at this . . . news."

Wei Pan Ch'ao said nothing and took a drink himself.

"Why am I still here?" Pao Shih said suddenly.

"Pardon?"

"My husband is dead and yet I have not been reclaimed by Heaven. I could die now, do you realize that? Just as any mortal. I was denied that while he lived, and upon his death I was to be taken back. Yet here I am. It is curious, that is all."

"Heaven quite likely has more on its mind just now than reinstating you. The Fairy of the Trees said they did not seem to recognize the significance of the murder. I suspect the Jade Emperor was relying on the Judges of the Court of the Dead to act upon that item of the sentence, but the Land of the Dead is in chaos. If the books have not been kept and your husband's name has not been recorded it is likely this error has not yet been noticed."

Pao Shih began to weep, small, bitter sobs, hugging herself as she rocked back and forth. "Ah, poor darling. What will become of him? His spirit is doomed to wander free; they will not even know to look for him when they gather the others up. His soul has no home, no wealth in the afterworld, there will be no shrine to his memory, no offerings for his soul, no prayers will ever reach him to comfort him. Ah, K'e-yung-ah . . . what has he done to you?" She moaned and fell onto the grass. "This is *worse* than death."

The dusk had turned to night and Wei Pan Ch'ao lit a fire and ate alone, for neither of the women cared for anything and Pao Shih was soon asleep again, though Yin Whun was awake. She was despondent but reasoning more clearly than Pao Shih, and she and the monk sat by the fire and drank the wine.

"She is right," Yin Whun said. "It is curious. But it is also possible the Jade Emperor does not know where she is."

"The fairies found us easily enough."

Yin Whun smiled a brief, sad smile. "Surely you must know that her Sisters have watched over her constantly from the very moment she was expelled from Hibiscus Village. Not a step has she taken nor an event passed in her life that one or more of them has not known of. They can do nothing for her but small comforts. Though she suffers in the summer the insects do not aggravate her. The Tiger of the Winter Wind may howl in the streets of Kaifeng, but not in her garden. There was never a plant that did not flourish for her. Such things are of little real use and they are much grieved that the one thing their vigilance could not prevent has come to pass, but they have never left her.

"Their spies are everywhere. It is how they found you when she needed it. But the Jade Emperor does not appreciate what the fairies are truly worth. He does not even suspect it and I doubt it would occur to him that such lowly beings might deceive him, for I am sure they have lied to him for her sake. In many ways the High Gods are fools. They think power and might are worth more than cleverness and efficiency. That is why Wei T'ai-Tsung is running them ragged. He has his father's intellect. The Court of Heaven has grown slow-witted with time."

In the morning Pao Shih awoke with a grim determination and a fierce desire to bring her son down in any way possible. Wei Pan Ch'ao was no longer concerned about her failure of heart, but her rage was consuming and it was fueled by the frustration of her all too human condition. In an increasingly rare moment of calm and rational thought, Wei Pan Ch'ao at last took out his inks and brushes and convinced her to help him draft a petition to the Jade Emperor to reinstate her power so she could help locate her son.

"It is risky, I know. If they have forgotten you we will give ourselves away by this. But I see no other choice."

"I will carry it for you," Yin Whun said. "Leave this place and do not tell me what road you will take." She pulled the monk's map from his pack and indicated a town. "I will return here and journey north along this road. Come to me when you are ready. They can pull nothing from my mind if I do not know where you will choose to overtake me."

"It is too dangerous," Pao Shih protested. "I have lost one whom I love . . . no, I have lost two. I would not lose you also."

"He cannot refuse this," Yin Whun said. "Heaven may have grown dull-witted, but it is not altogether *stupid*. You are the best chance there is to locate him. He hates you as much as you hate him."

The Jade Emperor was not impressed. In fact he was inclined to blame Ku-She and the monk nearly as much as he blamed Wei T'ai-Tsung himself. The taoist reprobate was responsible for the theft that had taken her into the mortal world, where she had fallen to temptation and brought forth the monster who was now wrecking both Heaven and Earth. And her stewardship of the child had proved disastrous. The Court of Heaven took no blame itself, of course, for Wei T'ai-Tsung's present attitude, and bitterly resented the implication, though

Yin Whun had tried to couch it in the subtlest terms, that it had any responsibility at all.

Yin Whun replied to all their questions honestly and with unusually bold forthrightness, but the Jade Emperor was greatly displeased and had her imprisoned, to be questioned under torture if necessary until she told them what they wanted to know.

The Eighth Month was waning and there was no sign of Yin Whun. Pao Shih had taken quarters near the small city of Leipo in the foothills overlooking the southern curve of the Szechwan Basin; a day-and-a-half by foot north of the spot to which Yin Whun had intended to return. They rented a little hut from a farmer who had housed his mother-in-law till she died. It had the multiple advantages of being cheap, available and within convenient sight of the road. The first few days they had lodged in the city itself and had taken turns loitering about the city gate, watching the road, but when it became clear she had somehow been detained, the hut became more practical and private. Almost at once she had shed the men's attire for the garb of a peasant woman and felt better for it.

Pao Shih's mood was erratic. It cycled from angry to guilty, desperate to determined, despairing to vengeful to worried to calculating and merciless. She often cried quietly to herself at night, which Wei Pan Ch'ao tactfully pretended not to have discovered. He, in his own way, brooded over the murder too. It struck at his mortality. Not just that his nephew was dead. He had lost track of the generations which had passed between his own son and this relationship to Wei K'e-yung. They all grew old and eventually died. But his line had narrowed too. Wei K'e-yung was the last of his male heirs. There were Liu Ch'ing's two sons—there had been a third, he recalled, a year younger then Wei T'ai-Tsung who had died at the age of eight—but these were of the woman's line; they belonged to another name, and they would likely inherit whatever Wei K'e-yung had left. Only the direct masculine lineage was venerated at the ancestral table. . . . Still in all . . . he decided it would not be an altogether bad thing to acquaint himself with Liu Ch'ing's sons.

He chuckled at the irony of what his own male line had come to. Directly or indirectly, he had been responsible for Wei T'ai-Tsung's existence and his immortality. Wei Pan Ch'ao himself was in an odd semi-immortal state. He had lived longer than any man he knew of, and would quite likely continue so as long as no extraordinary circumstances occurred. But unlike a true immortal of Heaven, it was possible for him to be killed. Only the Jade Emperor himself could pass a death sentence upon a fairy or a god and his agents and weapons were very specific. It amused him and sobered him at the same time to see that the serpent had come full circle and taken its tail in its mouth. His line had at last produced a *true* immortal with a magic quite likely the equal of his own, and it seemed likely this nephew would be the instrument of Wei Pan Ch'ao's artfully-postponed end.

Though it was the last admission he would ever make in his companion's presence, Wei Pan Ch'ao was worried. And more than a little afraid for his life.

The foxes scattered like autumn leaves, russet and red gold, through the halls and corridors of the Palace of Heaven, barking and laughing their high, cackling laugh. It was an evil sound, but even more so was the constant screech and howling of the monkeys, who now also ran madly through those same chambers, tugging at ornamental hangings, breaking crockery and attacking whatever moved. The monkeys were more destructive than the foxes, but the foxes were more feared, even in Heaven, for they were the bearers of evil omens; the harbingers of doom. The monkeys at least could be explained without much thought. Wei T'ai-Tsung had turned on the Monkey King when his humor had soured and he had no more use for him as a tool of harassment. He had tricked the Monkeylord and imprisoned him in an iron cage, which he suspended from a tree in the Western Mountains. The cage was so small the Monkey could not move about, and his tail hung down outside the bars where Wei T'ai-Tsung had set foxes to worry and nip at him. Swarms of angry monkeys and baboons had overrun the temples and forest towns, killing children and the sick and aged who could not flee them, and even invading the halls of the Palace of Heaven. The monkeys had been easily driven off, but the foxes were another matter. Everyone knew full well it was Wei T'ai-Tsung who had set them in there. His message was clear and, try as they might, the pages and clerks could not rid the palace of the vermin.

The usual placid, almost rigid order of Heaven was in complete chaos. Every vassal to every deity under the Jade Emperor's rule was on guard or actively in search of Wei T'ai-Tsung. Even the Jade Emperor had seen fit to change the accustomed ritual of his existence so as to remove himself from certain jeopardy. And the matter of the fairies, which normally would have been so small a thing as to barely attract his notice, was vexing in the extreme. At any other time he would have looked upon this as merely a petty annoyance, but this open stubborn resistance to his authority in the midst of such a crisis verged on treason. When affairs had been settled the fairy realm would have an accounting to do, and Madam Chou might well find herself with a severely revised roster, for he strongly suspected every fairy and elemental in Hibiscus Village of complicity in this.

With these omens so present even in the halls of the palace itself the Emperor of Heaven took an entourage of the best warriors history had produced and his closest advisors, and began an inspection of his realm. He no longer trusted the reports to be accurate, for the fairies were possibly conspiring and the Monkey King was openly allied with the renegade and the demon spirits aided whatever was in their interests to aid, and Wei T'ai-Tsung's actions had been a pleasure to them. There was an urgent need to know the true state of affairs in Heaven and it no longer pleased the emperor to be the jewel in the ring.

But his absence from the throne did not lessen Yin Whun's suffering and daily, by the measure of Earth, the questions were put to her and she answered truthfully as always.

"I have been gone so long now . . ." she gasped at last, "that they will surely have taken me for dead, or as I am, and will have gone on in search of him without me. They are lost beyond finding by now. . . ."

The logic of this struck her jailers as reasonable, but the Jade Emperor was not there to give them leave to stop what he had ordered and so, reluctantly, and sometimes gently, they continued to examine her.

Yin Whun lost track of time. It was easy enough to do in the palace but her service to the seasonal fairies had given her a keen sense of the movements of the Earth and it disturbed her that she no longer knew these things. Had it been so long? Or had it only felt so in her torment? She wished fervently for an end to the tortures she could well imagine might be eternal if the emperor so pleased, but when it came she did not recognize it at first and when she did the nature of it horrified her.

For the whole universe seemed to come apart around her; suddenly but with a fascinating, dreamlike slowness which made awareness of it unavoidable. She had never imagined it was possible. The ever-shifting layers of magic, which were reality in this place, seemed to tear like gauze curtains, the dark, evil layers of things seeping through, killing the glow and dazzle. The floor beneath her heaved and buckled, then shattered like ice. The dark places had become substantial and now they began to crumble slowly leaving a grey void.

"Come!"

She thought she heard a voice . . . like her mistress's . . . familiar . . . but not Pao Shih.

"Come!" it hissed again. "Quickly!"

All was silence, but the commotion of the destruction struck the ear, or the mind, like a crashing and a great roar. She could not be certain there were truly voices in there, and everywhere she looked was chaos. Nonetheless, weak though she was and in pain, she tried to stand and search out the voice.

As she stumbled across the shattered-porcelain floor she felt herself supported and through the shifting haze of dissolving magic she saw her mistress indeed, but it was Tung Shuang-Ch'eng. Behind her, beside her, on Yin Whun's other side she thought she saw the Fairies of One Hundred Herbs and One Hundred Grains and the Lady of the Silkworms.

"Come," Tung Shuang-Ch'eng said. "We must get you to a safer place. The village is as yet sound and we may hide you there."

"Please, no," Yin Whun begged. "I must go to my lady. She must know what has happened here."

"She knows even as you do, for the Earth is nearly as badly damaged as Heaven by this catastrophe."

"Then I must go to her certainly, for that mongrel of a monk will be of no help to her, and you would only jeopardize yourselves by taking me in. She may need you yet, but if I am found there none of you will be free to assist her."

"Very well," Lady Tung said. "Can you manage?"

"She is weak," said the Fairy of the Herbs. She called up the spirits of the healing plants and laid a hand on Yin Whun's brow as Yin Whun had often done for Pao Shih or her husband. "Things are too unstable here. I cannot do more than strengthen you. It will require a little time for you to heal, but you do not have that so you must manage as best you can."

Yin Whun thanked her, for she felt much stronger. Well enough that all her pains were clear and sharp now, but she ran through the shattered, crumbling, fading and shifting palace as fast as she could, following the Fairy of One Hundred Birds, who flew ahead as a swallow. In the throne room the tiles of the floor were tossed about like game pieces dumped carelessly from a bag. The throne itself lay broken upon a grey and brooding storm cloud, and a dark mist was rising from the cracks in the floor. The Golden Dragon had no doubt accompanied the emperor but Yin Whun was brought up short by what else was missing.

The Fairy of the Birds circled her head impatiently. "He has used the Golden Ax to chop down the Willow," she said. "See, the stump is still rooted in the clouds but the Willow itself has fallen to Earth."

"And that has done all this?" Yin Whun gasped.

"It struck the great Western Mountains when it fell and the quake that ran through the Earth has cracked and dislodged the pillars holding up the four corners of the sky. Since these pillars also support Heaven we are in grave danger of collapse."

"Can the damage be repaired?"

The monk looked dubious. "Your Sister of the Birds said so, but if they are spending all their efforts on your son, Madam, one wonders when they will have the chance."

"Of, course," she said. "That is precisely what he wants. They cannot ignore this. The palace and the Four Pillars of the World are too weak to be left as they are. The emperor must choose—to repair the damage or hunt him. It is likely they can do neither efficiently now. They are vulnerable on all sides."

"As are we," Wei Pan Ch'ao said, rising from the devastated trunk of a giant tree. "In the dream your Sister of the Birds said the Jade Emperor is suspicious of everyone, not least of all the fairies now, and may find a way to force them to locate us, though he does not seem to have thought of this yet."

"Pray my son's latest atrocity keeps him too badly occupied to think of it at all," she said following him toward what the day before had been a road. Then they had been going north, into the Red Basin. Now they were heading southward again, for the fairy who had visited Wei Pan Ch'ao in a dream while Pao Shih lay awake in her anger, had told of Yin Whun's plight and her escape and where the fairies had been able to leave her with so much chaos above and below to hamper their efforts.

Chou Ch'ung-i was grateful for even the smallest glimmer of reason in the Master of Heaven and Earth just now. His rage was immense and filled the skies like the worst storms of the typhoon. In light of the magnitude of this latest disaster she had pleaded the usefulness of having the discredited fairy as an ally—that there was no time for revenge, no matter how deserved, when she might serve her emperor well and truly as she always had before her disgrace. As for punishment, the necessity of destroying her own son should satisfy that requirement satisfactorily, and she had already suffered the loss of her beloved husband at her child's hands. She would more than gladly kill him herself if she had the means. But she needed her fairy powers back to be of any *real use* to them.

"Please forgive her," the fairy pleaded. "Or if you can not forgive her, at least grant her the means to *earn* your forgiveness."

Crisis is sometimes a superior condition. In the case of the Jade Emperor this was turning out to be true. For many eons the universe had run peacefully, the only difficulties being matters of the administration of the Earth and the doings of man. And while these difficulties were more or less grave by the lights of humankind, in Heaven they were but bureaucratic nuisances, to be resolved in one way or another, more or less efficiently. It had been a long time since Heaven and its emperor's strength and wisdom had been tested. And as with many things in a system which is too peaceful for too long a time, Heaven and the Jade Emperor had become unaccustomed to actual *rule*.

As things became more dire, the Jade Emperor began to awaken as from a lazy man's slumber; one which passed the time rather than strengthening the body, and he had begun to shed the pettiness which had, for a long time, been increasingly characteristic of him. Madam Chou was a faithful and reasonable advisor and he accepted the petition without further discussion, calling for his writing box. He was not particularly surprised to learn that Yin Whun had escaped in the chaos of the attack on the palace. But it would now be necessary to find the fairy and the monk and deliver the message.

In the Jade Emperor's retinue was the Seventh Son of the Dragon King of the South. His father's territories were as yet unaffected by Wei T'ai-Tsung's systematic collection of the Great Pearls and he was completely unhindered in all the ways of the dragons. He was also enraged by the murders of the vassals of the Dragon Kings robbed of their pearls, and he vowed to do whatever was possible to punish the culprit. The dragons had long been charged with a free reign over his destruction, being one of the Jade Emperor's principal tools for such tasks. But finding him had been another matter.

The Jade Emperor was also not entirely surprised when Chou Ch'ung-i admitted in a most roundabout and vague fashion that she just might possibly have some inkling of the general locale where Yin Whun was likely to have returned to Earth . . . but he was inclined to ignore the implications of that and sent the dragon off with the Lady of Hibiscus Village to pursue her "intuitions."

This land was not the land they had walked through two days before, though they followed the same road, where they could still find it, back in the direction they had come. The memory of earthquakes still rumbled in the bones and the meadows of the foothills looked like great heaps of rice paper that had been torn and crumpled and carelessly discarded.

When the Willow struck the Earth, smashing to pieces against the Western Mountains, which in turn had split with the force of the blow, the jade leaves had scattered in all directions, felling trees, leveling great patches of forest for many li. And from the sundered mountains the earthquakes had run, wave after wave. Cities and cottages fell with equal ease, rivers vanished or changed course, farmlands turned inside out and cliff-faced plateaus rose where there had been level plains. What trees the Willow did not claim had then to survive the earthquakes. The saplings had more success than the mighty warriors of a hundred years and a thousand storms. Terrified, the people and the animals rode the heaving land like sailors caught in mid-ocean when a typhoon descends too quickly.

And when all was still beneath them again, the quiet was sickening. Nothing moved. Nothing breathed. Nothing spoke. The moans and sobbing started long before the barking of the now-wild dogs or the curses of men. It was a full day before the birds began to call again among the branches of the fallen trees, and the people moved about in a daze.

Pao Shih and Wei Pan Ch'ao picked their way carefully over mounds of earth and huge shafts of upthrust rocks, skirting chasms that had not been an obstacle on their northward journey, but always trying to locate the remaining vestiges of the shattered road, for it was their only clue now to locating Yin Whun. Nearly all the other landmarks were drastically altered.

Near midday, having located a long and relatively unchanged stretch of road, they stopped beside a little brook which had not been there before. They took their rest in the shade of a copse of trees which were still standing, though listing strongly to the downhill side, and filled their waterskins. The brook was clear and cold, the water sweet, and Pao Shih in her sorrow and rage found a small, sad satisfaction in the knowledge that the land would repair itself eventually no matter what devastation was visited upon it. The brook had been born of a nightmare, but it was pure and beautiful and need not be ashamed of anything.

As they shared dried fruit and water, Pao Shih saw a man approaching from the south. It was the first person they had seen since the holocaust and there was something curious about him. Then it struck her. His bearing was tall and straight. He walked with a brisk, purposeful stride and he was alert, seemingly unaffected by the surroundings. But for some reason Pao Shih found it difficult to see his features clearly. She quietly spoke a word to the monk who was on his feet at once, quick and wary as a cat.

"What . . ."

"He wears the aura of magic," Wei Pan Ch'ao said. "Move quickly."

"He has seen us," Pao Shih said. "I am sure of it. Should we flee so openly?"

"I do not know what he is, but I do not think it can be good."

Pao Shih rose as casually as she could and turned to follow the monk to less open ground, but the stranger hailed them from the road and called them by name and they both froze. It was unlikely that even a friend would have recognized them from that distance."

"What is it?" Pao Shih asked.

"I cannot tell. It is a magical thing, though it wears the form of a man. I cannot see past it. I have become very practiced at that. It is a powerful magic and I am certain it is far more than a fairy."

"It knows us," she mused. "Why has it not destroyed us where we stand?"

The man had come much closer now and even Pao Shih could see the glow about it. "Dragon fire," she breathed. "This is an aura even mortal eyes can see."

"Most curious. Why indeed do we still live?"

Wei Pan Ch'ao stepped past his companion and entered the road where he and the "man" stopped on opposite sides of the stream. "Dragon," he said boldly.

The young man bowed and apologized for the disguise, introducing himself formally. Wei Pan Ch'ao was impressed.

Reaching into his tunic the man produced a scroll with the seal of the Jade Emperor of Heaven clearly upon it. In a grand and formal voice he said: "I have a warrant from the Jade Emperor of Heaven, Ruler of All Things in Heaven and Earth," he cleared his throat and continued quickly, not accustomed to speaking in audible words, ". . . for the reinstatement of the powers, rank and immortal state of the Fairy of Ku-She, lately known as Madam Ku Pao Shih, First Wife to the late Governor of Honan."

Pao Shih gasped and ran to the bank of the stream. "She did not fail!" she cried.

"It was Madam Chou Ch'ung-i who succeeded in convincing His Most Noble Magnificence of the wisdom of this course. Are you prepared to accept this boon?"

Pao Shih prostrated herself at once before the emperor's agent and the ritual of reinstatement was carried out quickly and efficiently. As she lay facedown before the dragon she felt a sharp tingling in all her limbs and a brief flash of dizziness and when she tried to stand she was suddenly overcome by a wave of vertigo so that the monk had to catch her and support her for a moment. The world had expanded to proportions she had long grown unaccustomed to and the fairy-sight left her reeling. But the dragon put out his still-human-seeming hand and steadied her where she rested against Wei Pan Ch'ao and the worlds fell into place again and she was steady. She felt as though she had been released from a dark, deep prison and could see and breathe for the first time in too many years. Though she had always regretted her diminished state she had forgotten what she had truly lost and she was suddenly overcome with the joy of it. She began to weep, but the dragon calmed that too with a touch.

"You must have strength now, Little Fairy," he said, "for there is much for you to do. I will go with you and do whatever you require of me. I will humble myself and place myself under your direction as long as it serves our mutual ends."

Ku-She thanked him most humbly and said that the first thing was to locate Yin Whun.

"She is not there," the dragon said.

"But my Sister of the Birds said she led her there herself," Ku-She protested.

"As she led me," he replied. "Still, she is not there."

"May we see this place?" Wei Pan Ch'ao asked.

"If you wish," the dragon said. "It is not far."

The place was a small cave formed by the upthrusting of several large boulders and a raw, new rift in the hillside. A dozen trees had fallen with that birth; one a venerable giant, which Ku-She approached with a tender sadness the monk had not seen in all their journey.

"Ah," she said, placing a hand on the gnarled, heavy-barked trunk. "My Sister of the Trees will miss this one. He has been with her a very long time."

Then she turned from the tree and found Wei Pan Ch'ao standing in the midst of the small clearing before the cave, straight as a rod with his eyes closed and his hands cupped before him like one holding a bowl.

"There is a strong residue of magic here," he said seating himself on a nearby rock. Stronger presences than the fairies and more than this venerable dragon would account for."

"Speak plainly, monk," Ku-She snapped, suddenly angry. "I well know you are capable of it."

"I believe Yin Whun is in the hands of your son's agents," he said. "And I suspect we are deeper into this game than we realized. Things may begin to move quickly now."

"They will move quickly enough now that I have some control of my resources again," Ku-She said hotly. "I do not know him. I cannot anticipate him. I was a fool to think I could find him or influence him in any way . . . save one. And I know that way well now. My bitter experience has taught it to me. Had I understood this earlier I do not know if it would have made any difference, for I was powerless, but I have a voice again with which I can call to the fairy world. I can be heard in *Heaven* if I so choose, and if I call to him, my son will not fail to hear me.

"Now he will come to me, and he will have no need to search."

In the dark places beneath the Earth, Wei T'ai-Tsung moved about quickly, safe from the eyes of Heaven which could not see beyond that barrier. When the Earth was formed it was crossed and recrossed by invisible trails made by the Great Dragon Lung Mei in his wanderings. These were the veins of the Earth, through which the natural forces flowed like blood. Such places were lucky for a man who might happen to build upon that ground, or who was fortunate enough to transact business or form an acquaintance there. The magic had sunk deep into the ground and was visible to special eyes. It was the very basis of the geomancers' art, but only in Heaven was there a true record of them. By his perfect knowledge of the

Heavenly map of those trails, Wei Tʼai-Tsung was never in a
moment's doubt of where he was or how to get from one place
to another with the greatest efficiency.

He paused in his present journey and listened . . . and
then began to laugh. He was quite near his destination,
however, and continued on his way at once, his delight almost
childlike in its simplicity and pure wickedness.

The two horses came to Earth a short distance away and
immediately as their hooves struck the ground they came on
toward Ku-She and Wei Pan Chʼao at great speed.

"This is your son's answer," Wei Pan Chʼao said as the
horses came to a halt, blowing and stamping.

Ku-She was uncertain. But as soon as her doubts were
expressed one of the horses spoke, addressing them with a
human voice and in a courteous but stern manner.

"We are the minions of Wei Tʼai-Tsung," it said. "Your call
has been heard. Our master sends us to you that we may carry
you to him swiftly and directly."

Ku-She was enraged and demanded her son appear before
her but Wei Pan Chʼao calmed her and drew her aside. "I see
no alternative," he said.

"If we go we will be in his hands at once and we will be
powerless."

"No, not powerless," the monk said. "I do not think he is
capable of such great control. He wields his own power
cleverly, but only the Jade Emperor could remove your fairy
portion and only he could restore it. If Wei Tʼai-Tsung was in
command of so great a capacity he would challenge the ruler of
Heaven himself. But he cannot. He nibbles at the fringes of
great power. He steals the tools that *wield* power. He destroys
the things that contain and limit power. He looses evil to take
its own course but he does not direct it. He scatters confusion
and sets annoyances in motion to distract attention from his
actions and their possible remedies. With all Heaven in an
uproar trying to contain what he has set free or repair what he
has broken, their efforts to combat him have little chance of
taking effect.

"Do not rate him higher than his worth simply because we
do not know the extent of his ability. Heaven is already doing

so and it is only to his advantage. In not coming to us he may have committed an error for, if we go to him, we will be *within* the scope of his power where we may observe its true shape and extent. And if, in the end, he *is* too powerful to stop, then it hardly matters if he kills us here and now or later . . . in a place our friends will learn of."

In her anger, Ku-She had forgotten the dragon who lay close by in hiding.

Turning to the horses, Ku-She called them in her sternest voice.

"Though my son's refusal to come to me is completely improper and his manners are reprehensible, we will, nonetheless, accept his hospitality. His choice of transportation, however, is unsuitable. You wear no saddle or bridle. How are we to ride?"

"You will not fall," one of the horses said. "Our magic assures that. But you may *only* ride. You may in no way guide our progress. Therefore, such gear is unnecessary."

The horses were of great size and broad across the back. They were difficult to straddle and, expert horseman though he was, without tack or trappings, Wei Pan Ch'ao found clinging to them difficult. Poor Ku-She was even worse off. Yet, though Wei Pan Ch'ao was frequently unseated and felt his balance to be constantly at risk, he began to note too that never once did the precariousness of his position evolve into real danger. The horses had said merely that they could not fall. Not once had they said the ride would be comfortable.

In the glade by the stream the dragon lay invisible. He waited and watched all that transpired on the road and when the monk and the fairy moved to mount the horses of his enemy, quick as the blink of an eye, he made himself small as a sparrow. Perching upon the bank of the stream he sought the rising vapors which carried him high up into the clouds, and as the great white horses sped into the evening sky, the Seventh Son of the Dragon King of the South, cloaked in the fullness of his power and mounted upon a great bank of grey and darkening clouds, followed at a discreet distance.

Angry and frightened, Ku-She clung tightly to the animal's neck all through the night. The horse's mane snapped sharply across her face in the wind, stinging her eyes and cheeks. Her hair came undone and tumbled down her back, pulling and tangling and whipping in the wind like the horse's mane. She, too, had soon realized she could not fall, but being bounced and flung about was too uncomfortable to endure, so she held fast to the animal's neck. It arched and stretched and bowed beneath her as the horse galloped the invisible roadway through the clouds.

As the sky began to pale, Ku-She at last saw before them the great towering crag of a mountain peak. Far off to her right she saw Wei Pan Ch'ao and his mount. As they drew closer to their goal the distance between the horses diminished till at last the monk fell in behind Ku-She and they began a rapid descent to the mountaintop.

There were great puffy islands of clouds below them now and banks of dark clouds massed on the horizon to her left, moving swiftly and curving around behind as if to embrace the mountain.

The horses clattered to a landing on a narrow ledge a distance below the craggy peak and, without breaking stride, clambered up the steep incline and into a cleft in the sheer rock wall. Within the slash in the mountainside the light quickly vanished till it was merely a bright streak upon the darkness at Ku-She's back. The walls of the passage were close, but within a few strides the sound of the horses' hooves changed, and it became apparent they had entered a cavern of considerable size.

Suddenly, amid a huge crash and grating of stone, the passage closed tightly behind them. She felt Wei Pan Ch'ao at her side, knee to knee. The horses had stopped.

Then there was only darkness. . . .

And a small, soft weeping. . . .

And laughter.

"Who are you, coward? And *where* are you?" Ku-She demanded. "Show yourself! We are your prisoners. Why do you still need to hide in the dark?"

"Coward?" a masculine voice said pleasantly. "No, Little Mother, this is *your* task. It is a small thing; well within even a fairy's limited powers . . . or have you forgotten how to use them? No matter. Think a moment. It will come to you. Then it is up to you to decide when you are ready to see *me*."

Ah, clever, Wei Pan Ch'ao thought. *His first test and it is well reasoned, perfectly aimed. She cannot hesitate in this. She must not.*

But even as these convictions settled upon him, the monk felt the tingle of magic being worked. Slowly the darkness brightened into gloom and Ku-She's form beside him began to separate itself just slightly from the darkness.

The cavern was large and Ku-She knew she could not light it all, even poorly, so she concentrated her efforts upon a small area, and gradually it began to brighten. She became aware of several figures huddled to one side. She dared not hesitate, and yet . . .

She had always imagined he would just *be* there. In the frenzy of pursuit, a door flung open, a corner turned, or dropping from the sky mounted upon some foul creature, the monster would be revealed to her with no time for thought. . . . But she knew it would not be so. She would see the child she had borne, sound of limb and well formed, grown into a man. And he would be beautiful as all fairy kind was.

The light continued to grow, steadily if slowly. The cavern was larger than she could judge, the roof low but sloping upward sharply as it reached the limit of her circle of light. The floor was littered with rocks, some the size of boulders but most mere stones or pebbles. On the walls were sconces, some of the torches still smoking from having been recently extinguished. Aside from the huddled group by the wall there was not another human figure in sight.

"Who is there?" she said, peering into the twilight. For a moment the weeping, which had been a constant undertone, grew and was quickly muffled again. The figures by the wall seemed to move closer together, but their shapes and colors were becoming clearer.

"Who is it?" she called again. "Yin Whun? Is it you? Speak to me!"

"No, Sister," the trembling voice of a frightened woman replied, ". . . it is I . . . Liu Ch'ing."

Ku-She was aghast. She willed the light to grow brighter and suddenly it did, even more so than she had expected. The monk was helping her. She wondered if Wei T'ai-Tsung would sense that. She slid from the horse's back, unhampered and crept closer.

What the light revealed was, indeed, her sister-in-law, crouched on the floor of the cavern. She was surrounded by a huddle of children. Liu Ch'ing's eldest daughter stood beside her mother and held Yin Whun's youngest child in her arms. Liu Ch'ing also held one of Yin Whun's daughters in her lap and this child appeared to be the source of the weeping. Liu Ch'ing's two sons stood on either side of Memi K'ai Hua as though to fend off whatever monsters might accost them. But the fairy maid was nowhere in sight.

Ku-She stepped closer, carefully examining the little tableau for signs of trickery. The child in Liu Ch'ing's lap cried louder and the woman covered its head with her long sleeve. Her garments were soiled and tattered and the children were also in disarray.

"Ch'ing-ah . . . Yin Whun, where is she?"

"Ah, Sister," Liu Ch'ing said in a tiny voice, "she was here. She *is* here, but . . ."

Again the laughter rolled through the darkness and Ku-She willed the circle of light to expand, but it grew dimmer as it did so. Wei Pan Ch'ao was too clever to give himself away that easily.

At once all the torches burst into flame. Ku-She could just make out the form of a man standing on the threshold of darkness.

"You have more courage in this matter than I thought," he said, walking forward. "If this little gathering had not distracted you, you would have revealed me quite quickly. Unless I had evaded you." He chuckled and the light began to clarify his features.

Ku-She could not take her eyes from him. Like a sparrow entranced by a snake, she could not help watching her doom approach. But she did not think of death. That was not what she feared.

With an extreme act of will she turned her face from him, looking to her sister-in-law and the children.

"What have *they* done to you? Or is it for my benefit they are here?"

"For my own sake," he said. "This is a reunion. You are all the family I have and, being the eldest son, I am now the family head. It was my desire that you all be together.

"The fear you see is as much on your account as mine. What

must they think to finally see you so? They hardly knew me . . . the little ones not at all, but you . . . you were known to them . . . and you have deceived them. You too, Uncle, but Pao Shih most of all. Have they ever heard your real name, Mother? The Fairy of Ku-She no longer resides in Heaven. Does the mortal world know this? Is her name spoken anywhere?"

As Ku-She watched the remnants of her family cowering among the rocks she knew Wei T'ai-Tsung was entirely correct. They looked at her without a spark of recognition or a sign of hope. She remembered how her husband had been when he had learned the truth and how he had never again trusted his once-beloved uncle. How much more terrible must poor Liu Ch'ing feel by this revelation, so callously done. Her life had not been luxurious, but it had always been sheltered. She was kind and patient and Pao Shih's most constant friend, but she was not strong and her disposition had always been somewhat fragile. And the children . . . what must *they* think?

Yes, of course, she thought. In working even this slight magic her fairy aura was about her. What Liu Ch'ing and the children must see would be awful indeed, for her form would be indefinite, her presence and beauty a trick of the mind rather than a thing the eye could know. No wonder they stared at her so; she was elusive and they were beguiled as well as shocked.

Abruptly Ku-She killed the light and the cavern dimmed to flickering torchlight. Her form became definite once more, though her appearance was permanently altered.

Anger overcame her fear. She turned on him sharply and her worst fears were instantly realized. Her son was the exact image of his father when Ku-She had first seen him nearly twenty years ago. Even had her husband still lived it would not have mattered. Wei K'e-yung had changed with time as all mortals did, but Wei T'ai-Tsung wore the look, the face, the form of the man Ku-She had sacrificed her world for.

"Is this truly you?" she said. "Or do you deceive me in order to torment me? Is this an honorable thing?"

Wei T'ai-Tsung took Ku-She's hands gently but firmly in his and began to tug her toward Liu Ch'ing and the children. "Come," he said, smiling. "Uncle, come. I want all of us to be together."

He released one of Ku-She's hands but held the other as they walked. "Such a gathering has been my heart's greatest desire for longer than you can know. And now . . . now my happiness is nearly complete. It would have been but for an error on my part."

He stopped before Liu Ch'ing and looked down at the terrified, miserable woman crouching at his feet.

"Sister," Ku-She said, but Liu Ch'ing would not look up.

"Please, Uncle, be comfortable," Wei T'ai-Tsung said, gesturing at the bleak emptiness with his free hand. "You retired from the family shortly after I was born. You have been away a long time. Do you know your relatives? I do. I have watched all of you for a great deal of my life. Shall I introduce you?"

"As you wish," Wei Pan Ch'ao said. He seated himself on a large rock with his arms folded across his chest and studied his nephew impassively.

"Yes, Uncle, watch me carefully. I know about you as well as the others. You are not as clever as you think."

"You say your family is all together at last, but I do not see your Second Mother. Where is Yin Whun?"

"In time, Uncle. She is here. You will see."

"*Where is Yin Whun*?" Ku-She demanded, anger like daggers in her voice.

"Patience, Mother. I said we will all be together, and we will. Shortly."

He held her hand in both of his now. "I *am* sorry about my father. I did not intend to kill him. That was not what I wanted."

Ku-She was struck by the sincerity in his voice. "What did you want?" she said.

"I wanted him to be here . . . with the rest of you. But I had been away too long. I had forgotten how *fragile* mortals are. Do I hurt you, Mother?"

Ku-She looked away from his face and down at her hands which he held in a crushing grip. She tried to pull free but he was very strong. He smiled at her.

"You are immortal again, Mother. Have you forgotten how that feels? It takes quite a bit to discomfit us. Much more than these. . . ."

Suddenly he released Ku-She's hands and turned sharply, catching the boy Tian Feng, with a sharp blow. Tian Feng reeled and ducked his head and Wei T'ai-Tsung seized him by the hair at the back of his neck, pulling his head up sharply.

The child yelped once in pain and surprise, and Wei T'ai-Tsung shook him hard. He was no longer smiling.

"No," he said. "Not like these. They are so easily injured. One must take care not to overburden them. They die much too easily."

Then he lifted the boy off the ground and tossed him at his sister's feet like he was no more than a rag toy. Tian Feng shook with anger and glared at his cousin with all the rage and hate of a grown man, but he did not put a hand to his sore head or his newly-bruised knee.

The child is brave, Ku-She thought. I hope he does not use it foolishly. But Wei T'ai-Tsung had lost interest in the boy.

"Where is Yin Whun?" Ku-She said slowly. The ice was in her voice again and hints of blizzards raged in her eyes. The monk sat by and was silent.

"The Little Mother is close at hand. Though she is the lowliest of fairies she is still an immortal, and like you she need not fear such rough handling as I gave the boy. Therefore, I would have gained nothing by employing it. Also like you and my uncle, she means to destroy me or, at the very least, betray me to those who could."

With his hands clasped behind him he went to stand between his mother and his uncle. Ku-She felt the pang of old memories. The stance, the gesture, the stride were all so like her beloved husband. She held firmly in her mind the image of a moment earlier; of Wei T'ai-Tsung and the boy and her son's face as he relished the pain he caused and his anger that the child would not admit it. This was *not* her husband, had nothing to do with anything her husband had ever been, and this she would cling to as much as need be.

"I may be young, Uncle, but my time, both on Earth and in Heaven, has taught me stern and difficult lessons. At my own mother's knee I learned to guard my trust, and in Heaven I learned whom to guard it most carefully *from*. I learned many things. I learned about the fairies and what they are capable of. Even with all her fairy powers restored my mother is merely that—a fairy. She is limited in both the magnitude and scope of her powers and influences. You, however, are another matter. I cannot say what the extent of your skills may be. But apart from that I must also remember that you are still mortal. This alone limits you greatly. So I treat you with caution and respect, Uncle, as is your due, but I do not cringe before you. You do not worry me overly much.

"As for the Little Mother . . . she did not worry me at all, being so much less than either of you, but she did vex me considerably. She was extremely uncooperative and in need of restraint." He saw Ku-She's eyes flicker and her gaze briefly rest upon his girdle where three amber drops hung.

"No," he said. "Such confinement is for those deserving of gems. The Little Mother does not please me in any way. She required a lesson. It is one I felt might benefit all here."

A child began to cry again and Liu Ch'ing moaned softly and hid her face against the little girl's hair.

At once the cavern was filled with the voice of a woman screaming with rage and pain. The boulder upon which Wei Pan Ch'ao had seated himself began to heave and the surface flowed as though molten.

Wei Pan Ch'ao leapt to his feet and retreated several paces from the suddenly writhing rock. New contours began to form swiftly. As they watched, horrified, the stone resolved itself into the head, shoulders and bare back of a woman. Her posture was bent forward in a low crouch and her arms, legs and lower torso were still firmly imbedded in the stone. Her head was bent forward and her hair, falling free about her face, was also caught in the stone, making it impossible for her to raise her head. Her back and shoulders bore the marks of recent abuse. She struggled against the rock with all her might till Ku-She thought she might tear her own flesh.

"Nothing the Jade Emperor has done to punish me is harsh enough for having brought so foul a creature as you into existence," Ku-She said in a fury. "What have you done?"

"Only restrained her, as I said. The rest is the result of the Jade Emperor's interrogation. If she were as troublesome to him as she has been to me I would say he did little enough to persuade her."

Upon hearing her lady's voice, Yin Whun strained her head as far to the right as she could and called out to her. Ku-She ran to her but at once the stone began to flow about her body again.

"Take care!" she called. "He cannot . . ."

Her words died suddenly as solid rock closed about her. Wei T'ai-Tsung wore a look of rage.

"She will not learn? Then I will teach her another way!"

From his belt he snatched the Golden Ax of the God of War. He crossed the distance to the stone in three long strides, swinging high as he did so. Ku-She leapt directly into her son's path but he swept her aside with an easy blow and struck the rock with the blade. A jagged shard nearly the size of Ku-She's hand clattered to the cavern floor and spun to a halt by her foot.

Once again Wei T'ai-Tsung released Yin Whun briefly from the boulder; just long enough for his mother and uncle to see the great, bloody wound upon her right shoulder. She sobbed once and tried to raise her head and within the instant was returned to stone again.

"I am a patient man," he said, calm once more, "but some things are beyond patience. You will both be well served to remember this lesson. If you make it necessary I can be very creative."

A deep chill began to settle in the cavern as Ku-She fought the urge to spring for his throat. The fact that he bore her beloved husband's resemblance so strongly now disgusted her far more than it compelled her. He demeaned it, fouled its memory and gave her more cause to hate the sight of him.

"I have much to do with the world and Heaven before I am satisfied, and you shall see them both destroyed—utterly—before you depart my company. Because neither was kind to me and because you loved them both far more than you ever cared for *me*."

"Forgive me, Nephew, but one of your lineage hardly seems likely to possess the strength for such a task. Though your powers are unknown—to nearly everyone it seems—if you were that mighty you would not have stayed your hand so long."

"Ah, Uncle, as you should well know it is not native power that is important but the ability to *acquire* power and the cleverness to use what you have acquired.

"The ax of the God of War," he said stroking the blade. "And in these three ambers, my current wives; the third daughter of the God of the Hearth; in this a minion of your Sister of One Hundred Trees, the Lady of the Mulberries; and in this the goddess of Healing. . . . I suggest that those of our family not blessed with immortality take care against injury."

He replaced the amber at his belt and reaching within his tunic withdrew a chain from which were suspended four pearls.

Taking each in his hand in its turn he said, "See how the color differs with its direction? This first is the Northeast. It is blue-grey like the winter sea. This one is the West and is pale blue like the distant mountains in summer. This one is the Southwest and is the color of honey. And this last is the East and is pink as the sky at sunrise. I have not discovered the colors of the other four yet, but I will soon.

"Once I possess the pearls they cannot refuse me. Even those dragons free in the clouds cannot harm me as long as I possess the pearls for their directions, and when I have all eight I will control the waters and the rains and I shall raise a flood that will cover the world to the very gates of Heaven. To the steps of the Jade Emperor's palace itself!

"You doubt me, Uncle."

"If there is one thing my very long life has taught me," said Wei Pan Ch'ao, "it is a healthy skepticism. I am content to wait and see."

"You are too easily pleased, Uncle. It is a shame I cannot offer you a greater challenge."

"Enduring your hospitality will be challenge enough I expect."

Wei T'ai-Tsung laughed once more. "I will try not to disappoint you, Uncle," he said. He made formal greetings of farewell to all assembled and, with a curt word to the horses, which fell in behind him, Wei T'ai-Tsung vanished into the darkness and left the cavern.

The torches continued to burn about the captives and Wei Pan Ch'ao could not help but notice that Ku-She was trembling visibly where she stood beside the stone. Rage and grief were at war upon her delicate face and her hands, her inner sleeves untucked and clenched tightly about them, rubbed constantly and mechanically at each other as though the cloth could scrub away her son's touch.

Her voice was bitter when she spoke at last. "What now, Monk? We are in his hands . . . what have we learned?"

Wei Pan Ch'ao spoke calmly. "She would be imprisoned so whether we had come or not," he said. "If he had come to us and we had succeeded in destroying him I have no way of knowing if his magic would hold without him. If it did, all of these,"——he gestured to the women and children—"would have been lost to us and she would *still* be in the stone."

"Free her."

"I do not think that is wise."

"Can you?" Ku-She demanded, flashing him a furious look.

"Possibly . . ."

"Then do so."·

"Have patience, Madam," he said. "I must study this place and what it contains. Calm yourself and help me if you can. His magic is everywhere and we must examine it carefully."

Ku-She stopped wringing her hands, seated herself upon another large rock some distance from Yin Whun and began to tidy her hair, removing the pins and combing out the snarls with her fingers as best she could.

"She was always stronger than I," Ku-She said to the monk who had come closer. His posture was of one listening carefully for small sounds in the distance, but he stopped by her and gave her his hand. She took it and stood beside him. "She was braver and often more clever. She had faith when I had not, and it was sometimes as much the fact that I could not dissuade her belief that we could do anything as it was my own duty that kept me going. And when I met Wei K'e-yung, even then she was right. I lost faith, gave in as much to my despair as to my love. If I had not stopped listening to her counsel . . . none of this would have happened. She is worthy of being a much higher fairy than I. The Jade Emperor will know this. I will see to it, even though I am not worthy to kneel in his presence, I will have him know this."

Then Ku-She removed a torch from the wall and she and Wei Pan Ch'ao began to inspect the cavern. As they passed the women and children still seated close together by the wall Ku-She could not help but see how they looked at her.

There was little to see in the rest of the cave. Several passages led downward deeper into the mountain but Wei Pan Ch'ao did not believe they went anywhere. All but one, which stood only a short distance into the darkness beyond the torchlight and was also blocked by a stone. The cavern was large but not vast and it took them some time to inspect it completely. When they returned to the light they found everyone asleep but the oldest of Liu Ch'ing's boys. Tian Feng sat before his sleeping family staring into the darkness in the direction of the lightly echoing footsteps of his aunt and uncle.

As Ku-She replaced the torch, Wei Pan Ch'ao sat beside the boy.

"How long have you been here?" he said.

"I don't know," the boy replied. "It has been closed like this, with only the torches, but it feels like a long time. Days. When he put out the lights we knew something was about to happen."

"Was Yin Whun here when you came?"

"No, Uncle. He brought her here later. The cave was darkened then too and she was here with the horses. We had already been here . . . I don't know how long by then. They began to argue at once but he did not put her in the stone right away. During one of their fights she suddenly seemed to understand something about him but before she could tell us . . . he made her into the rock."

"Has he any companions here?"

"We have seen no one but him . . . and the horses, but they have only been here twice."

"Can you free her, Uncle?" Ku-She asked again.

"I believe so. Though I will have to be careful. This cavern is full of enchantments. Especially here. He has not bothered with the stone walls farther on. They are very thick and, though I can move easily enough through walls, I cannot pass through an entire mountain. At this end where he has placed the stone and there"—he pointed into the darkness—"where he has blocked only the one passage, the enchantments are strong. The other passages cannot lead anywhere useful or he would have blocked them too.

"Releasing Yin Whun will be my first test of his strength. It will also be my first test of his arrogance. There is a great deal of magic at work in this place and if I am careful he will not easily detect a little more . . . unless he is waiting in the shadows. If his contempt for my own abilities is as great as I think it is, however, he will quite likely have gone on about his business."

"Then we must be about ours," Ku-She said, "for there is no way to know when he will come again."

Wei Pan Ch'ao left the boy's side and went to sit with his back to the small boulder that was the fairy maid. At last he looked up at her with that cunning, foxlike smile she had seen in the old days.

"We are at war, Madam. Are you prepared to do battle?"

Without waiting for the reply he shifted about into a crouch facing the stone and placed his hands upon it. He remained so for only a moment, then he slid his arms about it, bracing his knee against the floor. And suddenly Yin Whun was in his arms. They remained poised and motionless for a fraction of a second and then she slumped against him, moaning loudly in her pain.

"Silence, Little One," Ku-She said, rushing to her side and covering her with her own coat. "He may hear you. Speak normally but try not to cry out."

"MOTHER!"

At once Yin Whun's little daughter, Li-Wu, rushed across the cavern and threw her chubby arms about her mother's neck. The other two girls were close behind her. Liu Ch'ing kept her distance, but her own children crowded close, both curious and concerned. They crept nearer and Gui Li'ng reached out a hand to stroke her hair, and the rest formed a ring about her. The wound in her shoulder bled profusely, but she sat up with Wei Pan Ch'ao's help and clutched the sleeve of the coat firmly against the gash in her flesh.

"I must tell you," she said in a hushed and strained voice, "what I know of him. I have learned something of the nature of his power. It had begun to occur to me some time ago I think, but I could not quite get it all. When he brought me here we argued a great deal. He is inclined to boast and I found it easy to goad him into telling of his misdeeds."

"Easy?" Ku-She said. "Look what your resistance cost you."

"He knows he is not equal to a true god. He counts himself more clever, though, and I do not think he himself is aware of the nature of his power, which I believe is directly related to the nature of his lineage.

"His father was a mortal, a creature of the Earth. His mother is a fairy, which means an elemental, involved in things relating directly and solely to the benefit of the Earth. Therefore his power is largely bound to and in need of the Earth. I do not believe he is *capable* of killing a major deity, or possibly even a minor one. All his harassments have been in the form of theft or destruction of godly tools. Even the Hawk and the Hound of Yang Oerlang were mere *symbols* of his authority, tools of his godly function like the ax of the God of War, rather than deities or even fairies. His poor kidnapped wives and I were transformed . . . and all of us into stones. The Monkey King was imprisoned in wood, the Great Dragons are bound to him by his possession of their pearls but he cannot control them. The dragons he has murdered were all vassals and therefore lesser beings, and at that it was only possible for him to destroy those bound to the Earth.

"All those whose tools he possesses, though he cannot control them, are powerless against him as long as he holds their artifacts. They cannot act against their own power. In this regard I do not think he has realized that the destruction of the Hawk and the Hound was an error, for, though Yang Oerlang is somewhat diminished by it, he is still free to act directly against Wei T'ai-Tsung. Nor does your son seem to understand that the surest way to make *you* powerless against him, Madam, is to posses your Golden Chopsticks, or the White Mule, which would disarm both you and Tung Shuang-Ch'eng."

"Yes," Wei Pan Ch'ao said, thoughtfully stroking his beard. "There is much to what you say, though I do not believe it is all there is to Wei T'ai-Tsung."

"Nor I," Yin Whun admitted. "But it is a beginning. And it seems likely, based upon some of the things he has *not* done, that he is blind to it . . . for the moment at least. Please forgive your stupid servant. In one of our arguments I allowed myself to become too bold. He knows I believe I have discovered something, but he could not force me to say what."

Yin Whun looked very tired and could no longer sit upright, even with Wei Pan Ch'ao's arm to rest on.

"Please forgive my stupidity," she said earnestly. "I have not done well, allowing myself to be trapped so and then allowing our enemy to suspect me."

"You have done well, Little One," the monk said. "Rest and let the women tend to your wounds. Your lady and I must think more about this."

Liu Ch'ing had come forward as Yin Whun told her story and now knelt beside her sister-in-law and without a word began to tear strips from her own undergown. She had a jug of water in her hand, from which only half the contents had been drunk, and with Zou Ming's help they swabbed away the grime and blood. Ku-She recognized the article as kin to the magic pot she had left Heaven with so long ago. It would not run dry and Wei T'ai-Tsung would not have to see to their needs. Somewhere, she guessed, there was probably a basket or box for food.

Wei Pan Ch'ao settled himself some distance apart by the stone blocking the mouth of the cavern to meditate and consider his magic.

"How difficult could it be to break, Wei T'ai-Tsung's enchantments?" Ku-She said, somewhat disdainfully. Having freed Yin Whun with so little apparent effort, Ku-She's confidence in their success was rising, for, though she had paid careful attention, she had been unable to detect the feel of the monk's magic in the midst of her son's other enchantments.

"One small success is no more than one small success," he said. "It is not the strength of his magic that is important, but the unorthodox nature of it. The transformation was not sophisticated. Yin Whun does not suffer when she is within the stone because she has no awareness . . . of her condition or her surroundings. I believe he can allow her such consciousness for only a brief time and while he himself is present . . . as when he first introduced her condition to us.

"I do not worry greatly about breaking his charms. It is discovering the proper angle of approach which is challenging, for even that simple transformation was oddly constructed.

"Being mortal, my own power is unorthodox. For this reason I may be the best detective for our needs. I must open my mind to all that surrounds us here and meditate upon it a while."

Wei Pan Ch'ao quickly fell into a sleeplike trance and Ku-She returned to Liu Ch'ing and Zou Ming, who had improved Yin Whun's appearance considerably but were at a loss as to how to stop the bleeding of her wounded shoulder. Ku-She placed her hands over the affliction and attempted a small healing spell without success.

"It will do no good," Yin Whun said in a tired voice. "He

has the Lady of Healing in one of his ambers. It would take a stronger magic than any fairy's power to work a remedy without her."

"I believe you are right, Little One," Ku-She said, "but something must be done. You cannot continue like this."

"How could I die?" Yin Whun said. "I am still a fairy. It is only the mortal members of our family who must fear for their lives from such wounds. My blood could flood this cavern and I would be no different."

Ku-She sat beside her as the women pressed one more wad to the bloody shoulder.

"I have been *human* too long," she said. "I am not equal to this."

"You must begin to think like a fairy again," Yin Whun said softly. "There is no time to learn it slowly."

"Yes," Ku-She said, sitting up straighter. Something clearly had occurred to her. "You are right."

She quickly searched among the rubble on the cavern floor for the chip of stone Wei T'ai-Tsung had struck from the rock. It had not been returned to flesh when Wei Pan Ch'ao had unbound Yin Whun from her prison but perhaps it still could be.

She pressed the chip to the wound and it fitted neatly into the gash. At once the blood ceased to flow except for a tiny trickle at the lower edge.

"Uncle! Uncle, come quickly. You are needed."

But she could not rouse him. Reluctantly Ku-She left him deep in his trance, afraid now that she might have disturbed something important, for he must be very far from the mortal condition to be so completely unreachable. Once more she tried her own power upon the wound but could neither transform the stone nor bind it in place. In the end it was with a strip of Zou Ming's gown that the wound was kept closed. Only a small spot of blood escaped from time to time when Yin Whun moved about, but she was soon immobilized quite thoroughly by her two youngest daughters who fell asleep with their heads pillowed upon her lap.

Time passed. The torches burned endlessly, never seeming to diminish and the basket and jar were full again. The family ate and from time to time the younger girls played among the stones, but there was little to do but wait. Tian Feng and Gui

Li'ng took torches and examined the nearer reaches of the cavern, but they had done this before, even before Yin Whun had been brought to join them, and there was nothing new to be found; no visible traces of the magic their aunt and uncle had looked for.

Wei Pan Ch'ao did not rouse from his meditation and Ku-She began to grow concerned. Had he encountered her son in some way of which they were unaware? Had the battle been joined and lost? The body still breathed, but that was the only clue she had to his condition.

She kept close watch on him in case something should change and she might be needed and so she did not hear her son approach.

Suddenly, Wei Pan Ch'ao jerked to consciousness and leapt to his feet with a look of vast annoyance upon his face. The monk seized her hand and pulled her to her feet as he ran toward the women and children but it was too late. Wei T'ai-Tsung's laugh rang out at the edge of the darkness and he strode into their midst swinging an amber pendant at the end of a short chain. His coat was thrown open and he wore the look of a man thoroughly delighted with the news he has brought to his family.

Wei Pan Ch'ao stopped in his tracks and pulled Ku-She up short beside him. Wei T'ai-Tsung's gaze was fixed securely upon the two of them.

"Mother, Uncle . . ." he said, a seed of suspicion sewing itself in his mind. "I am delighted at your eagerness to see me."

He clasped the amber firmly in his hand and fastened the chain to his sash beside the others. "I hardly think your enthusiasm is due to the prospect of meeting my latest wife." He flicked the amber with his thumb. "Though I am sure she would find you suitable company, as she is another of your kind. What trivial matters have you been amusing yourselves with in my absence? Clearly it is something you do not expect me to approve of."

With a sudden great bellow of rage Wei T'ai-Tsung turned about and cast his gaze to where the stone containing Yin Whun had been. Ku-She would have thrown herself upon her son in an instant, but Wei Pan Ch'ao restrained her. He could feel the tingling of magic in his hands and he knew he could not hold her but he had stayed her just long enough that Wei T'ai-Tsung had moved beyond her immediate reach.

"Do not be a fool," he whispered. "We are no match for him yet."

Then Tian Feng, a large rock in his hand, stepped forward into his cousin's path and raised the stone to strike.

With hardly a thought Wei T'ai-Tsung struck the boy aside with the back of his hand and the child fell senseless to the cavern floor as the women and children scattered. Yin Whun sat with her back to the wall still wrapped in Ku-She's coat and stared up at him, calm and defiant.

He turned sharply once more and looked at the monk, a wild and excited expression on his face, but dark anger in his eyes.

"So, Uncle," he said. "You have the audacity to defy me after all. It was a simple test. I had no doubt you would try it. You succeeded more quickly than I thought you would. But you have also failed. There are consequences to such defiance. I had hoped you would have better sense than to *test* them. Know then that further attempts to thwart me will not be tolerated. You try my patience as this one did."

As he said this he seized Yin Whun's injured arm by the wrist. She gasped as he hauled her roughly from her seated position to her knees and dragged her from the wall. An icy wind sprang up and raced through the cavern and the torches sputtered and dimmed. But suddenly they roared and flared to brightness again, holding steady against the wind. With a moan Yin Whun was once more resolved into stone, though the surface continued to flow slowly as though the occupant struggled against molten lava. Then snatching the ax from his belt, he took careful aim and struck a large chunk from the rock.

A sharp but muffled scream echoed through the cavern and fell silent as the surface of the rock grew still.

"LOOK!" he bellowed, pointing the ax at the chunk of stone at his feet.

The rock was gone and in the flaring torchlight they saw the bloody severed right hand of the little fairy.

Liu Ch'ing screamed and fainted into her daughter's arms.

Then it was a stone again and Wei T'ai-Tsung snatched it quickly and thrust it into the pocket of his coat. The wind stopped, though the cold in the cavern grew glacial.

"You need wear your father's features no longer, you pathetic coward," Ku-She said in a voice brittle with rage. "You have fouled the memory of them quite enough that I no longer see him when I look at you. Show yourself. I would see the kind of filth that would do this thing!"

"You have been warned, Mother," Wei T'ai-Tsung said calmly. "As have you, Uncle."

Then he left the cavern once more.

Ku-She threw herself across the stone with a cry of rage that quickly resolved into sobs of grief. Zou Ming was sitting on the cavern floor sobbing almost hysterically while she held her mother, who could only moan and tremble in the girl's arms. Gui Li'ng sat beside his brother who still lay where Wei T'ai-Tsung had dropped him, but was beginning to come to a groggy awareness. Yin Whun's three daughters clung to each other and wept bitterly.

Wei Pan Ch'ao knelt beside Ku-She and tried to comfort her, but she would have none of it.

"Free her," she sobbed. "We must do something."

"No," he said. "She is better off where she is. She can do nothing to help us and at least for the moment she is safe."

"Then help my son," Liu Ch'ing sobbed. She crawled across the rock-strewn cavern floor to where Tian Feng still lay, awake now but in obvious pain. Wei Pan Ch'ao went to the boy and knelt by his side. The child's left arm would not move and there was no feeling in his hand. Wei Pan Ch'ao found that the boy had a broken collarbone and a considerable lump where the back of his head had struck the floor. His head ached and his vision was blurred.

"I cannot heal him," he said. "Wei T'ai-Tsung still holds that power locked in amber, but I can make him sleep and forget the pain for a while."

"No, Uncle," Tian Feng said. "I want to help fight."

"For that you will need rest." And so saying he laid a hand gently on the child's brow and the boy immediately fell into a deep, untroubled sleep, his head pillowed upon his mother's lap.

Wei Pan Ch'ao returned to his place by the mouth of the cave and called Ku-She to him.

"I have seen the dragon," he said. "He waits beyond the cavern upon a bank of clouds, but we have not spoken. I must be free of the cave. The impediment he has placed upon the stone is strong enough that I cannot, at the moment, free more than my sight.''

"And what of my son?" Ku-She asked. "Can you locate him within the magic?"

"He comes and goes. At the moment he is within the mountain, but often he is not. I will not make another error as I did with Yin Whun. He shall not enter unnoticed again."

Again the monk fell into his meditations, rousing himself only to eat and listen to his nephew rant and watch him strike more shards from Yin Whun's stone. And the dragon waited. But for how much longer he could not say.

At last the monk went to her quietly and said: "I have found the impediment blocking the stone, but I will need aid to actually remove it.''

"Then we are no better off than we were," Ku-She said, an edge of annoyance in her voice.

"Not so, Madam," he said, looking about for the family which was still some distance away and keeping his voice low. "I can pass *through* the stone now . . . and so can you. Your fairy power is sufficient for this if you follow me closely. Once free there are other powers to help me break this hold."

"Then I must stay, for if you cannot take them with you, I am their only hope. Besides, it will serve to hold him here."

"It is entirely possible that this is not the best battleground for our purposes."

"What other *have* we?" Ku-She demanded. "Out there he looks to be nearly invincible. In here we know how his magic is limited."

"I think not. Out there he deals by stealth rather than strength. He is a petty sneak-thief and vandal with a finely detailed knowledge of his victims. Here he is within the province of his power, for I believe Yin Whun was correct. He needs the Earth for his real strength. Within this mountain he is very strong."

"Are you his better?" Ku-She asked bluntly.

The monk looked annoyed for a moment, then thoughtful. "No," he said. "All pride and vanity aside, I think not."

"Are you his equal?"

"In many things, yes. And in some I am superior. But not in everything and possibly not in the most important ones. I do know that we would be best served to lure him away from this mountain and preferably from the land altogether. But first I must move that stone.''

Taking the hem of her sleeve in his hands he gave her the fox smile again. ''I have a thought, a small scheme. It may serve us to save the others from harm later on if I cannot find a means to move the stone before things come to a head. It needs testing and my absence needs to be disguised.''

With the aid of the children, Wei Pan Ch'ao moved a large boulder to a place beside Yin Whun. He put his hands on the stone and before their eyes it began to change. A moment later there stood two identical stones; every bulge and crack and streak of color was exact, but it was only an illusion, the monk said. If he had truly possessed the power to transform rock he would have been able to form a passage in the cavern wall for all of them to escape by.

Then as they all watched, he released Yin Whun from her prison.

She was dreadful to see.

Memi K'ai Hua stifled a scream but Zou Ming fainted and even the boys could not look at her, for poor Yin Whun was mutilated terribly. The rags of Ku-She's coat still clung to her and began to soak up her blood as soon as she was free.

Her pain was extreme and she could not help but cry out whenever she was touched or tried to move, but the fury and pain were beyond her control and she was nearly hysterical with rage.

The monk placed his right hand upon her forehead and at once her body relaxed against the wall and she fell into a deep sleep.

He removed his coat and wrapped it about her with a whispered word, and the bloody fairy maid vanished and the monk himself sat in her place. The face wore a look of deep meditation. Though she bled as before, the illusion masked all sign of it. Ku-She removed the torch from the sconce overhead, darkening the corner and making the deception stronger.

Then Wei Pan Ch'ao stepped into the shadows by the great rock sealing them in the cave; he became a shadow himself and vanished into the stone.

It is done, Ku-She thought. *Only do not be gone too long, Monk. For I do not know what he will do if your magic does not hold.*

When Wei Pan Ch'ao entered the cavern it required only a quick glance to see that all was not well. The chill was deep and half the torches were out and Yin Whun's altered form was nowhere in sight. Nor was the stone. Only the boulder he had laid his illusion upon sat, untransformed now, just where he had left it. Yin Whun was not present in any form. And Ku-She had changed.

She was the essence of all the most terrible aspects of winter and her bearing was that of a being who knows the extent of its superiority. She was magnificent and, small as she was, her presence filled the cavern. Her face was calm and hard and the look in her eyes froze him to the bone. There was an icelike translucence to her pale skin and he did not think he could have survived her touch.

"He was not fooled for even a moment. The cloak of your magic and his did not hide her fairy aura and it took no time for him to see it mingled with *your* image and not with the stone."

Wei Pan Ch'ao sighed heavily and cursed himself. It was not good that they were no longer together. His greatest fear was that Yin Whun now hung from a chain at Wei T'ai-Tsung's belt where it would be very difficult to retrieve her. Ku-She stood before him with her hands clasped and said nothing and her face never changed.

"Where is she now?" he asked, looking about for more recent signs of Wei T'ai-Tsung's magic.

Ku-She raised her hands and a rain of gravel and small stones escaped between her fingers.

"Madam . . ." he said.

"That is all that is left," Ku-She said. "Some of the pieces are bigger." She prodded a small rock with the toe of her shoe. "She is everywhere about you. We will never find all of it. Some is no more than dust."

"Ah, *no, no*!" he cried. "I had thought many things but not that! Forgive me, Lady Fairy. I have failed you and in my failure I have cost the life of another dear to you. But it is worse than even that."

"I know. He was furious and in his fury I do not think he understood what he did. His temper is still his greatest enemy.

"He has destroyed a fairy. Perhaps he cannot crush the lump

of coal in which Chang-O is held fast, but it is possible that he can. And there are many lesser immortals who may fall as easily to his wrath as poor Yin Whun. We must act upon him soon, Monk. *Soon.*"

"The dragons will help, but we must find a way to get the pearls from him . . . or destroy them. It is a great sacrifice but it will release all the dragons bound to the Earth and free the Lung Wang to act against him. As it stands they can do little against him here unless the pearls are destroyed."

"And what of Chang-O and the others?" Ku-She said.

"I do not believe his magic will hold without him." He hesitated a moment. "But for Yin Whun . . . There is no repairing that."

"Come," he said, "we must see to the others. There are dragons beyond this sealed tomb who will help remove the impediment he has placed upon the stone. With their aid we will all be free soon and then you and I must see to your son."

They set about gathering the family but almost at once Ku-She called the monk to her. A short distance away little Li-Wu was once again playing amidst the littered debris of rocks, but in the torchlight dusk of the cavern her face was strangely illuminated. She gazed steadily into her cupped hands, which were filled with a warm, rosy glow. It shone pink between her chubby little fingers and pulsed gently like the movements of a living thing.

When the fairy and the taoist magician knelt beside her and peered into her hands, to their amazement they saw she held a Great Dragon Pearl. The child was transfixed and did not move when Ku-She took the pearl from her hands, but her eyes did not leave it for an instant until Ku-She covered it with her own hands. Then Li-Wu began to cry quietly.

The fairy called to Zou Ming, who came quickly and carried Li-Wu to the front of the cave.

"When he shattered the stone I flew into a rage," Ku-She said. She told Wei Pan Ch'ao how she had attacked her son, blind with fury, striking him with her fists and slashing his face and clothing with a small shard of stone from the cave floor. Oddly and infuriatingly, he seemed to find this amusing. She could not hurt him and at the moment when she had needed it most she had totally forgotten her magic and had behaved as any silly mortal would.

"He will surely miss this," she said. "And soon. He has not been gone very long."

"Yes, he is still within the mountain. I felt him when I passed the stone. Here, Madam, let me have that."

Ku-She handed it to him and he felt the tingle of its magic rush through his hands and into his arms. The longer he held it the deeper the magic flowed into him and he began to feel the thrill and wonder that had captured the child. The magic was seductive. It could not be ignored and it was difficult to concentrate on anything else. His will was formidable but it was easy to see how the child had become so quickly overcome. He quickly returned it to Ku-She's hands and, looking about the floor, retrieved a chunk of rock of roughly the same size. In a moment it was identical in appearance to the Dragon Pearl in all ways but the most important. It had no fire and its magic was only a taoist shadow.

"It will take a good deal more than I can do to give this its illusion of reality," he said.

Ku-She took the stone in one hand and the pearl in the other and clasped them both together in her lap with her head bowed and her eyes closed. Presently the glow in her lap began to increase. It warmed the frigid paleness of her skin, which took on the look of late-afternoon sun reflected on an icy lake. When she lifted her hands two pearls burned softly side by side, and when Wei Pan Ch'ao took the new one into his own hands he felt the tingle in his bones. Ku-She looked tired.

"It will not last. Perhaps a day but no more. With luck that will be more than we need."

They placed the pearl in a spot where it could not be seen from the part of the cave where the family now sat gathered. Wei T'ai-Tsung would find it easily but he would have to look. Then, wrapping the pearl carefully in a bit of silk torn from Ku-She's hem, Wei Pan Ch'ao tucked the real pearl into the fold in his sleeve where he would not touch it nor see it and its effect upon him would be greatly diminished.

The children were excited at the thought of flying on a dragon's back—even Tian Feng who was still in pain—but Ku-She was worried about her sister-in-law.

Suddenly Wei Pan Ch'ao rose to his feet and stepped into the shadows. "He comes," he said but he was not there even as they heard the voice.

A moment later Wei T'ai-Tsung burst into the circle of light.

There was dark anger on his face and he cast a quick glance at the women and children huddled against the wall as far from his usual entrance as they could get. He stepped closer but stopped, spying the faint glow of the pearl among the rocks to his left and quickly scooped it up.

Ku-She held her breath. But her small spell had been sufficient and, pocketing the pearl, he turned abruptly away and without a word left the cavern and its miserable prisoners behind.

Ku-She was furious when the monk once again emerged from the shadows. He had been gone a long time. But he had taken the pearl to the Dragon King of the East and enlisted more aid.

"It is unfortunate," he said, "but our enemy still holds the pearl, limiting the power of the Lung Wang controlling *this* territory. The dragons can assist in the rescue of our people, but they cannot act directly against your son. Even were they free to do so and laid siege to this place, they could do little against him as long as he remains in the shelter of the Earth."

"Then we must lure him into the open."

"*And* somehow destroy the Pearl of the West."

"A dilemma," Ku-She said. "Truly. For if he is merely driven out he will most likely choose to travel within the Earth and seek refuge in another territory still under his control. So we must tempt him to a place where he cannot take refuge in the Earth . . . *and* . . . where whichever of the Dragon Lords who remain unbound are free to work against him without the constraints of territory." A sly note had crept into Ku-She's voice and a cunning light into her eyes.

The monk smiled his own foxlike smile, for certainly she was up to something. "Clearly there must be such a place," he said.

"There are two. Heaven is the first and most obvious. I think it would be difficult to lure him there just now considering the tumult he has so recently thrown it into. But the other . . . it will take some thought to devise the proper bait . . . but the sea. Ah, *there* are possibilities."

Wei Pan Ch'ao was most pleased by this line of thought. "In

the east," he said. "He would not attempt the southern ocean because he does not hold the pearls which would give him safe passage into those waters. But he mistakenly believes himself still in possession of the Pearl of the East and there he would not need to remain beneath the ground."

"An advantage, yes, but within the sea the Dragon Kings hold no territory and this would be our *greatest* advantage."

Liu Ch'ing was nearly hysterical when she heard that, though the dragons waited in the clouds beyond the stone, she and the children must not yet leave the cavern. Wei Pan Ch'ao silenced her with a spell of sleeping and he had Ku-She set about devising a lure commensurate with Wei T'ai-Tsung's ambitions and style. The children and even Zou Ming crowded close to listen and help if they could.

There were many things in the sea that might tempt him and most of the gods and spirits would be amply willing to assist in any plan that seemed likely. The Maid of the Sea might offer to become one of his wives as a bribe to leave her realm unmolested. He would surely take her, and her realm, too, once she was safely in amber. There were sea-demons with whom he might be tempted to seek an alliance as he had with the Monkey King, though the demons themselves would be of no direct help. There was countless wealth to be harvested from the sea and the power of the Great Waves if he could steal the artifacts of the Water Spirits. The children had many ideas as well, especially the boys, but they were largely impractical until little Yun-Chih Te-Hsing, who was growing tired and hungry and out of sorts, recited a story of a man in the ancient land of Chi in the Kingdom of Wei who had a daughter who was desired by a demon who refused to pay the bride price. Insulted and fearing the demon would steal the child, he went to the sea and called upon the Lady of the Sea Turtles, who agreed to hide his daughter for him if he would steal a casket of Wishing Pearls from a dragon for her.

When Yun-Chih finished the little tale she was on the verge of tears for it was one of her mother's nursery stories. "Maybe," she said in a small, unsteady voice, "she would hide *us* if we asked her to."

At once Ku-She swept the child into her arms and pulled her down into her lap, hugging her tightly. "Ah, my Little One, perhaps she might. But the dragons will carry you into the clouds where you will be safe. . . . I have something better for her to hide."

It was not difficult to goad Wei T'ai-Tsung into an argument when next he entered the cavern to boast of his latest theft. He had set free the horses that drew the chariot of the Sun, and the Sun God was now forced to draw the heavy vehicle across the skies himself. It was no mean feat and as a result the sun rode low in the sky and the world existed in a prolonged state of twilight.

But he had acquired no more pearls. His mother baited him and taunted him and allowed herself to be drawn into the passion of the fight which he well believed. Since his murder of Yin Whun she had flown at him in a rage whenever he came near enough, and he did not doubt for a moment the "slip of the tongue" which revealed that the Great Dragons had all placed their pearls in the keeping of the deadly Sea Urchins who were nominally their vassals but ruled the ocean floors with little interference.

Wei Pan Ch'ao did not reenter the cavern until he was certain Wei T'ai-Tsung had left the mountain. "He has flown," he said, "upon the horses. He is arrogant and believes himself to have a clear path across the territories between here and the Eastern Sea. I have done as you asked and instructed the Lung Wang to allow this so that in truth he will have an enemy at his back when he thinks he has a refuge."

"And the Sea Urchins?"

"As you warned me they are an uncooperative lot, but they dare not go against the interests of the Great Dragons and have agreed to assemble a vast array of Wishing Pearls so that Wei T'ai-Tsung may be required to spend a good deal of time searching for something which is not there, thus giving us time if we need it."

"Excellent," she said.

The monk looked sour. "It was their idea."

The removal of the stone was quickly accomplished and the monk awakened Liu Ch'ing, who fled to the ledge with the children in tow. Zou Ming carried little Li Wu who wanted earnestly to know if her mother was already awaiting them in the clouds with the dragons or if she was still hidden deeper in the mountain. Yun-Chih hid her face in her cousin's sleeve and began to weep.

When all had been safely borne away by the dragons, Wei Pan Ch'ao returned to the cavern where Ku-She had remained.

"I am loath to depart this place," she said in a sad, quiet voice. "Poor Yin Whun. When I took her from Hibiscus Village I had no thought of anything like this."

"No one could have guessed at it, Lady Fairy."

"I should have sent her back . . . when my exile began . . . but as always I was selfish and needed her company. Now I am loath to leave her here . . . alone."

"Could the Jade Emperor restore her?" the taoist asked.

"We are not like men. There is no Land of the Dead for us. Even if the body remained there is no spirit to restore to it for we *are* spirits. There is nothing left after that. Come," she said, turning toward the faded daylight beyond the cleft in the rock, "the dragons await."

Heaven was an awful sight, even for one who had lately borne it so little love. The proper passageways were difficult to recognize amid the chaos of transformed, ruined magic, but it was the quickest way to reach their destination. Ku-She paused there only long enough to send pages to Great Dragons and the god Yang Oerlang who was still unfettered, though Wei T'ai-Tsung did not seem to recognize this any more than he realized he carried a counterfeit passport through the Eastern Territory.

Wei Pan Ch'ao tread lightly and quickly, diminishing his presence as much as possible. He had always known he would one day visit the Court of Heaven, but he hardly expected it to be in such a state, or in a time and manner not of his own choosing.

"Time in this place is a muddle," Ku-She said, "but things are now so out of shape I cannot say if we will arrive before him or not. We cannot wait for the others."

There were many wrong turns which ended abruptly at nothing; a state of affairs which unnerved the fairy considerably. Her usual path to Hibiscus Village was nowhere to be seen, though she was certain it was in the same sector as the corridors to the Eastern Sea. But they hurried on, pausing only long enough to retrace wrong steps and choose a new avenue.

At last they heard the faint roar of the sea, and a breeze began to tug at them which was damp and laden with the smell of salt air and sea grass. But before they reached their destination, Ku-She turned left into another corridor and when they emerged they were in the watery realm beneath the sea. The taoist magician took the lead now and quickly guided his companion to where the Sea Urchins had laid their trap.

Wei T'ai-Tsung had indeed arrived ahead of them. Even before they came within sight of him Ku-She could feel the disturbance in the currents; his anger at not having found his prize at once. In the water the aura of his magic burned very brightly as the dragon fires did. It made him easy to see in the gloom of the deep ocean and the more he searched, the angrier he became and the brighter he burned.

Keeping to his rear they approached slowly and steadily, making as little motion in the water as possible. When they were as close as they dared get without springing the trap prematurely, they took refuge in a forest of tall sea grass and watched. Suddenly he stopped and held up a huge, black pearl. It was not a Dragon Pearl, Ku-She knew, but he would not be able to determine that till he got it free of the sea. It was enough, however, to prompt him to continue his search with renewed vigor and intensity.

Abruptly he ceased his searching and lifted the black pearl, turning slowly about. He held it before him for a moment, then with an angry cry and a sudden twist of his body, dashed it to pieces against the side of the casket. He spun about again and faced the stand of grass.

They had come too close. She did not know what slip had alerted him, but the trap was sprung and the dragons were not yet there.

For a moment Wei T'ai-Tsung looked startled, then a flicker of incredulity flashed across his face before the complete wash of comprehension.

"Of course," he said. "You have tricked me very neatly and that has given you the chance to get the others to safety. But I was greedy, and my mother gave such a fine performance I did not think to wonder how she *knew* what the dragons might have done. And now you have come to try to kill me and win the Jade Emperor's gratitude. I can hardly blame you. You are both sorely in need of his good graces. But I am afraid you and my uncle are much too clever, Mother. Though it grieves me to have to abandon my private plans for you I fear I cannot allow you to live."

There was little enough the wind and the snow could do beneath the ocean, but Wei Pan Ch'ao was a different matter.

"Test your power against me here, upstart," he said. "I think you will find it a different thing from the safe ground of your mountain."

And thus the battle was joined. Wei T'ai-Tsung's aura began to glow brightly. It was amber and grew ruddy as he gathered his strength, but Wei Pan Ch'ao's was multicolored, like the nine-colored silks which bind men with magic. It shimmered and shifted like the walls of the Jade Emperor's Palace and this was more power than Ku-She had imagined a Man could ever gather upon himself. She felt ineffectual but there was little her fairy power could do here and at its fullest her small blue-white light was insignificant beside the strength held by her son and his uncle.

There was little to see of the struggle save the shifting and flaring of colors and the growing anger on Wei T'ai-Tsung's face. His spells were failing to have any apparent effect here. No doubt he had first tried his favorite spell of binding but whether the monk resisted the spell of his own power or the ocean would not permit his landbased spells to take hold was unclear. Nonetheless, no stone appeared in the monk's place and there were no spells of confinement he could work in such a place where the nature of its substance was in constant motion.

Slowly the two combatants moved closer to each other, circling and circling, spiraling until they were just beyond touching. The taoist's face was a mask. Set and emotionless, it served to further pique Wei T'ai-Tsung's frustration and anger.

The water fairly burned about them now. The glow had grown till it moved outward from its close sheathing of the body like tongues of flame. The colors mingled and flowed and eddied and nibbled at the edges of each other's power like the peacock colors of lamp oil in a bowl of water. The thrust and counterthrust of these auras was virtually the only way Ku-She had of telling who was dominant from one moment to the next, but slowly, Wei Pan Ch'ao's vari-colored mantle began to encroach noticeably upon Wei T'ai-Tsung's auburn glow.

Wei T'ai-Tsung's movements began to slow and steadily and carefully the monk moved closer into the spiral, his right hand raised toward his opponent's face. Like a man moving in a dream, Wei T'ai-Tsung avoided his uncle's touch. The healing powers and the power of sleep made him sluggish and he backed away from the hand that might possibly even render *him* unconscious if he allowed it to take hold of him. But suddenly his back was to the huge casket of pearls and Wei Pan Ch'ao's right hand closed upon his shoulder.

The ocean burned and the russet flared and grew as Wei T'ai-Tsung pressed against the spell. He was drunk and groggy but far from helpless. Now the monk's left hand came up and his right shifted but he could not get a firm grip on his nephew's throat. Wei T'ai-Tsung grappled with his uncle too now, and the colors of the magic grew and dimmed and flowed around and through each other.

Then suddenly Wei T'ai-Tsung gasped and coughed and began to struggle like a man drowning. Ku-She knew at once what the monk was attempting and the colors of his aura became dominant as Wei T'ai-Tsung struggled fiercely in his uncle's grip. The water began to move swiftly about them and even where Ku-She stood aside she felt the rushing and the increasing warmth and then it began to boil.

For the first time Wei Pan Ch'ao's face betrayed signs of the strain of their combat and the ruddy light of Wei T'ai-Tsung's aura swirled about and through the rainbow of the other. Ku-She began to fear for the outcome of this duel and she saw her chance and knew what she had to do . . . what she could do.

Pressed against the casket with his arms upraised, Wei T'ai-Tsung's coat was thrown open, revealing the sash about his waist with its four amber drops and . . . only *two* pearls? For the first time she noticed that the East and West hung about his neck and there were four empty chains fixed to the sash. Opportunity was frequently unkind but it was the best she could hope for.

Ducking low she circled behind Wei Pan Ch'ao, for the sash was fastened on the farther side, and made a dash for her prize. It did not come free at once and the tugging distracted and enraged Wei T'ai-Tsung. He reached for her, but as he did so his lungs once again filled, and he began gurgling horribly. The heat of the water was unbearable but the distraction would cost him dearly and in a moment she had the sash free and fled for the shore as the two men struggled in each other's grip. Looking back she could see only a great, roiling tumult of fire and churning water, but when she cast a second look back she was being pursued. Her son wore a look of the darkest rage she had ever seen and he came on in her wake, still struggling for breath, but gaining steadily. The monk was not far behind him and neither looked at all well.

She wrapped the sash about her own waist as she ran but she had lost track of the passage to the Palace of Heaven and found she was approaching the shore instead. She prayed fervently that the dragons would be there waiting so that her son would not have time to vanish into the Earth, but she had no choice. She must keep what she had won at all costs now and there was no place else to go.

When she reached the shore the sky was dark with thunderclouds and there was a flickering of lightning on the horizon. The dragons were gathering but they were not yet arrived. They had lost their advantage of the nonexclusive territory of the ocean, and now she only hoped the Lung Wang of the East was in the forefront of those converging on the seashore. But how to hold him here till they arrived?

Behind her she heard a gasp and a cough and the thrashing sound of a body struggling in the surf. Without looking back she dashed up the beach, but the two white horses who served her son stood before her, stamping and blowing fiercely. One was saddled this time and both wore halters, but for all their more common appearance they were no less ferocious. They moved down the beach toward her at a menacing lope as she ran from the sea.

Close at her back she heard a heavy thud and an oath and suddenly the hem of her skirt was caught fast, pulling her to a stop. The horses pulled up short in front of her and she ducked aside to avoid being struck. She clutched the free ends of the sash tightly in one hand and whirled about tugging on the skirt with the other and kicking sand, but her son was already immobilized. Wei Pan Ch'ao had tackled him about the knees and he had snatched at her skirt as he had fallen. From the knees down the monk was still in the water and the rage on Wei T'ai-Tsung's face and the ferocity of his struggling indicated he could not retreat into the Earth unless he broke that grip. Ku-

She mustered her own strength and a chill swept the beach. She reached down and lightly brushed the back of the hand held fast to her skirt.

Wei T'ai-Tsung gasped and drew back, for the touch had frozen him to the bone.

"The horses!" the monk gasped. "While I still anchor him to the sea! I have released them. Flee now . . . *quickly*!"

She needed no further encouragement, for the two men were now rolling in the surf locked in each other's arms and the fire of their magic scattered like spray and sparks all around them. Seizing the halter of the saddled mount she climbed aboard as quickly as she could and fled down the beach. Within a couple of strides the beast was airborne and heading directly for the massing stormclouds.

Wei Pan Ch'ao was showing the strain of his phenomenal age. Though his magic was strong, he had never particularly thought of it as a weapon of personal combat and his physical strength was ebbing. No sooner had his mother wheeled her horse about than Wei T'ai-Tsung broke free and caught at the halter of the remaining horse, binding it to him once more. Then the monk tackled him again.

By now Wei T'ai-Tsung's anger had surpassed his reason. He was groggy from fatigue and the near drowning and the monk's opiate touch. He barely knew where he was anymore, but he knew this was the closest he had ever come to a true opponent and he knew his own life was at stake. As his uncle heaved himself up from the sand for another attack, Wei T'ai-Tsung unslung the Golden Ax from its thong across his shoulders and swung about in a mighty crosscut.

Ku-She looked back from her mount in time to see the ax bite deep into Wei Pan Ch'ao's left side, and a scream escaped her lips. The horse faltered and broke stride but she turned away as the monk fell, and kicked the beast mercilessly.

The pain of it was blinding but Wei Pan Ch'ao felt the blow rather than the cut and lost his breath. The other pain would come in a moment he knew, but he still had the strength for one more thing. Folded sideways over the blade he gripped the handle with both hands as he fell and said a little spell of binding. Wei T'ai-Tsung could not free the blade.

"Choose, Nephew," he gasped. "You have killed me for sure but you have lost the ax, and she escapes. You have lost everything. An honorable man would concede that, even in my dying, I have won.''

"Then an honorable man would lose," Wei T'ai-Tsung said, releasing the ax handle and snatching up the halter rope again. "Cherish your prize, Uncle. I will be back for it!"

Wei T'ai-Tsung leapt onto the horse's back and set out in pursuit of his mother without a backward glance. Wei Pan Ch'ao sank the rest of the way to the ground and rolled onto his back, gasping with the pain and smiling and trying not to chuckle. "An honest man . . . might have . . . lost," he murmured, closing his eyes. "But only a stupid man . . . would have gotten on that horse . . . and flown . . . into the sky.''

The horses were well matched but Wei T'ai-Tsung was a better rider. Ku-She's White Mule was a placid creature and the saddle on this giant made things only marginally better. But the distance between her and the dragons closed rapidly. Unfortunately so did the distance between her and her pursuer.

"Sisters!" she called aloud. "I am in need of your assistance!"

Wei T'ai-Tsung pressed his mount as hard as he could without the means to be really cruel, and saw his prize draw nearer. The dragons were angry but that was of no concern as long as he held the pearl. They could kill the horse beneath him but they could not touch *him*. As he flew on, however, a strong, chill wind sprang up and gathered force rapidly. Then he felt a sharp pain in his shoulder and twisted about to see a brown hawk falling away from him and banking for another attack. Her talons were like razors and she had the fairy glow upon her. As the Fairy of One Hundred Birds rose on the wind to strike again and Wei T'ai-Tsung composed a spell that would fell her like a rock, the sky became littered with swooping, screaming birds. They distracted him; struck at his face and bare arms and at his legs and at his horse as well. Amid the beating wings and sharp pains of beak and claws the horse rolled its eyes and began to foam and struggle. It fled in its own direction and Wei T'ai-Tsung was unable to control it, but the menace swept on around it and would not let it land or change course away from the clouds. When the first bolt of lightning sizzled past the animal's rump, Wei T'ai-Tsung knew something was seriously wrong.

The distance between his mount and his mother's grew greater by the heartbeat now and in mere moments she vanished into the thunderclouds with not a backward glance. He tried to turn the horse aside, but the birds attacked and pressed it on in the direction of a vast slate grey thunderhead that seemed to separate itself from the rest. The horse could fly in no other direction and it could not land.

Another bolt of lightning snapped past, even closer than the first, and now Wei T'ai-Tsung saw a remarkable creature seated atop the thunderhead. It appeared to be part man and part serpent, but the dragon head of the Lung Wang was unmistakable and beneath its chin rested the rose colored Pearl of the East.

It was the last thing Wei T'ai-Tsung ever saw.

Ku-She could not watch her son die. The monk . . . ah, he so richly deserved it, and yet she felt badly that it had had to come from the one worthwhile act he had ever done with his long life and great learning. She doubted the Jade Emperor would have granted him permanent immortality, but in a way he had his wish. He had always wished to avoid the Land of the Dead. With the court disrupted and the rolls untended he would very likely never appear on that census. Like her beloved Wei K'e-yung he would wander homeless forever. She had a sad, small hope that they might find each other somehow and wander that eternity together.

Yin Whun, her husband, her son, the accursed monk. All these things were gone now. The female side of the family would inherit Wei K'e-yung's wealth and Liu Ch'ing would take care of Yin Whun's children. There was nothing left to tie her to the mortal world and she could not deny that she had been punished.

The dragons were sent for the monk's body and the Fairy of Ku-She turned her stolen horse toward home, hoping that Heaven would have some small place for her amid the rubble and ruin where she could rest and prepare for the coming winter.

EPILOGUE

At the very onset of winter, when all the fairies were being charged with their particular duties for the coming season, the Jade Emperor held a rare audience. Madam Chou presented the Fairy of Ku-She at the exact time of his bidding to determine if she was fit to return to her duties. Madam Chou petitioned the court on her behalf and on behalf of poor Tung Shuang-Ch'eng, who had had to carry the burden of the task alone for nineteen years.

The throne and the audience hall looked nearly normal, though portions of the path from Hibiscus Village were still unstable and severely out of true. The Jade Emperor was inclined to be lenient, all the terms of his original sentence having been met and surpassed, but his inclinations did not extend to generosity and Heaven was still a shambles.

"Little Fairy," he said, his voice echoing hugely in her head and her bones aching with the beauty of it. "Do you love Heaven?"

"Ah, yes, My Lord . . . Most Magnificent Master," she stammered with her forehead pressed firmly to the tiles. "In all my mortal time Hibiscus Village and my Sisters were never out of my mind and I have greatly missed the performance of my proper duty."

The Jade Emperor was silent for a while.

"Where is the monk, Wei Pan Ch'ao? Tell us this and I may be tempted to greater leniency."

Ku-She gasped audibly and had to remind herself strongly to keep her head to the floor. "In all honesty, Most Sovereign

Ruler of Heaven and Earth, I truly cannot say. I saw him killed on the shores of the Eastern Sea . . . near Yingtien. Or I thought that was what I saw. My most foul and unspeakable son, whose name shall never again pass my lips, struck him an impossible blow with the Golden Ax of the God of War. I was already on horseback and on my way to meet the dragons so I could do nothing to help him. The dragons went for the body at once."

"They found none," the emperor said. "Nor did they find the Golden Ax."

Ku-She could not help but laugh, though she succeeded in silencing it before the emperor. *That jackal,* she thought. *That unspeakable vermin! He entered my life a liar and a thief and he leaves it the same way. Let someone else retrieve this thing and see if they have any better luck than I did.*

"And would you tell us if you *did* know, fairy?"

"Most Excellent Master of All the Universe," Ku-She said earnestly. "I would tell you in an instant!"

That winter the snow was the most beautiful sight anyone had seen in nearly twenty years and men wrote poetry to its perfection that has lasted the centuries.

Fontana Paperbacks: Fiction

Fontana is a leading paperback publisher of fiction.
Below are some recent titles.

- [ ] SHINING THROUGH Susan Isaacs £3.99
- [ ] KINDRED PASSIONS Rosamund Smith £2.99
- [ ] BETWEEN FRIENDS Audrey Howard £3.99
- [ ] THE CHARMED CIRCLE Catherine Gaskin £4.50
- [ ] THE INDIA FAN Victoria Holt £3.99
- [ ] THE LAWLESS John Jakes £2.99
- [ ] THE AMERICANS John Jakes £2.99
- [ ] A KIND OF WAR Pamela Haines £3.50
- [ ] THE HERON'S CATCH Susan Curran £4.50

You can buy Fontana paperbacks at your local bookshop or
newsagent. Or you can order them from Fontana Paperbacks,
Cash Sales Department, Box 29, Douglas, Isle of Man. Please
send a cheque, postal or money order (not currency) worth the
purchase price plus 22p per book for postage (maximum postage
required is £3.00 for orders within the UK).

NAME (Block letters)_____

ADDRESS_____

_____

While every effort is made to keep prices low, it is sometimes necessary to increase them at short
notice. Fontana Paperbacks reserve the right to show new retail prices on covers which may differ
from those previously advertised in the text or elsewhere.